KINGS OF DESIRE

M.o. Absinthe

If any of the following are triggering to you, this book may not be for you, please turn back now. Your mental health matters.

Abuse

Alphaholes

Attempted Rape

Attempted Somnophilia

Blackmail

Beggary

Bullying

Blood

Child Neglect

Degradation

Drugging

Dub Con (Dubious Consent)

Exhibitionism

Extremely explicit sexual content

Grief

Humiliation

Knife Play

Manipulation

Mental abuse

Mental trauma

Murder

Psychological Abuse

PTSD

Various kinks

Trauma Violence

Slavery

Voyeurism

Villain MMCs

For all you book babes who crave them dark, seductive, tattooed, and more morally black than gray.

I've got you!

THERE IS NO LOVE WHERE DARKNESS GROWS,
BUT YOU COULD LEARN TO LOVE THE DARKNESS

CONTENTS

PROLOGUE

Cole's deal

"I agree," I breathed so hastily that I wasn't even sure if he heard what I said. It was like taking off a band-aid. Quick and painful.

"You agree to what? I want to hear you say it." The way he was enjoying the fear and nervousness seeping from my pores was evident by the growing erection pressing into my stomach.

I looked around to check if everyone else was still staring, but I only saw a few students in a rush to walk away from the free show. "You know what, Cole. Come on, don't prolong this; classes are about to start." I wanted to leave, but his clenched hands were still there, pinning my arms against the wall.

He was an immovable wall. Nothing I said, unless it was the words he wanted, would stop him from the torture of making me say what he wanted to hear. He was so unbothered by the rest of the people here he wouldn't check what was going on around us. He couldn't care less about the classes or what everyone else was thinking. He was the king here, and that applied to everyone who set foot in this college—teacher or student.

His signature coldness was surging like an iceberg hitting an already sinking ship. "I asked you to say it. Now," he growled, gathering the pieces of me he was about to own.

"I...I agree to let you do whatever you want with me for a

month."

Brax's deal

"Let's hear it," Brax cut straight to the point, erasing every sentence that I was preparing to say and leaving me with only an undeniable truth.

"I need my family." I sounded weak, and that was going to cost me. All other words seemed to just fade away when it came down to the real reason I was here.

His eyebrows furrowed, yet before I could decide if it was from confusion or anger, his face was back to its usual stony expression. A moment so brief it may have just been my imagination, as the next words out of his mouth reminded me of who I was dealing with. "Take a seat," he said, hoarsely, relaxing his head back against the armchair, unwilling to lose eye contact with me even for a second.

I turned to take a step back, heading towards the only other chair in the room, though before I could reach it, he decided to clarify things for me, "Not there."

To be honest, I knew the first time he said it where the *seat* he was referring to was. I just willingly chose to ignore him, hoping that maybe if I played dumb enough, he would leave it be.

Taking a deep breath, I turned to look in his direction, where very clear instructions were waiting for me; the tips of his fingers were tapping on the upper part of his leg. He wanted me to sit on his lap.

*F*erris's deal

"I should take this as a *yes* to my offer."

"Yes, it's a *yes*." I nodded. With Ferris, it didn't feel so difficult to tell him that I accepted, as it did with Cole or Brax. But it felt much more difficult in every other way. "But we're keeping the condition."

"Okay. I'll have Alfred take you to your new apartment tomorrow," he continued. "I don't keep track of expenses, especially not with the people close to me." He struck a match and lit a few candles on the table next to him, letting the flames dance in the darkness of his eyes.

A wolf in sheep's clothing. I knew it from the second I entered his world a day ago, and yet an invisible power was subduing me to be his little lamb.

No angels allowed between these lines, no Prince Charming, just delicious villains.

CHAPTER 1

A *month ago*

-Bea-

"Natalia, I swear on everything holy, I will return for you and Sebastian." With the tips of my thumbs, I brushed away the hot tears that endlessly sprang from her bloodshot eyes. "I'll get you out of this hell and we will start a new life for the three of us. Do you believe me?" I needed to hear her say the words. She can't lose hope. Hope was the only thing we had left, besides each other. And right now, I was the one tearing us apart. Her voice cracked, filled with pain. The distraught look on her pale face, her brown hair a disheveled mess, and the endless pools of anguish I saw reflected in her eyes threatened to destroy my soul.

"Yes, I believe you. I know you are strong... I believe you will come back." She caught me in the tightest embrace, saying an anguishing goodbye. "I love you..."

"Until the end of time." I finished her sentence. That's what our mother used to tell us when we were children.

"I love you until the end of time."

Though her *end of time* was much sooner than anyone

predicted. She died a year and a half ago, leaving Nat, Sebastian, and I alone in the cruelest of worlds—the three Musketeers, neither distance nor time could ever divide us. Just me. I broke away from Nat's embrace and disappeared into the night. I couldn't stay a second longer. The fear and regret buried so deep within me were moments away from preventing me from taking another step further. The thought of leaving them behind, of abandoning them with a monster was twisting my stomach, making me almost throw up.

My feet felt heavy... my soul felt heavier, but I needed to go; for them, for our future.

It was our only chance.

I was our only chance.

Things weren't always like this, not back when my mother was still alive. We used to be happy, well, as happy as one could be in these times.

The world had changed, or so my mother used to say, because I only got to know the *now* version of it. Humanity had caused its own destruction. Uncontrolled dumping of toxic wastes along with excessive pollution from factories brought us close to the Apocalypse. The rich were busy keeping the money flowing into their pockets and never listened to all the warnings regarding environmental changes. No one cared until the smog clouds got darker and thicker, sometimes so dense that you could barely tell the time of day.

It only went downhill from there. Like a rollercoaster of events, once set in motion could never be stopped; tornadoes, hurricanes, earthquakes. It felt like nature itself was set to destroy humanity. With good reason, we deserved everything that came our way.

Resources became scarcer, the division of the social classes followed and everything became an undeclared fight for survival. The cost of living became so high that the middle class didn't survive the transition. The tenacious became richer while most of those who still had a shred of decency gradually fell into poverty.

These days the sky is always dark, reflecting itself onto everyone's soul, while a small ray of sunshine is a luxury most of us will never benefit from. The heavy smog, the unsatisfied basic needs, the poverty, and the pain all converged into a molten hatred, consuming everyone from the inside out.

My family was the last remnants of a once fading middle class. My mother was the direct descendent of a baroness, and that still opened certain doors while she was alive. With her passing we had hit rock bottom. Our father—and when I say *father*, it's with a mountain of disgust and regret because he could hardly be classified as that. He's never worked a single day in his life.

It didn't impact us while growing up. My late mother used to provide well beyond what any other low-class family could ever hope for, after her demise the effects were devastating. He couldn't get a job, not that he would have wanted one anyway. Instead, as a resolution to his problems, our *beloved sperm donor* was forcing *us* to provide the daily basics. Well, the daily basics, plus a few extra dimes for him and his drug-addict friends.

I couldn't say that he didn't love our mother. He did, but just her. He loathed us, considering that we *forced* her to share some of the time she could have spent with him to raise us. We were her greatest blessing and his greatest curse.

The shock of her sudden death changed him completely to the point he became inhuman. The grieving man who was left with three young children he didn't want, he became an exploiter, using my sister and me to beg for money and food. Yet, how could he expect us to get anything from those who had so little for themselves? My brother, Sebastian, got away from my father's *special treatments*, mostly because he was only six, and his health problems didn't allow him to venture off. My father couldn't risk losing him, especially since having legal custody of Sebastian provided him with a few dusty dollars each month from social benefits.

In a way, I was glad my brother was sick. I know that must sound like the most horrible thing to say, but his illness exempted him from experiencing so many worse things.

The beatings, the punches, the blows. I received them every time paranoia got the better of our father, and he suspected that we were keeping a part of our daily earnings.

The freezing winter that brought us close to hypothermia so many times while having to walk around half a city each day dressed merely in rags so we could receive people's mercy.

The damp summer heat that was descending from beneath the clouds, melting the soles of our shoes into the asphalt. That was on the days we were lucky enough for him to allow us to even wear shoes.

The humiliation of knowing you are worthless. Just a shadow that floats through murky streets, hoping you never run into someone you know. Until the day you begin wishing that no one would recognize *you*, that no one would see *you*. Until with time, you become invisible to everyone, even yourself.

If things weren't bad enough for us, my father thought about turning this beggary into a new business; having his little minions, working day and night to fill his greedy pockets.

Initially, when I heard him talking about it, I didn't think he had it in him to do it. I mean, my father never went through with a plan in his life. Why start now?

But I was wrong.

His dickhead friends convinced him it was time for them to become *entrepreneurs*. Using the one shared neuron wandering their minds, they decided to start the modern slave trade branch of his business.

People had so little hope these days that they would do anything for a mere piece of bread or a miserable roof over their heads. So he became the best at exploiting that.

I knew where this was going, human trafficking was just the next step in his *business*. You can guess who would be first on his list, given that he would stop at nothing to get what he wanted. After all, money was his ultimate goal.

I wanted to run away and search for a new beginning for the three of us from day one. I had my third year of college paid in advance by my mother before she died. That stopped me from going through with my plan, at least for a while. She used to place a great value on education and always made efforts to ensure that my siblings and I would receive one.

My father even tried to get a refund on my college fees. Fortunately, he was turned down. Not that he would let me attend the classes.

Still, I somehow managed to continue my education behind his back. With the permission of some of my teachers, I went on with my studies. I used to take most of my courses from a distance, helped by the notes of a couple of other students. I only had to show up for the exams. That helped me to pass that year, but paying for the following one would be next to impossible. At least, in the same city as my father.

The truth was, he was paranoid about Nat and me hiding money for a good reason. I managed to raise enough for me to be able to get through a month's rent and the first installment for my final year of college. That was my main motivation for running away. I needed to finish my education to have any chance of providing for myself and what was left of my family.

There was a single place I had in mind.

I heard rumors of a city where people had a higher standard of living, finding better jobs, and obtaining the so-needed daily basics more easily. That was my *great opportunity*.

I couldn't have been more wrong.

Echo City. My new city. Weird name for a place where no one hears your screams, no one feels your pain.

They said the sun shone here, and I believed them. I believed them until I saw how the toxic vapors coming from the junkyard on the outskirts of the city formed an aurora borealis, covering the whole sky.

That was their sun.

Death was their sun.

I had no choice but to remain here since the next city was too far, and the transportation alone would either use up an important part of my rent or my college tuition. Besides, this was proclaimed to be the richest city in the area, the only place where I had a chance of finding a job.

Everything was the same everywhere anyway. The rich lived in luxury while the poor were left to pick up the scraps.

Every day was a struggle for survival. Everyone acted like a predator, not even waiting for your corpse to get cold before they would strip you of your possessions.

That was what poverty did to people. The lack of a defined middle class created a bottomless chasm between these two types of inhabitants. The wealthy stayed in their ivory towers while we collapsed in the street.

How could they live so large and leave so little for the rest of us? It's human nature—the evolution of the species. The competitiveness of always being on top helps you easily forget what you had to do to get there. I was about to learn that the hard way.

I registered at Echo City University, managed to pay the first installment and find a shoebox apartment where they didn't ask for a few months' rent in advance.

At first, I had hope; finally, things seemed to be going my way. I even got a night job at a packaging company. It wasn't much. It would barely cover the rent, but it was a start— a chance I never got anywhere else. For the first time, things seemed to be going in the right direction, but with each passing moment, Nat and Sebastian were running out of time.

My first day at the university was two weeks after arriving in town. Day one of senior year. I knew the rules from my old college, don't ask questions and don't talk to anyone. Most of the students were representatives of the elite class, with minor exceptions of one or two who were here on scholarships. The lower class couldn't afford to go here, and in all honesty, I couldn't afford to be here either. I had always been a fighter, never known to give up, and I sure as hell wasn't going to start now. I just needed an extra job, or ten.

I walked down the hall, trying to figure out my schedule for the seminars, lectures, and labs. A pretty difficult task since at the same time, I felt the need to hide in the shadows of every corner so that no one would see me. Despite my best efforts, it seemed I'd quickly become the latest attraction. And not in a good way, more like in a freak show manner. My clothes were selling me out the moment I set foot in the building. Along with the fact that everyone already knew each other from previous years, turning me into an intruder. All eyes were staring at me with the disgust I was already accustomed to.

"Come with me, they don't want you here." A womanly voice accompanied the hand that grabbed mine, guiding me toward the other end of the hallway. Looking at her I noticed a shock of flaming red hair, freckles adorning almost every inch of her small lanky body, sullen cheeks and clothes that didn't look to be much nicer than my own. "What's going on here?" I asked, confused by her haste to get me out of everyone's sight.

A worried look spread across her face as she was getting ready to explain how things functioned around here. "You're breaking the hierarchy."

A hierarchy wasn't an unfamiliar notion to me. We used to have one at my old college where for certain people, you needed to have permission to address them. Even by glancing at those around me I couldn't distinguish the hierarchy here.

"What are the hierarchy rules?" I asked, letting her know that I already had an idea of what she was talking about.

"The main lobby," she answered succinctly, clearing everything up for me.

It all made sense since with each step I took further toward the end of the hallway, more pairs of consternated eyes seemed to be gazing at me.

The girl continued, "You're allowed to walk through there only if you need to get to class. And *only* if there's no way around it. The higher echelons stay at the entrance, and everyone descends from there, according to their rank."

I knew she wasn't kidding. This wasn't a joke. It was this place's normality, and let's face it, our world's normality. What went on at the university was just a reflection of the rankings used out in the streets.

"We have to use this back door." She pointed to the double glass doors behind us. I guess we weren't the only ones that were categorized as rock bottom, as the constant stream of students going in and out, made the doors virtually useless.

I rolled my eyes, though honestly, I didn't have different expectations. I knew my place, or at least, the place where they all thought I belonged.

"I'm sorry; I'm Jenna. That was rude of me." She giggled, slapping her forehead with her palm, like the thought of kidnapping a stranger without a proper introduction was comical.

I started laughing at the irony of the situation. "It's okay. I'm starting to believe you saved my life. I'm Bea," I said, smiling.

"Scholarship?" the freckled girl asked.

Don't tell me my luxury clothes gave me away...

"Not really, more like the work-my-ass-off type of scholarship." I adjusted my jacket slightly so I could cover up a stitched-up hole in my shirt. My thoughts remained on how obvious my financial condition should have been. My hair, a darker shade of brown than my sisters, while not unkempt; was not as glossy as that of the elite, with their daily vitamin enriched foods. My clothes were patched in several places and baggy in others as a result of too little nourishment over the past year since mother passed. My green eyes dull with dark purple bags under them from the lack of sleep from working overnights. It wasn't like the thought of other people knowing I was penniless really affected me, but indirectly, I knew it would. The poorer they thought I was, the more they were going to feed on my misery.

"The hardest one," she giggled again, searching for something in her own worn-out bag.

"I assume you're here on scholarship," I smiled, peaking

at the thick pile of notebooks that were one step away from tearing her bag apart.

"That obvious?" she asked.

"I'm sorry, I didn't mean to pry," I apologized, realizing I had given myself away from having looked in her bag.

"Relax, it's not like it was some big secret. I think I'm the only student around here who has something else besides makeup and drugs in there anyway."

"You and me both," I shrugged, opening my bag for her to see my personal stack of new notebooks. "But I'm not going to get the chance to use them unless I can figure out my schedule," I added, exhausted because I had no idea where to even begin looking.

"You're lucky that the right girl found you," Jenna winked, turning toward the glass doors. "Come on, it's on a panel outside," she said, walking through the exit and out into the back garden.

I rushed to follow. As soon as I managed to catch up to walk beside her, the lecture about ECU went on. That's short for Echo City University, if you didn't catch on.

Jenna strode through a long paved alley to the empty side of the yard, where metal panels were hiding in the back, almost covered by an overgrown green fence.

I found it weird that no one was there, but Jenna quickly shed light on the mystery, "I guess we're the only losers around," she observed, continuing to walk toward the boards. "I don't assume you have a smartphone or a viable internet connection?"

"Actually, I do have a smartphone," I chuckled, pulling the brick-like device out of my pocket. I had a smartphone, but it wasn't *smart* at all. It was an outdated version that used to belong to my mother. I could barely place a call, let alone have access to any kind of advanced technology. The only reason I brought it along was to keep in touch with Nat... if she could ever find time to call me.

"No offense, but *that* looks like it came out of a junkyard. Does that even have internet?" Jenna asked.

"I would be surprised if it even has reception." I made fun of my *modest* situation because, well, why not?

"Assuming it had, we wouldn't need to come here for our schedule. It's published online. Same as a part of the research material we need for some of the classes." Her shoulders dropped as if she had already been defeated by the system. It was the elite's world at the end of the day, and that's exactly what they called themselves—The Elite.

"Fortunately, we do have a little backup." She turned her gaze to look over her shoulder at two guys who looked like they just came from a comic convention. "I think I lied when I said that I was the only student to carry something other than makeup or drugs in my bag. These two nerds got in with even better grades than I did, they use notebooks too," she said with a chuckle.

One of the young men waved at us like he seemed to already be aware of our presence there. "Darrel and Thomas," Jenna pointed towards them. Darrel was around six foot one but he couldn't have weighed more than I did, so even if his sun-kissed hair and light green eyes could have made him attractive, the lack of basic resources for a decent living, along with his nerdy look were making him look dowdy. Thomas was substantially shorter, his clothing a little more fashionable than Darrel's, but keeping the same shabby look along with the nerdy one. His curly dark-hair and the glasses hanging on a string around his neck made him out to be the classic bookworm of the two.

Placing a hand on his hip, Darrel began examining me from head to toe. "New blood."

"Chill out, you're not a fucking vampire," Jenna uttered in disgust, mostly because his gaze had stopped at my neckline. Well, not exactly at my neckline. Maybe a few inches below, at the round shapes that I was doing a lousy job of hiding. I never liked people staring, and the fact that I was successfully heading toward a D-cup was making it hard to prevent that from happening.

In any case, he was harmless, nothing that I couldn't handle, and nothing compared to the lustful looks of my father's friends.

"These two relics are my only friends around this place," Jenna rolled her eyes as if she couldn't help but stand them.

A bitter smile emerged on my face. "Be happy you have them," I said, turning my head to see what courses I had for today.

Jenna had something I didn't—friends. At least, not anymore, anyway. It seemed my quick downfall took me out of their graces because the fact that they could afford a warm meal while I couldn't was the final straw that broke our *solid* friendship.

However, I clung to them as much as I could. Pathetic, I knew, and I despised myself for it. But the course notes they had, and the extra manuals they could afford to buy while I couldn't, made me try and keep the connections. I guess they were as happy as I was when I left. The problem was that, here, I was supposed to do it all over again for one final year.

Checking out the schedule, I couldn't figure out what was where because there was something still confusing me. The university was a lot smaller than my old college, even if the land where it stood seemed to go on for miles. Strangely, there were only three buildings, a few tennis courts, a hippodrome, and a covered Olympic swimming pool.

"Where are the dorms?" I asked, looking back at Jenna.

"Dorms?" Thomas cackled. "You think any of these spoiled asses would live in a dorm?"

How was I to know? Back at my old college, they had several dorm buildings, and the *spoiled asses* were often dumped there by their parents, as a babysitter was no longer efficient at that age.

"Look around you," Darrel continued Thomas's idea. "There's a reason why this place is up in the hills."

I did notice that the university was on higher ground but hadn't observed every detail since it took me forever to get here. Besides, I slept on the bus for most of the trip.

"The Elite don't need dorms because they all live here, in the Hills, while the Annelids live in the Pit."

"Annelids. Is that what they call us?" My amusement mixed with contempt.

"Yes," a sad Jenna answered, taking in a deep breath—like that could ever ease the burden.

"Annelids, as in worms?" I asked again, knowing too well from biology what the term represented. A phylum that consisted of different kinds of worms.

"Exactly, newbie, Echo City is separated into two categories —Annelids and The Elite." Thomas didn't seem happy with the nickname either. But it was just that—a label set by a snobbish group of people. In the end, we could call them whatever we wanted, couldn't we?

Things like this stopped affecting me long ago. These days,

I have more serious burdens to bear.

"I have to run; I have Calculus." The first class on my planner was about to begin.

"We'll be joining you in that one," Jenn snuck her hand around my arm and began leading me back toward the glass doors. "We're geeks, in case you hadn't noticed."

"Don't rush; it's only introduction day," Darrel babbled, trying to catch up with us.

The reality was I didn't want to make a bad impression on day one. I needed to have my teacher's support. With the extra jobs I planned to take, I would need to make a habit of missing classes.

We passed through the back hallway to reach the main lobby, and if things seemed weird before, now it was a freak show. The hallway was murmuring with endless voices, whispering. Some seemed to be in horror while others in admiration.

I raised myself up on my toes, trying to see what was happening, but Jenna's hand quickly came down on my shoulder and pushed my feet back on the ground. "What the hell do you think you're doing?"

Was that fear glinting in her eyes?

"Let's go, quickly," she scolded me, dragging me into a corner, but not before I caught a glimpse at what was happening. There was a demon—because there was no other word I could use to call him. A blue-eyed demon packed with a Herculean body of well-defined muscles and the most devious grin I'd ever seen.

His very aura was predatory, evil, dangerous. Whichever word you wanted to use. A full body shudder wracked through my small frame just looking at him.

A few strands of jet-black hair fell over his eyes as he was lifting a poor guy by the shirt in a display of force and superiority. The ultimate bully, followed by a pack of jackals to corner his victims.

What could the guy hanging in the air have done to receive such treatment, was it an innocent word misspoken, or simply flashing a look in the group's direction?

I knew the stereotype all too well, and loathed it all the same.

"Who is that guy?" I asked as Jenna was dragging me along a secondary hallway, far away from the show.

"Fucking trouble," Thomas answered with the annoyance of a man who was obviously speaking from personal experience. I wouldn't be surprised if he, too, had been on the *demon's* list throughout the years. And in complete honesty, I was only asking about that guy because I knew I would be on that list as well due to my financial situation. The strong always pick on the weak.

Jenna must have sensed that I wasn't going to drop the subject and decided to save me the trouble. "Cole Clayborne. He's a kind of king around here. The king of idiots, if you ask me, but don't let anyone hear you say it. Here even the walls have ears, and you wouldn't want to end up on death row over a few misplaced words."

"That bad?" I asked.

"That bad," she answered, stopping in front of a classroom. "We're here. Say hello to the first day of ECU." Her enthusiasm faded, almost ironically, as if emphasizing what coming to this town really meant. I was now officially an Annelid.

CHAPTER 2

Two weeks later, and I was nowhere closer to finding a second job. I had searched everywhere, from the sweatshop factories to the top luxury restaurants up in the Hills. Absolutely nothing.

A rotten sensation of constant worry began to gradually infiltrate my system, slowly turning into a fear that I didn't need. Not yet, anyway. I needed more time before desolation would take hold and my struggle would be in vain. My sister and brother were still so far away, and failing them wasn't, by any stretch of the imagination, an option.

I continued attending my classes; might as well take advantage as I paid for them. I wasn't going to let a single cent go to waste. I never skipped a course, and for the first time in a long time I'd actually found a friend, I even took the opportunity to dedicate a few hours to girl time. It felt almost normal. I hadn't felt normal in so long that sometimes I think I forgot I was even human.

Jenna and the two guys—Darrel and Thomas, tried to help me find some kind of work, but there wasn't much they could do. None of them came from money, and none of them knew anyone in a position that could provide me with a job. I even suspected that Jenna and Thomas had a more delicate situation back home than my own. I never asked—out of politeness—and they never told me.

This morning, I woke up feeling a little dizzy and with a slight headache. It must have been from the hours I put in at night combined with the time spent attending classes. Or maybe because I skipped a few meals. The few coins shining in the bottom of my wallet were only enough for transportation.

It didn't matter. Tonight, I get my first paycheck. Not that it would be enough for food *and* rent, but at least it would buy me a couple of extra days to finally find a second job.

Searching my *vast* wardrobe, I put on one of the two shirts I owned, then pulled a fabulous pair of authentically worn-out jeans on, and I was on my way. Though, the bus didn't seem to agree with my plans. The driver could only cross the unmarked border between the Pit and the Hills after having waited for over twenty minutes for a protest meeting to disperse. By the time we made it through, I was late for class.

It was too late for me to go to my first course and too early for my second, so I decided to go over a few class notes outside before the rain began. I could tell by the dark clouds that it wouldn't be long before that happened.

Finding a secluded bench next to the sports gym, I sank onto it, trying to decipher the scribblings I had made in my notebooks. With my handwriting, I should have registered for Med school.

"Come on, man, give me a break," a whimpering male voice caught my attention before I could get through half a page.

Who could be around? I asked myself, scouting the area with my gaze, without spotting a single soul.

"No, no... let me search my backpack." The same whining voice sounded, as I realized it was coming from behind the gym.

Initially, I wanted to remain on the bench. I even hoped deep down someone would pour instant glue on me and stick me to the wooden boards. But surprisingly, my body moved, carrying me to see what was happening.

I was like a moth flying to an open flame.

With cautious steps, I made my way through the narrow pathway that separated the gym from the labs. I managed to keep my presence concealed by hiding behind the thick leaves of a climbing plant that covered the walls of both buildings.

"All of them." I didn't recognize the voice, but I was certain that it didn't belong to the same guy that I had heard earlier. I needed to take a closer look. So, without a second thought, I took a step further, hiding my body beneath the plants.

Now that I could see, I noticed an unassuming blond guy, who must have been pretty low in the hierarchy ranks because I saw him all the time towards my end of the hallway, pressed against the English-style brick wall by a much more muscular type of animal—Cole.

"All of them I said," the brute roared at the student under the ecstatic gazes of the chipmunks that followed him—the *Golden Boys,* as everyone called them. More like the *Moron Boys* if you ask me. Ace, Jason, and Nick—three slaves to their king. Yet none of them were half as imposing as Cole.

Ace seemed to be next in command. Although his sharp facial features, along with the twisted look in his dark gaze, gave him the potential of making him out to be even more dangerous than their leader. The stabbing-in-the-back kind of dangerous.

In comparison, Nick and Jason were almost harmless. Both were trying a little too hard to live up to the *bad boy* image which made them seem desperate to belong to the group. Not just anyone would notice that aspect, but I had the bad habit of sometimes observing a person down to the smallest details. Their expensive clothes, expensive haircuts, luxury watches, and gym-toned bodies—even if Jason definitely skipped leg day—showed that they paid a little too much attention to how others perceived them. While the bad-boy attitude should have come with the *I don't care about what anyone else thinks* mindset.

"Break his nose," Ace said, encouraging Cole to step up his game. They were acting like they were back in high school, and certainly not like they were in their senior year of college. In an ideal world, they would just be a sick bunch of losers; but instead, here they were royalty.

The well-defined back muscles hiding beneath his black shirt tensed, creating a very angry version of the blue-eyed villain. "Are you fucking telling me what to do? Maybe I should break *your* nose for that," Cole snarled with his demonic gaze straight at Ace. Seemingly seconds away from taking his disciple by the throat and reminding him of the rules.

Without a second thought, Ace and the other two backed down. They created a distance from their leader and his current victim, who quickly regained Cole's attention. "If I have to wait for a second longer, I **will** break your nose," he roared at the guy who was curled into himself.

With hasty moves, pulling at his pockets, the caged student raised a hand with a generous stack of bills. He held them out to Cole. The bills shaking, not as a sign of defiance, but due to the difficulty he was having controlling the nervous trembling of his hands.

Not waiting for a second longer, the *king* yanked the stack out of his hands. With a thief's agility, separated more than a quarter, and shoved them into his pocket. He then threw the rest of the money to Ace. "I guess this should cut it for the final arrangements," Cole raised an eyebrow like he was doing the math on something.

"My place Friday night?" Jason questioned in a tone that was waiting for confirmation.

"Let them know." Cole nodded, freeing the student who was on the brink of a panic attack.

It was like the poor guy evaporated in a second, running as fast and as far as his feet could carry him while Ace and the rest of the crew took a right to enter the gym.

Strangely, Cole didn't move, he simply stood there like a statue for a couple of minutes. Even as the rain began and large drops started rolling on his face, filling the thick strands of jet-black hair and making it tumble over those cobalt pools of darkness.

I couldn't leave either, not without revealing my position. The plants were offering me a temporary shelter, yet it wasn't enough. I felt my clothes catching the cold drops of rain and heating as they hit my skin. The cold droplets cause me to shake harder than the leaves around me. But there wasn't a chance in hell that I would flinch and risk him catching a glimpse of me.

Cole turned and took a few steps away in the opposite direction, giving me hope I was finally free. But my sense of freedom was quickly shattered by the gruff sound of his voice. "Get out here," he snarled, stopping and turning his gaze straight toward the bushes that were hiding me.

I paused, not knowing what to do, embarrassed and scared

at the same time.

"Don't make me come and drag you out of there myself." This time his tone was much more menacing than before and angering him more than he already was didn't seem like a good choice at all.

I pushed the leaves away and took a step further into the pouring rain. Cole paused for a second as if he was waiting to see if I dared go closer to him. I didn't, and that made him stride in my direction, halting only a few inches in front of me.

Expecting the worst, I gulped, terrified of him possibly hitting me. Yet, he seemed to have different intentions. "You're cold," he smirked, angling his head so he was looking directly at my hardened nipples that were breaking through my t-shirt.

Embarrassed, I wrapped my arms around my chest, attempting to cover myself, only to see a wide grin spread on his face. I was sure it wasn't something he hadn't seen before. But it was something that I'd *never shown to anyone before.*

"Do you like watching me?" Cole continued, his arrogance leaking into his words. I was aware that he wasn't expecting an answer. He was just preying on humiliating me.

Before I knew it, his hand raced towards me, making my eyes instinctively close. I silently waited to feel the impact of the blow. It would be nothing I couldn't handle since I've had such thorough training from my father that I was prepared for anything.

Surprisingly, his palm stopped somewhere else, under my chin. Taking a breath, I opened my eyes to look at him, his tempestuous gaze falling on me. A lazy thumb rolled over my lips, stealing the oxygen out of my lungs, "Little Mouse, you're going to keep these sealed about what you've just seen."

He wasn't asking; he was telling, though I nodded to

confirm it anyway. Anything so he would let me leave.

I knew exactly what he was referring to. He didn't care about people knowing he was bullying that student earlier; he would have probably taken pride in that. He was referring to me seeing him take the money.

He must've had his personal reasons for doing that but I didn't care, I just wanted to disappear.

"Flee," he whispered into my ear. Blowing a breath towards me like I was a single ash flake, and he decided where I would end up. I didn't need him to tell me twice. I ran as fast as I could, straight into the girl's bathroom where I glued myself to a cold radiator, trembling and hyperventilating, with no real chance of finding the warmth I needed.

"Hey, hey, hey," Jenna greeted me around twenty minutes later while I was just preparing to detach myself from my new hideout. "Oh, did you get caught out in the rain?" She asked, turning on the faucet to wash her hands.

"Yeah, my bus was late," I muttered, recalling the real reason I skipped class and ended up on Cole's radar. "And I had the fortune of running into the Golden Boys," I whispered so that the rest of the girls that were in the bathroom wouldn't hear us.

"Oh my God, did they hurt you?" Jenna asked with concern and a tint of horror plastered on her face.

"No, I just overheard them talking about something." I wouldn't normally have told her about my encounter—not because I had something to hide, but because I didn't think it was even worth mentioning. I was curious about something, and she might have had an answer to my question, "Do you know about them having some arrangements, like something important coming up? They seemed excited about it."

"Oh, maybe they were talking about the party," she said, furrowing her brows.

"The party?" I asked.

"Two times a year, they throw a luxurious party. The first half of the hallway is generally invited. No money is spared—and that's because the money comes from the Herd."

I was confused. "What do you mean it comes from the Herd?'"

"They usually consider anyone outside their close contacts as a member of the Herd. You see, the money is like a protection fee. They use it to finance different parties—not that they couldn't afford it anyway, but it reinforces their authority. The more the Herd produces, the more expensive the bottles on the tables," Jenna muttered in disgust.

"And do the ones attending also pay the fee?" I needed to understand what was going on around here once and for all.

"Yeah, most of them need to pay it, depending on how rich daddy and mommy are. It's like a ticket to the ultimate party because anything goes there. And when I say anything, I mean ANYTHING. At least that's what I heard. I haven't been invited to one as you may have guessed by now."

I knew from her tone that the *"anything"* should raise my interest and probably make me start dreaming of getting myself an invitation, as any other student would. I had an idea of what could go down at an Elite party where overly bored people found any number of things to cure their boredom. A bunch of assholes clowning around with no real worries on their mind when I alone had too many for a single person to bear.

I cut the conversation short. It was just a small curiosity anyway, and I needed to go to class before I missed my next one too.

The day passed relatively quickly. I was excited about getting my first paycheck. The first money I ever worked for, and even if it was far from being enough, it gave me a strong feeling of independence.

***

I took off from the university, leaving everything that happened today behind. I needed to get myself into a working mood, but first I needed a nap. I never backed down from a challenge. Working nine hours every night and lifting twenty-five-pound boxes had an effect on me by the time dawn came. How long would I be able to keep running my body like this?

The boss never stayed until the morning, mostly because the factory had three shifts, and it would have been impossible for him to always be on duty. With that in mind, I stopped by his office to get my paycheck before going to fulfill my daily duties.

Heading toward the compounds' courtyard, where the containers that serve as the main office sat, I noticed a woman crying. She was hurrying toward the gate with eyes full of tears and a look of worry etched on her face that unsettled me. I knew her, she worked on a line next to mine, but I never interacted with her. I never interacted with anyone in the factory since we're paid according to what we deliver. Every cent mattered these days, and not only for me. We were human robots from 10 p.m. to 7 a.m. In a way, that was fine by me. I needed to focus on what was important and not be taking someone else's problems on myself. It was in my nature to sympathize with others' pain until it sometimes merged into me. And when it came to soul-destroying places, this factory could hold the lead.

"Can I come in?" I knocked on the metal door but didn't push the handle until I heard a confirmation echoing from within.

I must have had the most ridiculous, ear-to-ear smile splattered on my face. The excitement of receiving my first paycheck overwhelmed me. I was finally earning my own money, no more panhandling on the street for mere coins or scraps

"Ms. White, please take a seat," Randy, the man who hired me, gestured toward an empty seat near his desk.

I followed his instructions, then waited for him while he searched through some papers for something. "There it is," he uttered, pulling out a thin file and opening it up in front of me. "Sign below the marked line." He pushed it towards my end of the table as if I had any idea what the document was about.

"What's this?" I stuttered, noticing the word *finalizing* somewhere above the line he was referring to. I didn't get a chance to read everything that was written down, but from the one-second speed reading, I had an idea of what the document was about.

"It's a termination of our contract," Randy calmly said, as if that was our initial agreement. I never liked the man, I knew there was something off about him. But these days jobs were as scarce as gold, so that made the *liking* aspect irrelevant.

"What do you mean, I thought it was indefinite?" I didn't understand what was going on. My mind quickly became a blur, threatening to lose all sanity.

"It wasn't, haven't you read the contract?" he asked.

Big mistake on my part because I didn't. Not that I would have refused it anyway. I was just so excited about finding a job in only two days since I arrived in the city that I skimmed through the pages. I only stopped on the sections where they had specified the pay.

"To be honest, I would have kept you if it wasn't for what's happening in the streets," he said, glancing out the window.

"What's happening on the streets?" Between my time spent at the factory and the university, I didn't have any idea about what was going on around me. Plus, the lack of a TV was a black stain on me being up to date with the latest news.

Randy looked back at me with doubt—or as if I came from Mars. Lighting himself a cigarette, he breathed in thin strands of smoke. "Riots. The whole place is a fucking ticking bomb," his voice tense with worry.

"But what's that got to do with me?" I couldn't connect how my job fit into the picture.

"It's easy; we produce packages for clothing. Do you think the Elite will be so invested in shopping when all hell is about to break loose? I'll give you the answer to that. They'll be running like the scared craps they are."

You could clearly see in which camp he was playing. Still, none of this would solve my problems; on the contrary, it deepened them. "We are shutting down at least one of the shifts to cut the losses for now, and as you may have realized it, last in, first out," he concluded, leaving me speechless to stare into the ground.

Not only could I not find another job, but I was also losing the one that I had. Desolation wasn't enough to describe the tormenting fear that was sneaking into my soul. With every second that passed, I felt that I was approaching the end of the world—at least the end of my world.

"Here's your money," he pushed a few bills over the file, leaving me enough room to fill out my name under the marked line "Sign. It's only a formality anyway. The contract stipulated that our agreement ends today. Your signature is needed just so that I don't fill out some more useless forms."

"Please, give me a chance. I'll work harder than any employee you have. I need this. I can't leave this room without a job." I almost begged him to let me keep it. As I said, it wasn't even much, to begin with, but it was *something*. And now I was about to be left with absolutely *nothing*.

Randy smiled, but the curl of his lips had a devious amusement in it. "You think they all don't want the same thing? That they're not desperate? You should have heard the offers I received over a job. And don't think I don't know that this packager position is not much, but compared to what's out there in the Pit, it's everything. People are dying out there," he said with a dark satisfaction, as if people's misery was empowering him. He was the boss of a few putrid bills. But those bills could make a difference between life and death when you didn't even have food to put on the table.

"Please," I pleaded much stronger than I used to do back in the streets. Now, it wasn't for my lame attempt of a father; now, it was for my siblings.

Randy took a drag out of his cigarette, then paced toward a small window that was positioned to face the factory. "Come here and tell me what you see."

I almost jumped to my feet, hurrying toward the window. I was hoping that it was his way of finally telling me that I still had a chance of keeping my job.

I glanced through the window to try and figure out what he was talking about, but there was nothing out of the ordinary. "People," I replied, looking at the numbers of workers going in and out as the shifts were changing.

"Dull, murky people," he snarled, taking a step closer to

me. "You're not like them are you?" His lips touched the back of my head as a wandering hand wrapped itself around my waist. "You shine," he added, as my body froze like an Antarctic blizzard had just gone through it. "I may have another use for you around here." He was putting light upon his name, as his voice became *randy*, and his body leached against mine, forcing me against the window.

I admit, I was desperate but never desperate enough to accept the advances of a man well beyond his fifties, no taller than a garden gnome, with gray hair and an expanding bald spot.

"Get off of me!" I turned to push him around. There was no need to ask him what he was doing. Things were obvious enough.

A hand that caused my stomach to churn raced to tug on my t-shirt. "It will surely beat working on the packaging line."

Drawing my arms back to get enough momentum, I dashed toward him. I even managed to push him away for a second. But his force overcame mine and I ended up trapped between the metal wall and his reeking breath while his lips were searching for my own. I turned my head so he wouldn't reach me, yet his body came so close that I began feeling his whole weight pressing down on me. I had to get out of here. Yet, in this moment it seemed like an impossibility as I could barely even move from where he held me against the window.

"Ahem," the clearing of someone's throat stopped Randy, forcing him to turn his gaze toward the door.

In that second, regrouping my forces, I pushed him off me. Without waiting for him to recover from the shock, I ran toward the exit, taking a moment and using a speed I didn't know I possessed to reach over the desk and grab my money.

I thought I made it, but the moment I turned to get out the

door, my face smashed into what seemed to be a brick wall. The move unbalanced me. My palms opened to catch on to something, letting go of the measly dollars I earned that were so important to me.

The feel of expensive fabric under my fingers brought me back to the present I was just jarred from. The man who had just indirectly saved me from my assailant was standing right in front of me. "Get your shit together, Randy," he roared as I froze, glancing up at him. It was like facing a comet hurtling straight at me, with deep absinthe eyes and devious indentations in his cheeks—a perfect trap set out to destroy me.

How is it that someone could look like a God yet have the eyes of the devil?

Despite the instant mess his imposing presence made of my mind, I was no fool. Something evil was lurking beneath his perfect surface, so wicked that it had the potential to alter my universe. Just that one glance at the magnificence of his sculpted face and body, chilled me to the bone. The jet-black hair styled to perfection, the saffron note in his cologne, and that undeniable masculinity he exuded without the slightest effort were warning signs written in capital letters.

"He's not going to hurt you," the man snarled more in my ex-boss's direction than mine, while the chill-giving authority of his gestures was assuring me that he was right.

I dropped to the floor to pick up my money. Despite all the risks, I had to do it. If I didn't, it would have been *game over* for me once I walked out the door.

With rushed moves, I gathered the bills that were spread next to the Italian leather shoes the man was wearing. He didn't help me, and I didn't expect him to. I was just happy because if I was in the Pit, someone would have tried to steal them by now. Still, I was in the wrong place, and no matter what affirmation the businessman had made, I was in great danger.

As soon as I grabbed all the bills, my feet raced straight to the exit without having a second look their way. I didn't want to see them ever again—neither my despicable boss nor the strikingly handsome stranger.

I ran so fast that I thought my shoes might tear before I reached home. I only stopped running about three bus stops away from my apartment. It was impossible for me to go on at that pace. My heart pumped so loudly in my chest that I thought it would explode, and every single cell of my body seemed to be catching on fire. I was moments away from breaking down, but with the last of my strength, I crawled into the shower. This day had been an ordeal. As soon as I put some clothes back on, I understood how big of a nightmare it really was. Counting the bills, with tear-dropping desperation, I realized that it wasn't the whole sum I needed. Either Randy gave me less money, or I lost a few bills when I dropped them on the floor back at the factory. It didn't matter now since I would never return there.

I could no longer hold in my distress. Hot tears streamed down my face, soaking the bed sheet. For the first time ever, I felt defeated. It was rent day tomorrow, and I didn't even have enough to cover it. Not even a single dime for the university tuition either, and my stomach was twisting with a loud sound. It seems I have to try to make it through another night with no food.

I had to pull another blanket on top of me. I wasn't sure if it was even that cold in the room or if my body was beginning to cave in, but it managed to give me the comfort of insulation. I wanted to disappear. It would be so easy if I could just disappear. Yet, I couldn't do that, not to Sebastian and Natalie.

I think that I cried for hours, still hiding between the pillows, knowing it may be the last night with a roof above my head.

Sleep eventually found me, ravaged by tormenting emotions and utterly exhausted from fighting a battle every second I breathed.

I didn't wake up until morning, despite racking my brain last night before succumbing to sleep, I still had no idea what to do. I didn't even feel like getting out of bed, just lazily melted there into the mattress, hoping that I could find a supreme power to start everything all over again.

Where can I go? What can I do?

I wanted to close my eyes and go back to sleep, hoping that inspiration would find me. But as my lashes were preparing to unite, a small red spot on the floor caught my attention. My eyes blinked wide open, and I let my feet fall onto the ground, focusing on the object. An envelope.

Was it a bill? Utilities? Not likely since I didn't really have any except for the water—and even that came from a barrel that my landlord kept outside.

I rushed to open it, curious and intrigued since the paper seemed to be of high quality. As I unfolded the white sheet, dark handwritten letters revealed themselves. Letters, that little did I know would change my life.

Come to where two worlds meet and find the key to a new life— today 6 p.m.

CHAPTER 3

I folded the letter in half and placed it back in the red envelope.

While every single one of my instincts was telling me to throw it back on the floor where I found it and simply forget about it, part of me was hesitant to do so. My gut feeling was telling me this was the glimmer of hope that I had been trying so hard to find. Darkness lingered at the edges of my mind, threatening to consume me if I gave up hope. This could be my one chance to survive and accomplish my goals.

Maybe it was a trap, yet the 1% chance that this was real was forcing me to ignore my instincts. I just needed to figure out what the letter was about.

Reaching the sink, I splashed cold water on my face hoping to reconnect to reality. The room seemed to be spinning. I needed to smother my instincts so that I could wrap my head around this invitation that may be my last shot at saving my family from that monster. I had to do it. I had to pursue this last possibility, no matter how risky it could be. This was a world that showed no kindness, and deep down, I feared the price I would need to pay. Even if the words on the paper turned out to be true, in life, nothing comes for free.

I searched for the black skirt that I had brought when I left home. The only skirt I ever owned since I was more of a pants girl. But judging from the expensive paper, I had a feeling that my torn jeans wouldn't do me any favors this evening.

I didn't have a shirt. Not a decent one anyhow. I just tucked a white T-shirt into the skirt. It turned out to be one of those careful messy looks. Maybe they will think that I'm punky. In any case, it was the best that I could do.

Brushing my hair into a ponytail, I took a last look in the mirror. I was still a far cry from looking like an Elite, but it would have to suffice. I was already late for school and staring for a few extra minutes at my reflection wouldn't have gotten me a new set of clothes anyway.

A knock at the door stopped me on my way out. I was two steps away from twisting the doorknob when a voice that I feared to hear brought me to my senses. "Rent," my landlord barked, reminding me of the sum that was due that day.

What could I tell him? I didn't have the money.

I needed to stall him, at least for a few hours, until I'd figure out what the letter led to. That meant I couldn't go through the front door, so I decided to make a getaway. Opening the small window I usually keep tightly shut because of thieves, I threw my bag on the metal fire escape ladder and then sped down the stairs. With all the running I had been doing these days, I could participate in a marathon.

At least I managed to make it to the university on time. Yet, throughout the day my mind was nowhere near ECU, just drifting away *to where two worlds meet.*

It was a riddle. A complicated one, yet all too easy at the same time. The two worlds—the Pit and the Hills divided by a thin line—a street—half poverty and desperation, half luxury and opulence. An invisible border that divided our societies so well.

Now, all I had to do was to figure out the exact place I was supposed to go to.

I barely made it through my classes. I was constantly staring at the clock, counting each second. The minute my last lecture of the day ended, I was on my way to finding *the key to a new life*—whatever that meant.

The edge of the Pit, where I was hoping to find what I was looking for, was just about a mile away. I was too anxious, my feet couldn't be held still to wait at the station, so I figured I would burn off some energy and just walk there. Too much excitement, I guess. I could only hope it was real, and wasn't a trap to make me some involuntary organ donor.

When I finally made it to the street I was searching for, there were no open doors or large signs with my name written all over them waiting to guide me to where I needed to be. Not that I was expecting any in the first place.

Initially, I thought about asking around, but what exactly was I looking for anyway?

I had no option but to wander around and hope that I could figure things out on my own, maybe even find a small clue to where what I was searching for might be.

I analyzed each house as I went by, focusing on the luxurious part of the street. The quality paper was a sign that my location was most likely on that side of the road, and I was right. *The key to a new life* suddenly made perfect sense, a key-shaped door was right in front of me. It was a gothic building, unique in its architecture, as intriguing as the letter that took me there.

Realizing I was moments away from uncovering the mystery, every sensation known to man was racing through my body. I was cold while burning internally, shaking but driven by all the courage in the world.

I needed to know whether my little brother and sister were lost or saved.

With full sail ahead, I ventured to knock on the door.

No one answered.

This had to be it; I wasn't mistaken.

I knocked again, harder this time, until the metal door clicked open, revealing an empty room. I stepped forward, tilting my head just a little inside to see if anyone was around when a voice acknowledged my presence. "Just in time, Bea. Lobby—first door on the right."

The voice was a female one I didn't recognize, yet her knowing my name meant we had to have previously met, right?

Following her instructions, I entered the hallway and stopped in the doorway of the first room on the right. In front of me stood a tall, beautiful woman, her hair dark as the night and piercing eyes to match its color. She was in her late 40's, maybe early 50's. The only thing that really betrayed her age were the small wrinkles forming under her eyes because her body looked like she had just come out of high school.

A golden dress made of expensive material wrapped tightly around her waist, while every piece of her jewelry screamed luxury. She was distinct, glamorous in every sense of the word, maybe a rich businesswoman, high society for sure. However, I didn't get to linger on analyzing her. My thoughts were abruptly interrupted by the sound of her voice, "Good afternoon, Bea."

"Good afternoon, but how do you know my name?" There was something strange happening here that pushed me to try and find out where she knew me from.

She smiled, revealing a perfect row of pearly white teeth. "I wouldn't be in this position if I didn't. It's part of my job to know everything about the people I interact with." Taking a few steps toward her desk, she gestured for me to take a seat. "My name is Vanya, in case you're wondering. You were smart enough to decipher my note, which means you are worthy to sit in this chair. There is a certain level of cleverness I search for in a person, and you passed the test."

I needed clarification. "Can I ask why I'm here?"

"You tell me why you're here. Everyone has a reason. What's yours?"

"Hope," I gulped. "I need the new life you mentioned in the letter." I was turning my cards face up on the table.

"Then let me see what I can do for you. Ever heard of The Pleasure Room?" she asked so casually.

"What?" I replied, startled.

"It's not what it sounds like, not if you don't want it to be. But it does fulfill a man or a woman's pleasure, fantasy... call it whatever you like." Vanya reached for an elegant leather pouch that concealed a pack of cigarettes.

"I can't do this," I babbled. There had to be some trick, I knew it.

No matter how desperate I was, selling my body wasn't an option.

Lighting herself a cigarette, Vanya raised an annoyed eyebrow. "You didn't even give me a chance to explain. I'm not a patient woman, and you're almost taking the last of it." Her cold tone cut right through me, bonding me to my seat. "As I was saying, we have some simple rules here. The girls and guys here are like a family. I do not tolerate envy, jealousy or any behavior resulting from those in my establishment.

"The Pleasure Room is actually the room you wait in, along with the others that work here, waiting for the Pleasure requests to arrive.

"For each client you will receive a letter that stipulates their desire—The Pleasure, as we will refer to it from now on.

"Any one of you can read the letter and let the others know what it contains.

"Each letter will contain The Pleasure itself, the amount you will receive, and the duration. Some of them contain special requests, though not all, and some of them can be addressed to a specific person.

"You'll all take turns in getting The Pleasures. For example, if you were first today, you will be the last tomorrow, and so on, rotating with your colleagues so that everyone can have a chance.

"If you refuse a Pleasure, then the next in line can decide whether they refuse or accept it. Have I made myself clear?" she asks, waiting for me to process things.

I nodded, though, all I was thinking was that I had to get out of there. Yet, this was by far from being her intention. "Now, do you have any other questions?"

And here it came. The sensitive part that I knew she had purposely left out. "What am I supposed to actually do on a Pleasure?" I asked with a trembling voice.

"Whatever your client desires, as long as you are comfortable doing it. The initial Pleasures aren't of a sexual nature. I don't allow them to be, and if the client decides to raise the game, they also have to raise the paycheck. That usually means adding another zero to the sum. But it's your say-so where you go from there."

"If I accept or not?" I all but whispered.

"Yes, if you accept to let the Pleasure be of a sexual nature or not. I'm not going to lie and tell you that my clients don't usually want to go further. Most of them do. You're all attractive, and trying to satisfy a primordial need, well, it's a part of human nature. But you're the only one who decides if it goes further or not," Vanya continued.

Taking a deep breath. I needed to calm myself down. She wasn't done explaining things, I had to relax enough to stay in my seat while she finished.

"The jobs can differ. Some of our clients just need company because they feel lonely and need someone to talk to. Others want you to pretend to be somebody they need you to be... and some of them just want to take pride in having a pretty girl on their arm."

Everything the woman said sounded dangerous to me. Even the thought of having contact with these people was sending a cool shiver down my spine. "Is this legal?'

Her brows furrowed slightly. "The mayor and a few judges are among my top clients. It's legal. Very legal. But also, very discreet. Our clients usually like to keep their identities unknown, except from the person who they hire for The Pleasure, and me.

"And since we have reached the legal part, you will also sign a contract that stipulates the requests, and your limits. No one can reveal the nature of your job, but at the same time, you have to keep your mouth tightly shut about anything that could happen during a Pleasure. And about the person who requests it.

"There's one more aspect I believe needs to be mentioned. Our clients are only the elite society, so they spare no expense to make sure their Pleasures come to life. You can easily earn in an hour what you used to make in a couple of days, maybe even a week of working in the Pit."

"What if I want to back out of a job?" I asked.

"After you've accepted a job, you can't back out unless the one who solicited The Pleasure tries to harm you in any way. That doesn't usually happen. The compensation they'd have to pay cuts deep even into the largest of pockets. Plus, we have a few bodyguards that you can call on at any time.

"To sum things up, usual Pleasures can't be declined. If you refuse a Pleasure after initially accepting it, you are required to pay our agency the price of the contract, even though the client won't pay you."

Her words began settling in my mind, yet I was far from seeing myself involved in any of this. Still, my curiosity was pushing me to know more about this strange place. "You mentioned something about The Pleasure possibly requesting a certain person."

Vanya took a long drag of her cigarette. "Usually, it only specifies if they're looking for a man or a woman, but we do have clients that ask for some of our employees in particular. Most of the time, the clients that require a specific person have worked with that employee in the past. To make things clear, if the letter asks especially for you, then the rule in which you have to wait for your turn no longer applies." She finished her sentence, then rose to her feet, leaning forward on the desk, supporting her hands on the desktop. "I'll need a decision now, unfortunately, I'm two girls short. Two of my employees left without warning, and as you may have realized, I can't just put an ad in the paper for this job. "

The walls seemed to be closing in on me. How was I supposed to make a decision with no time to think this through? Whichever way I looked at this there didn't seem to be a correct choice. "Can I have a moment, please?" I ran out the door, unsure if she answered me or not. My heart was pumping loudly in my ears, making it almost impossible to think with all the adrenaline pumping throughout my body.

I wasn't the right person for this job.

But was it the right job for me?

The moment I got out the door, the thick smoggy air made it difficult to breathe. Yet something about it helped clear my head. *How was it that nothing and everything made sense?*

What was I going to do? There was nothing for me back in the Pit. I had searched everywhere I came across for another job, exhausted all the options. This was the only chance I had. Maybe I could even get enough Pleasure's to bring Nat and Sebastian here to live with me—hopefully without having to break my dignity.

There wasn't even a choice when I had a second to breathe, I would do anything for my siblings.

With my decision made I turned and ran back into the building and into Vanya's office. I couldn't afford to miss this opportunity. "I'll take the job," my voice trembled so hard that it sounded like an old cassette stuck in playing mode.

Vanya's palms glued together, her forehead furrowing in annoyance. "Never walk away from me again when I'm talking to you. Got it?"

I had rushed out in desperation and made a mistake. "Got it," I answered, hoping that my rude action wasn't enough to make her withdraw her offer.

"You're lucky I'm in a difficult situation with not enough personnel on my hands. I would have locked the door behind you if times were different," she hissed, searching through a thick stack of files that were placed in the corner of her desk. "You're hired. Go towards the end of the hallway and wait for a Pleasure. I'll prepare your contract by the time you're ready to go."

What?

Now?

As in today?

"Go, you'll know which room it is when you get there." Vanya didn't raise her eyes to look at me, continuing to search through the files.

I didn't give her the chance to get mad at me again. I just walked out of the room—this time with slow steps. Little did I know, I was heading to a point of no return. Once I passed through that door, my life was going to change forever. Maybe, it already had.

Misery or glory—I was moments away from finding out. One thing was certain, Vanya was right about me recognizing the room immediately. A large wooden door loomed in front of me, growing with size with every step I took.

Stopping in front of the door, I reached to touch the old wood carvings. Black and golden gargoyles masterfully sculptured into its surface, watching poor souls, ready to devour them. The door looked like it went directly into the underworld, as if screaming of an otherworldly magic. Everything that Echo City represented, and a little more—the gateway to heaven and hell.

Rise or fall—this was it.

I pushed the door open and stepped into a new world, finding myself in the middle of an imposing room where all eyes swung in my direction. I didn't even get a chance to see the people's faces clearly before a female voice greeted me.

"Welcome."

I raised a few shy fingers, "Hi."

"I'm Laura; Vanya usually assigns me to guide newbies around the place," the woman who greeted me continued while I kept looking around. Maybe around a dozen people, men and women, scattered all over the large hall, some involved in enthusiastic conversations while others were just hanging around the place.

"Bea." I smiled, though it probably looked more like a grimace since I just exposed my teeth. The situation I found myself in made it difficult to express a genuine smile, even though the woman standing in front of me seemed to have good intentions. The kind look on her caramel face appeared genuine, her warm soft brown eyes, so different from the cold gazes I usually encountered in Pit.

"Come, follow me," she walked toward a table where different drinks and snacks were carefully arranged. "Help yourself to whatever you want."

I wasn't sure that was a great idea. After not eating for the last two days, I could have eaten the contents of the table—plates included.

"Just a glass of water." I reached for the water decanter and poured myself a glass. Hunger or no hunger, I wasn't ready to stuff my face with all that I could find in front of so many unknown people.

"They're not that bad," Laura benevolently smiled, looking around her at the other people in the room, then placed a few tiny sandwiches and an apple on a small plate. "Let's sit at that table," she gestured towards a small byzantine metal table placed in a secluded corner of the room.

I followed her, taking the seat next to the window.

"I came from the same place," she nodded, placing the plate in front of me. "And I'm never returning there." The bitter gaze I know so well flashed through her eyes. "Eat, they don't care."

I wanted to say it wasn't necessary, maybe some dumb excuse that I ate just before I got here, but she knew. She knew *the hunger*. She knew the pain. There was no use in denying it, especially since my stomach was one step away from rioting on me.

"Is it hard? I mean, is it hard doing the Pleasures?" I asked while feasting on the first meal in two days.

"It was at first. Until I realized that it's a lot easier than working for a dusty fist of cents. I had enough of fearing every second of the day that I wouldn't be able to afford food or rent."

"Do you... you know... step up the game?" I was ashamed to intrude in her personal businesses, but I needed to know what was truly going on here.

She paused, raising her eyes to peer straight at me. "I... I personally don't, but almost everyone else here does it. Let's be honest; all the people in this room were hopeless at one point. You don't end up here otherwise. I guess accepting sex as a part of the Pleasure depends on how desperate you are at the time life opens this door for you."

A weight was lifted off my chest. There was a chance that I could do this job without losing myself. Maybe, in the end, coming here was the best decision after all.

However, I didn't get to fully weigh things before I noticed something being slipped underneath the door. It was a small red envelope, very similar to the one I received this morning.

"Hey, new girl," a tall blond man who looked like he could run in a fashion show for the Elite, leaned to pick it up, then looked my way.

Was I the new girl?

"He's talking to you," Laura chuckled, nudging me to go in his direction. Everything was happening so quickly that I didn't even have time to react.

"Don't look so surprised. Since you're new around here; we'll let you have the first letter. We do this with everyone."

Vanya was right. They did work as a team—a small family. Pretty strange when outside this door it was eat or be eaten by the bigger predator.

With shaking hands, I reached for the letter, slowly opening the envelope. My feet were seconds away from abandoning me. My eyes closed, hoping to avoid what had already become unavoidable.

30 minutes speed date—tonight 8 PM

Attractive woman in her twenties

$300

"You certainly fit the picture," Laura came from behind me, peeking at the letter over my shoulder. "Easy money. Not great, but easy."

$300 for half an hour wasn't great? I used to make that money in a week, maybe even a week and a half. There wasn't a chance in hell I was saying no to that.

"I'll do it," I answered even before anyone asked, mostly to convince myself not to back down.

A warm hand sneaked on the small of my back. "Welcome aboard," Laura whispered, catching my wrist and dragging me somewhere on the right. "Come on, you have to get ready. The time is so short. I have no idea what the one who pays the bill was thinking, giving you only half an hour to prepare."

I turned my head to look at the large clock on the wall—7:31 PM.

What was *I* thinking, accepting my first Pleasure less than half an hour away?

"Hurry," she rushed me, pushing a door open and guiding me to the middle of an enormous dressing room. If the white Italian custom furniture wasn't impressive enough, the exhibited display of gowns and shoes was absolutely stunning. Large showroom cases of colorful purses and shoes in all shapes and sizes defined an aisle that led to the most outstanding collection of dresses and outfits.

"What is this place?" I asked with wide eyes. Looking around, my gaze stopped at the gleaming sequins that were delicately twinkling under the light cast by a crystal chandelier.

"Hun, as I said, none of us came from money," she shrugged, pushing some clothes aside while she was searching for something. "All Pleasures are paid for by people belonging to the Elite society, and you can't really go to the Hills dressed in what you're wearing."

I turned my head to catch a sight of myself in the mirror. My black skirt and T-shirt could have been almost decent; if it wasn't for the cheap material. The hole it had in it was carefully tucked away in the hem of the skirt. But my worn-out shoes would definitely give me away, revealing my true financial condition.

"Please, don't be offended. I didn't mean it like that. It's just that you have to fit into their world, and you can't do it without selling the whole illusion. You should have seen the clothes I had when I first came in. Makes yours look like they came from a runway," she said, pulling out a red bodycon dress. "Here, try this on."

"But that's so tight," I uttered, looking at the tiny piece of red material.

"It's supposed to be that way. Put it on; you do want them to return for another Pleasure, don't you?" Laura practically threw the dress in my arms and walked away. "I'll be back in 5, give you some privacy. Put the dress on and do something about that hair."

Now there was also something wrong with my hair?

I was a little embarrassed to change with her still present there. I waited for her to leave the room, then got out of my clothes and put on the red dress. It slipped right on, just like it always belonged there—revealing a whole different person. The dress let out all the curves I usually kept hidden behind my baggy jeans and looser shirts, from my firm ass to my large chest, turning me from a nobody into a temptress.

Yet, there was something missing from the picture—Laura was right about my ponytail. Getting rid of the band that held my locks together sent a cold chill running down my spine. It was the best version of me, and I can't deny that it empowered me to the tip of my toes. At the same time, the change was also terrifying. In an instant, I had become an object of desire, and sooner or later this would have an irremediable effect on me.

The cheery sound of Laura's voice brought me back to my senses. "Yes, perfect!"

I could see her admiring me from a distance while I was having trouble arranging the dress around my defined shapes in an attempt to cover them up a little.

"Just take a deep breath and let it stay the way it's supposed to." Laura smiled, sensing my clumsiness but also my insecurity. "Here, you need shoes too." She handed me a pair of black heels, completing my *new* image. "And a hint of makeup." She smudged a brush over my eyes, then a little mascara and "You're done."

It was a brand new me staring back in the mirror—a *completely different me.*

"Two minutes left on the clock; you have to hurry," she rushed me.

Where did the half an hour go? I panicked, dashing out of the closet and heading toward the lobby as fast as I could in the new heels. Walking in these heels was almost like walking in tin cans.

"It's okay, you've got this." Laura quickly caught up with me.

She had better be right because only seconds were separating me from stepping into a new era.

"Sign here," Vanya's voice echoed from her office, stopping me on my way and forcing me to make a small detour to put my signature on the paper.

With no time to read the contract, it was just about blind faith. I was just praying that I wasn't repeating the mistake I made with Randy. Maybe I was sealing my fate, or maybe it was a pact with the devil. If that was the case, then the devil was personally dragging me out of my own hell.

Two seconds later, there it was: my name in black and white. The dice were tossed, and the game had just begun—my first Pleasure.

CHAPTER 4

I stepped out of the building, looking across the street. A brand-new luxury car was waiting for me, engine purring and the passenger door open.

"Hurry up, please," a male's voice was pressing me to move faster. And before I knew it, I found myself seated next to the driver.

"Wow, you look amazing," the man behind the wheel happily exclaimed, then, without a single explanation, drove off in a hurry.

My limbs were trembling, and I was trying to keep my anxiety from getting the better of me. He could be a freak, a rapist, a serial killer or maybe all of the above. The guy beside me was becoming, unwillingly, the vivid representation of a horrid abomination.

I took a quick sneak peek out of the corner of my eye, expecting to catch a glimpse of probably the last person I'd ever see. Funny, he didn't look so menacing, just a regular man in his late thirties, maybe early forties. Caucasian with dark hair, hazel eyes, an oval face and a small beard. Okay, okay, I was rehearsing in my mind a description for the police, if I'd still be alive to give one.

"Here's the deal." The man turned to face me with an even more concerned expression than my own. "I've never done this, but desperate times call for desperate measures. I need you to pretend to be my date for tonight. It's not even for the whole night, just for a few minutes while I drop off my kid."

I turned to look at the backseat, where a little boy was sleeping peacefully in a car seat.

What kind of killer takes his child along to a crime scene?

"My wife recently left me for one of her interns. Met him during surgery, probably confused the scalpel with his dick," he confessed.

"I'm sorry," I had no idea what to say. This Pleasure was quickly turning out to be something completely different than I had imagined.

"Not as sorry as I am, believe me. He's fifteen years younger than me." The man sighed, stopping at a red light. "I loved her, I still do, but I need her to realize the mistake she's making— what she's really losing. That's where you step in."

"How's this going to help you fix your relationship?" If anything, seeing him go his separate way may only deepen the gap between them.

"I need her to see that I'm still worthy. You know... that I can still get a pretty woman's attention."

I tilted my head to take another look at the man sitting next to me. What was he talking about? I don't usually look at men older than me, but he was like fine wine. The laugh lines on his face accentuated every single one of his manly features. I had no idea why he hired me in the first place when he could have found himself a real date, maybe one even more attractive than me.

"Then let's show her that," I smiled, determined to play along. "But I think that I should know your name first. You know, people that usually date tend to know small details like that," I giggled, causing a smile to erase the small frown previously marring his face.

"Michael. And my date's name would be...?"

"Bea."

"Even your name is beautiful," he flashed me a quick smile, before driving again since the traffic light had turned green. "My son was with my mother today, and we're taking him back to my wife now. Just so that you know what's going on in case she asks," he said, giving me a short briefing.

I was starting to feel like an actress preparing for her first part.

"We're here," he spoke after driving a few blocks, stopping in front of an impressive mansion.

"Come on, Nathaniel, it's time to wake up." Michael got out of the car, unlocked the back door, and reached for his son. At the same time, the main door of the house opened to reveal an attractive blonde woman in her thirties, waiting for him.

But the man suddenly had a change of heart, intimidated by the arch of his wife's eyebrows while looking in my direction and observing my presence in his car. "Shit, I can't do this. Please stay there."

Man up, for God's sake. I thought to myself but did nothing to help him yet. I followed his instructions and remained in the car while he walked down the front sidewalk, carrying his half-asleep son to pass him to his wife—if she could still be called that.

I watched his face change a million colors under her

inquisitorial eyes as if he was the one to blame for her infidelities. Even if I couldn't hear what they were saying, the desolate expression on his face needed no words. He was losing the game, and the only ally he had was staying still, in the front right seat of his car.

This was it, all or nothing; I pushed the door open and walked like a gazelle until I found his arm. Okay, maybe a wounded gazelle, since heels were still a mystery to me. "Michael, we're going to be late for the Opera," I whispered, leaning toward his ear, then stretching out my hand to meet the main target. "Bea," I smiled, making sure to show off my perfectly white teeth while a look of helpless anxiety was reflected in her eyes. Having a bimbo by his side could pose no threat, but having a beautiful, educated woman asking him to go to the Opera was a different kind of trouble.

"Come," I rushed him, catching on to his arm. "We do have plans after," my voice warm, filled with a seductive tone that was almost making me laugh. But for her, it was the real deal. *I* was the real deal.

She babbled something as I hung onto Michael's arm and walked back to the car.

"Thank you," he breathed. "You must think I'm such a fool."

That was exactly what I thought, but I knew the reason behind it. "You still love her. You can't dictate your heart. You're not a fool."

"I'll take you back." He drove us back to Vanya's, trying to avoid discussing what just happened. But before the car came to a stop, a beeping sound lit the screen of his phone.

"Can you come over and look after Nathaniel for a while? I don't feel too good. I think I'm coming down with a fever."

"It worked," he said while looking in disbelief at the screen.

"She's never been sick a day in her life. Kind of convenient to get sick for the first time on my date night." He parked the car, turning a warm smile toward me. "Thank you again."

"My *pleasure*," I returned the smile, "But I feel that I need to add something." I knew it wasn't my place to say this, but my mind sometimes could not find peace, "She doesn't deserve you."

That was when I saw it in his eyes—*he already knew.*

I walked back to the building, low-key satisfied with myself. Mission complete. It was so easy. Too easy, if you asked me.

In less than half an hour since I left for the Pleasure, it was payday. My problems were as good as solved. Rent was being paid by the end of the night. I had strong hopes that I would be able to raise the money I needed so I could bring Sebastian and Natalie here to live with me in around two months. If it was up to me, I would go get them tomorrow, but my father would probably call the cops on us since he was the one who had custody. I needed a lawyer, and we needed protection—neither of those came cheap.

***

I returned to The Pleasure room the next afternoon. In Laura's opinion, it was a slow day. Only a few Pleasures arrived, and my turn was still far away since I just had a Pleasure the day before. No need to get disappointed, there was always going to be tomorrow, and a better-paying Pleasure could get me back on track in no time.

Though tomorrow came... and the day after... and then the day after that too.

The letters still arrived, but most of them specifically asked for those who the clients had already worked with, while the others were addressed to my male colleagues.

I was panicking, even if Laura was trying to calm me down, explaining that the right letter would come soon.

But I couldn't **do** soon.

I needed *now.*

Soon would only delay my plan, but time was an asset that wasn't on my side. And just when I had almost lost hope, the red envelope opened for me.

Sex bomb for the night

$1000

Today 9 p.m.

"Wow, a classy one," Sonya, the girl who opened the letter, laughed, handing me the envelope. "You can pass if you don't like it," she reminded me of the rules since the one who was paying for this Pleasure sounded like an absolute dick.

My instincts were strongly warning me to pass it along and wait for an hour or so for another letter to arrive. But what if that hour turned into a day again, and the *one* day into many others?

Plus, there was the pay—$1000, almost enough to get me back on my savings schedule.

I shook my head, removing all doubts—and mental sanity along with them. Before I could get a chance to second-guess my decision, I breathed, "I'll take it."

"Are you sure?" Laura asked with a hint of concern since the classy **sex bomb** wasn't a usual request for a letter. Sure, they all wanted *attractive young women* or *sensual dates,* but the *sex bomb* must have been a first.

"I'm sure," I answered, thinking about what the money truly represented. Besides, what could go wrong? There was a certain line that couldn't be crossed without my consent, and I decided from the first second of my agreement with Vanya that the bridge would never be burned.

"Go get yourself pretty then; you have two hours to spare. Make a sex bomb out of yourself," Laura chuckled at the irony of the situation.

"Two hours... A bomb with a timer," I muttered, heading towards the walk-in dressing room.

My *timer* was rather long since the sex bomb look was ready in less than an hour. And I say *an hour* because I spent half of that time staring at myself in the mirror, making sure I'd left none of my *assets* unexploited.

My choice for the night was flawless. A short black lace dress that wrapped around my body in heavenly perfection, revealing every last curve of my voluptuous shape. It was exquisitely accessorized with a black pair of heeled sandals, and as for my hair—large waves of silky curls that rolled over my breasts. I added some makeup too. Fine black lines above my eyelashes to bring out the greenish color of my eyes, and a tint of lipstick to plump the sex bomb vibe out of my lips.

Now, all I had to do was wait. *For an entire hour.*

I was beginning to regret all the time I had on my hands. I think I preferred it the other way around, with my first Pleasure where I was rushing everything to the point it managed to take my mind off the pressure.

At least the hour to kill was finally giving me the time I needed to go through the Pleasure's contract. It wasn't a scam; everything was laid out clearly in black and white—benefits, and penalties together.

"Your car is here five minutes early. You can still wait if you want to, but I have to leave for a meeting," Vanya said while collecting her purse and heading towards the door.

"I'll leave now." It made no sense to delay the inevitable. I got up from the chair I was sitting in and followed her outside, where a cab was already waiting for her.

"Your limo," Vanya gestured toward a black limousine as she got inside her own transportation and drove off in a hurry.

I turned my head to look at the impressive vehicle that was waiting for me, a sleek black limousine, with chrome accents and fully tinted windows. I gulped, heading toward the door which opened to greet me. "Hop in," a male voice encouraged me to enter, and from the giggles and laughter coming from within the car, he wasn't alone.

"Don't be shy, we don't bite," another man said while I was climbing in, only to observe something that my mind could never have conceived happening.

In front of me, I found a familiar face—Jason, while on my right there was Ace, followed by Nick. The Golden Boys without their leader.

I braced myself, preparing to voice an explanation since their amazement at finding me in this position seemed to be inevitable.

"Fuck, she's so hot," Jason growled, biting his full lips as if I wasn't even present there.

"You're not touching her, I signed the fucking contract, and it's *my* ass on the line. That greedy bitch will sue me for everything I have if we break the terms," Ace rushed to remind his friend about Vanya's specific terms of service.

"Lucky fucker," Jason roared, rearranging himself better in his seat while looking at his reflection in the car's window to fix his light brown hair to perfection.

"Yeah, not so lucky tonight," Ace grinned, his devious smile reminding me of a hyena. Not that he wasn't usually acting like one.

There was something off about this whole scenario, and I was having trouble figuring out my part in it. At least they didn't recognize me, and that was helping me be more relaxed. I guess being a nobody pays off at the end of the day.

"Listen, babe," Ace decided to address me in his *oh-so-mannered* way. "One of our friends recently lost a bet. So, he's in for a penalty. That's where you come in. He can look but can't touch. That's gonna be a little tormenting for him since he's not the most patient person in the world."

A certain level of satisfaction was evident on Ace's face as the word *friend* didn't really fit into his story. "What he doesn't know is that you will try to seduce him. That's your job for the night, and I'll be watching to ensure that you fulfill your part.

"Vanya gave me a double contract. *He* will also have to sign it and respect the rules since you're going to be his companion for the night."

He. I had a fear I knew the *he,* Ace was referring too. An empty sensation began gnawing at the pit of my stomach since I had a strong feeling Cole was the one whom I was to keep company for the night.

At least they seemed to fear the consequences of breaking the contract. That was lifting a small weight off my chest. The smothering sensation was still there, pressing deeply on every nerve, killing all illusions I had that this Pleasure could be as easy as the first. This would be a test of endurance. Putting up with these idiots would probably prove to be much more difficult than I thought when accepting the letter.

"How much for the full show?" Nick decided to test the water, confusing the purpose of the Pleasure with a whole different thing. At least, different for me. He was smug, that's for sure. If only his IQ would have matched his physical appearance.

"You'll have to go to the piggy bank for this one; she's definitely pricey," Ace answered on my behalf as if he would have any idea of what my rules were.

"Excuse me?" I retaliated, extremely annoyed with his question. Just because I accepted the mission didn't mean I had to keep my mouth shut. "If you are searching for a different type of companion, I suggest you turn the car around and ask for a different person for your Pleasure. See if you have better luck with them."

I was expecting them to do just that—take me back to Vanya's place and ask for someone else who would probably be more open to fulfilling their fantasies.

Strangely, they didn't. My bitchy attitude seemed to agree with Ace just fine. "Nah, you're perfect." His eyes flared with devious thoughts like an evil mastermind seeing his plan come alive. He was up to no good, and I could only pray that his scheme for tonight wouldn't have repercussions for me. In the end, I just wanted this to be over so I could get paid and get on with my own plans.

"You know, I keep looking at you and I think I know you from somewhere. But I can't put my finger on it," Jason narrowed his hazel eyes as if he was trying with all his strength to get the rusty wheels of his mind to work, maybe even recognize me.

"If she ain't a stripper, the chances of you knowing her are pretty low." Nick was letting out the sarcasm. They were all the same, in my opinion—three spoiled brats with too much money to burn and too much time on their hands.

I wish I could say that the ride was a short one—or at least a pleasant one, but it felt like a never-ending bad dream. The guys' sexual innuendos kept rolling in for almost half an hour, while I either smiled through my teeth, or made them bite back their words. Nothing with any decent success since the hormones mixed with the bottle of vodka they shared in the car were making them even more obnoxious than usual.

I was almost happy when the limo stopped... *Almost* being the keyword since nothing involving this evening could make me happy in any way.

I stepped out of the vehicle, and it was like stepping into a different world. Sure, I've seen luxury before, but never on this scale, so glamorous that even the street seemed to be made of gold. A private piece of heaven—for those who could afford it. For the rest, an unattainable dream, especially since for most of those living in the Pit, their greatest achievement was putting food on the table.

There was a lot of fuss around the mansion, and I was starting to realize that we were arriving at a party. From my guess, the party I caught them talking about a few days ago. That meant trouble—a world of trouble since probably half of the university was going to be here.

How the hell was I supposed to get out of this one?

"This way." Jason's hand fell on my hip, skimming the curve of my ass while his alcohol-reddened eyes were trying to stare seductively into mine.

His moment of playing Casanova was short-lived as I moved his hand away before he got a chance to *feel me up.* "I can walk by myself, thank you."

"I think I'm falling in love." Deciding to pursue his juvenile pick-up strategy, Jason was insisting with his *seductive* gaze.

"Cut it out before Cole gives you a black eye," Nick tried to bring him back to his senses, confirming the thought I feared most—their *king* owned my time for the night. If the ride here seemed stressful, the rest of the evening would be catastrophic. "There he is," he turned his head to my right, where Cole was talking to one of the girls that I usually see hanging around their group.

It didn't take long for him to notice our arrival, and since I was the centerpiece of the evening, his night-blue eyes began scanning me from the moment he acknowledged my presence.

"My man, I brought you your victim for the night," Ace made sure to introduce me as the acquisition of the day, and when it came to Cole, that's exactly what I was—*a victim*.

CHAPTER 5

C ole seemed to know exactly what Ace was talking about. The king picked up a bottle of whiskey from the ground and strode across the lawn, heading to the back of the garden. "Let's go into the guesthouse; there are too many people here."

The guys followed one by one while my feet seemed to be stuck to the pavement.

"Are you coming? Or should we ask for a refund?" Nick noticed me hesitating and did what they all do best—feed on my misery.

That's exactly why I couldn't show any signs of weakness. "Yeah, I was just admiring the house."

"Just make sure nothing sticks to your fingers on your way out." Jason said, giving me a once over.

Great, now I was also a thief. What were they expecting me to steal? Some silverware?

We made our way to the guest house, which was practically a mansion in itself. It had a secondary garden, a tennis court, and a swimming pool—everything needed to entertain the *poor* guests who came to visit.

"I need to have a word with her first." Cole turned to look

at us and, at the same time, pushed the house door open so I could go in.

The thought of being alone with him, even for a second, was sending cold chills down my spine. The refund Nick was talking about earlier seemed to be the perfect solution to get out of here. But there was a catch, if they requested a refund for my failure to perform; *I* was supposed to pay that money to Vanya, and under no circumstances could I afford that.

There wasn't any other option but to take a step forward and go inside.

"Just don't touch her," Ace grunted out loud just as I was walking past Cole.

"Only if she asks nicely." Cole said in that tone of supremacy I feared, confirming every anguished thought I ever had about him. The blood rushing through my body caused a pounding in my ears as fear took over.

The door closed behind us, revealing an infuriated version of this devil, who took a step in my direction until our bodies almost joined.

What the hell have I gotten myself into?

"What are you doing here?" he muttered under his breath, so heavily that the words seemed to fall upon my face.

"What am I doing here? What do you mean?" I only managed to mumble, trying to understand what he was talking about. Didn't he know about Ace's contract? Because he didn't seem so confused a minute earlier in the garden.

I didn't answer, not because I wanted to infuriate him even more, but because I couldn't risk exposing myself just on a hunch.

If his friends didn't recognize me, then he wouldn't either, right?

In the end, I was just a nobody from the Herd, and that

served me just fine. Besides, what were the chances of him recognizing me since he doesn't even recognize the girls he sleeps with?

"Little Mouse, I asked you a question," his words like rocks crushing me to the ground.

Mouse... Deep down, I hoped that it was just an appellative he liked to use on everyone, yet I knew, *I* was the *Little Mouse,* and he was the Big Bad Cat.

"I'm here for the Pleasure," I whimpered, unable to hold my ground. He was taking control, and there was nothing I could do to stop him. It was his night from then on.

"Man, I hope you're not fucking her. That wasn't our agreement, and I'm not paying for that." Ace's patience had lasted for less than a minute, cutting our *wonderful* conversation short.

"No, *not yet,*" Cole answered him while his eyes kept peering through mine, then turned his head to the door. "Get in here."

He didn't have to tell them twice. All three of them came rolling through the entrance door in a heartbeat.

"Next room, now," Cole ordered his wingman while I was left with Nick and Jason. At least I didn't fear those two, but they weren't exactly the best company either.

"Jason, don't touch her," Cole decided to growl out, closing the door to the other room. He was making his friend sound like a dog in heat that needed to be leashed. And the more I was looking at him, the more I realized Cole might have been right.

"Why did you bring her here?" I could hear Cole talking from the other room since it was silent as a grave from where I was standing. And it seemed I wasn't the only one eavesdropping on them. Nick and Jason took a few steps to try and almost glue themselves to the door. It was all about hierarchy, and when it came to the important stuff, Cole and

77

Ace were the only ones whose opinions counted.

"*Her*?" Ace still hadn't caught on to what Cole was asking, and that made their leader take a long pause.

"Couldn't you find one less attractive? This bitch is going to give me blue balls by the morning," Cole quickly reverted to his usual obnoxious self, but somehow managed to avoid the real question.

As if I had mush for brains, some twisted feeling began to stir inside of me. He found me appealing. Even if he was admitting it in *his* specific manner, it still managed to have an unwanted effect on me.

I needed therapy, desperately.

"This is payback for fucking my girlfriend." I could hear Ace say. He was trying to sound ironic, maybe even turn his affirmation into a joke, covering the fact that his manhood had been seriously offended.

Not that Cole would give a shit about his feelings anyway. "The whole football team and me. Just because you're the only idiot who takes her out on dates doesn't make her your girlfriend. Now give me the fucking contract, and let's get this shit over with."

"Ace's been waiting a long time to get him with something." I could hear Nick and Jason whispering from their spot glued to the door.

"He's lucky Cole chickened out and lost the bet."

"That's only because he was wasted when he made it."

"Were you talking about me?" The door opened while the dragon itself was stepping into the light with flared nostrils. He was moments away from spitting rivers of fire over them and putting them back in their places.

They both became irrelevant, just small scared children in front of their leader. "We were just wondering how you'd be able to keep your hands off her. You know... look, but don't touch," Jason babbled, the words tumbling out awkwardly, annoying Cole even more.

"Fuck off, shitheads," Cole roared at them, making them all evaporate out the door. "You, come with me," his tone mirrored the one he used with his crew—exactly the same air of supremacy, as if he was ordering me around like a slave.

Without any other options, I followed him up the stairs and into a small bedroom, letting the thought of being all alone with him in the house gradually sink in.

The second the door closed behind us, Cole began searching for something in the room. First in the nightstands, then all around the bed, and finally heading towards the dresser in front of which I was standing.

I had no idea what he was looking for. I just took a step on the left so I wouldn't be in his way. But before I could get out of his space, an arm blocked my exit, trapping me between the dresser and the fine material of his leather jacket. His gaze was raw, visceral, cutting me to the bone whilst analyzing every inch of me.

An unknown feeling spread through my system. So intense that it compelled me to try and remove the arm that was barricading me. I needed to get out of here.

Nothing made sense anymore. He was intoxicating me with every breath of air that left his lungs.

His arm was much heavier than Jason's, almost impossible for me to budge, while his demanding eyes seemed to add new bars to my prison.

"Where are you going, Mouse?" He said, pulling his head back a few inches to take a better look at me. "Are you cold again?" He grinned, fixing his gaze on my cleavage where my breasts were betraying every reaction he was inciting in my body.

I wished so badly that I had chosen a different dress, one that would have allowed me to put on a bra and cover my hardened nipples—a consequence of our closeness. But how was I supposed to know that I would run into someone like him?

"You said you wouldn't touch me. It's in the contract," I tried to sound menacing, but my voice only came out as a scared whisper.

"You'll keep quiet about this, won't you?" He let the warmth of his breath fall on me while he traced his palms on the exterior of my upper thighs. As if I weighed nothing, he lifted me to his waist, then up onto the dresser that sat behind me. "How am I supposed to not touch?" he asked, drawing his tongue piercing between his teeth to play with it, as if it was mating season and he was displaying his best assets to get the female. *And why did it seem to be working?*

His fingers gently ran through the curtain of my hair, tucking some loose strands behind my ears.

Was this his game?

Seduction?

Whatever it was, it was affecting me, hardening my body on the wooden dresser in the last attempts to keep a hold of my sanity. It was still Cole, the ultimate bully, and now he was trying to intimidate his way under my skin. I needed to hold on to this thought, even though the alternative seemed so tormentingly real.

"Close your eyes; I promise it won't hurt," the whispered words instilled beautiful fear deep inside of me.

I thought he had a deal.

I thought *he* was the one supposed to resist me.

"Now, Mouse," he barked, making my legs close around his waist and draw a long groan from his lungs.

I apparently had no self preservation when it came to this man. Maybe I was scared, or maybe I was just weak, but my eyes closed, following his command.

Despite my legs secured around his waist, I felt him move somewhere on my left as I was trying to chase away the thoughts drifting through my mind. My intuition was telling me to start running, while my body was asking me to savor each second of whatever he had prepared for me.

Something was stirring in my hair as his wicked words made their way to my ears. "You reek of fear." He could see right through me. That was no surprise since I found it impossible in those moments to hide the obvious. But what surprised me was that he didn't even *bother* to hide it, "It turns me on." A thought that made my eyes squeeze themselves shut, desperately trying to conceal the perilous feeling that was building up inside of me.

His hands advanced to the back of my head, tightening something around my eyes. "You should be good to go. That is unless you want me to go on," he said, huskily, resting his palms on the upper part of my legs.

"What is this?" I asked, touching the material wrapped around my face and realizing it was a mask.

"You're not the brightest bird, are you?" Cole rolled his eyes, making me push him back to try and see myself in the dressing room mirror.

"No charm school classes for you, I assume," I snarled, since two could play that game.

"Watch that mouth of yours, Mouse. Or I'll have to watch it for you." Apparently, Cole could have said anything he wanted, but no one could offend *the king*. "Or maybe you would like that. You could close your eyes again and imagine it. Or I could make it a reality."

"That whiskey must have gone straight to your head." I just

couldn't keep my mouth shut since he kept insisting that every living soul should fall for him.

"Don't fucking test my temper," he roared, taking me by the upper part of my arm and whirling me around to face him. "I like you better when you shiver."

It was a threat, and it was also a pending promise, while flames of desire were sinfully dancing in his eyes.

"Why did you put the mask on me?" I asked. Was this a sick fantasy of his, or did he have another reason?

He let his eyebrows narrow into a frown. Explaining himself was certainly *not* a part of his usual routine, yet he managed to indulge me. "Just because my friends have the memory of a goldfish doesn't mean that anyone else won't recognize you. The whole fucking university is here; you're going to run into someone you know sooner or later for sure."

His answer surprised me. Yes, the mask would be a tremendous advantage, but why would he help me? "Why are you doing this?" I asked, determined to convince myself that there could be a living human being trapped behind the asshole layer he's so proud of displaying.

"Oh, you haven't realized it by now? It's because I fell in love with you from the first second I saw you, and all I want is to protect you," his tone so sardonic that he almost burst into laughter even before he got to finish his sentence.

A wake-up call, emphasizing so thoroughly that fairytales don't exist. There are only urges, needs of the body, and of a troubled mind; no happy endings, only hollow hopes drifting in a sea of doubts.

"It's fine if you don't answer, but you don't need to patronize me," I muttered.

"Why do you think I put it on you? I don't want people to see me around you." At least he was telling the truth; I was a nobody. No matter what dress I put on, how pretty I would look, or how smart I would be, I would still be the girl at the other end of the hallway.

I turned again toward the mirror in an attempt to dodge another bullet—I felt him moments away from explaining my true place in society. "How did you know you'd find this mask here?"

"It belongs to the blonde who's friends with Jason's ex. I forgot her name," Cole said as the girl he was talking about was irrelevant.

I managed to change the subject. Although his new answer seemed to be bothering me. There was a 99% chance he had slept with her. How else would he know the mask would be in the bedroom? And no matter how much of an obnoxious jerk he was, I still had hopes in that 1%. Apparently, when it came to Cole, I was running in self-destructive-mode.

"It looks a lot better on you," he was still playing his game, alternating ice with fire.

I puffed, decided not to let him get to me. "Are we done?"

"Yes, unless you'd like to take a seat on the bed," he whispered, seductively yet mockingly at the same time.

I raced through the door without providing an answer. The only thing that would come out of my mouth right now were smartass or sarcastic replies and that wouldn't work in my favor.

"I'm starting to think I'm going to have fun tonight," Cole deviously whispered, rushing to catch up with me as I was walking back through the garden. "Take a left through here," he continued, showing me the way since I had to stop, unsure if he wanted to stay outside or go inside the main house.

For some reason, a knot got stuck in my throat. I spotted too many familiar faces from the university through the double glass doors. *Luckily* for me, I didn't have time to brace myself since Cole was a master of giving instructions. "Inside," his heavy palm fell over my ass, sending a painful chill to travel through my body.

"Why did you smack my posterior?" I turned irritated towards him.

"You mean your ass?" Now, *he* was playing dumb.

"Fuck off!"

"Let me get this straight, you can say fuck off, but you can't say ass?" His laughter filled the overcrowded room just as we were entering the house.

My teeth clenched, turning my head to the right to look at him. I decided to give this spoiled brat a piece of my mind, though before I got to say something, another person caught my attention. Ace was staring angrily in my direction as if reminding me of my mission for the night.

Damn... I was supposed to seduce him.

I suspected *fuck off* didn't fit into *the words of love* dictionary.

"Come, I need another drink," Cole walked toward a table. His bottle of whiskey seemed to have gotten lost on the way, and he was in need of a new one.

I didn't enjoy following him around like a lost puppy, but I needed to play the seduction card and at least try to fulfill my part. "Let me," my fingers traveled over the back of his hand as he caught a new bottle of whiskey. "I'll pour you a drink," I reached for a glass and filled it with the amber liquid.

His eyes flashed with suspicion, and the next thing I knew, he took the glass out of my hands, placing it back on the table. "I'm a drink from the bottle kinda' guy." And he had every intention of proving that. The bottle glued itself to his lips, and he was taking more than a few large sips.

My eyes rolled all the way to the back of my head. "That's not water, you know? I would like to have you sober for the night."

"You would like to *have* me for the night. That's an interesting thought," he whispered in an aroused voice.

"Do you have to twist every word I say?" I muttered.

"I like getting you fired up." The devil confessed while gazing at me, assuring himself *every* sense of the word got to me.

"And do you think you're succeeding?" My tone low, warm, almost seductive.

"I think you want me to succeed. I intrigue you."

I couldn't deny that, at least not the second part. I wasn't even sure what I was doing anymore. The consequences of my actions seemed to have a stronger effect on me than they did on him, but I needed to give it a try. The seduction plan was still on.

I needed a gesture, maybe even a kiss to fulfill my part of the Pleasure—as outrageous as it might have sounded. "What if I would admit that to you? That you intrigue me." I was playing with fire, but I could constantly feel Ace's eyes burning on the back of my neck. I couldn't leave this party without giving it my best shot. Getting into trouble with Vanya because of some spoiled rich asses was unacceptable.

However, I guess I shouldn't apply to an acting school any time soon since my plan was far-fetched. "Either you have multiple personalities, or Ace put you up to this. Don't try to fuck with me, Mouse. I'll fuck you back. Or maybe you'd like that. *ME. FUCKING. YOU.*" Cole's words hit a sensitive spot and probably elicited an uncontrolled reaction on my face. One that betrayed my *delicate* condition.

"No way... Are you like the little Virgin Mary?" The corners of his mouth rose into a grin. "You are, aren't you? I can see it written all over your face. Oh, Mouse... you have no idea what that does to me."

How the hell could he tell? I was even wearing the stupid mask. Was it that impossible for me to keep my reactions under control?

"I would have helped take care of that problem for you, but I won't be losing this bet tonight. I can't. Though that doesn't mean you won't be tomorrow's challenge."

The dickhead thought he would be doing me a favor. "I don't see it as a problem," I muttered, offended by his offer.

"You're missing out on the best part of life. You should see that as a problem," he took another sip, looking straight in front of him only to spot Nick who was heading in our direction.

"Hey, man. What's with the mask?" Nick asked, turning his attention to me.

"It's my new fetish," Cole said without showing any sign as to whether it could be a joke or concealed sarcasm.

"Cool... Listen, I came to tell you that I'll be leaving earlier tonight. I found myself a hookup, and I'm not really in the mood for partying," Nick went on as if nothing was out of the ordinary.

"Okay. Leave," Cole turned his back on him as I was left mute, looking in Nick's direction.
Did he really come to ask permission to leave?

However, I didn't have time to linger on that thought since Cole's attention was back on me again. "How can this even work?" I guess he had questions of his own regarding me. "How does a girl like you get involved in something like The Pleasure Room? What were you thinking signing up for this? You're a fucking virgin, for fuck's sake."

I wasn't going to explain myself to him. "What do you care?"

He shrugged. "I don't. I'm just curious. What was it,

money? Clothes? Did you want to get out of the Pit?"

I felt offended. It wasn't about clothes or a better life for me. "Family. I have two siblings who I want to bring here into the city to live with me. I need money to do that. It's complicated."

"Enlighten me. I have time; besides, there's not too much to be done around here, and if I keep making out with this bottle, I might put a smile on Ace's face and break the bet."

He did have a point, but I wasn't going to pour out my heart just because he couldn't keep it in his pants. "I've said enough already. Let's change the subject."

"Oral sex," he said, smiling.

I couldn't hide my shocked expression. "Excuse me?"

"I've changed the subject. Let's talk about that," he snickered, enjoying the blush that covered my cheeks.

"You're not going to drop this, are you?" I raised an eyebrow, hoping to intimidate him.

Of course, it didn't work, "Not unless you can find other subjects to get my attention."

"Fine. I need the money to pay for a lawyer since I need to get custody from my father. He won't willingly let them leave. Plus, I need other things too. Like, pay for college, rent, food, give them a better life. Satisfied?" I ask, crossing my arms.

Cole took another sip out of the bottle of whiskey, "I don't get satisfied that easily, but this is boring me. I thought it would be some exciting reason."

"Sorry if I'm not living up to your expectations." My eyes seemed to roll to the back of my head again. How could someone from the Elite ever understand? Even though I suspected him not to be so *Elite* after all.

"I could teach you to live up to them," a whispered promise that instilled both anger and a certain level of uncontained curiosity.

"Do you have a moment?" One of the girls that I usually see at his end of the hallway cut in on us, licking her pumped-up lips while trying to bat her eyelashes as seductively as she could.

She was flirting with him right under my nose, and even if our connection wasn't real, it crushed something in me. Even looking as I did, I still wasn't enough for these people. I was being stomped over once again. "I see that you have enough disciples," I said, trying to hide the tremble in my voice.

The words seemed to hit him differently than I suspected they would and turning his back on the all too eager marionette, he whirled to look directly at me. "Yes, but they don't fear me as you do," his words felt so heavy and serious that they seemed to halt all things around us. The people evaporated, and the music stopped just so that his affirmation would sneak into the deepest corners of my being. He wanted me to fear him; he thrived on my fearful reactions, every single one of them confirming his supremacy.

I was empowering him.

"Ahem..." The girl was still behind him, not being too successful at processing the obvious message.

He never even bothered to address her, ignoring her presence completely. That should have made things clear, in my opinion. However, it seemed Cole had a certain power over the ladies, as I came to find out, after two similar attempts followed in the next few hours. The bimbos, and the crowd of people who wanted at least a nod of him acknowledging their existence, kept him busy, distracting his attention from his main *victim*—me.

I was *almost* out of the woods. The party was slowly dying, and everyone appeared to be gradually evaporating, leaving the premises, or seeking discretion in some secluded corners of the house. Though, *almost* didn't quite cut it, especially with Ace's eyes pinned down on me. I had to give it another try at seducing Cole, and it had to be something that his friend would get to see. Mission impossible since the king had already caught onto our plan. But I still owed it to Ace, by the terms of the contract, to have another shot at this.

I kept thinking of a strategy as another one of the contenders to a warm place between his bed sheets showed up. The notion of self-respect had died, brutally slaughtered by these girls. To complete The Pleasure I was supposed to act the same as them and try to coax him into making a move on me.

My back glued itself to Cole's chest, drawing my head far back to look at his cobalt eyes. "My feet are killing me," I whispered, and with a good cause since we had been standing for the whole night.

"I don't like couches; they give me *ideas*, and I have enough of my own for now," he smiled, looking down at me, straightening his posture until I felt every rocklike muscle of his body, along with the hard shape of his cock.

The sexy scent of his leather jacket, the faded hint of whiskey, and the devil dancing in his eyes were all conspiring to make anyone fall under his spell. To be honest, if I had met him a couple of years ago, there was nothing that could have stopped me from doing it.

"I'm going to go and get myself a drink, then return," Aria, the girl who seemed to be stuck like a keychain to him, despite my presence there, excused herself. She probably finally noticed that it was impossible to raise his interest.

Still, that wasn't leaving me at an advantage. One way or the other, Cole was seeing straight through my game. "Don't try to play with fire. You may find me to be the perfect match." He was evil and sublime at the same time, recognizing the absolute intensity of *everything* he was doing to me. "He's watching you, isn't he?"

"Ace is an idiot," Cole continued. "I've lost a fucking bet, and this shithead took advantage of that. Now, I'm stuck with you. So, unless you're in for a threesome when Aria returns, I suggest we get out of here."

Well, that statement quickly brought me to my senses. I kept confusing Cole with a human being, and not the jerk he truly was. His *let's get out of here* seemed to be a double-edged sword. I just hoped he didn't mean into a room.

He left, and I was compelled to follow, exiting through another part of the house to an interior garden where a swing bench was waiting for my tired feet.

"What are we doing here?" I asked, balancing my body on the swing to catch a little momentum.

"I didn't have anything particular in mind, I just wanted to escape the house. But I'm sure that I can think of something if you want me to." Every single one of his words had a double meaning, always testing the waters and my reactions.

"We could just talk," the dumbest idea slipped from my lips since I'm sure the talking was far from being his favorite activity.

"Okay, talk," he shrugged, waiting to see what went on in my head.

Well, there was a question that I wanted to ask all night. "I was curious what the bet was about?"

"Hmmm," he trailed a few of his fingers over his lips as if he was thinking of something, right before coming up with the most absurd request, "Kiss me, and I'll tell you."

I wasn't that curious.

Though he decided to continue what was turning into a ravishing torture "You can do it here." He raised his shirt, revealing a sculpted V-line and placing an index finger right where the line was beginning "or here." His hand went up along with his shirt, showing off the exquisite art of his tattoos, then stopping at his pecks, above a glinting metal piercing. "It doesn't count as losing the bet as long as *you*'re the one kissing me." He was playing games under the delusional impression that I could ever be one of his pawns. No matter how mesmerizing his muscles shone under the moonlight, they were far from being enough to get me to consider such a thought.

"Does it have something to do with the fact that you no longer have money?" I took a wild guess that this was the reason he kept a part of the money he took from that student in the courtyard a few days ago, especially since he took it without any of his friends noticing. I was only trying to change the subject without giving in to his absurd request. But it seemed I had screwed things up. I had struck a chord.

His eyes narrowed, a flicker of something dark passing over his face. "What the fuck did you say?" His voice dropped, low and menacing, changing his attitude entirely, and catching the string of my swing, making it stop, and keeping my body above ground.

"I'm sorry, I didn't realize what I said." And truthfully, I didn't. I just thought he would understand it was safe to talk about something like this with me since I was probably the only person he knew who wasn't in a position to judge him.

"My father just put a lot of money into some congressman's election. It's just a matter of time before we cash in on it." He suddenly was calm again. Too calm, if you ask me... "Which brings me to my next point," he continued, raising the corner of his mouth so diabolically high that I recognized on the spot nothing good could come from what he was about to say next. "There is something about you that I want, and there is also something that I have, that you need."

"What could you possibly have that I need?" This wasn't about money. I knew he was having his own problems. And even if it was about money, I would have never accepted it. Besides, I didn't want to find out what he wanted from me. I had a feeling that nothing good could come out of asking *that* question.

"Protection. You said something about needing the money to get custody. I can get you the custody and all the legal protection you may need. My father owns some politicians. And I control my father. No institution would dare to come after you in this city. All that, without you having to spend a dime."

"You would do that?" The foolish girl in me forgot for a second that she was face to face with the devil himself.

"For a certain price, of course." There had to be a catch. And some prices don't need to be paid in money. "You think that what you tried to pull on me tonight would go unpunished, Mouse? You think that I could let things go after you talked back to me, and especially after you teamed up with Ace?" This was the Cole I knew at the university. The cold, insensitive bastard who thought he could always get what he wanted. "I could always have charmed my way into those pretty panties of yours, but it will be a lot more fun like this."

"Like what, Cole? You think that I would sleep with you?" The thought made me laugh. "You said it yourself, I'm the Virgin Mary."

"And I will let you keep that. For now," he said with the certainty of a man who already had the deal in his pocket.

I looked at his bottle of whiskey to convince myself that he was drunk. It was almost full. Strange. "Sorry to disappoint you," I said, certain that nothing could convince me to give him what he wanted.

"Don't need to be. You're not going to." He let go of the

strings of my swing, and I drifted away from him. "You will agree to be mine for a month, and I, in return, will give you what you need." He spoke so determinedly that even *I* found it difficult not to believe him. "Now run along, Mouse. Our time together is over—for tonight." He caught the strings again, halting the swing so I could get out and leave. And who was I to disobey his command when it meant my freedom?

"Go fuck yourself," he roared towards Ace, who was watching over us from a distance. He then sat on the swing, bringing his bottle of whiskey to his mouth, studying me as I walked back to the door.

Well, he should've taken a good look, 'cause it was the last of me he'd see outside the university. I was such a fool to think of him as being slightly human. That's what I got for always trying to see the best in people. Sometimes, *the best* doesn't even exist.

Leaving the party behind, I finally found a cab to take me to my apartment. I crashed the instant I saw my bed, throwing my clothes somewhere on the floor. It had been an agonizing evening, but, in the end, I had brought a thousand dollars home, and that was all that mattered.

I was one step closer to winning back my family and three steps closer to losing myself.

CHAPTER 6

I went to bed around five a.m. What was left of the night flashed by in what seemed a second, but it didn't matter. I was waking up to a new morning—hopefully, a better one.

The memory of Cole was still fueling the trembling in my knees, but I was determined not to let him take over my first hours of relaxation since I left Salt City. Since I arrived in Echo City, I split my time between ECU, searching for a job, or actually going to work. I couldn't even remember the last time I had an hour to myself, and today I was going to make up for lost time—at least until 5 p.m. when I was expected back at the Pleasure Room.

I wasn't the most exciting person in the world, my day being divided between cleaning and looking over some course work, then spoiling myself with an afternoon nap—mainly trying to catch up on lost sleep. Before I knew it, I was back on duty, sitting on the sofa of The Pleasure Room and listening to the stories of Sophia, one of my new coworkers. Apparently, most of the Pleasures were tedious and pretty easy, but once in a while, you could get the misfortune of running into a more difficult one. And from what she was saying, it didn't get much worse than Cole.

Lucky me!

At least that will keep me out of trouble for a while—according to her statistics. And it wasn't possible that I could be the only one drawing the short straw all the time? Right?

To be honest, I wasn't expecting to receive a letter today, even though the weekend was the busiest time of the week. There were enough guys and girls waiting in line, and even if the odds worked in my favor, I probably wouldn't get a job earlier than tomorrow night.

But as they say, never say never. Only about an hour after arriving, I heard my name being called out. "Bea," Matt—one of the guys, was calling for me while holding one of the red envelopes in his hand.

"It's not my turn," I let him know just in case he had the order mixed up. Even if I was indeed desperate to obtain any mission I could get, I wasn't going to cheat my colleagues out of one.

"I believe it is. Here. Read it." He stretched out the envelope along with a large smile.

I wanted to explain to him again that he was making a mistake, but something made me take the letter.

24-hour City break

$1500

Requirements: Bea

Now

The letter was specifically asking for me. But who could it be that knew me?

I first thought of Michael. Maybe he was making another

attempt at getting back together with his wife. Though the city break didn't seem to fit the picture.

Then my mind raced towards Ace.

I immediately had the urge to decline, yet the sum made it impossible for me to do.

Besides, *the statistics* were leaning in my favor.

The timeframe of *now* wasn't leaving me with much time to think, so before I was even sure that I could do the Pleasure, I found myself answering, "I'll take it."

I rushed to the dressing room, disposed of my clothes, and put on whatever I grabbed first. Vanya's contract was signed while jogging through the hallway. Less than five minutes after receiving the letter, I was climbing into a black Jeep, and heading off to an unknown destination.

There was no one else in the vehicle except the driver, but I suspected it was Ace who asked for the Pleasure since the interior was even more luxurious than the one in the limo the other day. Or maybe it was Cole? However, with his financial situation he wasn't the prime suspect.

Bracing myself for the second night of mingling with wolves, I laid my head back against the headrest and waited to arrive wherever I was going. I found it weird that we were drifting away from the Hills, heading straight towards the heart of the Pit. I never imagined one of the Golden Boys would ever enter the ghetto or have any form of contact with the Annelids—except for me. Though I highly doubted that any of them knew my origins, besides Cole.

The car pulled to a stop in front of a club, which although having a hint of glamor to it, lacked the opulence demanded by the Elite. The place reminded me of a knock-off of some luxury brand, but for the Pit, it was as close as one could get to riches.

What on earth could one of the Elite be doing in a place like this?

"Follow me," the driver instructed whilst getting out of the car. Before I knew what was happening, he opened my door and then walked me inside the club through a metal back door.

Something was off. There was no way that this was either Ace's or Michael's doing.

So, who was behind this?

A narrow dimly lit hall led me through a maze of doors and corridors, guiding me towards the place where I suspected I needed to be.

"Get inside," the driver ordered me. He had definitely skipped charm school. At least he opened the door for me to go in.

It was pitch black, and even though I had just come from a shadowy hallway, my eyes couldn't adjust, leaving me clueless as to what was in the room. A hurried beat pumped in my chest as fear of the unknown set in, heightening my senses and bringing me to the verge of a panic attack.

"You're late," a manly voice that I'd heard before cut through the darkness.

"I needed to change first," I murmured, trying to jog my memory and figure out who the voice belonged to.

"Did I ask you to change?" The mysterious man questioned me as if I was supposed to have known what he had in mind.

In any case, I don't think he would have appreciated my initial choice of clothes for the day. The outfits I had back at my apartment weren't suitable for pretty much anything. "You wouldn't have liked the type of clothes I was wearing."

"And do you think I appreciate these?" He grunted, unsatisfied that I wasn't a mind-reader. *What the hell was he talking about?* He could barely even see my shadow, let alone make out my dress.

"I don't care what type of clothes you usually wear. If I were to base my decision of hiring you on that, you wouldn't be here today." The light in the room suddenly went on, revealing a face that had been haunting my dreams for more than a couple of nights. The man that I met in Randy's office was standing right in front of me. Dominant. Powerful. Astonishing.

The memory of his image bestowed upon me that day served him no justice. I remembered him to be alluring, when in fact, he was more like sculpture chiseled by Michelangelo himself. A defined jawline, framing the perfect features of his face while the contrast between his raven hair, sun kissed skin and the two deep jade orbs that glared at me was melting my kneecaps into some kind of jello.

He seemed too good to be true, that is until I got a better look at his eyes. The piercing blueish green tint of them showed no sign of goodness. There was a ruthlessness to their depths, something about them spoke to his personality. This man had the capacity to be evil, dominant, a mastermind; and yet everything about him screamed temptation. He was bad news. I had no doubt about it, yet there I was, face to face with the most tantalizing danger.

"Take them off," his tone calm, confident, as if he had done this a hundred times before.

"Excuse me?" I retaliated.

"Your clothes, I want them gone," he reaffirmed his request, although I already knew what he was referring to. I was just having a hard time believing his nerve.

"Who are you?" I asked hoping to gain some clarity as to what was going on.

"That's none of your concern, nor is it a requirement of this job. Now we are already late, so remove your clothes."

"I think you got the wrong person. I don't accept those kinds of Pleasures."

"I've got exactly the right person, Bea. Now TAKE. OFF. YOUR. FUCKING. CLOTHES." He wasn't giving me any room for negotiation, and the anger hiding on his face was forcing me to comply.

Who was he? *And what was he going to do with me?*

Unzipping the dress I had on, I pushed it down to my feet, standing there only in my underwear. My self preservation made me draw my arms around my chest so I could at least try to cover some of the exposed parts of my body. Hot tears began rolling to the ground as I was praying that he wouldn't hurt me.

"Cut the drama and put this on," he said, picking up a garment bag from the couch and handing it to me.

"What's this?" I asked, pulling on the zipper to reveal a beautiful golden dress.

"I need you dressed... for now. And unless you want to put on a private show for my men on the way to the car, I suggest you slip that on." I could tell that he wasn't kidding around. He wasn't the type to do that; on the contrary, he seemed deadly serious. From the way he pronounced every single word to the way his body managed to remain completely still while he talked.

The dress wrapped around me, molding on my form as if it was custom-made to fit me.

"Could you please turn so I can remove my bra?" I had to ask since the straps were showing from underneath the dress.

"No," he answered with a calm in his voice that was instilling fear into my soul.

"No?" my voice trembling.

"I own three strip joints, amongst other businesses. Believe me; you don't have anything I haven't seen before." He spoke with arrogance.

"Fine," I muttered, without any real intention of exposing myself in front of him. With Houdini-like skills I slipped an arm under my dress, unclasping my bra and removing it without showing any skin. "I bet you haven't seen this one before," I wiggled the bra in his face and then threw it next to my clothes.

"You've got quite a mouth on yourself for someone who was so desperate less than a week ago." He did have a point. I sometimes tend to drift off and forget my main goal. I never was the most obedient person. I guess I needed a little time to become accustomed to following so many orders.

"This isn't a coincidence, is it?" I asked, having the impression that I was part of a plan.

"Let's go. I'll tell you what you need to know in the car. It's a two-hour drive, and I'm already falling behind schedule because of you."

I could have nagged him about how he could have asked for the Pleasure earlier today since he seemed to have had, whatever this was, planned for a while. But the man was a ticking time bomb, and I wasn't going to be the one to set it off.

We were soon climbing into the same Jeep that initially brought me here, which then pulled away to continue our journey.

"We're going to attend a party for a few hours. You'll do exactly as I say, and you'll be sleeping in your bed by the morning with the money in your hands." The boss of all living breathing things was ordering me around, placing me as if I were a pawn on his chessboard.

"Why did you ask specifically for me?" The question was still tumbling around my mind, and I couldn't find peace until I had an answer.

Ignoring me, he took a bottle of whiskey from the car's minibar and poured himself a drink. It was clear that he was only going to talk when he wanted to, or when he felt that it was necessary.

I think he left me to stew for almost half an hour while looking out the window, shifting his glass and stirring the ice cubes in his drink. "Did you know that Vanya hires only on recommendation?' He finally decided to speak, asking a question that I completely ignored. In the rush and madness of everything, I didn't get to ask how she found me. But I had a feeling that soon enough it would all begin to make sense.

"I didn't find it necessary to ask. I was just thrilled to have the opportunity." After all, it wasn't appropriate to look dumb in front of him, was it? "But who would recommend me?"

"Someone you should be *grateful* to." The smug tone of self-satisfaction left no doubt that he was talking about himself. Not that I wouldn't be eternally grateful to anyone who helped me like this, but the way he said the word grateful had a certain connotation to it. Making certain he knew I now owed him, while somehow ensuring I was aware that where he was concerned no debt would remain unpaid.

There was no point in playing the fool and pretending that I didn't understand who he was referring to. "Why would you recommend me?" I asked.

He downed the whiskey in two mouthfuls, then gazed straight at me. "I need you for a *job* without any unnecessary headaches. I wanted to make sure that you wouldn't talk. Vanya has her ways of seeing that through."

"What kind of job?" I had to ask since I feared what the word *job* meant to him.

"All you need to know is that we'll go to a party and pose as a couple. I will handle the rest. You just have to look pretty and smile."

"Probably like most women, in your opinion," I mumbled, seeing a stereotype in him.

Before I realized it, my mouth had gotten the best of me again. His eyebrows narrowed while his eyes were peering through me. "What did you say?" the weight of his body leaned against mine, completely trapping me between him and the seat. "Do you think this is some game?" his eyes were losing the shades of green, darkening till they were black as a starless sky.

"No," I whimpered as one of his palms locked on my waist.

"Then you better start acting like it. You will do what I say the second I say it. Understood?" he spat at me. I would have had to be insane not to listen to him.

"Yes," I muttered while trying to calm my racing heart, it felt as if it was trying to beat out of my chest.

The man was as deadly as he was impressive. It seemed that agreeing to whatever he said would be the easiest way to get through this, although I don't give myself much time before finding another way to screw something up.

"Tonight, I will be Joshua Davis and you, Milenna Russo. I am an entrepreneur and often do charity work. We met when you came to my foundation seeking financial assistance with setting up a local soup kitchen." The look on his face and the tone of his voice were both so serious that I was struggling to maintain my facade of simply being his eye candy for the evening.. Everything he was saying seemed like an all too obvious lie, and I was struggling not to laugh in his face. There was no way that anyone would believe his story.

"Do I amuse you, Bea?" I guess it didn't take all that long for me to screw up after all.

The smile on my lips suddenly disappeared. "No."

"Then what is it?" His tone seemed all too tranquil to be anything more than a front.

"I was thinking that if you want to come up with a plausible background, maybe we should change the part where you do charity work." He seemed so far off from the type. More of a taker, than a giver.

"There are five diners in the Pit that every night, after 10 p.m., serve warm food to whoever needs it. All of which belong to me. Do you have any other stupid comments to interrupt me with?" The annoyed raise of his eyebrow, suggesting I was skating on thin ice yet again.

Speechless. That's exactly how he left me, a cold chill running down my spine. I was the last person in the world that should be judging someone and that's exactly what I had done.

"I didn't mean-"

"Then just keep your mouth shut and listen," he warned.

I nodded.

"We've been together for five months, and we currently live together in Salt City."

The name brought painful memories back to haunt me.

"That's where I'm from."

"Good, then, you'll know what to say if anyone plans a visit there. Main attractions and places. Though I doubt there is anything of interest there."

And he was right. Just dirt and poverty covered the streets. Even the elite there seemed like peasants compared to the luxurious parts of Echo City.

"We should have everything covered. But if something emerges, we'll improvise," he continued.

"Can I ask a question?"

"I'm sure you'll ask it at some point anyway if I say no now, so we might as well get it over with." I was starting to believe he was the best judge of character that I've ever met because he was 100% right.

For some reason when it came to this man, I needed answers. "Why are we doing this? Why not just go alone?"

"I need access to someone. He has never seen my face but knows of me. I don't want him or his guards to suspect anything. A couple draws less attention, and if I play my cards right, I'll get what I want. Now, if you're done, I have some work to do before we get there." His attention turned towards his phone, where it remained for the rest of the drive. Not that I had anything against it. I didn't want his focus on me in any way. There was something very twisted about him. Even though he wasn't the definition of a regular textbook psychopath, I reckoned that he wasn't far from it.

After around an hour's drive, the car stopped in the middle of nowhere. "Come on, we need to go," he said, waiting for me to get out of the Jeep, then followed me.

"Where are we?" I couldn't see anything around us for miles, and the most sinister thoughts began prowling my mind.

"We're not there yet, just changing cars," he said as a couple of headlights lit up in the foggy darkness, revealing a limousine similar to the one Ace rented the other day. "Get in before you freeze to death."

It was a lot colder out here than in the city. The few minutes spent outside were already making me wrap my arms around myself, to preserve body warmth.

The limo drive was pretty short. We reached the luxurious destination right after we entered the city.

"Just stay calm, and everything will be fine," *Joshua* wrapped an arm around my waist to escort me from the car. He made sure it remained there from where our names were checked by the doorman until the majestic ballroom where the event was taking place.

I was stunned, having never witnessed such luxury before. Black marble floors, Roman arcades, and massive chandeliers made a grand statement, while the elegantly dressed guests looked as if they were attending a royal wedding. "There are so many people here," I whispered, looking all around me.

"You only have to focus on one person. Me." His grip tightened as his voice changed from rough to extremely seductive. If I didn't know better, I'd say he was trying to charm his way under my skin. "Let's go to the bar for now. I need another drink."

"What will the lady have?" the bartender rushed to ask, ready to prepare us drinks.

"Water, please," I answered the bartender, who looked at me as if I cussed at him.

"And a double whiskey for me." *Joshua* responded, followed by a nod to the bartender. "Slow down. You wouldn't want to get too drunk," he chuckled, looking at my glass.

Was that humor? I suspected him of a lot of things but not that.

I quickly decided that I should let him know that it didn't go unnoticed, "Your mood seems to have improved."

"You started acting more... How should I put it... Docile? That's a quality I appreciate."

Well, he wouldn't be appreciating me for long because my mouth had a time lock on it. "I bet I would look real pretty on a leash." I purred, rolling my eyes. Sarcasm, here I come... although when I actually took the time and thought about it, it was a bad joke.

"If you behave, maybe I'll consider putting one on you, later." He emptied his glass in one swallow, making it clink on the bar.

Was he for real? I hope he didn't take me literally.

But I was starting to think he did, since without warning, he fastened an arm around me, pulling me to his chest.

"What do you think you're doing?" I asked, glancing straight at the carved lips that seemed to be closing in on me.

No answer. At least not before his lips skated along my collarbone, and up my neck towards my ear. "We're supposed to be a couple. What's so hard to figure out?" This time, I could feel the irritation in his voice. "The man I'm looking for just went upstairs. I need to get there without looking suspicious. *You* will get me there. It needs to look like things are getting heated up between us, and we're searching for privacy."

"Doesn't that sound a little juvenile?" I asked since it seemed to be something Cole would do.

"The world evolves the same. Fifteen, twenty-five, or even

forty-five. People live for the thrill, and tonight, we won't be seen as any different." The words didn't even finish reaching my ears before his lips fiercely met mine.

A charade. That's all this is. I kept repeating the words like a mantra, hoping I could convince myself this was nothing more.

That's until his tongue snuck inside my mouth.

Except instead of feeling like a violation, it felt real; I felt alive, like he couldn't live without ravishing me. Like a tidal wave crashing on the rocks only to caress them each time it was retreating to the ocean. A dream and a nightmare at the same time. Deep down, I knew I should loathe it, but the thought was far from connecting with my body. I was mesmerized, kissing back the illusion of him, already losing a game that I had no idea I was playing.

"Let's go," he took my hand, guiding me to the bottom of the staircase, only to catch me in another kiss. This time, much more intense than before, like he wasn't just kissing me, he was trying to consume me.

Things were happening a lot faster than I thought they would. He wasn't the man to miss any opportunity. I was certain of that, especially since his hands fell to the curve of my ass, pressing me dangerously close to his rock hard cock.

Did he feel it too? *The magnetism? The passion? The heat of our bodies?*

But I couldn't have that. Not when my main mission was of so much more importance.
"This is a little too much, don't you think?" I asked amidst the pulsations of his tantalizing tongue.

"Is it?"

His fingers wound their way into my hair, steadying my

head while he explored my mouth so deeply that he left no corner untouched. "I'll pay extra for the inconvenience," he paused, sucking my bottom lip roughly between his teeth.

Inconvenience? Was that what this was?

"Or I could ask you to join me for the night?" He pulled me in even tighter against his body, digging his fingers into the small of my back and leaning in to continue our kiss.

"*Joshua...* I can't," I whimpered.

"It's Brax. *Joshua* is only for tonight."

The name seemed to fit him a lot better. The X at the end hardened the letters, reflecting his true self.

"You don't have a boyfriend or a husband. I asked for a file before I hired you. So, what's wrong? You are obviously attracted to me. I'll *try* to behave if that's what you're worried about."

I was sure that the word *behave* meant something different to him than to the rest of the world. But I had other motives to refuse him. "I am not in the habit of doing something like *this*."

"Make it a habit with me." Now he was really pulling out all his weapons of seduction while trailing a line of kisses along my jawline and moving his lips toward my ear.

I had no idea how to explain this to him. "You misunderstand. It's not in my habit *entirely*."

"You mean...?" He stopped to regain a much more normal position and looked at me like he was having a revelation.

And cue the embarrassment.

"Mmmm," he groaned as if contemplating plan B, though he didn't seem to want to share it with me. "You never know how the night might end." He traced his tongue against my lips, urging them to open and receive him once again.

Closing my eyes, I hoped the tingling sensation taking over my body would cease. Maybe I would get used to him kissing me. Or maybe I'd find a way to detach from everything, that the effect he seemed to be having on me so far would ease. Yet, judging by the sensations flowing through me, it was a pipe dream. The tingles were turning into fireworks, and my body was exploding with need for him.

"Let's get you upstairs." It sounded more like a promise than a mission. I needed to keep my head on; remember that this wasn't what we came here for.

My feet seemed as light as feathers, walking on invisible stairs, then drifting off into nothingness. Our lips were still tightly joined, like nothing could tear them apart. Nothing except for his plan.

"Wait," he made us pause in front of a room where three men in their late fifties were having a conversation. "Shit, he's not alone." I felt Brax tense, scanning the area while analyzing all possible scenarios. I had no idea what was really going on, but it sure seemed crucial to him. "Here." He pulled me outside on a terrace that led to the lobby, then closed the glass door behind us. The plan was still on. The terrace had a clear view of the room where the man Brax was following was. "We need to wait until they leave and hope he won't join them," he explained, walking me through the scheme. "Get back here." In one swift move, he grabbed my wrist, rotating me so I fell back into his arms.

He was heavily armed when it came to the power of seduction, and my innocence was turning me into his prey. "We can't afford to look suspicious if anyone passes by." He smiled, flashing the devastating dimples in his cheeks. "In case you were wondering..."

"What if-," I didn't get to finish my idea before a ringtone I hadn't heard in so long interrupted us. My phone. But it never rings, *unless...*

CHAPTER 7

"*B*ea?" *The cracked voice brought me to* *my senses the minute I picked up the phone.*

"Natalia?"

"*Bea, I don't have much time. I took one of the guards' phones,*" my sister whispered.

"The guards?" What guards was she talking about?

"*Yes, we're guarded now. You have to come back to get us out of here.*"

"What? What's happening?"

"*Father has gone mad. He's planning on sending me away. I think he wants to sell me for a pretty sum; at least, that's what I heard him say to one of his friends.*" Her words shocked me so strongly that I almost dropped the phone.

"No... no, I won't let that happen!" I screamed, trying to figure out something that I could do that very second.

"He said something about me leaving at the end of the month. That's less than two weeks from now. I don't know what to do. I'm scared. I've tried to run, but he's got all these people watching us. There's no way out."

The pain and fear in her voice were killing me, like a rock crushing me to the ground. "I'll find a way." Even if it would kill me. "I'm coming for the both of you."

"I love you; I have to run before he sees his phone is missing." The line went dead before I could say a word, and so did everything around me. I wasn't on the terrace anymore, just in a dark place, needing to escape.

I had to go and get them back; I need to get out of here to make a plan to get them out of there.

I started walking, feeling as if the crushing weight of the ocean was drowning me. I was maddened by the thought that I would never get to see her again or that my father could hurt them in any way. I kept striding in an unknown direction, everything around me a blur, just pushing myself into the ground to advance faster and leave this place. I didn't seem to be moving, just stuck, a captive of this house.

"Bea... Bea... Bea." The calling of my name brought me back to a fractured reality. I was still there, Brax's prisoner. My body, trapped between his arms, glued so tightly over his chest that I was having trouble breathing. "Calm yourself. You're making a scene," he muttered under his breath, whirling us both around so he could still look inside for the man he needed to meet. "Who was that?" The question wasn't his to ask. He had his mission, while I had my own.

"None of your concern," I snapped back, trying to break free from his grip.

"I asked you a question. I think it would be wise of you

to answer," the tone of his voice had lost all trace of warmth. Reality was once again crashing down around me. This man was as dangerous as it got, and I needed to still be breathing in the morning, so I could go after Natalie and Sebastian.

"Answer me!" His palms caught the upper part of my arms, shaking me back to my senses.

"My sister... my father has her and my brother." I inhaled deeply, bracing myself to tell Brax what happened. Not that I thought it would matter to him. But with each word I spoke out loud, I realized that going there in this state would only end us all. "My father has her guarded. Plans on selling her." I'm sure I wasn't making much sense, yet nothing seemed to make sense anymore. "I have to go get them," I said with my last remaining strength, acknowledging that I was embarking on a suicide mission. I had to try. It was my duty to try and protect them.

"Shit, they left," Brax looked through the glass window behind me, catching the moment when he would have full access to his objective. "Don't move an inch. I'll be right back, and then we'll talk about this. Okay?" He didn't expect an answer before storming off to meet the man we came here to see. Little did he know he should have waited to receive one. I was still teetering on the line between desolation and reality. A minute, maybe two... hell maybe even an hour flashed by as I was drowning in a river of emotions, with fear at the forefront of them all. So strong, that it was subduing me under its wings and washing all reasoning away.

My feet carried me back to the lobby. I couldn't wait any longer, no matter what that meant in the end. I was leaving with or without him; heading straight back to my old city.

I tried to see where Brax went. As I approached the room, I could hear men's raised voices arguing. I didn't care anymore. I just pushed the door open to inform him of my plans. As far as anyone else here was aware I was his girlfriend, interrupting their meeting for a headache should be a valid excuse. Though, my *plan* was far from seeing the light of day. The instant I pressed my hand to the doorknob, a muffled roar rushed through the air. A bullet hitting its target, finding its way between its victim's eyes and filling the room with his blood.

It wasn't a private meeting that I was helping Brax to achieve.

It was an assassination.

My eyes filled with horror, staring at a killer while my voice let out an uncontrollable scream. The next few seconds were foggy. Before I knew it, all the air seemed to have abandoned my lungs. I was up against the wall, struggling to breathe while Brax's hand was tightening around my neck to the point I thought I would hear my windpipe crack under his pressure. "Shut the fuck up, or you will get us both killed, and *I will end you* before I let that happen." The look on his face and the vitriol in his voice brokered no room for argument.

Although there wasn't much room for my head to move, I desperately nodded in agreement; in an instant, I found the relief I was searching for, sucking in gasping breaths of air as soon as he released my neck.

"Put this on." He took off his jacket, wrapped it around me, then drug me out the door. "Things got heated, and you had a little more than usual to drink. That's how you will act on our way out, and that's the story we're sticking to if anyone asks. Got it?"

"Y... yes," I mumbled as we made our way through long corridors back to the stairs that led to the main room.

"You'd better." The snapping sound of his voice seemed to be even more threatening than the muffled sound of his gun.

We were cutting through the vibrant crowd, my arm pinned between his own, as we floated towards the exit. We almost made it. That was before someone caught up to us. "Leaving so soon?" The hostess placed at the entrance stopped us to ask. However, I didn't even realize what she was saying at that moment. Everyone appeared to be plotting around us. It seemed like every single person in the room knew what Brax had done.

My face was transfigured, changing colors as I barely kept myself standing, my body weight supported on his arm.

"She needs some one-on-one time." Brax winked at the hostess, putting on display his charming smile and escorting me out of there.

The excuse seemed to appease her, as the hostess stepped aside. We were free from everything except our consciences.

"You will keep quiet until we get to the Jeep." He nudged me to get inside the limo, waiting for the driver to close the door behind us while he was looking at the tears springing from my eyes.

The privacy window went up the instant the limo took off, bringing Brax's index finger to my shivering lips, "Shush."

And I did, for the rest of the trip, bottling a mixture of sensations that were close to making me throw up.

Upon reaching the same sinister field where we changed vehicles earlier, the Jeep awaited us. We switched cars, and once we were inside Brax's vehicle, the true nature of his personality surfaced. "What the fuck were you thinking?" His shushed voice turned into a roar while his countenance was revealing the burning eyes of a dragon.

"I... I...-" I had no idea what to say or even what I was really thinking in those moments. I was just babbling away with words I didn't understand myself.

The inside of the car turned into an oven under Brax's threatening gaze, everywhere his jacket was touching me felt like a branding. With the last of my strength, I pulled on the sleeves to remove his tux jacket from my shoulders, letting it slip onto the seat next to me. Only then did I grasp the reality of the situation I found myself in. Red dots were splattered all over my dress, the realization of why he was so quick to throw his jacket over my dress becoming clear. I was covered in blood.

A state of dizziness spread throughout my entire body. Natalia's words, along with the blood on my skin and clothes, were causing a heavy pounding in every corner of my mind. "Blood...blood..." I scrubbed at my skin so roughly that it was starting to tear, though without any results. The blood was still there, but now mingling with drops of my own.

I was freaking out and had every reason to. However, my panic attack was short-lived. A few seconds later, I felt a small sting somewhere around my neckline, and everything turned black.

***

I woke up with strange music humming in my ears, not something unfamiliar to me, but not anything I expected to hear—Chopin's Preludes. My mother used to be a fan of the classics, and it didn't get much more classic than this collection.

But who did I know that would listen to this? And more importantly, where was I?

My eyes shot open as I tried to raise myself from the bed. Only to discover, to my horror, that I was only in the bottom part of my lingerie.

"Jesus!" Though there was nothing sacred about my

whereabouts. "What happened to my clothes?" I said to myself as there didn't seem to be anyone else in the room I could've asked.

"They're on the chair next to the window." Surprisingly enough, someone answered. As a presence I now feared made its way into the room.

Brax took a few steps in my direction, motioning towards my clothes. Luckily, my instincts kicked in before he could reach me and I snatched the quilt off the bed to cover my exposed chest.

"As I said yesterday, no need to cover yourself," he snarled, glaring straight at me.

I was starting to think he was right since he had already seen most of me anyway.

"You undressed me," I quivered, holding on tightly to my fluffy shield.

"And washed you. Some gratitude would be in order." The man always wanted something in return.

"Gratitude? You're the one responsible for all of this," I snapped.

Brax didn't seem to appreciate my tone. "Don't blame me for your decisions. I never forced you to go to Vanya or accept the Pleasures. That was your own choice."

As much as I would have wanted to deny that, it was true. He merely set the stage, and I charged ahead willingly.

I cast my eyes downward, still holding on to the quilt for dear life. "Did we...?" I felt embarrassed to ask him the question.

"No. You will be very much conscious when *we* do that. Now get dressed. I'll be expecting you in the living room."

Rushed steps carried him out of the room as if he was exerting the last of his control to vacate the space. His arrogant attitude was very much there, encouraging him to hallucinate that he'd ever find me in his bed again.

I dressed as fast as I could, ready to leave Brax and his whole world behind. He was a killer, and I wanted nothing more to do with him. What happened the other night will remain buried between the contract's pages, while I, on the other hand, had other urgent matters on my mind. I needed more time to raise the money, especially since I would need the finances for Sebastian's medical treatments—at least until the papers came through. As if that wasn't bad enough, I needed a viable way to get them out of there. But this was neither the time nor the place to think about that. I decided to come up with a solution to this after I had returned to my apartment so that I could think through every aspect of this in peace.

"I'm ready to leave," I announced to Brax as soon as I stepped into the living room, though his agenda was far from being close to mine.

"Who said that you were leaving? Sit down," he ordered in a voice that couldn't be ignored.

Without too much fuss, I found myself a place on the couch. I couldn't argue. It would make no difference as this was his house. His rules.

Initially, I was in too much of a rush to notice, but looking around, the place had nothing in common with the club where he took me to yesterday. It far more resembled the luxury mansion where the party had been held. Numerous pieces of art were proudly arranged on display, from valuable paintings to unique sculptures, revealing a part of him I knew nothing about. I thought of him being much more thug than an erudite. But the selection of art exhibited and the large bookcase that I could spot through the open door to his home office was making me rethink everything.

One way or another, there was one thing I was still certain about—he was the villain, and I was just moments away from finding out exactly how much of a *villain* he really was.

"I'd like to extend the terms of my contract," he said, lighting himself a cigarette.

I had a feeling something like this was coming but I dreaded even thinking about it.

"That option isn't available, in my case." There was no point in beating about the bush.

"It will be, I assure you. Everything and everyone has a price. And you right now desperately need the money," he casually answered, like he already had this all figured out.

I couldn't deny that he was completely right; I desperately needed the money. Still, sleeping with him was definitely not my way to get it.

"But you need something else, even more than money. You need a way to get your family out. And that means escaping your father's guards. Isn't that right?"

A knot was clenching my throat from trying to speak, and I barely let out a "Yes."

Yes, he was right; even if I could raise enough money, I would still need to find someone able to get them out of my father's house without harming them.

"I happen to know some very skilled men for these kinds of operations. The type of men you don't find advertising in the local newspaper." Brax was king of the underworld, and he was making full use of that title.

"What do you want in return?" My voice demanded, waiting to hear the rest of the deal, only with that knowledge would I be able to leave without looking back.

"As you may have noticed, I collect many different items of my liking. Things are simple. I see them. I like them. I obtain them. And you, Bea, are playing hard to get." His fingers rolled over the dining table, tapping it in a rhythmic yet cranky beat. "I'm not going to pretend to be the good guy just to get under your skin. I don't have the necessary patience to do that. Besides, I believe you would be better off without me trying to seduce you. I want you to get out of this with a satisfied body rather than a broken heart."

"You think that I could fall for you?" I laughed.

"I *know* that you would fall for me. But we wouldn't want that, would we? You see, I'm a pretty complex individual, and when I set my mind on something, there is little to no chance I'll let anything stand in my way. And as of now, I have decided that I need to cross your name off my list and for you to start your *habit*—as you like to call it—with me."

He must have been out of his mind. I couldn't even hide the shock on my face. "You want me to have sex with you?"

"You make it sound like a bad thing, but basically, yes. Full access to your panties for one night." He paused, his eyes twinkling devilishly. "You're right. It does sound bad when you say it out loud. Can't help it, I have a foul mouth."

He was just plain evil and, at the same time, delusional if he ever thought that I would enter his game.

"So, to sum things up, I get to have the unspoiled version of you for a night, and your family gets an express trip to your apartment in Eco-City. Win-win, as I see it."

I needed to get out of there. "Are you done?" I asked.

"Did I say I was done? Don't make me bring penalties into this equation," he snarled, reminding me of the full extent of his reach.

I may have pissed him off, but his plans were never going to see the light of day anyway. He was even more dangerous than my father, and getting involved with a man like this could never end well.

Brax took another drag of his cigarette before he gave me his ultimatum. "You don't have to give me an answer now, but I expect one by tomorrow night. I run a club on Orchid Street. That's where you can find me."

I won't be looking, though I didn't get to tell him that. I didn't want to get into another situation where I'd be crawling at his feet.

"Now, we are done. A car is waiting for you outside to take you home," Brax said, finally putting an end to the Pleasure.

Without waiting for him to tell me twice, I seized the opportunity and said my goodbyes, then walked straight outside.

I can't do it... I can't do it; my mind was on auto-play. Even as the words were echoing through my mind, another thought was starting to take its place. *Did I even have an alternative?*

CHAPTER 8

The seclusion of my apartment didn't bring me an answer to my problems. The fact that Brax's offer was still on the table was making me queasy. There was no way that I could say yes, but I couldn't refuse it either. I needed support to be able to get my siblings out, and right now, it seemed, Brax was the only one who could provide that for me.

I also needed money for lawyers and hospitalization, and the two grand I had left after rent and groceries was far from covering either of those.

There had to be another way. Life couldn't be that cruel. At least, that's how I was trying to reassure myself.

When I really started thinking about it, there was one other person that I could try to ask for help. Maybe a loan that I could pay back, even with interest as I completed the Pleasures. Vanya, my boss, came to mind. She was the only person I knew who was wealthy enough to be able to support me, even if it felt like I was using up the last of my pride to do it.

It didn't take me long to get changed and head down to the Pleasure Room. However, I managed to arrive there by late afternoon. I guess *morning* in Brax's bed was somewhere around 1 p.m.

The first person to greet me was Laura. I bumped right into her as I was preparing to go through the main door, and she was just returning from buying coffee. "I thought we had an espresso machine," I said.

"Yeah, but we don't have the cute barista guy across the street," she giggled, walking inside.

"I need to talk to Vanya for a second," I said, stopping right in front of her door, so Laura knew I wouldn't be walking back with her all the way to The Pleasure Room.

But my plan didn't seem to fit Vanya's schedule. "She's not in today. I'll be handling the contracts." Laura shrugged.

"She's not?" Of course, she wasn't. Fate was playing a trick on me once again.

"What did you want to talk to her about?" She said stopping next to me, curious about what I had to discuss with Vanya. "That is, if you want to tell me."

I wasn't sure if I should, but asking for her opinion before I spoke to Vanya seemed like a good idea at the time. "Actually, I wanted to ask her if she could help me with some money. I would pay her back by completing Pleasures. Maybe with interest if that would help her agree."

"No, never do that." Laura was wiggling a finger in front of me as if I was committing the greatest blasphemy. "She has a strict rule about loans. Asking her won't get you anywhere except getting her to see you... differently. The thing is, she helped a few employees in the past, and they all screwed her over at some point. She's the kind of person who learns from her mistakes, so the only result you may get is probably being unemployed again."

Laura seemed so determined to prevent me from doing this, for all the right reasons. All I could think about was that my very last chance had just been blown away.

"I guess I should leave then." There was no need for my presence here today since I just took two Pleasures in two days.

"Not really. It's good that you're here. Things got crazy last night after you left, and the letters came flooding in. We get that during the weekend sometimes. I think there are only one or two people left before you now."

I couldn't deny I was a little flabbergasted that I had a chance of getting another Pleasure so soon. And since I couldn't get Vanya's help, I was definitely not passing up on the money.

"Come on, I need to put up my coat, then head back to Vanya's office in case someone comes to see her," Laura rushed me, walking inside.

I followed her to the room, where, despite the two coffees I made myself and all my attempts at staying awake, I dozed off on the couch. Exhausted was an understatement, as fatigue was already becoming a part of my daily routine. Lately, I had been bouncing like a ball from Pleasures to the university, just to be tormented nightly by the problems running my life. It was beginning to get to me.

"Wake up," Sophia's voice made me realize that I probably looked like a homeless woman falling asleep on a park bench. I even began checking for any signs of drooling. Temptress of the day! "I just got a letter, and I need to leave. You're the last here, so I suggest you drag your eyes fully open and watch the door. Laura has already called Julie and Maria from home so that we won't have to refuse any of the incoming Pleasures, but the next one is yours." My coworker rushed out like a whirl wind on her way out the door.

That was a comforting thought. However, no matter in what way I added things together, the money would still not be enough —especially since I wouldn't have another chance any time soon of getting three Pleasures in three consecutive days.

"Okay, bye." I waved her goodbye, then got up to pace the length of the room like a wild cat trapped inside a confined space. My heart didn't want to be here for a second longer. I needed to run back to my old city and at least get to see my siblings. But my mission was keeping me grounded, waiting for the knock on the door that would contribute to the funds that I needed so badly.

It didn't take long to arrive. The red envelope that I both feared and expected slipped under the door.

Company Throughout the Night

Woman early to mid-twenties

$2000

9 PM

The sum was a little over the average, giving me more reason to be worried about this, especially after rereading the title, *Company Throughout the Night*. But that didn't matter. None of it mattered. *I* didn't matter anymore.

"Is the contract ready?" I knocked on Vanya's door.

"Yes, come in." Laura seemed to be buried in papers, her hands pulling on the roots of her curly black hair, a sign of being in over her head. Still, she managed to provide me with the agreement that I needed to sign. "Just be sure to pack something to sleep in," she added before I got a chance to leave.

It was strange for her to tell me that. "I didn't see that in the request, but I will pack something," I reassured her, although a little confused.

I guessed she sensed that since she decided to clear things up for me, "This guy has asked for Pleasures before. I know from the other girls."

"Oh, then why didn't he ask for a particular person that he has used for Pleasures before?" It was kind of strange since the clients that return usually ask for the same person that they worked with in the past.

"They don't work here anymore. The last left a few days before you arrived. Just be careful with this one." It felt like she was giving me a warning.

"What's that supposed to mean?" I was beginning to freak out because her warning, combined with the *Company Throughout the Night*, was giving me a strange vibe.

Not that what she had to say next brought me any comfort, "I'm not sure how to explain it. I'm not sure even if I should say, but the girls that took his Pleasures seemed to have fallen in love with him."

"Do you think they went further? Slept with the man?" I asked, the thought unsettling me, especially coming after the last two Pleasures where the guys wanted the bar raised.

"I'm not sure. I didn't ask, and they didn't tell. One of them I knew for sure usually took the Pleasures further. So, if he offered, then the chances are that she accepted." A precedent that didn't sound good to me. Precedents create expectations, and there wasn't any way that I was going to live up to them.

"Thank you; I'll leave you to it. I need to get dressed anyway." I left for the dressing room, not necessarily because I was on a tight timeframe—I had almost an hour and a half to wait—but because Laura seemed to be busy enough, and my presence there would have just gave her more to worry about.

Dressing up was becoming a routine. It didn't take long for

me to get ready and pack a pair of silk pajamas to bring along. The rest of the time didn't pass quite as easily. The same math was still circling in my mind, adding the sums that I needed for my rescue op. I was always coming up short, needing much more money than I could ever raise in the given time frame.

The clock eventually hit nine, and it was time to walk out the door, though what I found in the street managed to surprise me. A regular yellow cab was waiting for me, no limo or glitter and gold luxury transportation.

It suited me just fine, feeling more aligned to my true condition than to the person I needed to pretend to be. Though, the feeling of relaxation didn't last long since after we took a few turns, I realized that we were heading straight to the Hills. The top of the Hills, to be more precise. I watched through the window as the luxury and opulence grew proportionally with the altitude. And still, we weren't stopping, going higher and higher, passing almost every house as we headed for the rooftop of this world.

"Mr. Ayers's delivery is here," the driver announced to a security booth that stood at the gates of an overwhelming estate.

Great, now I was nothing more than a pizza.

"She can go straight up." The person on the other end didn't keep us waiting. The car continued its journey for almost half a mile before the taxi pulled to a stop in front of a gothic mansion, or maybe it was even a castle.

"Have a nice evening." The man who drove me here opened the door, waiting for me to get out.

"Thank you," I murmured, heading toward the front door, overwhelmed by the grandeur of the place.

With timid steps, I reached the front door. After saying

all the prayers and graces I knew, I decided to knock, though the instant my hand made contact with the wooden door, it opened.

I should have felt fear, instead I was migrating from anxiety to numbness, both stunned and terrified at the same time. I was expecting everything and anything to happen. Nothing was tying itself together. *What was I to find here?*

What I had thought when I first got into the cab, and where the cab had brought me were worlds apart.

The place was remarkable, yet unusually dark. The weighty darkness filled the air with an atmosphere of mystery but also with warmth, inviting one to easily lose oneself within.

Shaking my head in an attempt to break free from the trance, I followed the guard's instructions and climbed the mahogany stairs, going straight up.

The first floor opened up in front of me and appeared to be endless, with rooms visible on each side of a twisted hallway. There was definitely a North wing to this building, maybe even an East one. Yet, somehow, I knew exactly where I needed to be. A small glimmer of light from underneath a door to the lobby was inviting my presence. That was it, I just needed to drag my feet and find out what Pleasure was really waiting for me.

Nudging the door to open, I found myself in the middle of a space I was slowly falling in love with—warm and dark, very similar to the main lobby. This particular room stood out like a shining star in the middle of the night.

Red flames were dancing in a black marble fireplace while hundreds of candles were leading the way toward two glass doors, and out to the balcony. I delayed following them. I couldn't go there yet. Not before I had taken a good look at the Victorian black sofa and the extra large bolstered bed that completed the room—if you could even call it just a room since it was the size of an apartment.

The place was spellbinding, and I was about to meet *the enchanter*. Little did I know that he would really live up to his newly gained nickname.

My eyes were drawn to the glass doors, my steps following my line of vision. Reaching the double doors and taking a peek outside, I realized on the spot why Laura's words couldn't leave my mind through the entire evening. *The girls who took his Pleasures seemed to have fallen in love with him.* Why wouldn't they, and how could someone even prevent it when an angel with the eyes of a demon was to be the *company throughout the night*?

Slipping between the doors of the balcony, I stepped outside to meet my target. *Or was I the real target in this case?*

"Hello, I hope that I'm in the right place," it took everything inside me to speak as I was already falling under a spell, looking at the sandy bronze strands of hair bathing in the moonlight.

"That remains to be seen." The man almost ignored me, turning his attention to an apple he held in his hands, which he was meticulously trying to peel, as he was lost in thought.

Just what I needed, another one with an attitude.

Strangely, he didn't seem to elicit a snapback reaction out of me, as another emotion was potentially growing—sympathy.

A glint of madness flickered in his pitch-black eyes, intertwining with something so beautiful yet so broken, reflecting the ultimate void and, at the same time, the entire universe.

I don't know if it was his 6'3" stature, the way his all-black designer clothes clung to his defined muscles, or the undeniable *lord of darkness* vibe surrounding him, but I had to take a step closer. For some inexplicable reason, nothing in this world could make me stay away from him.

When I said I usually take all human emotion upon myself, I wasn't kidding. By the time I reached his side, despite knowing nothing about this man, I was drowning in his silent pain.

"We're so high that we could almost touch the sky," I murmured. Taking a step closer to the ledge, I noticed that all I could see were the billowing clouds of toxic smog that permanently engulfed the city. His home and the balcony we were currently situated on were so high that I could see the clear night sky; for the first time in my life.

"The Hills—as everyone calls them, used to be part of a mountain range that eroded over the centuries. We're currently standing on the highest ground that's left. The closest and the furthest from divinity." The words of a man who knew exactly what he was talking about. "What about you? Where do *you* stand?" he asked, and I knew he wasn't referring to where my feet were grounded at the moment.

"Down there." I took a step to reach the railing, "Body and mind." Hiding from him served no purpose. His eyes leave me no room for obscuring the truth. He could see straight through me, no matter what lies I could have fabricated.

I glanced downward at the bottomless pit, seeing nothing but darkness. We were standing at the edge of our world.

"Maybe you need a miracle." In an instant, I felt his presence behind me, colder than the night's air. "But miracles don't exist," the strange vibe or his words made me turn to face him, only to discover myself standing face-to-face with the blade of his knife. "Do they?"

The metal was getting closer to the collar of my shirt,

making my body shake to the same insane rhythm as my heart.

One reckless gesture and it would be the end of me.

"No, they don't," I breathed, but not before I swallowed the lump forming in my throat so that I could speak. "What are you doing?" I was looking straight at the knife that was tracing a line on my shirt, yet without damaging the material.

"You are mine for the night. Or am I mistaken?" he asked as the path of his blade didn't stop. It continued in a straight line to the center of my chest.

"I'm pretty sure that Vanya has rules about this. And penalties." I tried to threaten him indirectly but only managed to raise a dark grin to spread on his lips.

"Look around you. Do you think I would be afraid of losing any sum of money?" He was right; in those seconds, I was just a name on a document. And even when it came to Vanya, a nice check would make my whole existence vanish from all archive files, wiping me off completely from the face of the earth.

The thought made me quiver, and so did the lack of rational judgment mirrored in the dark depths of his eyes. But I saw something more than the psychopathic façade he was trying to display. And I wasn't going to play his game. "So now what? You brought me here to hurt me?" I asked with a strange calm that matched his own.

"Is that what you think?" His question didn't hide concern, but rather pure curiosity. He was feeding on each shiver of my limbs, and despite my best attempts to control it, the fear was still there.

"You tell me what I should think," I said, trying not to pay attention to his knife.

But the blade ascended to the corner of my jawline. "Are you afraid of me?"

He wanted me so desperately to say *yes*. **For him to be the monster**. To be completely lost.

"No. I'm afraid of the blade, but not of you." The words came from the heart, unwilling to give him the satisfaction of self-destruction.

"Then you're a fool," his voice rasped, strikingly cold, though the gesture that followed reflected the opposite of that. His knife pierced the apple, jabbing it on the railing and, at the same time, freeing me from its entrapment.

My eyes blinked slowly in relief as I supported my weight against the balustrade behind me, ensuring my feet wouldn't fail me. This was a test that I had just passed. I think he needed me to prove myself to him, to prove that I could handle him, splinters and all.

"It's colder here than in the rest of the city," I said a few minutes later, clutching my hands to my chest. My blood had stopped boiling, and the cold atmosphere outside was beginning to freeze even my pulsing veins.

"It gets like this at night, because of the altitude. You should go inside. I'll be there in a little while." He turned to look into the void beneath us, leaving me to return to the candlelit room.

I must have waited for over an hour, staring at the flames that sparkled inside the fireplace, while trying to figure out how this man could have such an effect on me.

I must be losing my mind.

The thought was fast becoming a certainty, as I couldn't stop myself from feeling an insane magnetism toward him. The sound of footsteps snapped me out of my thoughts, looking to him I noticed he had changed. He was still the same man, same body, same expressions yet somehow he seemed calmer; tamer.

"Are you okay?" he asked, taking a seat on the rug in front of the fireplace, right next to me. "I'm sorry for the way I acted," he continued. "Sometimes my past seems to get the better of me."

I wasn't going to ask why he was acting that way, already knowing that there was no point in getting into the subject. Not now, at least.

"I've been through worse. I'll live," I answered, and although I wanted to, I couldn't hide the bitter aftertaste he left me with. Willingly or not, he hurt me, no matter how hard I tried to deny it.

"I'll make it up to you... Somehow." The promise of the man who had nothing and everything to give.

"Then you can start by answering one of my questions. What am I supposed to be doing here?" Simple and to the point, yet the answer based itself on something so complicated.

"First of all, I want to ask you a question. Do you know who I am?" He looked at me as if I should have already recognized him.

I had a feeling that I had missed something. With all I've been through lately, the news was the last thing that would concern me. "I'm sorry, but no. I just moved into town a month ago."

"Don't be. It's better that you don't." Sadness emanated from him again.

"I did hear the guard at the gate call you by your last name —Mr. Ayers. But that didn't ring any bells," I explained, having absolutely no idea who this man was—except for being my employer for the night.

"Yes, Ferris Ayers." His name, like a symphony, snuck beneath my skin. Everything about him seemed to be molded to seduce, not intentionally just by perfect beauty but by that unknown attraction building up to make him undenible. "I'll probably get to that later, but now to answer your question." He paused, then let a smile that held no humor within it appear on his face. "Still, you're here to keep me company through the night, and yet, I don't even know your name."

"Bea," I whispered, gleaming at the darkness in his gaze.

"I like that... Bea," he breathed each one of the letters out like my name had some divine magic to it. My body was reacting to his calling, raising a fluttery sensation within me. "You see, I can't usually sleep before dawn, and I don't really enjoy being alone," he continued in a much more relaxed tone. "I have a butler, Alfred, who usually keeps me company, but once in a while, he has to go out of town."

"Alfred?" I giggled, thinking about the cliche of his name.

"His real name is Halifaster. Couldn't go around calling him that," Ferris shrugged while smiling at me. "Can't help it if I like Batman. Even if at the end of the day, I think I may be the Joker." The serious ardor that grew on his face as he spoke was leading me to believe that the role would suit him just fine. Besides, The Joker was my favorite character of them all.

"Should I have called him Igor?" He put a hand beneath his chin, raising an eyebrow.

I chuckled. "Don't tell me you're hiding a pair of fangs."

"No, a pair of fangs is one of the few things that I don't hide," a mysterious tone coated his voice.

Should I be scared or fascinated?

"I won't try to pry, I promise." And I planned on keeping

this promise. This Pleasure should be like a heist—in and out. No more complications needed, especially since I had a feeling that this man could complicate my life at a whole new level.

He curled his lips into a deliciously charming smile. "Don't make promises that you can't keep."

"Cocky much?" I crossed my arms, looking straight at him.

His sadness suddenly resurfaced. "More like damaged goods."

Well, that makes two of us. "We all are damaged goods one way or another, Mr. Ayers."

"Mr. Ayers? Really? In the hour you've been here with me, I think it's safe to say you've seen all of my shades by now. I would say it's okay to call me Ferris."

"Okay," I nodded, stretching my feet closer to the flames. "This room is the most amazing place I've seen."

"For a second there, I thought you were about to say that about me." His laughter brought me a strange joy since he was slowly detaching from his initial state. "Seriously now, it was made at my specific request. I needed a place where I could feel my best, especially since I don't usually leave the house."

"You don't? How come?" I asked, surprised. He was rich, in his mid-twenties, and incredibly attractive. I would say it was the perfect time to be out there and living his best life.

Still, deep down, I could feel it: he was broken.

"Just not a fan of the outside world," he answered. "Besides, I only need a laptop to control everything around me."

"You can't control everything," I said, even though I knew rich people always thought they owned the world and everybody in it.

And apparently, they did own the world. "Maybe not me, but my money can. I just sign a check, and things get solved," Ferris said. I didn't continue, just lost myself for a short while in my own world. What if things could be that easy in my case? Write something on a piece of paper and, voila, all problems solved.

"What's wrong?" My absence was quickly noticed.

"Nothing regarding this night." I wasn't going to burden him with my own problems when I felt he could barely carry his own.

He suddenly reached for one of my hands, capturing it between his own. "I have time. Try me."

I know he was trying to make me feel it was safe for me to talk, but it just didn't seem fair to come to him with my problems. "You have enough burdens of your own. We don't need to talk about mine now."

"Okay, okay... I didn't mean to upset you, although it seems I'm quite good at it." His thumb began stroking the upper side of my hand, comforting me, like he just made a mistake and was trying to make up for it.

"On the contrary," I whispered, shaking my head.

"Don't tell me that you discovered the bundle of joy secretly hiding inside of me," he chuckled.

"At least I got you to laugh."

"Yes indeed," a genuine smile raised the corners of his lips. "So, tell me about you. What gets to you? What makes *you* smile?"

It hadn't been about me for so long now that his question seemed to be addressed to a whole different person. "Not that many things make me smile lately."

He squeezed my hand gently. "Maybe I could try and change that."

"Oh, and what do you have in mind?" I asked, not knowing exactly what to expect.

His answer came as a surprise, "A big screen TV and a comedy show."

"You really are The Joker, aren't you?" I laughed at what must go on in that mind of his. I knew from the start that there had to be something decent, and good within him. I just needed to unveil it, one step at a time.

"It seems the villain managed to make you smile."

We must have talked for hours, losing track of time, until my eyes began gradually closing despite all of my efforts to keep them open.

"We should go to bed." Ferris stood up from the carpet and offered me his hand to follow him.

As in the same bed?

Although this was the part I dreaded most, I couldn't put up a fight. I was supposed to do whatever he wanted as a part of this Pleasure, as long as it wasn't sexual. Even if that meant sharing a bed with him.

"Do you want me to give you something to change into?" he asked, heading toward the opposite corner of the room.

Somehow, I managed to answer him, even as my throat was clogged with emotion, "No, I brought pajamas."

"Okay, I'll go to the bathroom to get out of these clothes and give you some privacy." He disappeared through a secondary door, leaving me all alone.

I rushed to change, closing the pearl buttons of my navy-blue silk pajamas at the speed of light. Though my choice for the evening didn't seem to agree with him. "Some granny is crying after her pajamas," Ferris cared to observe, as soon as he entered the room and cast his eyes over my appearance.

Well, I couldn't say the same about him. He was dressed in a pair of black shorts and a matching tank top. More than a few extremely alluring tattoos peaked out from beneath the material along with the heavenly shape of his muscles.

Please, God, spare me this torture.

Still, I couldn't let him see that he was having any kind of effect on me. "Was this the charming part of you?" I muttered, trying to seem annoyed, although I didn't think that I was doing a good job at it. I was far from choosing a seductive type of nightwear, especially as I didn't want to encourage any other type of behavior. However, my words only managed to get me in trouble.

"I'd like it if you were out of those clothes and wearing mine instead. For you to know how it feels to be so close to me." He took a few steps, reaching my side. "*That* was the charming part of me. The one that tells the truth."

With one hand, he raised the quilt off the bed and, in one gesture, invited me to get in.

Sheepishly, I settled onto the mattress letting go of any hope that maybe I could have the couch.

"Don't worry, I'll stay on my side." He slipped between the sheets and arranged his head on the pillow. "But before you drift off, there's something I want to ask you."

I turned to look at him. "What is it?" I asked.

And it seemed he wanted an introspective look into my soul. "Where did you go earlier? When we were in front of the fireplace? What thoughts plague your mind?"

I wasn't entirely sure if I should answer that or not, but something made me, even if it might have been wrong of me. I couldn't continue to carry the burden alone. I needed, even for a second, to share it with another living soul.

"Too many things, for my own good," I sighed involuntarily. "I left my hometown to try and make a new life for my family and I. Well, a part of my family; my sister, Natalia, and my brother, Sebastian. I couldn't bring them here with me when I left, and my time to collect them is running out. It's complicated." I stopped, thinking he wouldn't be interested in the rest.

But he proved me wrong. "What does *complicated* mean?"

"I would need to work day and night for a month at The Pleasure Room just to cover the rent, the university, and my brother's hospitalization. I can't use his health insurance as long as I'm not his legal guardian."

Ferris showed more and more interest in my life story. "What is his illness? What's he suffering from?"

"Kidney failure. He's been on a transplant list for ages, but he's getting nowhere with the elite class in my old city having priority. He's on dialysis almost daily—," I paused. The memories of days spent sitting at his bedside were drifting farther and farther away in my mind. "I'm sorry, I can't... I can't." I needed to stop, even though initially I thought that I could talk about it with Ferris. My brother's illness was always a delicate subject for me, and thinking of his pain would only bring me to my knees.

Ferris gently traced my cheek with the back of his index finger, "I'm sorry, I didn't know this would upset you."

"It's okay. It's just a sensitive subject," I murmured, feeling his touch as a medicine that took away some of my pain.

"I think it would be better to let you sleep." His hand rested on my cheek for an extra second, then arranged some loose strands of hair that were falling over my eyes. "Goodnight, Bea."

"Goodnight." My eyes closed under the burden of my thoughts, and I managed to drift away.

It was dawn before I knew it, but it wasn't the faded light that got me to wake up. It was Ferris's arms, clenched around me so tightly that I thought they would stop me from breathing. His body almost curled into a ball, wrapped all around me, while he kept mumbling words I couldn't understand.

He was having a nightmare, one I feared may be impossible for me to wake him up from. Shivers of cold sweat were rolling down his forehead while a horrific tremble wracked his limbs.

"Ferris... Ferris...," I called him to come back so many times that my voice lost all power, "Ferris, please!" I begged, catching him between my arms, even though I was beginning to have serious trouble breathing.

As if by some miracle, his eyes slowly opened right before I felt like I had fainted. "It's okay... It's okay," I murmured, running my hands through his hair and keeping his head against my chest, waiting for his awful tremble to begin losing its intensity. "It's okay," I repeated, adjusting my body on the mattress until I could face him, fingers still intertwined between his brownish strands.

His heartbeat, pumping against me so powerfully that I thought it would escape from his chest. "I'm sorry, I—" he spoke with a hitched breath, resting his forehead on mine while he fought to chase away the last of his demons. "This hasn't happened in so long," he whispered, rolling his thumbs over my cheeks.

"It's over," I murmured, impossibly close to his lips. Suddenly, it was too hot between the sheets. His heartbeat seemed to be having an effect on my own, as the craziest rhythm was humming in my head.

He might has well have been the fucking devil, but I would gladly burn in his hell. Crashing my lips to his, following an instinct I never knew hid within me, I should have been scared of him. I should have been terrified of the thought of even being in the same room as him, but in his presence, my own sanity was slipping away.

It didn't take long before the role reversed, and *his* kisses began devouring *me*, nibbling on my lips, causing electric waves to take hold of my body. To make things worse, or straight damn amazing, I could feel a metal piercing in his tongue as it was brushing against mine. I had noticed it before, as we talked, but I never imagined I would end the night feeling it crash against my teeth. The sound almost erotic, yet altogether strangely intimate.

I didn't want him to stop, although I feared at the same time that soon, he wouldn't be able to stop. A groan of desire throbbed inside his throat as his tongue was claiming my mouth, leaning his body weight on top of me.

Burning passion was causing my top to slowly melt away, button by button until just one was left to hold my pajama shirt together. I was close to losing myself. And that could have made me drift too far away from my objectives. "Ferris, I can't."

His kisses didn't cease completely but gradually slowed their intensity until his lips finally parted so he could look at me. "What's wrong?"

"I just can't," I mumbled, hoping that there would also be a way to be able to convince myself of these words.

The tone of his voice suddenly changed, losing its warmth. "Why not? Is this about money?"

"No. Jesus! It's... it's about me." Impossible to explain, but at the same time, extremely easy, "I've never done this, okay?"

And of course, he didn't get the whole picture since my kind was as extinct as the dinosaurs. "Sleep with a guy you just met?"

"Any of it." I rolled my eyes as if thoroughly explaining it seemed a little absurd. "I'd better go. It's morning." I had to leave his place before the lust running through my body would get me to do something that I would later regret.

Yet, he didn't seem to agree. "I want you," he whispered, letting his gaze dominate my own. "Whatever that might imply."

"Ferris, I can't sleep with you," my voice came off low, and somehow scared, but not of him. I was scared of myself while I was around him.

His arms drew me in to rest against his chest while his lips fell to kiss my forehead. "I don't want you to return to the Pleasure Room. I'll take care of you." That sounded so good, more than good, that sounded amazing, but not now, maybe in any other situation. But right now, I couldn't see it as a solution to my problems because I wasn't alone. I had my family to think about.

"I'm sorry, but I can't do that," I whispered against his chest.

Another kiss fell on the top of my head as his arms wrapped tighter around me like he wouldn't let go. "You didn't let me finish. All I want is for you to *just* sleep in my bed whenever I find it necessary."

"I can't do that. You will want more, maybe in a day... maybe in two. It's inevitable. And I don't think I can give you that part of me." The truth was that even if I rejected Brax's offer, it wasn't completely off the table—no matter how badly I loathed it.

But Ferris wasn't backing down, "I'll make you a deal. I'll cover all your expenses, rent, college, you name it, including Sebastian's treatments. And in return, we will share a bed at night."

"I just told you that I can't—"

"You didn't let me finish. I am a man, and I know myself. I can't guarantee hands-off, but I can guarantee that I won't cross *that* line. Not as long as you don't want me to." He seemed sincere, though from what I'd experienced of him earlier I had no other rational choice other than to decline. The fervor was too surreal, leading me to a point of no return. And I wasn't sure that I wouldn't cross *that* line with him.

There was just something about him that was making me lose control of my body and mind. "I'm sorry, but I can't be here any longer," I slipped from between his arms and jumped out of bed, grabbing the clothes I came dressed in.

"Then perhaps I should call you for another Pleasure." He was testing all possibilities, confused by my reactions. And how could he not be when I had no idea myself what I wanted?

"Please don't. I can't return here." At least not if I wanted to keep my soul intact.

The darkness of his eyes deepened as resignation set in. I had no idea if the time we shared together was something special for this man or just an ordinary night. But the sadness spreading over his face led me to believe he wasn't mourning a missed opportunity for a one-night stand. "Alfred should be home by now. Look for him downstairs. Just tell him where you live, and he'll make sure you get home. I'm not too good at goodbyes," he said, getting out of bed then disappearing onto the balcony.

It was better this way. I think if I spent any more time with him, I would take back my decision to walk away. I left in search of Alfred. An extremely hospitable man in his late sixties and a spirit probably younger than mine as I discovered as soon as I found him. He was the sparkle of hope that shone through the darkness of the villa, and this place was in desperate need of a glimmer of light. Though I couldn't remain there and socialize because my mood was far from allowing me to be in any way social. So, I simply asked him to take me back to my place.

The bed from my apartment lay beneath me before I knew it, as every dark thought was making room inside my head.

No matter what I did, I would fail. Even if by absurdity I would accept any one of the offers, none of them, on their own, would be enough for me to get and keep my family here with me.

Cole had the legal background and connections, Brax had the underworld links to sneak them out between the guards, and Ferris had the money that made the world go round. But even if I were to negotiate with Ferris; he still wouldn't have been able to get me the unlimited support with the authorities, or the streetwise Brax had.

Separately, they couldn't help me, yet put together, they were exactly what I needed.

If I was going to do this, I needed to assure myself of success.

I didn't need one of the deals.

I would need all three of them.

*But would that mean three separate deals with **three** devils?*

CHAPTER 9

D ay one of my new life starts today. I had initially thought it would have been the day that I first arrived in Echo City. But I was wrong. This was the day that would change my life for good.

Confused, yet never seeing things as clearly as I did at this moment, I needed to make the ultimate decision. It was either me or Natalie and Sebastian. And that choice made everything so simple. There was no going back. If I had to sacrifice myself in order to save them; there was no question when it came to choosing between me and my family.

For the first time, I dreaded going to the university. It wasn't because of my empty pockets, my ratty outfit, or even because I was part of the Herd. It was because I dreaded seeing Cole, although it was the one thing I urgently needed to do.

The plan has been set into motion, all three deals will be seen through to the end. I just prayed *I* would still be standing when that happened.

I couldn't fall asleep, even though my eyes were closing from exhaustion. There was something within me much stronger keeping me awake. Panic, anxiety, and hope were alive within me, ravaging my very soul.

It seemed like an instant, but it was already time to leave

for classes, even though learning was the last thing on my mind at this time. Changing my clothes, I packed my bag and followed the same route I usually took, straight through the gates of ECU.

Not straying from the rules, I used the back entrance to the corridor, then slowly headed toward the middle of the hallway. It was as far as I could go, at least, without having every Elite student staring at me. And after the party, that was the last thing I needed.

My eyes scanned the area in search of my target, though if I actually thought about it, I was the target in this case. Cole and his crew were occupying their end of the hallway, and despite him noticing me, he showed no interest that I was around as if I bore no relevance. He never even bothered looking at me, which would have brought me joy on any normal day. But right now, I need his attention.

I recognized his game. There was no chance that he would ever come to me, so taking a deep breath, I began walking toward him.

The Elite soon noticed my defiance and began buzzing like a swarm of angry wasps all around me.

I didn't care anymore. I had one goal. "Cole," I said so loudly that I instantly made Ace and the other guys freeze to look at me.

"You're—" Nick finally recognized me but didn't get to finish his sentence before Cole intervened.

"Keep your mouth shut. You signed the fucking contract." Looking around he seemed to notice all the eyes ping ponging between the two of us. "Leave us," he ordered, clearing the space around us in an instant as everyone seemed to evaporate at his request.

"What do you want?" His blue eyes peered straight into my soul. He already knew what I was going to say—that

I was about to engage myself in his twisted game, leaving everything aside in the name of the unconditional love I had for my siblings. "Look around you; they're almost forming a line to talk to me. Make it quick." He ran a hand through his thick strands of raven hair, leaning his head over to one side to look behind me, where two sophomores were giggling and whispering to one another while gazing at him. Sorry, more like drooling all over him. Though I wouldn't ever admit to it or to willingly recognize the melting power he held over almost every breathing female. It made me feel dumb, mesmerized by some pretty package like the rest of the Herd. I was far from that, at least I hoped so.

"I'm sorry, Prince Charming, if I'm standing in their way to the throne," I spat out in irony, hoping that he wouldn't notice that low-key my body was reacting just the same way as those sophomores when around him.

It was just my self-defense mechanism kicking in.

Dumb move on my part.

"I would watch my tongue if I were you." His palms locked on the upper part of my arms so tightly that I was certain they would leave bruises. "You don't want to bring out the worst in me, do you now?" With the super strength those carefully built packs of defined muscles provided, he whirled us around, merging my body with the wall behind me. "Especially with what you're about to say," he continued. Those thick lips of his leaned right in to reach the crook of my neck, exactly like an animal sniffing out his prey.

How the hell did he know?

Was I that oblivious? That desperate?

"How did you—" I didn't get to finish the sentence as the tip of his tongue ran against the side of my neck, tasting me.

"You can't stay away," he whispered, tracing a warm, damp line with his tongue, inches away from my earlobe while I looked around us in horror, noticing curious pairs of eyes staring straight at us. Jealousy, hatred, admiration, and a myriad of other expressions all aimed directly at me.

I suspected no one could notice what he was doing since my thick curls covered his lips. But the Herd and the Elite seeing him even whispering something to me was almost like stepping into a new era. I would probably be an outcast in both camps now. And if that wasn't enough, Cole's grip on my arms tightened to the point where it became unbearable. "Your earlier remark is going to cost you," he breathed heavily, barely containing his excitement as to what I was about to say. He was certain I was going to agree, and he was right. I had no other choice but to do so.

"I didn't accept the deal yet," I muttered as if I even had a way out of this in the first place.

"Do you want us to go to my car so I can force the words out of you?" He smirked in full temptation, totally aware I had no way out. In a matter of moments, I knew I would relent, I had no other choice.

My teeth clenched, staring into the darkness of his eyes. The blue was almost gone, leaving just a deep black, filled with wicked desire. I wanted to scream, to run, maybe even slap him for being the obnoxious jerk he was. Yet, all I could do was gasp like a wounded deer. I was pathetic, but the times required me to be so. It was just that my sharp tongue didn't get the full message, "I can speak here, just fine."

I was heading for trouble at the speed of a runaway train, and I could do nothing to help it since there was something burning within me. That same fire that had gotten me into difficult situations so many times before, was fanning the flames that fueled my determination to go on.

"You want it, don't you? To test me? You want to see the worst of me," he cackled with a false amusement lingering in his voice. "Oh, Mouse, you have no idea." There was something so diabolically cruel in his tone that a cold chill ran down my back, leaving goosebumps on every single inch of my skin.

I chose to ignore it. I needed to ignore it so I could go through with what I came here to do. "I agree," I breathed so hastily that I wasn't even sure if he heard what I said. It was like taking off a band-aid. Quick and painful.

"You agree to what? I want to hear you say it." The way he was enjoying the fear and nervousness seeping from my pores was evident by the growing erection pressing into my stomach.

I looked around to check if everyone else was still staring, but I only saw a few students in a rush to walk away from the free show. "You know what, Cole. Come on, don't prolong this; classes are about to start." I wanted to leave, but his clenched hands were still there, pinning my arms against the wall behind me.

He was an immovable rock. Nothing I said, unless it was the words he wanted, would stop him from torturing me until he got what he wanted. He was so unbothered by the rest of the people here, he wouldn't even check what was going on around us. Cole couldn't care less about the classes or what everyone else was thinking. He was the king here, and that applied to everyone who set foot in this college—teacher or student.

His signature coldness was surging like an iceberg hitting an already sinking ship. "I asked you to say it. Now," he growled, gathering the pieces of me he was about to own.

"I... I agree to let you do whatever you want with me for a month," I trembled, forgetting an important part. "Ex... except —," I stuttered.

"Except *popping your cherry*," he devilishly laughed, as if I was going to willingly offer it on a plate eventually.

I felt mocked and insulted. "Do you have to say it that way?" I snapped.

"I can say it any way I want. Maybe I'll even make you repeat after me just to punish you. But I told you, I don't need to sink my cock into that pussy of yours to find satisfaction. I have so many other ways to have my fun." His lips moved toward mine, pushing his tongue against the corner of my mouth. "Ways that will make you scream." His palms clenched harder, forcing me to lean against him from the pain. "Ways that will make you beg," he continued, sneaking his tongue deep inside my mouth with demanding swirls as if he was reaching for my very soul. His tongue piercing, like a rattlesnake warning me of the danger. Cole was poisonous in all the right ways, the type of man who could easily take control of your body. But what made him lethal was that he could effortlessly get inside your mind.

I hated him. I *wanted* to hate him and the sick intoxication he brought along. He was evil, so deranged that he was almost psychotic. *And now he owns me.* A lame trick that fate was pulling at me in another attempt to break me.

"Finances, in two hours. You sit next to me," he suddenly ordered. Without waiting for a sign that I would obey, he released me from his grip and headed straight toward the gym as if nothing had happened.

I was in shock, still looking around me and trying to understand what I had just done. I was having trouble accepting the idea and even more trouble processing the information as a whole. I was now his and I was certain he would take full advantage of whatever his new position would have to offer.

Advanced math. I had to go through this for the next hour, when I felt there wasn't anything *advanced* about me in those moments. My brain froze, and there weren't any neurons available to process the equations that were being scribbled on the blackboard.

"I'm so lost, Bea," Jenna sobbed, turning a few pages from

her notebook where stars and hearts replaced the numbers in the equation, then began silently laughing.

I puffed, amused, and, at the same time, discouraged by my staggering lack of concentration. "What are you, five? What's with the kindergarten drawings?" I asked, running my fingers through a few of her pages to see that I wasn't the only one drifting away to another place during this class.

"I'm bored, and I don't understand one single word of what this bitch is saying," she rolled her eyes, laying her head on the backrest. She was probably hoping the class would be over soon, while I, on the other hand, could have stayed and listened to the impossible algorithms and equations for hours. Anything to delay what was to come.

"What's your deal? You're usually hanging on to each and every one of her words?" Jenna halfway busted me for being off. But there wasn't a chance in hell I would explain to another living soul what I just agreed to.

I shrugged as if nothing important was going on. "Just one of those days..."

"Oh, you mean a Cole Clayborne day?" raising her eyebrow, like she was onto something. Or maybe that was just the paranoia screaming inside me.

"Cole is...," I tried to explain our connection, but nothing plausible came to mind. *He's what, my new best friend? My tutor? My boyfriend?* Nothing that I could come up with would make any sense.

"Trouble," she cut me off, giving me a pass from the lie I was about to tell. "Trouble, written with capital letters... In bold!"

She had to spell it out for me, as if the turmoil threatening to break me wasn't enough. "Okay, okay, I got the message, don't go over the top about it." I raised my hands in a defensive way, laughing.

I wished she was right, that he would be just trouble. I could handle trouble, but for me, he was so much more than an inconvenience, more than a bit of trouble. He was the fucking devil.

Next class: Marketing. I messed up signing up for this course, considering someone from the Pit could never find a job at this level. This is where the big money came from, and the social division ensured we had no access to that. Ironic, since they let us study it in college. I guess they let us hope. Because hope is the most treacherous thing. Hope had kept the rebellion from igniting all this time and kept the Pit under total control.

I took my usual seat at the back of the classroom. No one I knew came to this course, except for the Elite's. All Cole's jock *friends* were here, yet he was missing. It wasn't unusual for him to skip classes, but I found it strange that he chose to *see* me during the next one and not now. Not that I was complaining. *Never* seemed to be the best time for this encounter, and if there was any chance that I could run and never look back, I would take it.

I tried focusing on demographics or whatever our lecturer was putting in the effort to teach us, but Ace's cold, incessant gaze was driving me out of my mind. I was beginning to feel so small and insignificant that I wanted to crawl under my desk just to avoid it. Why the hell was he even gawking at me?

Yes, I knew he had something on me, but he also signed a bulletproof contract that assured me he'd keep quiet about me working at The Pleasure Room. There was no way he would defy Vanya, Cole's reaction assured me of that. However, it didn't stop him from attempting to mess with me at a psychological level, trying to make me feel like the tramp he now thought I was. It didn't come as a surprise since the *Golden Boys* saw every breathing female as a piece of meat. So, I shouldn't really have felt utterly offended for being tossed in with the rest of the female population.

The class ended the same way it began, under Ace's careful supervision and with that putrid feeling still twisting and turning in the pit of my stomach.

What could happen during a class?

It couldn't be that bad, could it?

It wasn't like I hadn't already zombied through today's classes. Worst-case scenario, he would say some dumb shit and get me all twisted up.

Still, I needed a few minutes to collect myself. I was starting to fall apart, and I wasn't going to give him the satisfaction of pulling the strings to my emotions. It was enough that, on some twisted level, his best friend owned my body. Cole didn't need his help to feast on my soul.

I almost ran to the bathroom, stumbling on Jenna on my way there. Yet, I somehow managed to ignore her in my rush to try to get a grip on myself. My palms cupped together, splashing so much cold water over my face that, at one point, I thought I would drown. I wish I did; that way, I would be spared the embarrassment of what I would need to go through next.

A soft hand found its way to the back of my neck as I was still trying to use all the water on the planet to calm my nerves. "Are you okay?" Jenna's friendly voice reached my ears.

Was I okay? I couldn't even see straight.

"Y... yes. I need to get to Finance," I answered her, feeling another of her questions coming my way, and I was dodging it at all costs. Besides, I was convinced that my class was about to start.

But it seemed I was mistaken. "Class started like ten minutes ago," Jenna sheepishly murmured.

"W... What?" I stammered out, confused.

For how long have I been here? And what was she still doing here with me?

As if hearing the questions piling up in my mind, Jenna decided to spare me the interrogation and shed some light on our schedule. "It's Monday. I get off an hour earlier than you do, remember?"

She was right; we didn't have the same schedule on Mondays, and she would always end up waiting for me to hang out together.

"Oh crap, crap, crap I'm so late!" I ran out the door, hoping that it wouldn't be too late for the teacher to let me in. I might not have wanted anything to do with Cole, but the reality was, I needed everything to do with him.

"Should I wait up for you?" Jenna called out after me. The truth was, I had no idea what Cole's plans were for today, and I had no intention of letting her get involved in any way in them.

"No, we'll talk tomorrow," I called out, having almost reached the classroom.

I slowly pushed the door open, like a thief trying to sneak in, only I was sneaking into a class of twenty-plus people in broad daylight.

"Excuse me for being late," I apologized to the teacher, hoping that she would still let me attend the course.

"My lectures aren't based on excuses, and if you can't arrive on time, then I don't have words for you to hear." The old hag didn't even look my way as she spoke, as if the ultimate trash had just dropped in.

I scanned the area to find a very annoyed Cole sitting in the back of the classroom, eyes betraying every single thought. He shook his head in disapproval as if he was scolding me, but before I got to turn and leave, the teacher had a sudden change of heart. "Go to your seat, and do it fast, you're already interrupting my class."

Was Cole's disproving gaze meant for me or the teacher?

"Thank you," I mumbled, not having to be told twice, then headed toward the two-seater desk Cole was already at.

The pulsing jawline and clenched fists were announcing the trouble I was really in. "You kept me fucking waiting. No one does that," he snarled, looking at me like I was next on death row.

Oops... I just offended the *King* of ECU.

I couldn't say anything back. I was bad at lying or finding excuses anyway, and telling the truth would only have been a complete acknowledgment of his powers.

"At least you know your place and keep quiet," he muttered between his lips after a few minutes of dead silence on my end.

"You do know that the situation compels me to do this. It's not because I'm some one-neuron bimbo who has fallen under your spell," I retorted, inadvertently opening Pandora's box.

I fucked up, and I immediately recognized it as the corner of his lips curled into a diabolical smirk.

What have I done?

Running his fingers over the collar of his black leather jacket, he took it off, carefully arranging it on his lap. *Too carefully, if you ask me.*

"I'm going to enjoy every single second of this so much. Especially knowing that you'll hate every moment of it," he said, smirking like he was the fucking devil, devising a plan that would have me burn in his hell.

I sucked in a strangled breath, shifting to set a small distance between us; it wasn't like I could exactly run away.

What did he have in mind? I recoiled, knowing that no good could ever come out of that non-existent conscience of his.

Without warning, thick, strong fingers searched for my fragile ones, and to my surprise, his thumb was running in circles over the top of my hand, caressing it.

What the hell was going on?

It didn't take long to answer that question as his hand guided my own under the leather jacket, freezing my body on the spot.

"Are you fucking crazy?" I asked, my hands trembling, my pulse pounding in my ears.

"Yes," he casually answered, unbothered by my stupefaction, guiding my hand on top of the growing bulge in his pants.

Once I realized what he wanted, I had the impulse to pull back, but his other arm wrapped itself around me, sneaking his free hand on the side of my breast. "Don't complicate things for yourself," he snarled with dead serious determination, making me realize that it was either: obey his request or let him feel me up while everyone would be watching, including the teacher.

His palm guided mine over his hard cock, sliding it up and down over the material, trying to establish a rhythm. Only my own palm was a sort of melting dough at that moment, fingers shaking like I was experiencing sudden paralysis. But Cole wasn't giving up that easily, clutching onto my fingers to fasten around his throbbing cock, over and over again until my hand began moving on its own.

Drops of sweat began gathering on my temples as I was looking all around me. I had the feeling everyone knew I was about to provide some sinful pleasure to the university's most infamous villain.

"You do know how to unfasten a button, don't you?" Cole asked as I was lingering for more than five minutes over the fabric of his jeans that was concealing his pulsing hardness. I wanted to tell him to go to hell. But his hand, almost resting on my full breast, stopped me. I had to keep quiet before our actions became even more obvious to others attending this class.

Unhurriedly, I lifted my hand to the top of his jeans, uselessly hoping to duck the unavoidable. With sloppy fingers, I opened his belt, searching for the button he was talking about. Maybe I really *didn't* know how to unfasten it since I kept fumbling around it, trying to pull it open.

To my surprise, he wasn't mad about it; instead, a delicious flicker of lust twinkled in his eyes. "The longer you let *it* recover, the longer it will last." The demonic grin was back, making me aware of an unfamiliar aspect of the male anatomy.

How the hell was I supposed to know that?

Under no circumstances could I prolong this, trying to quicken my movements and unsnapping his pants without drawing attention to what was going on. If I took too long to get him to the finish line, I would be risking sending myself into a panic attack.

Freeing his cock from its imprisonment, I slid my fingers beneath the black boxers he had on, reaching for the hardened piece of him that was so eagerly waiting for me. His cock was much firmer than I had imagined it would be, my clumsy fingers still had no idea what they were doing. Instead of preparing to quickly give him the release he desired, they seemed to be stumbling on their path. Deep down, I knew he didn't want just the release he was about to receive. He lived for the adrenaline, relished in the pumping heartbeats our indiscretion provided. And something else too—he wanted to humiliate me, to make me feel low, insignificant.

Cole was using a successful global strategy—the smaller they feel, the harder and better they'll obey you. A trait that must have stemmed from his Elite heritage.

I couldn't help myself from looking around the classroom again, and even if everyone else was scribbling something in their notebooks, I still felt like we were being watched.

In my attempt to do *something*, anything to get this over with as soon as possible, my fingers ran over the damp part of his tip, feeling the complete effect I had on him. My gesture made him flinch and slide his chair along the wooden floor, releasing a sharp noise. Now every pair of eyes really was on us.

Sure, they couldn't see anything because of the jacket, but that dumb feeling of guilt was still within me.

Did they know? Did everyone know?

I stopped, forgetting to even breathe for a second. I felt like I was caught with my hands in the cookie jar. But suddenly, their startled gazes began turning one by one.

With eagle eyes, Cole peered straight through them, instilling a paralyzing fear on every single one of their faces. They all quickly understood that even the air they breathed here was owned by him. He was king of ECU, taking full advantage of his ridiculous display of power while both the Herd and the Elite were obeying him without a single second of doubt.

"What did I tell you?" he whispered, throwing me the same possessive gaze.

I looked at him as if I had no idea what he was saying, but in reality, I knew exactly what he was talking about. That by stopping every time I felt I was being watched I was only going to extend my agony.

"Don't play dumb," he growled as if I were attempting to insult his intelligence. "Fucking look at me while you're rubbing my dick. Is that so hard to follow?" The final order was bringing the last pieces of his plan together.

It seemed impossible to follow. The embarrassment I felt hit epic levels. And he was feasting on my misery, becoming more and more turned on by it. My eyes glanced straight into his cobalt pools while my hand began moving on his hardened cock.

Something about this degrading act was making my own body respond. A crescendo of pressure gathered in my mid-waist with every stroke of my hand that was causing his own pupils to flare.

I stroked my hand faster and faster, helped by the damp signs of his arousal, hoping to finish my job as fast as possible. And, strangely, I was beginning to feel in control, noticing his eyes instinctively closing and opening from the pleasure. He was losing the iron gaze he was usually using to subdue me, and for a second, my demon looked almost human.

However, it was short lived as the sexual energy he was releasing began having serious repercussions on my own body. A deaf pain was pulsing right above that sensitive spot between my thighs, while the bra I had on seemed to be tormenting my overly sensitive nipples.

I needed to end this. I linked the path of each of my movements with every twitch and expression blooming on his face. I noticed how the rise of pressure was spiking his breath and how the quick finger that ran over the smooth part of his tip was making his jaw clench. I was always a quick learner, and his release was building stronger moment by moment.

I owned his ass now... Well, it was actually the other way around, but a girl could dream, couldn't she?

With only a few more repeated moves, his feet buckled into the ground, teeth grinded, and jaw clenched, while the warm liquid signaling his release covered my hand.

The king got his wish, and I was quite certain this was just the first of many. But looking back up into his eyes, I noticed they were more shocked than filled with some sort of relief. Strange since I was expecting to find him at least a bit satisfied, and maybe even showing a hint of *gratitude*. I know that was a good one...

I couldn't waste my time analyzing him, or his possible mental issues. I had a messy situation on my hands, which I had to get rid of. With my free hand, I reached for a pack of tissues I had in my jacket to rid myself of Cole's cum while he never said another word. He was just expecting me to be done, eyes even colder than before and fists clenched so tightly they turned white.

What's wrong with him? I thought this was what he wanted.

"Ms. White," the teacher called out my name at the same moment I was finally breaking free from under his jacket. Shit, I was in trouble since I didn't have the slightest idea what she was talking about.

"Yes," I floundered, not knowing what she wanted from me. But before I could play dumb and pretend to have on-spot amnesia, the same disapproving shake of Cole's head got her to quickly reconsider.

"Not you, I meant Ms. Brunswick," she mumbled, annoyed yet helpless at the same time.

How much power did Cole really have around here?

Earlier, I thought that maybe I was just imagining things and that the teacher probably had a change of heart to let me attend class. Though I wasn't sure she actually had a heart to begin with. But now he was making use of his title, which provided him an authority that seemed to stretch out to the highest levels.

I should hate what I had just done. Even loathe myself for it, I felt so dirty that nothing could wash it from my mind. Yet, I was also certain that I made the right decision. Cole was definitely the man I needed to help me because I had the feeling that his family authority and connections ran as deep as he told me.

"You're dismissed for today." He rose from the chair and walked straight out the door without any further explanation and without anyone asking him a single question.

I tried clearing my thoughts to pay attention in class, although it seemed useless. I even took out a pen to get some of the notes down on paper, but my mind wandered to a *whole different place*. I had another encounter scheduled for tonight. One that I couldn't postpone.

CHAPTER 10

C lasses were finally over, and I managed to sneak out without running into Cole again. Brax was next on my list, but first I needed to go home and change before I met with him. The only problem was that I had nothing to change into.

I had to go and buy myself a dress. It pained me to spend even $40 on something for myself. But I didn't own anything that I could wear to a club, and it didn't seem fair to stop at The Pleasure Room to borrow something for personal use.

I found a black bodycon at a discount store, and took it home to get ready for the night. Much easier said than done since I didn't seem to be able to get a single thing right. My hands kept shaking at the thought of seeing Brax again, and my heart seemed like it was trying to beat out of my chest.

Leaving my apartment, I signaled for a cab. There goes another $15, but there was no way I was getting on the bus in this dress. I was already feeling uncomfortable in my own skin without a bunch of skeevy perverts ogling me. "To Orchid

Street, there's a club there. Do you know it?" I asked the driver since I had no idea where the location could be.

"Yeah, some bigshot kingpin owns it. Classy place. I took a broad there once," the driver answered, a hint of pride in his voice at his great *accomplishment.*

Kingpin... The word shook me, reminding me of Brax's undeniable street cred but mostly of what exactly I was getting myself into.

We arrived much faster than I would have wanted to. The strange feeling that I was about to face the executioners' scaffold gnawed at me deeply. But remaining in the cab for the rest of the night wasn't an option, so after paying the driver I made my way to the club.

"I'm here to see Brax," I announced to the massive bouncer, who was standing in front of the club door. He didn't seem the least bit impressed, making me wonder how many times he actually heard those words.

"Get in line," the man gestured for me to look behind me at the line formed in front of the club.

How the hell could Brax get so many people from the Pit to spend their last dimes here?

"Let her pass; she's the boss's woman," another guard said, coming from somewhere behind me. I recognized him as the driver from the other day. But the man had his facts all mixed up. I was far from being Brax's *woman.* Deal or no deal.

"Come on, I'll take you to him. He's at The Underground, on the other side of the club," the same man offered.

"Thank you." I followed him, walking beneath the colored neon lights until we reached a secluded part of the club. There was no one around, just the clink of doors opening and closing and maybe a pair of heels echoing through the corridors.

"Take a left, and the door will be right in front of you," the guard indicated, just as a thin girl with fire-red hair was coming toward me along the corridor he had just told me to follow.

I gulped, watching her try to fix her ruined makeup as she walked straight past me. She was cleaning the smudged mascara beneath her reddened eyes, while also checking on her messed-up ponytail. It was Brax's doing, I had no doubt. I was just wondering how long it would be before I'd be forced to fill her shoes.

I guess I couldn't delay finding out since I reached the door. Knocking quickly before opening the door; I came face to face with the man that I needed to see tonight.

Brax immediately raised his eyes from his whiskey glass. Their jade color burning right through me, destroying any confidence I may have had before walking into the room. "This is a surprise. I didn't think you would show up." Every word he spoke had a certain cadence to it, a mixing of lust and superiority, acknowledging my reason for being here, without missing out on the chance to point out to me that he knew he already owned me.

I had so many things to say and yet so few. Out of all the deals I had to make, I feared coming here the most. Not because I knew what Brax was capable of, but because I was aware of what he was capable of when it came to me. The fire burning in his eyes, the raw, unhealthy desire of a man incapable of human emotions, instilled a level of anxiety in the deepest corners of my being.

"I may not be as weak as you think." I said, trying my hardest to not let my emotions bleed into my words, I couldn't let him sense the fear flowing through me.

"We'll see about that," the green in his eyes twinkled under thick lashes, while he tilted his head to examine me. The corner of his lips curled into a smirk as his hungry gaze seemed to be unraveling every single part of me.

I had never felt so exposed, so vulnerable, as if I were standing completely naked in front of him. With every second that passed between us, I could so easily have imagined myself turning to leave through the door. But no matter what was waiting for me here, leaving without an agreement was not an option.

My throat suddenly dry from the unbearable heat that seemed to be fueled from somewhere within me. "May I have a glass of water?" I asked with what I felt was the last of my strength.

One of his fingers gestured towards a small table where an icebox containing a bottle of champagne and a decanter of whiskey seemed to be waiting for me. "I don't drink water after 6," he grinned, lying back in his armchair.

I didn't move since I usually don't drink alcohol at all, and now was certainly not the time to start. Though Brax seemed to have other plans in mind. "Whiskey? Or are you bringing me good news? If so, we'll go straight to champagne."

I hated him for being the perfect bastard he was. He knew exactly how hard this was for me and he was thriving on every second of my misery. I wasn't willing to let him exploit this any longer. Or at least that's what I thought, "I don't drink."

"Pour me another glass of whiskey and get yourself one too. If you want to stay in this room, then you'll have a drink with me." As usual, he wasn't asking; his tone left no room for negotiation and thwarted any chance I might have had of proclaiming independence.

Things were simple. I had something that *he* wanted, and he had something *I* wanted. The only difference was where we drew the line, I could be replaced, but I couldn't replace him. And that made everything so much more difficult for me. He held the upper hand, and that was going to cost me.

I couldn't refuse his command, especially since refusing it meant getting a bus ticket straight back to my apartment.

With timid steps, I reached for the table and filled the damn glasses.

"Put some ice in it too," another order coming from Brax, making my fists instinctively clench with frustration and contempt. Every sentence he spoke was intended to test me, and I was moments away from failing.

I brought him the drink, placing it on the side table next to his armchair. The only thing helping me hold onto my sanity at this moment was going over my acceptance of his proposal in my head. I was so overwhelmed at the moment that I needed to repeat it several times to remember it. The simple power of his presence seemed to control every cell in my body, numbing my mind and igniting my senses.

"Let's hear it," Brax cut straight to the point, erasing every sentence that I was preparing to say and leaving me with only an undeniable truth.

"I need my family." I sounded weak, and that was going to cost me. All other words seemed to just fade away when it came down to the real reason I was here.

His eyebrows furrowed, yet before I could decide if it was from confusion or anger, his face was back to its usual stony expression. The moment so brief it may have just been my imagination, as the next words out of his mouth reminded me of who I was dealing with. "Take a seat," he said, hoarsely, relaxing his head back against the armchair, unwilling to lose eye contact with me even for a second.

I turned to take a step back, heading toward the only other chair in the room, though before I could reach it, he decided to clarify things for me, "Not there."

To be honest, I knew from the first time he said it where the *seat* he was referring to was. I just willingly chose to ignore him, hoping that maybe if I played dumb enough, he would leave it be.

Taking a deep breath, I turned to look in his direction, where very clear instructions were waiting for me; the tips of his fingers were tapping on the upper part of his leg. He wanted me to sit on his lap.

If things were any different, maybe I would be irredeemably seduced by a man like him. He was the purest form of temptation, created to entice all breathing souls, drawing a perfect picture of exquisite masculinity. The posture, the dominance, and even the tone of his words were vibrating so deep within me that I was terrified to even approach him.

"Don't keep me waiting," he snarled with the impatience of a man who always gets what he wants. Things were easy in his world. He asked, and he received—no complications, no overthinking pickup lines, or planning romantic dinner dates. Just satisfying basic needs, or adding to his collection, as he liked to see things.

One thing I knew, I couldn't keep him waiting any longer. Dragging my feet across the expanse of the room, I reached his side and finally *took the seat.* In reality, I was more on my tiptoes than actually making contact with his leg, but it was the best I could do.

"Go on," he instructed after I finally succeeded in following his directions.

Was it even necessary to tell him why I was there? I suspected that he had already figured out the answer.

"You have five minutes before the show starts, so you better start talking before it begins," he casually said, putting an indirect timer on our meeting.

I guess he *did* want me to tell him. Didn't manage to dodge that bullet.

And what show was he talking about anyway?

I turned to look to my left, where a large glass wall seemed to reveal another room. I hadn't actually noticed it when I came in, being much more focused on what I came here to do than the architecture of the place. But now that he brought it up, I did find it rather strange. Although I didn't ask, though not because I wasn't curious. I didn't ask because he had mentioned the timeframe, and it felt like I needed days to gather my courage to tell him what I had come here for.

I guess the five minutes he gave me would have to do. "I need you to get my family. I want them here with me."

"You do understand what me helping you implies?" The wicked grin was back as he tilted his head to crack the tension in his neck, getting ready to delight himself with my misery.

I nodded instead of a direct answer; eyes tightly shut, trying to take in the effects of my decision.

"Good, we'll discuss the details tomorrow when I have all my men together." His tone was calm and calculated, concealing all signs of humanity.

Was that it?

Was I free to go?

I tried to stand and spare him the *effort* of carrying my

weight, but a determined hand wrapped itself around my waist. "Did I say we were done?" The coldness in his tone struck me, turning me into stone in his arms.

His nostrils flared out in anger, a stark warning sign of my disobedience. He knew I was no fool, and it was about time I stopped behaving like one.

With agonizingly slow movements, he reached for the top button of his shirt, pulling it open. "This shit has been annoying me all day." And then another button popped, revealing the black patterns that so majestically covered his skin.

Under no circumstances, did I want to look at him. My gaze struggled to stay away, but the magnetism of the drawings running over the defined shapes of his body was too much. And I was weak... so, so weak in front of the feral display of pure masculinity.

Taking my glass off the table, he pressed it to my lips. "Drink." His earlier words suddenly came to mind, *If you want to still be in this room, you will have a drink with me.*

With agonizing movements, I opened my mouth to take a sip of the liquid, telling him no wasn't an option. I could hardly swallow, clenching my lips to stop from spitting the whiskey out the second the taste hit my tongue.

"Come on, finish it all." Brax said, raising the glass until the contents managed to flow down my throat.

I coughed, trying to survive the burning sensation that seemed to set my lungs on fire while trying to get the bitter alcoholic aftertaste off my tongue. "Good girl," he spoke with self-satisfaction, moving his hand underneath my chin, then gently tracing a line downwards, between the curves of my breasts, and stopping over my navel. "The burning sensation... That is what I get when I look at you."

It was a confession, not one of *love*, since this man had no love to give. But one far more dangerous, of lust. He was *in lust* with me.

What worried me most was that I recognized exactly what he was describing. The heat spreading through my body, affecting my thoughts and reactions. The desire growing in my lower belly, that would be so easy to do something about in present company.

I decided to ask him another question, hoping it would distract me from the feelings flowing through me. "Do we need to go to Vanya about this?" After all, she was still my employer. Since the only reason this arrangement was being made was due to the Pleasure I accepted from him, would we still owe her a percentage?

"As long as you don't get a check or cash, Vanya doesn't care. I am going to spend a great deal of money seeing this through, but it won't count as long as I don't give the payment directly to you."

At least that cleared things up. I was having doubts about telling another soul of the agreements I needed to make to free my family.

"But if you also need cash, I'm sure that I could think of something to add to our deal." He just couldn't hold that thought to himself, probably already scheming up some new ways of owning me.

Luckily, I had Ferris's offer to cover that aspect, and despite his psychotic temperament, it paled in comparison to Brax's chilling demeanor.

Nothing he could say or do could convince me to extend our deal in any way, especially since I'd already agreed to give him such an important part of me.

"I don't need your money," I snapped, my mouth getting the best of me.

"Have it your way, but from my perspective you do." His voice shook slightly from the anger he was trying to control, needing to offend me back to prove superiority. It wasn't just a game that he was playing with me, but *the main* game in his world, establishing supremacy. That's what kept the money rolling and the loyal subjects bowing at his feet. That's what made him *King* on the streets.

"I'm sorry, I didn't—," I wanted to apologize in some way to avoid him getting mad at me. I'm not usually the apologetic type, but getting on his wrong side didn't seem like a good idea, at least not until he had fulfilled his part of the deal. Yet before I could finish my words, I caught sight of a bright light coming from the glass wall.

I turned away from him and noticed large spotlights shining on what appeared to be a stage with an upholstered table sitting in the middle of it. It was none of my business what was going to happen there, yet thinking of the possibilities gave me goosebumps. And since *the show* looked like it was about to start, it was my cue to leave.

"I should go," I babbled, refraining from trying to get up without permission this time.

"No, you shouldn't." His words, full of a pathos not customary from him. I must have been losing my mind, but I found myself both craving and fearing them at the same time. "What you're asking of me is a lot... A lot of money and a lot of time. I think it's only fair I should see a sign that you're as excited about this deal as I am... Call it an act of good faith on your part."

I knew it had to be a trick, an extra deal that I unwillingly agreed to. "What does that mean?" I couldn't conceal the whimper in my voice as it was cracking under the uncertainty of what he had planned for the night.

"Relax," his voice was so warm this time that it instantly wrapped around me. My body was melting onto his under the pressure of every anguishing need that had been tormenting me since I first made contact with him. "It only means you get to watch the show with me," he said in a tone that I knew hid so much more than just the words that had left his lips.

And I was right. With a gentle move, he turned me to face the glass wall, raising my body further up his leg until my back rested on his chest. Through the thin barrier of my dress I could feel every beat of his heart, I just hoped he couldn't feel mine because it was beating like that of a scared little mouse. Suddenly, the lights in our room went down, leaving just a few tiny bulbs to glimmer in the darkness. Caught by surprise, my shaking feet pressed on the floor, trying to find stability yet involuntarily arching against Brax's crotch. I froze, feeling his cock stiffening under me while his arm raised me a little further, bringing my head to rest on his shoulder. "I said, relax," he whispered, lips inches away from mine, heavy with desire.

I was certain that he was going to kiss me. Although I wish he wouldn't, the memory of his tongue against mine brought a wave of liquid heat to flow down my body.

My eyes closed, waiting for his mouth to cover mine, but the warmth of his lips never came.

I reopened them just in time to catch a glimpse of him carefully studying my neckline. Then pushing a few strands of my hair aside, his tongue began trailing a long line from my collarbone to that cursed spot behind my ear that made me tingle with uncontrolled need.

This was supposed to be nothing more than a job for me

and a game for him, yet my body seemed to have other ideas. Things were pretty clear at the start, but allowing his touch to have any effect on me would only complicate everything.

That was it. I was strong. I had to be so. At least that's what I tried telling myself. I had no idea that the atmosphere in the room was going to heat up so quickly.

Slow music began playing from the speakers while another set of spotlights brought the room behind the glass wall to life.

"What is this?" I asked, looking at the stage where an astonishing blonde woman, dressed only in a tight black lace corset, made an appearance.

"Shush, just watch the show." Brax's tongue began skimming the exposed part of my neck, in long swirls, making my skin crawl with the intoxicating sensation of *him*.

I was so fucking lost in his arms, hating myself for every single second I was trembling with desire. And I needed to do something—anything, to take my mind off him. So, I decided to follow his advice and focus on what was going on in the other room.

A half-dressed man with a herculean muscled frame seemed to have entered the glass room while I wasn't paying attention.

His curly ash-blonde hair, deep gray eyes, and milky complexion made him extremely attractive, and I couldn't deny that he could easily have been the object of any woman's desire, yet he didn't hold a candle to the man behind me. His hands would feel cold traveling my body compared to the heated palms that were now exploring the defined contour of my breasts.

The woman seemed excited to see him, approaching him with luscious movements, like a wild panther stalking her prey. They had magnetism, and you could see it from miles away. Her arms opened to greet him, running her fingers through the thick strands of his hair. Their mouths crashed, searching for one another in fluid motions. They were on fire, and the stage seemed to be burning underneath them.

The woman broke off the kiss and ran the tip of her tongue along his jawline, descending to the rock-like squares of his chest, all the way down to the V that formed the perfect arrow toward the hard bulge in his pants.

Moving her body in a sensual way, her knees hit the floor. A satisfied grin splattered over her face as her eyes went up to glance at the eagerness filling his features. He knew what was coming next, the eager rise and fall of his chest betraying his anxiousness.

With stagnant movements, as if feasting on his excitement, she unbuckled his belt, throwing it on the floor. She then slowly unbuttoned his jeans. It was becoming more and more clear to me that it wasn't only going to be a strip show.

Blushing with shame I wanted to look away, but I couldn't shake the feeling of Brax's intense scrutiny burning into me. This was a test of obedience. One that I wasn't going to fail, no matter how hard my ego was pushing me to riot against it.

Brax's gestures were beginning to match the atmosphere in the other room. His lips still on my neck, alternating small nibbles with a tormenting rotation of his tongue, enhancing the storm that he was building inside of me.

Trying to ignore my body rioting against me, my focus went back to the stage where the blonde woman had just tugged her partner's pants down along with his boxers, revealing his very aroused cock. Rivers of embarrassment ran down my spine as I watched her taking the length of his erection disappear between her lips. She was pleasing him with slow, lustful moves, revealing *him* from time to time, only to take *him* deeper in her mouth again the next second.

It was completely erotic, and their game seemed to be drawing me in like a magnet. I no longer wanted to look away, curious as to what would happen next.

Wish granted, I guess, as within moments, the man's long fingers entwined themselves between the long-styled locks of her hair. He slowly pulled her up and then lifted her in his arms, placing her atop the table. With expert hands, he made quick work of her corset, revealing a pair of voluptuous breasts .

I couldn't help but compare my own breasts to hers. Sure, I had volume; too much, in my opinion, but the perfect shape of her fake breasts were making me feel insecure.

I was completely unable to understand why the idea of Brax comparing me to her was tying knots in my stomach. In the end, why wouldn't he, when I was already doing it myself? Yet, being in his arms while he looked at another woman, whom I found more attractive than me, began to unsettle me. Suddenly, I didn't feel so comfortable anymore. The need to get up and leave was becoming so overpowering I was on the verge of a panic attack..

As if feeling my anxiety, Brax gently slid the thin straps of my dress down, kissing the skin he just revealed. His palms moving up my torso to cup my breasts as he seemed to mirror the gestures of the man who was on stage, making a gasp echo from my lips.

"You're so fucking beautiful," he whispered, knowing exactly what to say to chase away any thought that I wasn't the most attractive woman in his eyes. It was strangely arousing to feel his hands all over my body. The shock I initially imagined having was turning into decadent pleasure, the first step on a path from which I could never return.

The strap of my bra fell, revealing the naked roundness of my breasts. Panic lit my senses up again as a growl emitted from his throat.

"They can't see us," Brax whispered, assuming my anxiety was due to the possibility we might be watched. As if my quivering breath was fueling him, his fingers began circling my sensitive nipples, gently pinching them and gradually replacing my apprehensiveness with the pure need for something I had never felt.

My gaze returned to the stage where the beautiful woman was now lying on the upholstered table, and the man was making room between her long legs. She was as eager as he was earlier, smiling as he removed the last piece of material that covered her body.

Pressing her legs even farther apart, he dragged two of his fingers over the length of her pussy, causing her eyes to roll to the back of her head in pleasure. Her body arched instinctively as his tongue fell to follow the path of his fingers with long, thorough moves, extracting moan after moan out of her lips.

I swallowed the knot in my throat, trying to imagine how that could feel. Being an introvert, I always wondered if I could ever get that kind of pleasure, convinced that the embarrassment I would feel at that moment would stop me from fully engaging in the raw pleasure of the moment.

As if reading my mind, Brax's hands rolled over my hips, then down to the hem of my dress, raising it just enough to expose my panties.

You know that saying: *be careful what you wish for because it may come true.* Apparently, I wasn't careful enough. My kingpin's fingers were already testing the edge of my panties, moving the material against my pussy and raising a fluttering sensation within me.

"What are you doing?" I shuddered, overwhelmed by everything that was happening.

"I'm not going to spoil my prize if that's what you're worried about... just play with it a little," he said in the most seductive voice, kissing his way up to my earlobe. So heated and so soulless, ignoring the anxiety in my voice, his fingers slipped underneath the material, gliding over my sensitive skin. "Good girl, you're so fucking wet for me," he grunted between gritted teeth, enjoying the damp signs of my arousal while I felt his cock twitching beneath me.

I hated that expression—good girl. It was demeaning, and he knew that perfectly well. It was like congratulating a dog on a trick well played. Words that were empowering him to be the master. And I wasn't one to be subdued, at least not as a result of my own choice.

I fought it at first, unwilling to give him this kind of control over me, but move after move my body began betraying every conscious thought that I may have had.

Looking at the stage again, I noticed the couple had advanced to another chapter. The man buried himself deep within his partner, moving so intensely that it seemed the table they were on top of would break under his weight. Tiny drops of sweat were rolling off their bodies, shining under the spotlights, heightening every emotion that they were feeling. Her face seemed to express certain anguish—beautiful, bonding anguish, not the one that came from pain but one that came from pleasure.

I wondered if they were real lovers, or maybe just actors paid to perform on stage. The lustful sparkle in their eyes and the united lips while slamming into one another led me to believe that they were more than playing a part. Unfortunately, it was more than just playing a part for me too. I was enjoying Brax a little too much for my own good.

Closing my eyes, my hips seemed to have a life of their own. They were arching in ecstasy with every shift of his hand, making his smothered groans match my increasingly loud moans. Covering my mouth with my palms, I realized my body was refusing to obey me as a violent tension was building within me.

Brax didn't seem to agree with me silencing myself. Removing my hands he replaced them with his lips. His coldness turned to fire again, and his damn fingers danced against my swollen clit. He was turning me into a prisoner of desire while his tongue was probing against mine with a passion so fierce I was struggling to breathe.

Tearing my lips from his and turning back to the window, I fought to get myself under control. I needed to follow Brax's command and watch the couple on the other side. It just seemed impossible to do so. Their movement was hypnotic, yet somehow insignificant in comparison to the devastating turmoil that was *torturing* my body.

I watched the woman squirm with ecstasy while tears, not of pain or happiness, but supreme satisfaction, were glittering in her eyes. I couldn't help from letting the same shuddering sensation take control of my body, sending bolting flashes of pleasure straight to my core.

As if feeling my oncoming devastation, Brax's fingers began grinding on my pussy faster and faster, while his hand squeezing my breast was approaching a thin line between pleasure and pain. His groans no longer silenced by my lips, echoed in my ear, each one accompanying the movement of my hips along his cock as he continued his ministrations.

I no longer had control. Heaven met hell, and the most violent storm took over my body. All my muscles spasmed, uselessly trying to find the ground beneath my feet. I was convinced that I couldn't withstand this sensation for long. "Brax," I pleaded with him to stop or to keep going, I didn't know anymore. I only knew these new sensations he was making me feel were raising my panic levels. I have never felt so weak before.

He didn't care, just turned my head and kissed me harder, with a passion he kept buried so deep within him, moving his fingers over and over again against the source of my agony.

It was game over in seconds. I curled into a ball, crashing on his chest, giving him exactly what he wanted—my surrender.

"Good girl, you came so hard for me." His teeth stopped to graze my bottom lip into a final kiss. He just had to ruin the moment, trying to establish a dominance he had already won a long time ago. Yet, it wasn't enough to get a reaction out of me. I knew better than to say something about it to him and start an argument I had no chance of winning.

I was just trying to recover, melting into his arms while his lazy fingers twisted a lock of my wavy brown hair. It felt good, maybe almost normal, but the lights coming back to shine into our room brought a crushing reality back. Jumping on my feet, I rearranged my dress, trying to think of anything I could say that could serve as an excuse to get out of there.

However, Brax hastily spared me the trouble of finding my words. "I'll see you tomorrow. Erick will take you back to your place. I can't have you walking the streets in this *condition.*" He smirked, revealing what a bastard he really was.

Without saying a word, I turned to walk out the door, leaving his infatuated piece of ass behind. In his eyes, I was no different than the girl that left the room before me. Yet at the same time, *different in so many ways.*

CHAPTER 11

My visit to Brax was shorter than anticipated. It was only 11 p.m. when I got back home. Perhaps late enough for the rest of the world, though not too late to see Ferris. He had said he never goes to bed before dawn. So, what was the point in delaying?

Changing into the same black skirt that I wore when I first met Vanya, and a shirt that unfortunately had seen much better days, I decided to leave again in search of a cab. A little difficult in this part of town and at this hour, though not impossible.

This time, I paid much more attention while climbing to the top of the Hills. It wasn't about social classes any longer but about a means to an end. And the higher I ascended, the closer I was to my family.

The darkness of Ferris's mansion felt like a beautiful sonnet, letting the aura of mystery infiltrate my senses and carrying me through divine rhythms to knock on the main door.

"Is he with company?" I asked Alfred, praying that Ferris would be alone. I had just let my cab go, and there was no way I would find a ride back from the top of the Hill to the Pit at this hour. Besides, postponing things even for a day was something that may have me rethinking all of this.

"He's never with any company unless I'm away." The man opened the door so I could step in. "You know your way up," he nodded, bowing his head as I walked past him, then vanished along a long corridor that formed from the main lobby.

The stairs felt like trying to climb towering mountains, each step a struggle under the weight of the burden on my shoulders. I had two of my deals in place and just needed one more. The final one, the deal that would help me reach my goal, even if the price I was going to have to pay seemed impossible for most people.

With trembling hands, I pushed the mahogany door open and entered Ferris's room. The same warm atmosphere emanating from the fireplace embraced me from the first step I took inside this magic world. The scene seemed to be drawn from one of those fantasy books I loved to read, yet I feared that the Prince Charming in my story would turn out to be a seven-headed dragon.

I took a good look around, yet no one seemed to be present.

"Ferris," I called, trying to decipher his location, pacing the full length of the room right up to the balcony to see if he was there.

No answer.

Maybe he stepped out for a little, or maybe he was in another room.

In any case, I wasn't leaving before I got to talk to him, so I decided to wait there.

I was heading to take a seat on the sofa when the unlit candles caught my attention. I loved their flames the other day, so taking a match, I decided to light them up one by one.

"You said you wouldn't return," Ferris's husky voice startled me, echoing from somewhere toward the back of the room and making me turn to acknowledge his presence.

A dim light coming from the bathroom was framing his sculpted body. With only a black towel wrapped around his waist, the wet drawings that decorated his chest were out on display.

My eyes feasted on every divine contour of him. My throat went dry as if his torso had absorbed all the water left on the planet. I found myself forcing down the lump that hindered my breathing, struggling to find my voice to say even a word. "I changed my mind," I barely whispered, lowering my eyes to the ground so I could focus.

As usual, his sense of observation was spot-on. It didn't take him long to pick up on the distress that his body was causing. "I should put something on."

"Yes, thank you." More like *thank God!* since him standing there in nothing other than a towel was making a difficult task seem almost impossible.

The air in the room seemed to lighten as he left to change, only to return just as breathtaking as before.

Donning tight black jeans and one of those t-shirts that had the arms cut out. His top left most of the ink on his chest in sight, everything about him was tempting me to go over there and tear off what was left of his shirt, if only to study the patterns drawn into his skin.

"So, in what way did you change your mind?" His question made perfect sense. I hadn't stated whether I was referring to continuing with the Pleasure Room or actually agreeing on his deal.

"About your proposal, *and* not wanting to go back to the Pleasure Room." It wasn't that I didn't see the chance Vanya gave me as a tremendous opportunity, but I was certainly not able to withstand another Pleasure like one of the last three.

"You won't ever have to," the reassurance of a man who

could guarantee exactly that. Despite the warmth of his promise, he seemed to keep his distance, like he would need to remain lucid enough to be able to weigh his next words.

"But I still have *other* arrangements I have to fulfill... at least for a while." I felt that I should add this part, even if it could jeopardize my final deal. I felt keeping it from him was a form of betrayal, and I didn't want to risk anything that would add to his suffering.

He took a moment to think things through, acknowledging exactly what I was saying. "I understand. I should take this as a *yes* to my offer?"

"Yes, it's a *yes*." I nodded. With Ferris, it didn't feel so difficult to tell him that I accepted, as it did with Cole or Brax. But it felt much more difficult in every other way. "But we're keeping the condition."

"Okay, we're keeping the condition. I won't cross *that* line." Ferris smiled, maybe as deviously as Cole did, but I chose to ignore it. "I'll have Alfred take you to your new apartment tomorrow," he continued.

I had thought our deal only implied he'd cover the rent for the apartment I currently live in. "To my new apartment?" I responded, surprised.

"It's at the base of the Hills, but I'll ask him if we have anything closer available." Ferris was just counting the green houses on his Monopoly board and chose Boardwalk for me.

What was he talking about? "In the Hills? I can't live here; it's too expensive." I retorted, shocked at the preposterous amount of money he was willing to spend on me. The truth was, I hadn't had someone take care of me properly in so long now that it felt off, allowing him to give me such a privilege.

"I didn't realize that we were on a budget." He smiled, having rolled the dice for a final time, and declaring himself the winner. "I don't keep track of expenses, especially not with the people close to me." He struck a match and lit a few candles on the table next to him, letting the flames dance in the darkness of his eyes.

A wolf in sheep's clothing. I knew it from the instant I entered his world a day ago, and still, an invisible power was subduing me to be his little lamb.

"Wine?" He asked, taking an old bottle from a collector's shelf and removing its cork.
At least he was asking and not commanding like Brax did again earlier this evening.

I didn't usually drink, but tonight, it felt like I needed the wine he was offering. I needed to drift off for a while, to escape reality, if only for a moment, and he was a master when it came to that. He had his world, his safe place, and I yearned to join him there.

I nodded, taking a few steps closer to him. "Yes, please."

With Ferris, I couldn't premeditate my moves. Yet strangely, I didn't feel the need to. Everything was natural, fluid, like the red liquid swirling in our glasses.

"Tell me, what should we toast to?" He handed me the drink, searching my eyes for an answer.

There was no room for sarcastic or smartass responses when it came to him. He only wanted to see what it was that I considered worth toasting and without realizing, I was even more clueless than he was. For me, the toast was for a new beginning, with both ups and downs. I just wished I would get over the things that needed to be done and focus on the joy of getting reunited with my loved ones.

"It's complicated. I don't even know what to say," I wasn't lying to him, but I wasn't telling the whole truth either.

To my surprise, he seemed to have all the right words and he didn't waste a chance to use them. "How about you, for sleeping in my arms tonight."

"You don't have to charm me; we already made the deal." I didn't want it to come off as an offense. "I'm sorry, I say the stupidest things when I'm stressed."

Ferris looked displeased with my observation. I didn't expect him to be any different since I just managed to make the connection between us seem like it was all because of the money he was offering when in reality, things were much more complicated than that.

However, once more Ferris managed to surprise me. His hand slipped on the small of my back, pulling me to his chest, so close that our eyes were drowning in one another.

"Do I make you feel stressed?" he asked, pushing a few wayward curls away from my face and shifting somewhat so his mouth was only a breath away from our lips touching. "Do I?" he insisted, the movement of his mouth making his lips brush over mine in an agonizingly delicious gesture.

"Just a little," I answered, merging our lips, and feeling the world around us stop. The room started spinning, and there we were, trapped in a loop of time, lost in small unhurried kisses.

One... two... maybe a hundred times, our lips joined before our tongues met, discovering one another all over again. It was as magical as the sparkles dancing in the chimney and as dangerous as the flames flicking beneath them.

His lips—so warm, so welcoming. His palms slowly glided down on my waist, removing my shirt from the waist of my skirt so that he could make room beneath it. Electric tingles crackled in the tips of his fingers, moving on my skin and turning my body into the lights that twinkle while hiding in the Christmas tree. I was numbed and alive at the same time, lost in his spell, and dreaming of the place his fingers would get to pamper next. Higher and higher, they advanced until they found the base of my breasts, then gradually slipped underneath my bra. The piece of material seemed useless in seconds, and for the first time, I was waiting for the moment to rid myself of it. Though before he got to dispose of my burden, his kisses lost their intensity with lightning speed until his lips drifted away from mine and his palms fell back from underneath my shirt.

"I need to step outside for a second." He stormed out the balcony door, letting the wind rush in.

I was confused; he had a gift for making me feel exactly that way. But it felt wrong to leave him alone with whatever demons were haunting him. So, I followed, hoping to get some answers from his sudden change of heart.

"Are you okay?" I asked, stepping outside onto the balcony.

"Yes, I just needed a smoke," Ferris said, as he lit himself a cigarette, although I knew that he was lying. There was something more to it. I just couldn't tell what. "It's cold outside. Put something on." He gestured for me to go back inside and get dressed.

Well, he wasn't too dressed himself. "You're one to talk. You're in a tank top," I pointed out.

"I guess you're right, but go and put a blanket on." He was sending me away, almost as if he wanted to get away from me. I wasn't sure if he just needed a moment, or if he really cared about me not catching a cold. However, the almost freezing temperature made me listen to him and snatch a blanket off the couch to wrap it over my shoulders.

"Come here." I opened my arms the moment I returned to him and got his body beneath the warm material.

Strangely, he didn't seem to be cold. A smile that hid more bitterness than happiness rose on his lips while he lifted his arms so I could catch him in a hug. Gently, I wrapped my blanket over his back, making us a human burrito, but left one of his hands free so that he could smoke.

"So, what's wrong?" I asked, gluing my head to his chest,

listening to the music of his heartbeats.

He gently huffed, inhaling the night's air. "I don't know. It's hard to explain... It doesn't have to do with you."

"It sure felt like it," I murmured, considering honesty to be the best card. Although, I suspected him of not playing fair.

He let out another heavy breath. "Okay, it does, but it's not something that can be put on you. It's not your fault in any case. It's mine. Just promise you won't push me to talk about it."

"No, I won't. Do you want me to leave?" I felt like I had to ask since he didn't seem comfortable in my presence anymore.

"No, never," he rushed to speak, although *never* seemed a bit extreme. "I mean, I didn't act like that because I want you to leave." His free arm glided beneath the blanket, then after one last drag, his other arm found its way around me. "Although you should do it for your own sake." A smirk appeared on his lips, while something diabolical flashed in the two onyx pearls looking back at me. "Better now?" He questioned, clutching his hands on my hips until our bodies met, then driving his lips to fall on mine.

"Yes," I was telling the truth. A truth I was better off keeping to myself.

I could feel the corners of his lips curl again. "You're right. It is better," he answered, losing one of his hands beneath my shirt. Such a contrast between the cold outside and the heat generated inside our blanket. Without any apprehension, he began exploring every inch of my breasts, taking advantage that my arms were pinned on his shoulders, keeping our shelter in one place.

One by one, the buttons of my shirt were coming undone, making room for him to find my hardened nipples, and begin to gently twist them between his fingers.

A grunt of wild satisfaction left his lips. "You shouldn't

have come outside," he barely got out the words, nipping at my lower lip before kissing me again. "But you enjoy playing with fire, don't you?"

His question unsettled me, yet at the same time stirred up a storm within me. I recognized from the first time I met him the power he could have over me, and despite that, nothing could keep me away from him. I wasn't here only because of a deal, but telling myself it was just a contract kept things less complicated.

Ferris's kisses were getting stronger, and that was causing our height difference to become an inconvenience. So, leaning toward me, he dragged his hands beneath my knees and lifted me to turn us around and place me on the balcony balustrade. He wanted better access to explore my body. But that left me sitting precariously on a narrow stone railing at the edge of a cliff.

It felt like I was hanging on a fine line between life and death. "What are you doing?' I asked, panic coating my voice.

As if deaf to my question, his kiss grew hungrier, releasing an untamed storm to devastate me. We were both teetering on the verge of insanity. The blood in his veins quickened, driving his tongue against my own.

"Let me down from here," I pleaded between kisses. Useless. I was speaking to deaf ears as his mouth fell beneath my blanket to search for the round shape of my breasts. "Ferris," I whimpered, fearing that his actions would unbalance me.

"Shush." He pulled on my hips to tighten the distance between my core and his aroused cock, making my skirt rise so high that the thin material of my panties was glued to his jeans.

We may not know each other well yet, but I had never seen him look more alive. Eyes burning with desire as he raised his head to look at me. "I need you to trust me," he whispered, disappearing beneath the blanket again. Instantly, I felt him merging his lips to taste my nipples, leaning over me so much that the upper part of my body was left, hanging outside of the balcony, directly over the cliff.

"Stop it, Ferris," I let out a muffled scream, trying to push him back. But he wouldn't budge an inch; he seemed to be made of stone.

My efforts only seemed to drive him further. He was roughly sucking the soft skin of my breasts between his lips, leaving bruises along his path, while his iron hands were digging deep into my flesh, steadying me against him.

His mouth began moving harder and faster, hurting me, yet bringing me so close to ecstasy at the same time. He was propping me against himself, raising me almost completely off the ledge. "Ferris!" I cried out while real tears were rolling down my cheeks. I recognized the madness that I saw two nights ago. It felt like I was flying and dying at the same time, terrified that he was fucking insane but also terrified of the thrill of life coursing throughout my body. "I said, stop!" I tried to get a better grip on his shoulders but only managed to let go of the blanket, letting it slip off the balcony and fall lazily into the abyss. Catching a glimpse of it from the corner of my eye brought me suddenly back to reality. I no longer knew if he was playing or genuinely intended to hurt me. I was starting to think he wasn't even there anymore; as if his soul had left his body and I was face-to-face with a demon.

"Ferris," I screamed as loud as I could. I felt like I was slipping away. With the last of my power, I pushed my feet against the stone balustrade and propelled us backward inside the balcony.

The momentum unbalanced him. In his attempt to protect me, he fell to the floor, dragging my body on top of him.

For some strange reason, he began smiling. "You don't

trust me," he whispered, whirling us around on the stone floor until he ended up on top of me. "You will always be safe with me." He was making room between my limbs, bringing his mouth to claim mine, slow and unhurried again, as he did back in his room. And that was raising a thousand *questions in my mind.*

What was he actually doing? And what was he doing to me?

He was death, and he was life, slowly killing me while lifting me impossibly close to the sky.

Tears were still streaming from my eyes. The uncertainty of whether he would have hurt me or not was still there. But they were flowing for another reason too—the closeness, the union, the hands roaming my body, and the wetness pooling between my thighs. They were unstoppable, sending me on a road of no return as he was kissing his madness away. "It's okay... It's okay, Bea." He must have said it a hundred times, until I ended up believing it. It was going to be okay... in the end.

Minutes, maybe even hours passed by as we remained under the dark sky, moving our lips in an intoxicating rhythm.

"You're cold," his hand skimmed the goosebumped skin of my breasts, making him close a few of my buttons back together. "Let's get you inside." He helped me off the floor, and then walked me next to the fireplace. "I'll get you a new blanket." Leaving my side, he went to bring me a new blanket, while the scary memory of how I lost the first one was still haunting my thoughts.

As soon as he made sure I was covered, and with a glass of wine in my hand, Ferris put a small distance between us and went to take a seat on the couch.

"You're not joining me here?" I asked, surprised. Just a minute ago, he couldn't seem to take his lips off me—not that I had any reason to complain about that.

"If I were to join you right now, there would be a 99% chance that I would break my promise." He flashed a grin that quickly got lost in his glass of wine. "Don't worry; we will be sharing the bed tonight," he said while taking another sip.

"Is that a threat?" I chuckled, unsure if the warmth in my cheeks came from the fireplace or the wine.

That grin was back on his lips, "Only for the weak of heart. I see it as a challenge." He certainly had something wicked in his mind. I just prayed it wouldn't be as extreme as those moments on the balcony.

To carry on with this deal, I needed to pretend there was nothing wrong with the way he was behaving, even if it was becoming more and more obvious he suffered from a bipolar or split personality disorder. The time spent with him was even making me doubt my own sanity. He was the charmer, the jack of hearts combined with the wild card, perfectly synchronized into the most dangerous weapon of seduction. And I couldn't stop myself from falling into his trap.

After a couple of glasses of wine, feeling began to return to my hands as my body was coming back to life. I was finally warm, stretching my feet while letting the blanket slip off my back.

"Is it better now?" Ferris asked as if he had waited for me all along.

I turned to face him, "Yes," I answered, wondering when he was planning on joining me on the rug. It took me a while to warm myself, so I guessed his urges should have toned down.

I was wrong.

"Bea, I need you to do as I say. Think you can handle that?" His voice carried a warmth that bordered on manipulation, his words carefully chosen to mask the underlying directive, thinking that I couldn't tell it was still an order.

In reality, he didn't need to do that; we had a deal. One that

I had all intentions of obeying.

"Yes," I nodded to confirm the answer, even though I feared what was coming next.

"Take off your shirt," he said, looking at me like he was going to wait until I followed his instructions.

Where was he even going with this? It wasn't like he hadn't already seen what was underneath it earlier. I found it strange that he didn't personally come to take it off. But I couldn't oppose him.

With sheepish moves, I rose to my feet and then began unbuttoning the parts that were holding my shirt together, letting it fall to the ground.

"Now, your skirt," Ferris continued the instant I finished. He was waiting for me to follow through, slowly watching the material turn into a black pool at my feet. "Perfect, now get on the bed," his voice cracked with excitement.

My body arched against the mattress, but it wasn't in some overly arousing gesture. It was more like trying to hide between the sheets before Ferris could come up with more ways to make me feel embarrassed.

Yet, it didn't take him long before he continued with new instructions, "You're doing great, Bea. I'll be there shortly, but I need you to do something for me first."

That sounded like even more *trouble*.

Ferris positioned himself better on the couch as if trying to get a better view. "Put one of your hands over your navel."

"Ferris," I whimpered, knowing that he was up to no good.

"Shush... Do as I say," he ordered in a much firmer tone.

My eyes closed, sensing what was to come as my thighs squeezed into one another, protecting the sensitive place between them.

"You can keep your eyes closed if you want; it's okay." My new *master* granted me permission. At least I didn't have to look at him as *he* watched me.

"Now push your hand lower." He waited until my hand followed his voice and moved to the hem of my panties. "Now lower, underneath the lace. You know where I want it to be."

I gasped, squeezing my eyes tightly closed while my fingers found the dampness of my core. At least he wasn't the one to find out what devastating effects he had on me, although I suspected this was what his game was all about.

"You know what to do next. Or do you want me to explain it step by step?" His voice drenched in lust, waiting for me to go on.

Words weren't needed. I didn't come from Mars, but the embarrassment seemed to be freezing me on the spot while, at the same time, melting me on the bed. It didn't take long for Ferris to notice that I was stalling and offer again to walk me through things. "Do you want me to say it? To tell you how to touch that tight pussy?"

"No." I blushed and immediately began moving my fingers slowly over my sensitive skin, even though I knew I didn't have much chance of success. The truth was, I had tried this a few times in the darkness of my own room, yet without having any success—almost to the point I was starting to believe that nothing could ever come of it. At least not until this evening, when Brax showed me differently.

I tried to focus on the path he indicated, tracing it again to find a reaction—anything to satisfy Ferris's request and end the night. Come to think of it, he was no different from Cole and Brax; he just had a smoother way of saying things. I was certain that if I were to deny his requests, it would have some sort of repercussions. And I didn't want to test that theory, not because I was afraid of angering him, but because my body craved to obey him. Ferris held some invisible ropes, tying a part of me to him, no matter how hard I fought to oppose it.

Strangely, my body was reacting differently than before. Still, something was off. I found it difficult to put it into words without blushing again, but the only thrill I was getting was from the thought that he was watching me.

It didn't take Ferris long to notice, he left the couch, coming in my direction. Next thing I knew, he was beside me, causing my hand to stop moving as I opened my eyes to look at him.

"Go on," he said in a low tone, taking a seat on the bed beside me. "You look stunning," he leaned over and slipped his hands behind my back to unclasp my bra.

But I didn't want to go on. "It doesn't actually work," I whined, setting my shame aside to confess that I knew it would lead nowhere.

"It will," he said, his tongue tracing the round of my nipple while his hand overlayed mine, guiding it over my pussy and increasing the pressure.

Still nothing. Or at least that's what I told myself for less than twenty seconds until I felt his fingers intertwined with mine. He was leading an assault to that spot that made me arch in pleasure.

And he wasn't taking any prisoners.

Maybe I needed a man's touch to set me on fire, and with Ferris's gifted mouth on my nipples, I was burning. Something divine was taking hold of me as I felt the same tightening sensation rushing to build up under the tips of our fingers.

"See, I was right," he whispered, raising himself to reach my mouth, entrapping me between him and the bed. "Now, come for me, Bea."

I can't recall him even finishing the sentence before the perfect torment was ripping through me. I groaned and purred as his clasp on my hand tightened, forcing me to brush over my clit, which seemed to be becoming too sensitive to be touched.

I thought it was supposed to be game over as soon as he got an orgasm out of me. But he didn't let go of my hand, pushing me from one orgasm to another. It felt like I was hallucinating, drifting off to a new place where every single one of my nerve cells was being put to the test.

He was fucking mad, and he was trying to make me mad about him while I was both kissing and cursing him. In a final attempt, I managed to break free, squeezing my thighs so that he couldn't reach me again. The thought of withstanding him for a second more seemed impossible. "Enough, Ferris," I whispered, the tremble in my body transferring into my voice.

"You need me," the pain in his tone was confirming my suspicions—his ultimate goal was to control me; for me to need him beyond any other limit.

Reaching for his kiss, I got him to release my hand. I murmured, "I do," trying to stop the uncontrollable shaking of my limbs.

It was a lie. I didn't need him the way he wanted me to. I feared to need him that way and to madly give myself to him. I needed to remain detached so I could complete all the deals. And I was already losing at that game.

I didn't get to recover before Ferris's lips were exploring my body again. "Did I do this?" he asked, brushing his thumb over one of my breasts. He was looking at one of the bruises he caused on the balcony. They were mixed with the ones I caused myself after the mission I was part of with Brax when I tried to scrub that man's blood away. However, I was too ashamed to admit to the second part.

"I'm sorry." He let his tongue trail over it, licking my purple wounds while tugging me beside him and pulling a blanket over us. "I'll let you rest. Close your eyes, Bea."

And with that, I slowly drifted towards dreamland under the touch of his warm lips.

CHAPTER 12

I woke up with the strangest reflection burning in my eyes —as if someone was pointing a bulb straight at my face.

"What's wrong?" Ferris asked, sensing me almost jumping out of bed.

I couldn't tell myself what exactly was wrong, especially since I could barely manage to keep my eyes open. But after a few moments of acclimatization, my eyelids slowly parted, only to see the light of.... of the *sun*?

Was that actually **the sun**?

"Ferris...," I could barely call for him as I snatched the blanket off the bed and ran straight outside on the balcony. "Is this it?"

Ferris got out of bed. "We're high above the Pit and the smog level. So, yes. That would be the sun," he said, stretching his arms like a lazy bear coming out of hibernation.

"I... I've never seen it before," I murmured, embarrassed yet mesmerized by the picturesque view. It was the most stunning thing I had ever seen, warming me with the golden rays and bringing sparkles of unexpected hope into my soul.

However, Ferris didn't seem to be as charmed as I was by

the view. "The blessing of my royal heritage," he muttered, as if this was much more akin to a curse than a miracle.

"I didn't know that you were royal," I let out a chuckle, thinking that he was just kidding.

But it wasn't a joke to him. "Yeah. Blue blood is supposed to run through my veins. Funny, it was still red the last time that I bled. Though I'm beginning to believe that it may be black by now."

I could hear the bitterness in his voice but I couldn't stop myself from being surprised by his origins. "I'm pretty sure it's as red as mine. But royalty, really?" It felt strange since, less than a month ago, I hadn't even thought that any level of royalty still existed. And now I'm sleeping in a *royals* bed?

"My grandfather was the direct descendant of a king, but the monarchy is long gone. It's only politics. Senators and governors now," he said as if he wasn't interested in his title.

But it was something too important to be ignored. "So that would have made you king?" I asked, still trying to process the information.

Ferris grabbed my waist, pulling me against him. "A very uncrowned one, but who gives a fuck anyway? Not exactly leadership material, as you can see."

I buried my head in the center of his chest. "That's not what I see."

"You see the lies your imagination wants you to. The real me is the fucked-up version that you met last night." He was backing down again, and I had the feeling that I was losing him with the anger gradually building up into his every word. But I wasn't going to let him return to the shadows, not with the sun burning up there, just for the two of us. There was no chance I would let him chase me away just because he got scared, but I did need to get to school. "I need to go to ECU." I kissed him quickly, trying not to get into any disagreements that I couldn't win, especially not while I was already going to be late for classes.

At the speed of light, I ran back inside to get my clothes, making sure to remain somewhat out of the sunlight to avoid showing off the not-so-*perfect* state of my shirt. I knew Ferris understood that I didn't come from money, but I didn't want to give him more authority over me when he would realize exactly how bad my true financial situation was.

"I would like to see you tonight," he whispered, coming from behind me as I was fixing a few rebellious strands of my hair.

"I will do my best to be here, but you do know that I have other commitments." The truth was, I had plans to meet up with Brax to talk about my family. And that was a meeting that was impossible to cancel.

I could hear Ferris grunt, and the fact that he was unsatisfied with my answer was reflected in the tone of his voice. "So you mentioned. But we need to discuss you quitting The Pleasure Room."

"Can we please talk about it later, because I'm going to be late?" I tried excusing myself.

"You're not going to be late. Alfred will get someone to drive you to the university. Now go, we'll speak later on the phone." I recognized the irritation in his voice as he dismissed me, but there was nothing I could do about it. The deal was to sleep in his bed, not for him to own my life.

I gave him a kiss. "Thank you," I murmured, "I promise that we'll talk about this." I said, as I ran out the door to find Alfred.

"A limo for the lady," Alfred smiled, showing me outside to find my transportation to the university.

It felt a little uncomfortable leaving in a limo. "I was thinking more like a cab."

But it seemed I wasn't aware of how things functioned around here. "The cabs are only for trips to the Pit. A limo would attract too much attention there. Here, it's the other way around," Alfred explained to me the mindset of the Elite. And, come to think about it, he was right. A limo was a lot more normal here than a cab.

Welcome to the land of the rich. However, my choice of clothes didn't match my transportation, so regardless of the luxury ride, everyone could see from a mile away that I was still from the Pit.

"Thank you, Alfred." I said, climbing in the car. It quickly left descending the hill to reach ECU.

I almost crawled out of the limo when the door opened, trying to hide behind the driver so that no one would see my ride.

Mission accomplished. At least partially since there were a few pairs of eyes pointing at me, including Jenna's.

"How the fuck did you get your hands on a car like that?" she asked the instant I reached our side of the hallway.

Busted.

The truth seemed like such a bad answer at that time. Maybe a normal person would understand dating a rich guy for money... maybe even understand the deal. But having three demons own you was inconceivable in any book.

Still, I couldn't lie to her either. I was terrible at it, so I preferred the silence. Yet Jenna didn't. "Sugar daddy?" She chuckled, looking straight at me. "Details! Is he cute?"

I rolled my eyes.

"Is he old?" She stuttered, a bit repulsed.

"No... and yes, and no..." I guess I did owe her some answers. She did tell me every single aspect of her life, from the time she accidentally kissed her cousin—yuck, whatever the hell was that about—to the time she lost her virginity to the Math State Contest champion—double yuck.

"He's more like a guy I'm seeing—not exclusively. And he's not old! Mid-twenties," Come to think about it, he was around Brax's age. "I just needed a lift, and he let me use his limousine." I shrugged, hoping that I was off the hook.

But the interrogation went on. "Are you two...? You know..." Jenna asked.

"I don't know, and I don't want to know," I cackled. "No, nothing happened."

Her eyes lit up as if the most outrageous thought had crossed her mind. "Don't tell me that you're saving yourself for a prick like Cole."

"What do you know about Cole?" Why did she even bring him up?

"The other students were talking. They saw you together in the hallway. He's got his eyes on you." She raised a disapproving eyebrow.

Great, now I was the main subject in the school's local newspaper. You don't even have to print it for it to get to every single person walking these halls.

"They're even saying they noticed you two at a party in the Hills together," Jenna hysterically laughed. "Like, are these people on drugs? Someone from the Pit, going to a party in the Hills. Imagine that."

"Yeah, imagine that," although at this stage my tone was losing its irony as I realized that it was only a matter of time before everyone would know I belonged to him. "Cole just wants to get under my skin, and I need to find a way to avoid that." As if such a way could exist.

"Just stay low; it's only a matter of time before a new attraction grabs his attention." Jenna was trying to comfort me. But for some reason, her words only managed to upset me. It wasn't because I didn't want him off my back. Yet, knowing that someone else had his attention was a whole different deal.

Suddenly, a blank expression appeared on Jenna's face. "Shit, he's walking over here," she stuttered.

I pretended I had no idea about his presence yet it only worked for two nanoseconds because Jenna kept staring directly at him. And so were the rest of the students present in the hallway, since *the king* had strayed so far from his end of the kingdom.

"Are you trying to ignore me, Mouse? That wouldn't be very wise of you," Cole muttered as I felt his body gluing itself to my back. He was so close that I could feel every single one of his stiff muscles as his posture was towering over me.

"I'd better go," Jenna tried to excuse herself.

Though Cole didn't seem to agree. "Did I say you're dismissed?" he snarled.

Who did he think he was, the fucking principal?

"No, I'm sorry," Jenna almost shed a tear, showing signs that she was actually terrified by him.

My teeth clenched so tightly that I thought they were about to crack under the pressure of my wrath. It was one thing coming after me, but quite another coming after my friends. Our deal didn't involve making Jenna's life a living hell.

I needed to find a way out for her without infuriating Cole at the same time. "She was just leaving for classes," I tried to excuse her.

"If I'm not mistaken, we all have Marketing." Cole let out a devious smirk. He wasn't mistaken; he knew exactly what he was talking about. "Come, I'll save you two a seat next to me." Now, he was just acting strange. And I was fully convinced that it had something to do with his supreme pleasure in tormenting every second of my existence.

Grabbing hold of my arm, Jenna glued herself to me as we walked to class. She was hoping I could defend her from Cole, who was also tightly on our trail, panicking her to the extreme. "What are we going to do?" she whispered, unsure what he wanted from her.

I didn't have an answer to her question. But I knew I couldn't let him pick on her, and I would have done anything to stop that from happening.

"I'll handle him, don't worry," I tried to reassure her. Though the truth was, I had no idea how. Hopefully I could improvise, but when it came to Cole, there was little room left for anything other than his desires.

As soon as we entered the door, he showed us two seats somewhere in the corner of the classroom. "Ladies first."

I had a bad feeling about it, especially since I knew what happened the last time I had attended the same class as him.

I gestured for Jenna to occupy the one next to the wall so that I'd be left with the one next to Cole. I needed to keep her as far as possible from his tyrannical behavior.

And he noticed. "You're afraid of what I'm capable of. Good, you should be." He let a diabolical grin slide onto his face, tilting his head so he could look at Jenna.

"Leave her alone. She's got nothing to do with our agreement," I muttered, hoping no one would hear me, except him.

But I only managed to infuriate him even more. "Since when do you tell me what to do?" his tone annoyed.

"I didn't mean it like that... It's just that she's not involved in what's between us," I lowered my voice, trying not to anger him any further.

"And what exactly is it that's between us?" His question

made perfect sense in a normal world, but when it came to us, I wasn't sure if either of us held the answer.

"I know what it *is* between me and you... You should tell me about the rest." In my case, it was simple, I needed legal protection, and he was the one who could provide it. But when the wheel turned, I often wondered what made him so determined to chase me down.

"You were the only one who ever said *no*." His words hit me so very differently from how I ever thought possible, fueling the last remnants of my pride. I was the only one to refuse the king. Yet my ego didn't take long to burn down, as the flame of my newfound self-esteem was instantly hosed down. "And I'm not going to let that go so easily."

There was no *in between* when it came to this man, and I just realized that. No matter what I did, he wouldn't soften up on me and risk injuring his own pride.

Without warning, he pushed a thick notebook in front of me. "Here. Write my notes," he ordered.

I looked back at him, surprised that he even carried a notebook around. "Can't we just copy the notes later on a copy machine?" I was trying to find a way out.

Not that he was willing to let me. "No. I always lose papers, so I want them handwritten here." He pushed the notebook even closer to me.

Of course, he did. Finding a new way of torturing me was his favorite hobby.

"Okay... okay. I'll write them down for the both of us," I groused, taking out my own notebook and preparing myself to write the essentials down in both.

I knew that there had to be some trick. And I was to be proven right the minute the teacher started his lecture. Cole's hand *magically* slipped over the hem of my skirt, trying to find its way underneath it.

I guess it was just my luck that I was wearing a skirt so tight that his palm couldn't slide beneath the fabric. And yet, he wasn't one to give up so easily. Dropping our bags between us, he covered his arm to advance higher and higher, roaming the upper part of my leg.

The previous time we managed to duck intrusive eyes, this time he was making sure his gestures wouldn't go unobserved. This was how Jenna fit into all of this, a means for him to bring my embarrassment to a whole new level.

"Cole," I whispered, pleading for him to stop.

"Write," he ordered, pausing for a moment, but continued on each time he noticed that I was falling behind with the notes. "One mistake and I'll be sinking my fingers into your soaking wet pussy while everyone is watching."

My cheeks started burning. I had to finish transcribing everything on paper in time, or his hand would move. And I could feel how eager he was to reach for that spot between my thighs. It was a cat-and-mouse game, and he was enjoying pushing my anxiety to its very last limit.

It was impossible for me to focus, but I wasn't going to let him win, especially with Jenna keeping an eye on us. For her, it was like witnessing a murder scene. You want to look away, but you just can't.

My fingers were burning on the pen. The notes were coming together in both notebooks, and the adrenaline rush was reaching heightening levels. I could feel how badly he wanted me to fail so he would get to touch me. But at the same time, I knew he wasn't going to break the rules he had just set. Cole loved the chase as much as he loved the prize. And that was keeping me safe as long as I wasn't falling behind.

The skirt I had on, was only momentarily preventing him from reaching my core. It was just a matter of time before he would try to explore it again from underneath. Only, I wasn't going to allow him to go there, especially as every second I could catch a break, I was crashing into Jenna's confused stare.

Whatever Cole would do, Jenna would have noticed, and I was struggling with each minute to prevent him from putting on the show he wanted.

The rest of the hour was a nightmare, a race against time and my own powers. That was until the clock finally struck noon. I felt like I was crossing the finish line, but I knew better than to gloat. When it came to Cole, things couldn't be that easy. It would only be a matter of time before he would find new ways to torture me.

"You did good, Mouse." He smiled like the devil he was while packing his bag as if nothing had happened. "You turned me on." He leaned to whisper in my ear, making sure to brush his lips against the erogenous zone of my neck.

What the hell was he even talking about? I didn't even have a chance to say a word or make any kind of gesture except for that damn writing?

But deep down I knew how much of a sick bastard he really was. It was my fear that had turned him on, my stumbled breath whenever I felt him move, and the pain from my hand clutching so tightly to the pen so I could write as fast as I needed. I suspected he wasn't done with me. "After the break, meet me in the chem lab," he whispered in my ear, then walked away like nothing had happened.

Why the chem lab when neither of us was registered for that class?

It didn't take long for me to find out.

It was empty.

Closing the door after me, I breathed with relief. He wasn't around yet, and I desperately needed a moment of freedom after I managed to duck Jenna and practically everyone else during the break.

I gained a few minutes to relax since Cole was running late, not that I was really complaining about that. I dreaded the moment the door would open, and he'd find his way into the room. Every second passing was fueling a tremble in my legs at the thought of what was going on in his mind and what plans he had for *and* with me.

His arrival couldn't be indefinitely postponed, and the dark reflection of Cole's presence slowly filled the room. His steps unhurried, based on the anxiety they were provoking, he moved inch by inch to reach me while his lustful gaze was studying every round shape of my body.

"I underestimated you," a whispered groan of annoyance reached my ears as the large contour of his silhouette clouded everything in front of me.

Strangely, it seemed Cole was more irritated with himself than he was with me. *He* was the one who made the mistake of allowing me to get to that point of having an effect on him. But I knew all too well who was going to pay for that error—me.

His tongue traced over his lips while visibly craving my own. "I've been generous today." He actually believed that it was *generous* of him to stress me out to the point where I felt my legs almost failing me. "Don't you agree?" he asked, as if I should thank him for stressing me out completely.

No, of course, I didn't agree; how could I ever?

But how could I ever disagree either? Especially since I knew the consequences if I did. So, once again, I felt forced to swallow my pride. "Yes, I agree... you have," *your fucking majesty*. As you may imagine, I had to leave the last part out.

This was what Cole did best—break my pride, trying to get me to submit to him one way or another. And if I had any trace of a doubt, the satisfied glimmer in his eyes as I spoke confirmed my initial thought. "You know, I didn't even get to unwrap my present." He grinned, his body melting onto mine.

I uselessly tried to back down, only succeeding to entrap myself between him and a study bench. With slow-motion gestures, his hand sought to find the first button of my shirt, provoking an instinctive reaction to flash through me. I jumped, almost leaning back so he wouldn't reach me. I was strongly under the impression that all the lights were pointing straight at the recently exposed surface of my breasts, even though it was almost completely dark inside the room.

"Careful now. We wouldn't want me to break one of the buttons by mistake and you find yourself walking around the university half-dressed, would we?" he warned, slipping a hand around my waist.

It would be hardly a *mistake*, but I quickly got the hint.

"Relax," his voice calm and eager at the same time while he was unfastening another one of my buttons. Silence filled the room, broken just by the throbbing sound of our breathing, as my shirt came open and the cups of my bra came into sight. "I can feel your excitement. You were eager for me to touch you, weren't you? I could feel it from the first second you looked at me," he murmured, lifting me on top of the bench and pulling the last of the material that covered my breasts down to fully expose me.

That was it, I had reached my limit. "Are you on drugs?" I muttered. "Do you actually think this would bring me excitement?" I asked, surprised at his infatuation, even though, in reality, he did touch a sensitive nerve. I had felt a strange attraction toward him ever since the first time I saw him. But I put it on the bad-boy vibe that always seemed to have a strange yet unwanted effect on me.

I just needed to blow off some steam, even for a second. Besides, keeping every single one of my thoughts to myself was never my strong point. Cole maybe wasn't as dangerous as Brax or Ferris, but the adrenaline he provoked could not be matched.

"Oh, that mouth of yours. I told you I'll take care of it someday." His thumb came up to my lips, brushing them while his own parted with eagerness. Then it drifted again, applying pressure to the center of my bottom lip as his other free hand cupped one of my breasts.

A startled gasp escaped me as his palm closed in to fully weigh the roundness of my bust. Taking advantage of the breathless moment, his thumb slipped in between my lips. I froze, looking at him with shock as his finger began moving inside my mouth—in and out—over and over again, while his gaze was fascinated with every single action. He was in awe, living to witness the motion that culminated with my lips obliging and forming the perfect O.

His hard cock was anxiously threatening to burst his jeans, as his lips descended to trace a long, warm trail over my quivering nipples. "Fuck, Mouse. I might want to keep you," he muttered, almost in ecstasy, sucking my nipple between his teeth.

My blood was boiling with a strange desire. I felt my core tighten with need, trying to withstand the melted heat that seemed to flow like a river through me. I wanted him to evaporate, disappear, and never return... but maybe still leave me with the mesmerizing movements of his tongue and lips.

It was craving versus hate, always battling inside my mind when it came to Cole, to the point where sense would give in to pleasure.

I let out a moan as he drew my body to arch against him while still savoring the soft skin of my breasts. He recognized his impact and within seconds he abandoned his new playground and captured my lips. The tip of his tongue found room between the moving finger, stealing a kiss while pressing his thumb against my tongue.

Anger was an understatement when I came to realize what exactly I was doing. However, I couldn't tell if I was angrier with him or with myself for savoring the intensity of the moments as if it were to be the finest piece of cake.

"I know you like this as much as I do." His tongue skimmed my bottom lip in a wet trail that seemed to be mirrored inside my panties. Exhaling a heavy breath, he created a bit of distance to properly look at me. "I want you to come to my place tomorrow after classes. I'll text you the address." It was an open invitation into the lion's den.

If these kinds of ideas were crossing his mind in such a public place, what could he think of in the privacy of his home?

That thought alone was terrifying to me.

A small commotion in the corridors was telling us that time was up. No matter how eccentric Cole might have been, putting on this kind of show in front of an entire class was a little out of his league. "It's a shame that I don't have time to properly enjoy my present right now." He gave me a small peck on the lips as he was regaining possession of his finger and gliding it out of my mouth.

"These are only for my eyes to see." Brushing his tongue on the surface of my breasts as if saying goodbye; he rearranged my bra before someone could burst in and witness our indiscretion. "You're in so much trouble," he mumbled in a playful tone, lifting me from the bench and setting me back on the floor, not before he squeezed my ass strong enough for me to arch against him.

"I'll leave first." And before I could put two and two together, he disappeared from the room, leaving me to fix the rest of my buttons, just moments before students started flowing into class.

I wish I could have been angry, or even cried, screamed, drowned in agony, or maybe just had time to reflect on everything around me. But my life was running on fast forward, burning minutes and hours with the speed of light.

Before I knew it, I was staring in the mirror back at my apartment, getting ready for my meeting with another of my personal demons—Brax.

CHAPTER 13

The thought of going to see Brax unsettled me. It did every time, but now it was bringing me to the verge of an anxiety attack. There was something so complex about him that I couldn't fully understand. Yes, he was a psychopath, a killer, a user, fucking Evil Knievel when you draw the line, but there was something else too—like a smoldering fire, hiding a passion so intense that it could mystify everything in its path. The silent volcano that lay within him, entrapping sheltered emotions at the point of being set free.

For some unknown reason, his touch was still alive on my skin, making it crawl with the vivid memory of *him*. I was hopelessly fighting it with the last piece of my consciousness. And I couldn't go to see him tonight as emotionally weakened as I was. I still had a mission, and as intriguing as unveiling Brax's true nature may have sounded, nothing could distract me from my path.

Slipping into the same dress I wore the last time I went to see him, I grabbed a jacket on my way out and signaled for a cab. Before I knew it, I was in front of the club where he told me to meet him.

"Boss is in his office." The same guard, Erick, rushed out

to indicate his boss's location. "Down the stairs, then take a left through the metal door." This man always seemed to be around my mafia boss, which led me to believe he must have been his right-hand man.

Just how many offices did my mobster even have?

Following the instructions, I found myself in a narrow lobby with only a door separating me from my *benefactor.*

After praying to all gods that he'd have mercy on me this time, I gathered my courage and gently pressed the door handle to open. However, I didn't get to enter the room. Right before I could let Brax know of my arrival, I heard voices coming from inside the room. I recognized him speaking with another man. And let's just say he didn't sound pleased.

Before they realized that I was around, I pulled the door back to close it without actually shutting it completely. The noise would alert them to my presence, and drawing Brax's anger on me because I ruined some who-knows-what business deal was the last thing that I needed.

My intention wasn't to eavesdrop. I didn't want anything to do with Brax's businesses, especially when I knew most of them were illicit. The last thing I wanted was to overhear something and risk ending up under the police radar, or worse. Still, I couldn't help it since the discussion echoed through the small hallway where I was waiting.

"The people want a war, Brax. They're tired, and they're hungry. With every given month, the rations they are able to put on the table are getting scarcer," the unfamiliar voice said.

"I know. I feel it in the takings. Plus, some of them are loyal to me. One of their leaders came to me seeking financial support, promising some exaggerated interest payback rate for the money. Fools. Wars burn money, they only make fortunes for the winners, and in this case, the Annelids don't stand a chance against the Elite. Sure, the royals don't know shit about fighting, but they have weapons and finances. Just a group of mercenaries, and they'd get the Pit burning before dawn." It was Brax who spoke this time.

"What do we do then? Our investments will be at risk," the other man asked with concern.

"You have one investment, Patrick, and we both share it— this club, while I own half of the city. With everything frozen in assets for now. People aren't in a rush to buy properties around here, in case you hadn't noticed. Besides, even if I were to find someone to dispose of a few buildings and get some cash flow back on track, the sum I would get would be insignificant compared to what I spent on the construction. No one wants to buy a city that might burn."

Brax's visitor was panicking. "There has to be a way to keep things under control."

"There isn't," Brax said, anger lingering in his voice. "Best case scenario—just prolong the inevitable, and we can sell some of the goods to survive this, while still remaining on top. The money that would be needed to support a movement like this is way more than we can even fucking dream of. Think about it, weapons, mercenaries, maybe whole armies to mount an assault on the Hills.

"Impossible," Brax continued. "It's the food chain. The rich get richer, and the poor get poorer. If the Annelids oppose, the Elite will wipe them off the face of the earth. And believe me; others will follow to take their place. It's Echo City we're talking about. The last oasis of hope. If only those poor bastards knew the reality—there is no hope anymore. Let's just cross our fingers that our business won't become too affected in the transition." Brax casually said, proving once again he was perfectly adapted to survive anything, even though I could detect a hint of worry in the tone of his voice.

But his companion didn't seem to be as calm as he was. "You're talking about eradication!" The man seemed shocked.

Brax huffed, "I don't know what it will come to. But I am talking about survival of the fittest. And right now, I have my mansion up in the Hills where no one can touch me."

"Maybe I should leave the city."

"And go where, Patrick? Everywhere is the same. Maybe even much worse. Resources are becoming scarce because of the pollution. Things are simple. The Elite want lands for lavish gardens, tennis courts, and who knows what else, while they expect the Annelids to grow wheat in the one square foot of their homes."

"You think that's the main cause of starvation?" the man asked.

"I think that's the solution. If they can find the resources to grow miles of grass with artificial light, then they can fucking also grow a carrot." Brax was proving to be not only street-wise but also a good strategist. "I don't know; no matter how big I am on the streets, I'm too small in this game, and I never enter battles I know I can't win. And speaking of battles, our meeting has come to an end. I have something to take care of before shit hits the fan."

"Anything that I can help you with?" Brax's visitor asked again.

"I'll let you know if I need anything, but I don't think it will be the case. It's more like a kidnapping." Brax was talking about my family.

"Oh, a ransom. I hope it's profitable."

"No... not for ransom. Let's just say retrieving lost goods." I could sense the smirk on my mobster's lips as he said it.

"Then good luck with that. I'd better be going."

The second I heard him leaving, I backed down the lobby, then pretended I was just arriving. Under no circumstances could I allow Brax to suspect that I had overheard anything, especially since I didn't want to be privy to that information. I was just in the wrong place at the wrong time, managing to take the burden of the entire city upon myself.

Maybe the truth was that I was saving Sebastian and Natalie only to doom them.

But I couldn't think like that. I shouldn't think like that. I have to find a way through this.

At least Brax was committed to his promise, even though, initially, I had some doubts about his truthfulness. I was hesitant when it came to him, maybe even when it came to all of my *kings*. But Brax's wicked nature was making me suspect him most of being the most likely to not follow through with his promise.

"You're late again." As soon as the door opened, he roared, noticing me approaching from the other end of the hallway.

What could I have said? That I was there ten minutes ago? I couldn't let him suspect I had been spying on him, however unintentional it may have been. I simply nodded and slipped into the office as he stood aside to let me pass.

"Was that one of those nods women give to shut men up?" he hissed.

I shrugged, trying to appear much more relaxed than I really was. "I thought it was a man thing to nod rather than answer questions, not a *womanly nodding*."

"Don't throw some feminist crap at me right now; I'm not in the mood," he barked, making his way towards his mahogany office desk, and settling into his presidential seat. Come to think of it, it resembled a throne more than any seat I had ever seen.

"You seem stressed. Is everything okay?" I felt compelled to ask, noticing how his attitude mirrored the nervous twitch of his perfect jawline.

There was a ninety-nine percent chance that it had something to do with the visitor before me, but I couldn't reveal that I was aware of it.

"With recovering your family... yes, everything is okay," he paused, staring for a second into an empty corner of the room in an attempt to clear his mind. "Sit down."

I looked at the two chairs on the opposite side of his desk. Though, once again, I knew where he wanted me to sit, and my hesitation was quickly noted. "Don't play dumb. You said it yourself that I already seem stressed. You know where to sit," Brax snarled, pushing on his chair to move it away from his desk to make room for me to join him.

There was no way around this. Before I knew it, I was standing next to his muscular body, glancing into the absinthe in his eyes.

"Here, Bea." Sneaking a hand beneath my knee, he pulled me to get on top of him, making my legs straddle his waist. "Not close enough," he growled, lifting the hem of my skirt high enough to push my thighs all the way open. My pussy was joining with his growing erection, and my body instantly recognized that animalistic instinct that lies dormant in all of us. Only it wasn't so dormant anymore, especially when it came to Brax. Thank God for the layers of clothes we were both wearing, or else he would have claimed his *prize* right then and there.

Without paying too much attention to my visible distress

and flustering, his index finger wandered to the strap of my dress. "I like this dress." He deviously smiled, letting it roll off my shoulder.

"Good, 'cause it's the only one I have." I giggled, making fun of my own misery, as the warmth of his lips replaced the missing strap.

"I'll get you a new one," he whispered against my skin, alternating kisses with arousing nibbles.

His attention quickly moved to my other shoulder, repeating the actions, and disposing of the second string that had held my dress together. His kisses were so different than before—an unhurriedly searching for something over every inch of my collarbone, delighting himself with the taste of me.

"What are you doing?" I asked, noticing the top of my dress slipping on my breasts to the point that it barely covered my nipples.

"Do you want me to explain myself step by step? Because I can be extremely explicit." He didn't even bother to look at me, just pushed my dress lower, allowing him to hide one of my nipples between his lips. His gesture sent a devastating shiver through my entire body, instinctively making me arch against him in the chair. "I'm de-stressing myself," he murmured, nibbling on my now-hardened nipple. "And from what I can tell, you could use some de-stressing yourself," he said, sneaking both hands around my hips and getting me to arch again a couple of times against his crotch.

"Weren't we supposed to talk about retrieving my family?" I tried to get to the reason for my visit since things seemed to be going in a whole different direction.

Not that Brax cared. "My men are not here yet," he said, without breaking the union of his lips with my breasts.

"But what if someone walks in?" I shivered at the thought. Lately, the idea of public exhibitionism seemed to be following me everywhere I went.

"No one comes to my office unannounced. They know better than that," Brax muttered, annoyed.

I guess I was the only one who didn't, considering less than ten minutes earlier I had opened his door without knocking.

"Did anyone tell you that you ask too many questions?" he seemed pissed off.

I didn't get to answer as he grabbed my head from behind, crashing his mouth on mine. The kiss—raw, pure, searching within the depths of me and bringing out all the sensations this man could give. His tongue was spinning in delirium as both of his hands were searching for my breasts, cupping them from underneath and probing against my aching nipples. I couldn't explain the way he owned my body, but I couldn't deny it either. "This is cheating," I whined as every single action was raising a tidal wave to crash inside of me.

"No, this is." He abandoned my lips to bite into one of my hardened nipples so lustfully that he got me to almost crawl into a ball. The bittersweet chill of pain and ecstasy was spreading through my body, causing my legs to instinctively close. I was uselessly trying to protect the small drop of composure I had left.

His tongue rolled on my chest, slowly tasting the satin skin of my breasts in long, luscious strokes, making me melt into liquid longing on top of him. I could tell he wasn't there anymore, just a hundred percent focused on pampering his two newfound toys. The pleasure flashing through his eyes was so much more than simply erotic, hiding utter satisfaction, but most of all feral passion.

That exact impulse to arch against him was warning me that I needed to try and stop this before we would reach that point of no return. "I think we better stop before someone comes in." That idea may not have agreed with my body, but it agreed with the real reason I was there— saving my family.

"You really think so?" he groaned, clasping one of his hands on my breast while the other was finding its way beneath my dress. "Let's check that, shall we?" One of his fingers glided underneath the lace of my panties and straight to that sensitive place between my folds. "Ohhh, Bea. Someone's been lying, you don't really want me to stop," he grinned, retrieving his damp finger and letting the signs of my eagerness shine underneath one of the small wall lamps hanging in his office. His victorious laughter echoing throughout the room.

I babbled, hiding my face in my palms, hoping for an electrical meltdown to shield my shame. Not that he cared. "I really need to check that more thoroughly," he whispered, pushing my panties aside as his lips continued their journey over my breasts. But time wasn't on his side. Before he got a chance to continue his sweet torture over my skin, a knock on the door alerted that we weren't going to be alone for long.

I jumped as if I had stepped on hot coals, rushing to rearrange my dress while Brax shook his leg, trying to hide his visible erection. "Come back," he ordered me, pulling me back to sit on his lap—this time without turning me to face him.

Allowing him to get away with almost anything while we were alone was one thing, but enduring an even more dominant version of Cole and risking public humiliation was pushing me to the brink of sanity. "Are you insane? There's someone at the door?" I couldn't keep my mouth under control as his plan of me sitting in his lap during a meeting seemed totally absurd.

"They're my men. Don't worry; they'll probably put more effort into it knowing that I'm fucking you." Brax—*the gentleman*—lifted me a little higher on his legs to glide an arm around me. "Come in."

The driver, Erick, and another tall dark-haired man who appeared to be in his mid-thirties, pushed the door open and stepped into the dim light.

"Sit," Brax ordered his men, who strangely enough, didn't seem at all surprised at their boss having me in his arms.

"Good evening," they both nodded, bowing their heads as if I was of royal origins.

I also greeted them with a flustered *"Good evening,"* embarrassed at the temporary position as queen of the underworld. And when I say temporary, I mean just until I could get out the door because I was certain that the *seat* wouldn't even get cold before a different girl took my place.

"Who did you talk to?" Brax asked the driver while lighting a Cuban cigar.

"I've talked with Showman and Wrench about coming with us for support, but they each want ten grand."

Brax looked at me while his hand advanced upwards on my leg. "You're pricey, Fox," he smiled. "Tell us what you think we should know first.'

Where should I even start?

Before coming here, I was sure I was a hundred percent ready to give them all the intel they needed. But now that we needed to come up with a plan, I had no idea what I needed to say or do. "I've never done this before, so I'm not exactly sure what info would be helpful."

"Just tell us who we need to get out for now," the man

accompanying the driver gave me a hand before I would manage to exhaust the last of Brax's patience.

"My siblings. I have a sister and a brother. My sister's name is Natalia. She's thirteen. Brownish hair, green eyes, kinda looks like me. Now for my brother, his name is Sebastian, and he's six. Dark hair, also green eyes. But there's something that you should know about him. He's on dialysis—kidney insufficiency. You need to be extremely careful while moving him; shocks or sudden movements can trigger a seizure." I tried summing things up without giving them useless details.

"We'll need an ambulance to transport him safely," my kingpin thought out loud. "Now for the people around your father. Tell us about them," he continued.

"My father was a nobody, just a frustrated man who used to beat up his kids so that they could go on the streets and beg for money to satisfy his greed. That was before he befriended some lowlifes, probably even bigger screw-ups than him. They managed to set up a small human trafficking network; getting others to beg for them." I had to stop for a second as the memory of his fists throwing me to the ground was making hot crystal tears roll off my face and onto Brax's shirt.

Before I managed to gather my strength and collect my thoughts, I felt the arm around me tighten as I realized the body beneath me was tensed to its limits. "Did he beat you?"

"Yes." The answer brought a deep frown to his face, although it had nothing to do with some newfound feelings for me but everything to do with the fact that I was his property now. Plus, his men were carefully watching, and he couldn't let something like that slip as if nothing had happened.

"Give me the address, and tell us about the location... Rooms, entries, windows," Brax spoke between gritted teeth.

"It's on Fourth St., the first building as you turn left. It looks abandoned, but our family used to live in apartment 1B. The apartment itself has two rooms, both windows facing south. Although, I don't think there's where he would keep them— at least not Natalie. She said something about being guarded, and even in the good days the apartment could barely fit our family of five. It's almost impossible to set up a prison there. So, I suspect she's on the floor below. That's where my father set up his new *business*."

"Are there any apartments on that floor?" Erick asked.

"Not exactly. It's more like a large basement with a few rooms for storage where the new *workers* used to sleep." I tried my best to explain.

The tall man was writing everything down in a notebook. "How many people do you reckon are on the premises?"

"When I left a month ago, it was just my father and four or five of his so-called friends. I'm saying four or five because one of them is usually so high on drugs that he doesn't even count as being there." I paused again to look at Brax who downed the two fingers of whiskey that were in his glass. He was infuriated. I could tell even from the way he was breathing, and I couldn't deny that deep down I wished that one day someone would act like this just in need of protecting me. But it was far from being the case. I was the only one who could ever protect myself, and at the same time, I was the one who was selling my body.

"I received a call from my sister a few days ago telling me she was being guarded. I'm not sure what that meant because she couldn't talk for long. But I bet if it was someone I knew who was guarding her, she would have called them by name. So, I suspect that they hired new people, possibly recruited from the beggars. I don't know for sure."

"Entry points for the underground?" Erick asked.

"Only the main entrance of the building. There used to be a back entrance, but it was blocked some time ago due to robbers. They placed several dressers in front of it. You can't get in through there, at least not without making noise."

"Fucking perfect," Brax muttered, pouring himself another glass of whiskey from the crystal decanter on the table.

"I'm afraid it gets worse when it comes to the underground floor. It has a few ventilation windows, but they're only big enough for a cat to sneak through. I know because Nat got stuck climbing through one when she was just a baby, and we could barely get her out." I continued, realizing that things would be a lot more difficult for them than they initially assumed.

"That means more men for a frontal assault," the tall man spoke, transcending another of his ideas on paper.

"Any more *good* news for me, Princess?" Brax's nostrils flared with irritation, probably cursing himself for getting involved in this mess.

"I hope not. That is if the gentlemen don't have any additional questions," I said, looking at his men.

"This should do it. Just let us know if you remember any other aspects that you didn't cover," the driver said while looking at his boss.

"What's the damage?" Brax asked, taking a drag out of his cigar.

The tall man looked at him, then scribbled some more numbers in his notebook, trying to do the math. "Three mercenaries of 10k each, plus 2k, I would say, for the ambulance and five of our men, so we don't run into any surprises. We need two teams so we can go in at the same time. One for the apartment and one for the underground."

"Thirty-two grand plus expenses," Brax rolled his eyes, then turned to look at me as if I was the one who did something wrong. "Okay, go for it. Just make sure we have enough men. Failure is not an option on this one."

"It won't be. I'm taking Rodriguez with me, and we'll head there in the morning to keep an eye out on things," the driver spoke, getting up from his chair.

"Okay, how long do you think before we can go in?" Brax was probably counting the days left until he got to unwrap his gift.

"I'm not sure. I would say three days to a week. We need to study a routine, patterns in their behavior, maybe even see if they take shifts in guarding. Only then can we decide on the best time to act," the tall man spoke, also standing up from his chair, and heading towards the door. "We'll let you know as soon as we have something."

"Okay. I have a meeting with Ignacio in a few minutes, but come back to see me in about an hour. I want to discuss something about the gambling debts at the Lucky Royal."

"Sure thing, boss." And with that, the men evaporated through the door, leaving us alone again in the room, although in a much different atmosphere than the one at their arrival. You could cut the tension with a knife, and I'm not talking about that panty-blowing heated atmosphere. No, it was filled with anxiety, hidden worry, and irritation. I just wasn't sure if it was about the money or about the plan.

To be honest, the sum was absurd. I initially did the math on how much money I would need to retrieve my siblings, but I was wrong. I could never have thought of reaching even a third of that amount. I would have needed to work at Vanya's for a year to get close to raising that sum. And that was without eating.

"Your ass is expensive." Brax was keen on letting me know how much money I was taking out of his pockets. "Over 35k with travel expenses, plus the time of five of my men." His hand slipped under my dress again, heading straight towards the hem of my panties. "I'm a man of my word, but this is way more costly and complicated than I suspected. I deserve a bonus prize."

"You said it's a one-time thing," I whimpered, feeling his hand back between the folds and already playing with my core.

"And that it would be. Although right now I would fuck you against this desk until you would cry out in happiness. But, as we agreed, I only have one shot at this and don't want to waste it. Who knows, maybe you'll return begging for more."

I didn't reply since the one thing I could think of saying was *In your dreams.*

"I need a little something extra," Brax continued, "A test to see if you're going to keep good on your side of the deal."

"I thought that I already showed you that," I mumbled, knowing that nothing good could come from this, especially with the atmosphere being as heated as it was. But once again, I anticipated more absurd requests to follow, ever since I decided to make a deal with him. After all, he was a businessman, and he was milking our unwritten contract for all it was worth.

"I would love to start now, but I have a meeting in..." He looked at his watch. "Five... And I definitely don't want to rush this." His hand abandoned the inside of my panties before things could go to that point of no return. "Wednesday night, at my place." He took another drag out of his cigar.

I rolled my eyes. "I didn't say yes."

"You didn't have to. One of my men will come and pick you up. I don't like you walking in the Pit alone." Brax wasn't taking no for an answer.

"Awww, I didn't think you cared." Oops, sarcasm on the loose.

"We wouldn't want you to get into who knows what kind of trouble and leave me without my payment after all the effort I'm putting into this. Would we now?" He sarcastically asked, as if I wouldn't be able to take care of myself in the Pit.

How was it that I managed to get myself into trouble every time?

"Now go." He pulled me into a final kiss, biting on my lower lip. "I'll have to teach you when to open this mouth and when to keep it shut." His heavy palm collided with my ass as I was standing, making me gasp in molten pain. "A car is waiting to take you home."

I didn't reply since I was too busy cursing between my lips. I just strode out the door and into the designated car to take me back to my place.

CHAPTER 14

T he shake in my knees was still there, reminding me of the hold Brax has over my body. The one thing I couldn't allow was for him to infiltrate my mind. I was holding onto that last line of defense against all three demons who owned me.

I often wondered what could be so terribly wrong with me that my body preferred subduing rather than trying to withstand them. Because, no matter how many silver linings my relationship with them may bear, in the end, there was nothing aside from rot supporting our bond. I am a slave with no chains, tied to all of them in one way or another, trapped in a perpetual game of cat and mouse.

I looked at my phone to find three missed calls from Ferris. It was impossible not to keep my phone on silent during my visits with Brax since any questions coming from him regarding my other Pleasures were the last thing on my mind.

I almost pressed *call*. That was before I took a look around me and realized that I was still in the car with one of Brax's men. I didn't take an oath of total purity, but it just felt wrong to call Ferris from within the ride provided by my mobster.

"Have a nice evening," the man assigned to drive me home nodded while I glanced around me, noticing a yellow cab parked right in front of my apartment building. I needed to call Ferris as soon as I got inside, yet the sight of the cab left me with the feeling that he was already one step ahead of me.

There was no need to search for my keys. My apartment door was open, and a few empty suitcases were lying in front of it.

"Bea!" Ferris's butler, Alfred, greeted me as if I was the one coming to visit his place.

"Good evening," I looked around me, spotting two cups of warm tea sitting on the small coffee table sitting in the middle of the room.

"Had to warm them up a couple of times." Alfred reached out to offer me one while gesturing for me to take a seat on the bed since my *luxurious* apartment didn't even have a couch.

"I'm sorry, I was... busy"...*with selling the last part of my soul.* But I couldn't tell him that.

"No problem, I'm good at waiting." He took a sip in a totally relaxed manner—a relaxation that betrayed his British origins. "I'm just surprised that you weren't in a rush to get here and find out what I have in store for you. Ferris did tell you that I would be coming, didn't he?"

"Yes, he did mention something about you showing me to my new apartment, but I didn't think it would be so soon."

"*Now*, were his specific instructions. So here I am, ready when you are." He gestured around him, as if it were time for me to leave this place.

Maybe for any other living human being, escaping the Pit would be the supreme blessing. And I couldn't deny that my heart was trembling to open the door of my new apartment... hell, even the tiniest room sounded good. But with everything going on earlier, I had managed to forget all about it. That's how I caught up I was with the severity of the situation. Being deeply wrapped up in the new challenges I was facing, that life was moving at the speed of light around me.

"I brought some empty bags to assist you in packing your things," Alfred said, heading toward the door where a pile of empty luggage cases was waiting. Apparently, he didn't know that my entire life could fit into one medium-sized shopping bag.

"I'm pretty convinced that you won't have to do much assisting," the faded bitterness in my voice made him realize that he was far away from his royal palace. Here, in the Pit, things were a little different.

And it seemed that Alfred had already figured things out. "I understand. I'll ask the driver to take a few back to the car."

My sight fell to the floor. "Not just a few..."

"Should I leave two?" he asked.

"One will be enough," I murmured, still avoiding eye contact.

"I'm sure that Ferris will take care of this *inconvenience* immediately." He tapped my shoulder in consolation, assuring me my life was about to change.

"Can I ask you a favor?" I stammered.

A kind smile lit up his face. "Of course."

"Don't tell him. I don't want him to feel obligated to do anything beyond what we've already agreed upon." I was so far from doing this with any personal gain in mind. Our deal was only about my family and my responsibility of taking care of them. It was never about me.

"You don't know him." The man smiled again while rising from his seat to arrange a few cushions on the couch. "We should start. It's already late, and he was asking if you could visit him after I've shown you to your apartment."

It wasn't that I didn't want to see Ferris; it was more like a mixture of fatigue or maybe even being physically and psychologically drained. I was already carrying a feeling of guilt toward him since I was going to go to his place while I was somehow functioning solely on emergency batteries. I wasn't giving him the best version of me, even if that's what he deserved.

"My clothes are in here," I opened a small dresser and picked up all of my things from a shelf, then laid them inside one of the bags.

In less than five minutes, I was all packed and ready to walk out the door, carrying just one piece of luggage in my hand.

"I'll take that." Alfred snuck his hand between the handles of the case to steal it away and escort me to our ride for the night.

It felt as though I was leaving an entire world behind. I couldn't help but feel guilty that while I was heading for luxury, my siblings were still who knew where and suffering. But when it came to the suffering part, I was with them with my entire soul, absorbing their pain into my own heart.

"Can I ask something of you?" Alfred asked, while I seemed to be lost in my thoughts.

I showed interest in what he had to say since he didn't seem the kind of man to ask for favors. More like the kind of man who is always asked for favors. "Yes, of course. What is it?"

"Don't give up on him too easily. Everyone else seems to do it lately." And how could I ever, since this deal was securing treatment for my brother? Not to mention the part where Ferris had that secret-something that made any thought of giving up on him impossible for me.

But deep down, I knew exactly what Alfred was referring to; the madness, the darkness, that special part of him that made him undeniable. And at the same time, the kind of craziness that would make you run to the other end of the world, without ever looking back. "I'm starting to think that we're codependent," I said, looking out the window. I guess that was the truth; for some strange reason, we were linked by fate, needing each other in some strange way. However, I often wondered how much he needed me. Was I girl number twenty-something on the disposable list, or did he need me for me—Bea? Maybe only time would tell, and that was an asset that we held in abundance when it came to him and me. Our deal, unlike the ones I had with Brax and Cole, was *indefinite*.

"Now it's my turn," I flashed a sad smile, preparing to ask something that had been on my mind for a while. A question that I couldn't address directly to Ferris yet—at least not without risking triggering another one of his bipolar phases.

Alfred nodded. "Go ahead."

"I was wondering what happened in his past. I know there's a reason behind the way he sometimes acts." I said, barely gathering the courage to ask.

Alfred's gaze suddenly became lost. "I wish that I was in a position where I could answer that. But it's not my place to say. This is something that he needs to tell you himself when he considers the time is right."

I didn't push; how could I, when I already suspected his answer before I even asked? I was just curious, secretly hoping that he would at least give me a hint—prepare me for what to expect, because I felt like with Ferris, anything could happen.

"Okay, I'll let things come naturally," I said, turning my head again to look out the window and noticing that we were climbing higher and higher up the Hills. "Are we going straight to Ferris?" I asked, confused. From what I could tell, we were only a few streets away from his mansion.

"No, your apartment is right after the next turn." Alfred took a glimpse outside to reassure himself. "Here," he announced to me on our arrival as the cab stopped in front of a three-story mansion.

"Here?" I spoke in awe, looking up at the wall-sized windows while staring at the impressive display of wealth.

Alfred nodded again. "Yes, here. Ferris owns the building but had the first and second floors already rented out. You and your family will occupy the top level."

"Top level?" I repeated, the words stuck in my mind as if my last neuron had just burned out.

It didn't take long for Alfred to notice my almost shocked reaction. Every one of my delayed gestures betrayed the wave of emotions brewing within me. "Take a deep breath, and let's go inside. Everything is going to be okay."

In an ideal world, this was where Prince Charming had just come to my rescue, turning my life from rags to a fantasy dream. But there was just one catch—I didn't have a Prince Charming, I had three of them, and if their physical appearance could fool anyone that they came straight from a fairytale; what they held within them was as far as it got from a happily ever after.

"I hope that you'll find the accommodation suited for all of your needs," Alfred said, opening a double wooden door that revealed a living room the size of a tennis court.

I blinked slowly, trying to take in the view and struggling to comprehend that I was the one who would live there. It was as if some royal decorator had come and arranged my new living space following the most eclectic tastes. I knew how well Ferris mastered the element of surprise. And he was refusing to fail this time.

It all felt surreal; as if it wasn't supposed to be for me; as if I didn't deserve it to be for me. Surely every single object in the room would have a price that I was undoubtedly going to have to pay at some point. Still, it felt too much for someone with my background.

Thoughts began swirling in my mind, like a merry-go-round. Cole, Brax, and Ferris were all onboard, spinning faster and faster in my world, day after day, hour after hour, draining the last drop of strength left. The deals, the promises, the rush each one of them provoked, the sleep deprivation and the dark thoughts, the worry, and the pain, were all building up inside of me, consuming me from within until my body seemed to be melting into a pool on the floor.

"Bea, are you all right?" Alfred's startled voice sounded in my ears. Though I couldn't respond with even a single word, just floating around on my little black cloud, losing myself to the impossible exhaustion that was steering me into a dream.

***

I pulled on the blanket, clutching onto it as I was snuggling into the warmest spot on Earth. It felt so safe, as if I was secluded in my own piece of heaven, with a citrus and

243

wood perfume gently pampering my senses.

"Are you cold?" Stray fingers danced in my hair, following each strand only to twist on its tip.

Where was I?

My eyes barely opened, only to find myself in the place where the destination for the night had been about to lead me just before I lost all contact with reality.

"Ferris," I whispered, realizing that I was on his couch while he was sitting on the floor next to me.

One of his arms was securing my body close to his while his lips pressed against my forehead. "I'm here." The place that he just stroked with his lips warmed with a comforting sensation that was spreading throughout me.

I only remembered entering the new apartment; then everything went blank. "What... what happened?" I asked, confused.

"You fainted, and Alfred called me." He leaned his head to meet my gaze. "I should have remained there with you until you regained consciousness. I just have trouble being out of the house for too long. So, I brought you here instead. I hope that's okay with you?"

"I was coming to see you next anyway. I guess I took a shortcut." A girl could still be funny, right? "I was just preparing to call you when I stumbled upon Alfred waiting at my apartment in the Pit."

Ferris curved the corner of his lip into a smile, letting a hand slip beneath the blanket and around my waist. "So you missed me."

"Is there any world where I wouldn't?" I asked, although my voice lacked strength.

"Not with me, there isn't." He slipped a glass between my fingers. "Drink, you'll feel better."

"Tea... It's delicious." I praised it, enjoying the strawberry flavor that warmed my senses. But unfortunately, it didn't manage to bring me back to my normal self. "I think I need coffee," I said just as my hand started trembling, spilling a few drops on me.

"I'm pretty sure that you need sleep, not coffee." Ferris was scolding me as if I said something wrong, when in fact, all I ever did was try to keep up with my end of the deal and get myself back on my feet to spend time with him.

"What about you?" I asked, knowing that he couldn't sleep until dawn.

"What about me?" He shrugged, although I could see in his eyes that he knew exactly what I was talking about.

I lifted my body weight on my elbows so that I could try and recover a little from my coma-like state. "Nothing..."

"Come here." He gently pulled me, making me roll off the couch and join him on the floor, landing on top of him. "Tonight, I want you to get some rest." He rested his head on the carpet where he found a place to lay, just so that he could take a better look at me.

But clouds of doubt were rising around me as I realized that it was becoming harder and harder to keep up with my end of this deal. "I'm not the best company, am I?"

"Why would you ever say that?" With careful moves, he tugged my legs on both sides of him until I was straddling his lower waist between my thighs, pressing my pussy directly on top of his growing hardness. "I love your company." He jerked from beneath me, grinding on the spot that was already craving for his presence. "And I'm starting to think you *already* noticed how much I really *enjoy* it." Sneaking a hand to the back of my neck, he moved me lower to meet his lips while my hips arched instinctively against him.

"I told you—" I tried speaking.

"Did I ask for anything?" He cut my words right before I was going to remind him of the terms of our deal. "I was just minding my own business on the floor when you decided to attack me."

I gave him a condescending look. "Aww poor innocent Mr. Ayers being shamelessly attacked and seduced by an evil witch."

"I wouldn't go that far... You're not evil, though I haven't decided on the witch part yet," he said, smiling.

"How come?"

He ground his hips into mine again. "You seem to have an inexplicable effect on me... Dark magic, I presume."

"I was about to say the same thing about you, Mr. Warlock."

"Then it must be karma." He raised his head from the carpet to kiss me while my lips eagerly met his, melting into the throbbing rhythm of our bodies. It was slow and fast, burning minutes while letting them infiltrate us, as his palms were gradually exploring every part of my body.

"Go take a hot bath, and I will be waiting in bed." He let the back of his finger slip over my cheek, probably sensing that, although the atmosphere between us was becoming incendiary, I could barely support my own body weight.

A bath was just what the doctor ordered, especially since my batteries had just a few final sparks remaining before their dying breath.

"I'll give you something to change into." He helped me up, then paced toward his walk-in dressing room from where he returned with an oversized tank top. "No match for your granny pajamas, but it's the best I can do on such short notice."

Looking at the top, I crossed my arms, seeing right through his *wicked* plan. "This has like 90% less material than my granny pajamas have."

"Do you want me to ask Alfred to loan you one of his? I'm pretty convinced that he must have a museum-like piece from last century lying around on one of his shelves."

I snatched my new pajamas from his hand. "No need for a midnight intervention, but you have to admit that my pajamas had their charm."

"Cockblocking doesn't equal charm," he chanted.

"Oh, so that's why you were so eager to take them off." I giggled, heading to the bathroom.

"Don't light *that* match, Bea," he playfully threatened me while I closed the door of the bathroom.

Throwing my clothes on the floor, I slipped into the hot water, trying to let all my worries dissipate into the steaming vapors that were flooding the room. I had to admit that he was right; a hot bath was exactly what I needed. It just wasn't the best possible option for me at the moment since my body was still having trouble staying awake.

It couldn't have been in the bathtub for more than fifteen minutes. And still, as I stepped out, I realized that my clothes were gone, leaving me with just Ferris's tank top to serve as a full pajama set.

"Are you okay in there? Do you need help?" my king of darkness decided to ask, just as I was returning to the room.

"That answered my question." his sculpted lips showed off a smile.

"What happened to my clothes?" I muttered, a little annoyed that I couldn't find any pieces of underwear.

"I gave them to the maid to get them cleaned by the morning." He casually shrugged.

"Then can you please give me a pair of shorts?" I raised an eyebrow, knowing that he got rid of my clothes on purpose.

"No," he answered, taking a few steps in my direction. "Don't be so stressed, just trust me." Taking my hand, he led me to the bed.

How could I trust him when the last time he asked this of me, we ended up floating over the balcony?

And still, the silk sheets beckoned, waiting to caress my body. And at that point who was I to resist? Besides, my hand was tightly secured in Ferris's grasp, who made sure I found myself a place on the bed next to him, then cuddled me tightly into his chest.

Small kisses soon began melting in a suave line on my neck while daring fingers sneaked up to raise the hem of my tank top. It was all too much—fighting him, fighting the will of my body, and ultimately fighting to keep my end of the deal with Brax. Too intense, too abundant in emotions that I couldn't continue to keep them bottled up within me. Tears began soaking the bed sheet as my eyes tried to hide against his chest, seeking what little comfort I could find. I was drained, tired, exhausted, and at the same time left to bear the weight of my three promises.

The three deals. The three devils that now rule over my world.

It was too unbearable. Too much for my tired body,

which had been deprived of decent sleep for too long.

However, my motives weren't clear to Ferris, and he interpreted my outburst as if it were his fault. "You're crying? What's wrong? Is it because I'm touching you?'

I didn't have an answer since there shouldn't have been a question in the first place. My body was helplessly burning under his fingers, losing track of reality in his embrace. And that's exactly what was draining the last drop of strength I had left. That gradually maddening rhythm in which I fought with my own cravings, along with some thoughts turned towards my other two *kings*. A cumulus of everything in between, crowned with the guilt I felt because I couldn't be fully present here for Ferris, even though we shared a bed.

It was never my intention that he would see me cry. I just wanted to crawl into a corner for even just an hour and be completely alone. But as each minute passed, I realized that wouldn't be possible any time soon.

"What's wrong, Bea?" he insisted, as my face was still buried deep into his chest. He was becoming my only refuge, clinging to fake hopes of normality.

"I'm sorry... I'm sorry." That was all I could say.

"You're just tired," he whispered, cupping my face to look at me. "I don't care about the rest."

I had to be honest with him. "You should...," I breathed out the words. Of all the guys, he seemed to be the only one with a soul—as broken as it may have been. "I still have other agreements." I knew I told him before, but I felt that he needed to understand that my other commitments wouldn't end with my decision to leave The Pleasure Room.

But he wasn't giving up his mask. "I remember our deal; besides, I'm not afraid of competition. But I do want to talk to

Vanya tomorrow about the compensation needed so that your resignation will run smoothly."

"I should go in tomorrow and tell her myself."

"There's no need; she'll come here tomorrow evening to discuss things," Ferris said, giving me a small kiss.

I was a little confused since Vanya didn't seem the type who made house calls. But then again, Ferris deserved special treatment. "She will?" I asked, surprised.

I felt his palms slip beneath the blanket to lift my tank top above my hips, leaving me naked in my lower part. "Yes, but I'm not worrying about her right now. I have much more important things to focus on."

"Ferris," I said exhaustedly while squeezing my legs together. I was just realizing that I had a very long night coming my way trying to withstand him.

With slow movements, he pulled a strap of the tank top over my shoulder, then the other, pushing the top down to my waist while I was still hidden away beneath the blanket. "Shush, I know the limits. All you have to do is close your eyes and get some rest."

"How could I rest?" I giggled as his words and his actions weren't related.

"Easy. Just close your eyes." His lips quickly brushed over mine in a good night kiss while his thumbs fell over my eyes to get them to close. "Good night, Bea." His words danced over my flesh as he disappeared under the blanket.

Now how could I rest when his lips were slowly skimming the surface of my body, searching for my nipples as the metal piercing from his tongue was moving in circles to fondle them?

"I said sleep, Bea," he chanted from underneath the cover as my body tensed to its limits.

I tried closing my eyes again, savoring the way he was playing me like the finest Stradivarius violin, letting his heaving breath flow like the summer breeze on my skin. It actually felt so delicious, surreal in a way, as his sweet caresses were making me feel so special. Losing count of the kisses, I finally felt myself drifting to sleep.

Though, before I could finally reach my dreamland destination, an electric lightning bolt discharged its crashing shock within me, almost causing me to jump to my feet. His daring tongue was pressing its damn piercing against my lower stomach, charging me up and dropping me on the floor at the same time. It was sending a wave of crazed longing straight from my belly button to my core. I was vibrating with need as that erogenous place between my thighs was damp in fervid expectation.

"Sorry about that, I got carried away. I promise to behave." He raised the blanket to have a quick look at me, then disappeared back, decreasing his actions to a much slower rhythm.

It seemed impossible to sleep, but fighting with my body, I somehow managed to calm my senses. I knew exactly how things stood—his slip of the tongue wasn't a mistake, but a demonstration. One that almost tricked me into welcoming him to completely have me. It was a master's touch, shaking an already trembling leaf and bringing me exactly where he wanted me to be—*under his spell.*

CHAPTER 15

T he night passed with his delirious lips never leaving my body, present there between sweet dreams and total relaxation. At first, I thought it wouldn't be possible for sleep to find me. Besides the storm he created brewing inside of me, Ferris seemed to also have a therapeutic effect on my mind. He was my healer and the fountain of energy. By morning, I felt brand new — except for my conscience. There just weren't enough therapists in the whole city to ever fix that.

"Morning." I opened my eyes just to find the most amazing smile gleaming back at me while wandering fingers were still moving over my body. "Haven't you slept?"

"I have all day to sleep... while I only have you at night." A hint of regret captive in his voice.

I let my arms wrap around his neck while I moved in search of his lips. "Someone is greedy."

"Tease. You only kiss me because you know you have to leave in the next five minutes," Ferris grunted, sneaking a hand on the small of my back.

Was it that late? I didn't remember sleeping for that long in ages.

"Thank you," I whispered, kissing him again. I knew it must've been difficult for him to hold back, but I felt he was putting in the extra effort to do it for me.

"If you're thanking me for this, I wonder what you'll say about tonight?" Ferris asked as if he had a surprise in store for me.

"I was thanking you for being so understanding," I chuckled. "But what's tonight?"

However, he didn't seem willing to divulge the mystery. "You'll see... after the meeting with Vanya."

"Oh, yeah... I forgot all about meeting Vanya." Not that I was too eager to give her the news. But I needed to let her know my decision. It was the fair thing to do, as after all, she was the only one who offered me a chance when no one else would.

My eyes widened at the time on my phone screen. "I should go."

"You should. Wouldn't want you to be late for class," he said ironically, and with good reason. He couldn't understand my struggle; his money could get him any degree he desired. I, on the other hand, had to work hard, hoping that eventually I would have a chance to get a decent job.

"I didn't go through all that trouble just to give up on it now." I tried explaining.

"Of course not, especially since they just cashed in on your final installment. Go make use of the money," he playfully scolded me, revealing a little something he'd *forgotten* to mention.

I raised myself on my elbows to look at him. "You paid my

university fee?"

"Wasn't that our deal? Why are you so surprised? I told you that I would take care of everything. Just ask, and you will receive." He kissed the top of my head, making a statement of his power.

My lips merged with his again. "Thank you," I said, slipping beneath the blanket to wrap myself in a sheet I took from the bed. "I really have to go." Raising myself to my feet I went in search of my clothes.

"Can't wait for a Saturday morning when the university won't be an excuse for you to escape my bed," he laughed while I was still spinning aimlessly around the room. "Hold on. I asked for some new things." Before I knew it, he was out the door, and all I could do was wait for his return. There was no way I could leave the room *dressed* in only a sheet. I was heading towards the university, not a toga party.

Luckily, it didn't take long before he returned, carrying a few pieces of clothing and a shoebox. "I had no idea what to get you, so I asked my maid to buy something." He shrugged, arranging the clothes on the couch. "I'll be on the balcony while you get dressed."

As soon as he left, I began searching through the small stack of clothes he had just brought. And he seemed to know everything I needed—in every sense of the word. The maid had brought in a few essential pieces of underwear, a pale blue dress, and a jacket—elegant enough for the university, yet not stepping over the limit to turn me into the First Lady. And although I wanted to give the woman credit for my outfit, I had a feeling this was all Ferris's doing, as the items matched too perfectly to be chosen by the staff.

I twirled in front of the mirror a couple of times before my king of darkness returned to the room. I knew that he saw me naked, and he definitely explored my body before, but never in broad daylight. So, his decision to give me some privacy while I had changed was making him grow on me.

"What time will Vanya be here?" I asked to ensure myself that I could return in time since I had to pay a house call after classes to a certain someone.

"Later tonight. Nine, maybe ten. She didn't say."

"Okay, I'll be here by then," I rushed to kiss Ferris again as I felt him slip something between my fingers.

"Keys to the apartment." He winked, letting the rays of sunshine rest on the sculpted shapes of his face.

My Prince Charming.

The rest of the day went by rather quickly. Luckily for me, Jenna was the only one who noticed the luxury brand of my new outfit, convincing herself this time that my *sugar daddy* was living up to his name. There was no point in denying it. It was all too obvious—the luxury transportation, the clothes, and maybe even my more relaxed vibe when it came to basic things that I used to lack, including a meal during the day. I just prayed that things would remain the way they used to be, and that I was to remain invisible, not attracting intrusive looks.

I didn't have much time to think about that. Skipping out of the last few classes, I took the path to Cole's residence.

Getting on the bus, I ventured to search for the address that he texted to me a day ago, and discovered it was just a couple of streets away from my new apartment. An impressive mansion, much larger than Jason's and showing even greater luxury, stood in front of me. But there was a trick—a small detail

—that was betraying the momentarily dead-end his family had stumbled upon. Small tell-tale signs of dilapidation were blooming over the facade of the house. Issues that wouldn't have been left unattended by the usually vigilant eye of the Elite, especially since it was these details that set out their rank in society.

I'm here.

I texted him the second I arrived since I didn't know where to head, and getting lost around this place didn't seem like a good idea.

Up the stairs, third door on the right. I left the front door open for you.

My phone lit up with his *command,* and my feet soon moved to follow it.

The place was almost similar to Ferris's when it came to impressive decorations—on a smaller scale, but still, you could see in every corner the opulence it meant to display. However, I didn't have any time to waste, as much as I wanted to delay seeing the king of ECU.

Following his instructions, I found myself pushing open the door to his room. I had no doubt that it was his. The hurricane that seemed to have swept through the place was making it all too obvious.

I looked at the pile of books thrown on the floor next to some worn sports gear and a baseball bat. The sight left me hoping that somehow he might have called me here to clean his room. The space was in such desperate need of that. Though I knew all too well that it was far from his intention. Things never were that easy when it came to Cole, and this visit wasn't going to be any different.

"In here." Recognizing my presence, the king himself spoke

from behind a wooden door located in the opposite corner of the room.

Taking a moment to pull myself together, I walked toward the room he called from, unsure if it was a dressing room or a bathroom. Twisting the door handle, the sight that greeted me almost left me breathless, forcing me to remain frozen in the doorway.

Cole was waiting for me in the bathtub. He was divine. So stunning that it couldn't have been anything but pure evil lying within him. No angel could have ever looked like this besides the fallen one—Lucifer himself. Nothing but an astonishing display of muscles and tattoos were covering his torso, allowing every drawing to reflect majestically in the blue mirrors of his eyes.

For a second, I forgot to breathe, helplessly staring at his body. The last power of conviction lingering within me was fighting with the primal instincts that were ravaging my very being. Yet, the fear was still there—that tormenting anxiety, knowing all the wicked thoughts that could go through that devious mind of his, especially in this moment.

"Close the door behind you," he ordered, letting a dangerous grin bloom on his face.

I hurriedly followed his request, not because I had some hidden urge to submit to him, but because I was worried about the consequences of any rebellious behavior.

"Lose the dress, Mouse," he ordered, immersing himself a little more under the water, relaxing every tantalizing muscle of his body.

"Why?" I quivered, afraid of his plans for the day.

"You'll see. Just do it before you make me get out of here and get the job done myself," he snapped since the *servant* didn't comply in due time.

"Arrogant piece of—" I cursed between my lips, though I was interrupted right before I got to finish the sentence.

He instantly arched an eyebrow. "So rebellious, when I decided to be so generous with you today," his tone, so ironic that it immediately stirred a rush of panic to race through my body. "Now, make it fall." It was an ultimatum for his *generosity*.

Without lingering to think about it, since there was nothing I could do to oppose his will, I unzipped my dress and let it slowly slip down to my feet. And that left me only in my underwear under Cole's cut-through gaze, as he was scanning every inch of my body.

"So, you can obey," he said, getting on my nerves again, and driving me to the point of a breakdown. He was perfectly aware that there was nothing I could do to defend myself and was taking full advantage of that. "Now, come here, Mouse." Tapping a spot somewhere in the middle of the tub's edge, he called for me to join him there.

My eyes couldn't help but widen from the shock. *What the hell did he have in mind this time?*

Barely making a few steps, I reached the edge of the bathtub, lowering my eyes to see where I could step into the water. I didn't get too far in following his command since my sight stumbled upon something that made me blush with uncontained shame. He was completely naked! I know that people don't usually take baths in their bathing suits, but maybe I watched too many romantic comedies since I was hoping I would have some accommodation time on my hands. Yet what he called me here for held no romance and was far from a comedy. Cole seemed to get straight to the point when it came to human anatomy, probably because he had all the reasons to preen on his perfect construction.

And still, I froze, having never been so close to a naked man before.

"You can look because you'll *get to touch* sooner or later." He grinned as my hesitance seemed to have been quickly noticed by his vigilant nature. "Or, maybe not... I was just saying earlier that I was thinking about being generous if... you kiss me."

If only things would have been that simple. "Kiss you?" I asked.

"Yes. It's easy. You'll kiss me, and we will play a game that could bring you your freedom." That smirk was back on his face, but I didn't seem to have any other option. I knew that there had to be a trick here somewhere. Still, it couldn't hurt to try to get out of this in any way I could.

"You just have to do it like you mean it." As if I didn't have enough trouble already telling my heart and my mind not to listen to my body, now I had to pretend that I would be enjoying sharing a kiss with him. I just needed to convince myself that I really was *pretending*.

Without a second thought—so I wouldn't change my mind —I leaned over the tub and went directly for his lips. My tongue hastily pushed between them to explore each corner of his mouth, rediscovering that small piece of pierced metal that would cause me so much anguish.

It felt real... I let it feel so real that small moans echoing from my throat managed to merge with his lustful groans as his hand cupped one of my breasts, causing a delirium of restlessness to spread through me.

"Mouse," his eyes drenched in lust. "Now pick a number between one and ten."

Somehow, I felt that no matter what number I picked, I was

destined to be the loser from the start. In no way did Cole ever seem to enter a competition that he couldn't win, even if I did know of one that he lost—the bet that brought me to him as his company at that party. Maybe I did have a chance after all.

"Seven," I answered, thinking that it was best to be somewhere above the *in-between* section.

"Lucky seven." My choice brought a large grin to his lips. "You're making things too easy for me." His smile enlarged as he was just about to explain the rules of *his* game. "I have chosen a very easy game for today. It's simple. You just have to withstand me for 7 minutes."

"Withstand you? What does that even mean?" I quivered, knowing that nothing good could ever come out of this.

Cole shared a grin. "Don't worry. I'll walk you through it."

How thoughtful of him, especially when sympathy seemed to be the feature he lacked most.

"Hop into the tub." He offered me his hand to join him in the tub when all I wanted was to run away. Another piece of me was to be broken that day, and he was just about to feast on every single sign of my anxiety.

Following his directions, I stepped into the tub, placing each of my legs on either side of his hips, though without lowering my body to take a seat.

Little did I know that this was exactly his plan.

"Good. You'll need to stand for this one." He shot me the most devious look I've ever seen, his hand moving to the hem of my panty line.

I had an idea where this was going, "Cole..."

"Don't rush; you'll get to call out my name in a few minutes." The arrogant devil flashed his tongue between his teeth to play with his piercing while my eyes seemed to roll out of my head, trying to seem unimpressed.

"In your dreams," I snarled.

I felt his hands resting between my thighs. "No, but I will be in *your* dreams, Mouse. I'll make sure of that in around... seven minutes."

"So, if I win, you'll leave me alone but still help me with the custody?" I was still trying to hang on to any piece of hope.

"Yes. I've already talked to my father about it. It's being taken care of as we speak." He seemed serious enough for me to believe him. I'm not sure why, but even if he was the definition of evil in every other way, I had a feeling that when it came to a promise, he was a man of his word.

"But if you lose—" he continued.

"If I lose?" I was only focusing on winning since the prize would spare me from my misery. But I needed to also take losing into consideration, even though it was inconceivable that it would be one of my options. I had to be strong.

"If you lose, you'll get to take care of me." He looked down on himself through the water, gleaming at his eager cock. "And Mouse, you will need to do it as if you enjoy it. Exactly like you did with that kiss."

Dark clouds were gathering in on me and the notion was making my stomach twist. He was serious about it. Even though the thought of such a request crossed my mind, I was never quite ready for the moment to come.

I didn't need to think like that. I was going to win. I was going to be free again, free from his deal after the next *seven* minutes!

"I will even play nice and give you a minute head start," he casually said, reaching for his phone to set the timer. He placed the device back on the tub's border, with the seconds counting downward.

It was game on. Only lust was reflected on his face, as he was bringing his arms to draw me closer to him and his lips shifted to kiss the thin material of my panties.

All I could think about was how much I should hate everything related to him; his touch, his selfish attitude. His teeth gently grazed my panties, drawing them slowly down over my thighs. The place he craved so badly to explore was revealed while an electric storm seemed to be igniting within me.

"Such a perfect pussy. And all mine to play with." He let out a hungry snarl. "You have twenty more seconds to relax." He flashed that fucking tongue piercing again straight after looking at the countdown on his phone—6:20.

How could I ever be relaxed at a time like this, when my heart seemed to have moved into my ears, pumping so loudly that I was convinced that he could hear it? Before I knew it, my time was up, and his tongue slipped between my folds, running along the full length of my core. "You're already so wet. This is going to be too easy." He smiled again, disappearing between my thighs to move the metal in his tongue over my clit, pressing it against my skin.

I was in so much trouble, and I knew it from the second he made contact with my pussy. When he first came up with his game I was convinced that no matter what, I could pull through this, now I seemed to be drowning in the ten inches of water lying at my feet. His mouth was sending a wave of lust to tingle each one of my nervous receptors while my body was uncontrollably responding to them.

My eyes uselessly stared at the countdown, trying to

focus only on the passing seconds. Because each one of them seemed to be bringing a new sensation, building an anguish impossible to break.

Cole was groaning loudly as he was feasting, so deliciously rough that it was igniting every cell along its way. This was turning him on, and although I didn't want to look into the water, I couldn't unsee the effects tasting my core had on him. He was hard as a rock and even more driven to have me take care of his erection as soon as he was done with me. I was in agony, and I was in ecstasy, quivering as my legs were betraying me and at the same time wanting to run and escape.

2:22—not sure if that was a good or a bad sign as I caught those exact numbers on the timer. I couldn't help but curse myself for not choosing 2—the day of my birthday. I would have been saved by now—or maybe not, because the instant he noticed me looking at the phone, Cole's eyes also turned at the countdown. He was running out of time, and the concept of not winning did not fit well with his plans. "Don't worry, Mouse. I'm not going to lose. I'm going to make you come so hard that you won't even know what happened to you."

I wasn't worrying, but without a second thought, his lips merged to nibble and suck on my clit like his goal was to extract all signs of life from me.

It was too much for me to handle. Wave after wave of ecstasy was shaking my very last cell, weakening my knees to the point they turned to jelly. And he decided to end me. A slow bite on my swollen flesh, brought the hurricane that rose inside of me to finally tear me apart. "So sweet," he whispered, finding the signs of my uncontained exhilaration. "You're tough, Mouse. I'll give you that. I wouldn't have suspected that you would last more than three minutes," he spoke as if in a blur while I found myself shipwrecked against his chest. I lost, and the ticking of the phone was announcing my failure somewhere around a minute after my body was wrecked by euphoria.

But he didn't give me much time to rest. "My turn," I could hear him say, preening on my failure while drawing his body backward to hop onto the large rim of the tub. "Like you mean it, remember?" The words seemed to be stuck in my mind since now I had to fulfill my part. In the end, it was a fair game. I lost.

"Can we turn off the lights?" I asked, barely glancing at his aroused cock that was so ready for me.

His head leaned back to look at me. "Funny how you didn't want them turned off while *I* was attending you."

I didn't even realize what was happening, let alone figure out how to turn off the lights. It's not like I dared to look at him anyway when the embarrassment was hitting epic levels, and my eyes were only pointed to stare at the timer.

"No, we can't," he continued, annoyed by my request. "I want to see you. I want to see you enjoy me."

Like that could ever be possible...

"I want to see you take my cock between your lips," he grinned as I felt my cheeks burning with shame.

I looked at him with disgust lingering on the tip of my tongue. Yet, when it came down to what I needed to do next, it was the result of my choice. I knew what I was signing up for when I accepted his deal.

Truth be told, I had no idea what I truly needed to do, let alone enjoy it. Kneeling down, I just gently made his length disappear between my lips, remembering the actions the blonde back in Brax's glass room made to bring her partner to ecstasy.

The slightly sweet-salty taste of precum made my body

jerk in response, like my nervous system knew the effect I had on him and was eagerly responding to it. But I refused to get aroused by it. I didn't come here for pleasure. I came here to fulfill a task—my part of the deal. For my own sake, I better remember it every damn second. I needed things to be done with, as soon as I could. I was taking all precautions to do just that, guiding myself after each one of his groans.

I began moving up and down, gliding my tongue along his cock with each motion I made, slower at first, then faster and faster until his hand wrapped itself in my hair, guiding my exact moves. He was mine now, and even if he was controlling my body, for a few seconds, I was the one in control of him, having the *king* in complete need of me.

In reality, I always thought that I would find getting my lips on his cock repulsive. That I would force myself to resist the moments I needed to bring him to euphoria. But somehow, the exact moments in which the pleasure was reflected on each one of his facial expressions were making me enjoy this. After all, he seemed so satisfied by having his lips on me just minutes ago.

With each one of my glides, I could see Cole becoming weaker and weaker, almost shocked by his body's reactions, like the damn thing was going rogue on his commands. "Look at me," he growled out, close to his breaking point, holding my head in one place for a second to take a proper glimpse of me.

I refused to look. Embarrassment flushed down on me. I was ashamed of the degrading position he put me in, even if, by the lustful twinkle I found seconds later gleaming in his eyes, I was miles away from the humiliation I imagined. This was all about pure pleasure.

"Eyes up," he ordered again, and I couldn't deny him any longer. He had a message that I needed to hear loud and clear, and let it infiltrate into my system. "I'm starting to believe that I will need you for much more than a month," he groaned ferally. And I could see how badly he was craving me the moment my eyes rose to crash into his.

I just climbed the first steps to conquer his kingdom, even though I knew all too well this particular *king* had a heart of stone.

His hand began moving again, guiding my head along the length of his cock at a pace he enjoyed. He was so close. I could feel it with his every throb, roaring his approaching release as one of his hands snuck inside my bra to play with my aching nipple.

Suddenly, he pulled me in closer, thrusting himself so deep that I couldn't even breathe. His delirious movements were building the closer he got to his release. I couldn't withstand his hunger, trying to push him away even for a split second to catch my breath. However, it was impossible to move from his clenched hand. I was only a rag doll in those moments, with hot tears springing from my eyes, ruining the faded hints of makeup I had worn that day.

When all the oxygen seemed to have been leaving my lungs, I felt his hand pinch one of my nipples so badly that my eyes came open from the pain and he managed to push himself a little further inside my mouth. "That's it, my Mouse, be a nice girl and open all the way for me. You look so pretty when you cry." The devil was feasting on my anguish, finding his strongest ecstasy between my tears as he continued to move, letting his warm liquid fill my throat.

I shook my head to be set free and dispose of the thick evidence of his release. But the second he slipped himself out, he brought a hand under my chin to make me close my mouth again. His head shook in a sign of a no, his blue eyes peering straight at me. "You belong to me, don't fight me marking you."

I had to follow in his steps and swallow the liquid part of him. If looks could kill, he would have been dead the next second. Bolts of anger darted from my eyes, yet with no use. His hand didn't release me before he considered my task was fully accomplished. And as soon as I felt his grip on me slacken, I rose out from the water, searching for my drenched panties in the tub, then slipped back into my clothes.

"Are we done?" I asked, trembling, while looking into the mirror. I was trying to stop the tears from running down my face because I somehow needed to fix my makeup before I left his room.

"For the day. I'll see you tomorrow at school," he said in total relaxation, drawing his head back to rest on the tub border and enjoying that lingering satisfaction still residing in his veins.

I envied him for the cold-hearted bastard he was, because I was still trying to get my shaking legs to leave the room. But remaining there with him for even an extra minute wasn't an option. His mind was as devious as it got, and it would be only a matter of seconds before he could come up with the next *game*.

CHAPTER 16

I loathed Cole. I hated every single cell of his arrogant nature. And still, that quivering sensation lived inside my body, reminding me of the devastating power he held over me.

Rushing down the stairs, my gaze fixed solely on the entry door. I longed to leave his house before I even needed to catch my next breath. Yet, something stopped me. I could hear screams and shouts coming from the living room, so loudly that the walls reverberated from the intensity of an argument.

I should have left, lived in total ignorance for as long as possible—yet the sudden decision to stop on my way and listen in on what was happening was the catalyst about to put *all wheels in motion.*

"You bastard. I'm getting a divorce!" A woman yelled, her words compelling my curious nature to venture toward the place where the arguing was coming from.

Yes, I have many qualities, yet eavesdropping seems to be my greatest flaw lately.

"Where have you been? Have you been to the roulette table again? You've already driven this family to ruin." The woman's voice could be heard again.

"Shut up before Cole hears you! I wasn't at fucking roulette!" This time, a man's voice answered in an angered tone. "Our son asked me to take care of a custody problem for his girlfriend, and I was handling it with the mayor all morning."

A huge weight had just been lifted off my chest. Cole's promise was going to come through, alleviating some of that horrible guilt I was having over what I had just done in the bathroom with him.

"Girlfriend? Why is it the first time I'm hearing about her?" That must have been Cole's mother asking.

"Because you tend to overreact and ask all sorts of embarrassing questions. That's why neither of us tells you anything." His father seemed to be growing angrier with each passing second.

"Then, if you're having a breakthrough with all that honesty, why are you so afraid to confess to our son that the money isn't coming back? There is no governor or senator, or whatever lie you told him. You didn't invest our money in the next election. You invested it on a goddamn white ball hitting 13 black. And you lost!" The anger in the woman's voice equaled the situation he had put them in.

"Shut up, Debrah. He'll hear you. I still have connections. I will make the money back in no time, especially with the riots only one step away from breaking out."

"You're still the same gullible fool, Frank. The riots will break us, not build us."

"No, they won't. We still have Elite blood running through our veins." Cole's father appeared to be in on something.

"What use is there for it if it's not supported by money? We're more likely to be thrown in the Pit with the rest of the

Annelids, to become slaves of the Elite! We must prevent the riots, not stand by them. Just think about all the people who will die in the war. It's inhumane to turn the already poor Annelids into slaves. Haven't they suffered enough as it is?" Coles' mother seemed to be the only one in the family with a soul.

"That's the problem. The Annelids want more at a time when there is less and less to give. The Elite would never back down."

"Then the rebellions will destroy us." The woman's voice trembled. "Just think about it, in the eventuality of a war, the Annelids will be crushed. And then who will be left to work for the Elite? Us?"

"Not us, Debrah. The word is they want to enslave everyone who can't claim royal origins. Even those on the Hills. The governor is talking about hiring mercenaries to see his plan through."

"This is insane! You have to talk him out of this. He listens to your advice. You've been friends since kindergarten." Cole's mother tried to reason with him.

Although her husband didn't seem to have a say in the matter. "Money is the only thing that drives him on. And that's the one thing I lack at this moment. Besides, if the riots ignite, there's nothing stopping this."

"Then we have to do something while you still have power over them. Before they find out about our financial situation."

"Like what, Debrah? Enlighten me," the sarcasm in his voice matched that of his son's.

"I don't care. You didn't ask me what to do before you bet away all our fortune. Go back to the casinos and ask for a refund. Just get us out of this!"

"Do you think it really works that way?" Frank rasped at his wife.

"Then maybe you should talk to Cole. He has colleagues in high places, and he knows all your well-connected friends— some of them even better than you do. You keep talking about getting him to step into your shoes. Maybe it's time to ask for his help." Cole's mother sounded desperate.

"All his colleagues and friends will turn their backs on him when they discover that he's broke. It's the way the world works. We don't have real friends up in the Hills. Only acquaintances."

The sound of an opening door alerted me to the reality of my current surroundings. It wasn't a great moment to meet the parents. There was a chance of my cover being blown, so I ran out the door, searching for my momentary freedom.

Was what I just heard true? Were we on the verge of slavery, or worse, extinction?

I couldn't process all that information at that moment. Just left to go straight home—to my new home, that is.

It was the first time I was alone there, and the grandeur of the place didn't cease to amaze me. I finally set out to find out how many rooms my apartment hid, only to discover that the place was almost a mansion of its own. Five luxury bedrooms, including a master one; who knows how many bathrooms and closets, and the grand *pièce de resistance*—a rooftop pool. All for me, and my family, as soon as I would be able to get them here.

And then, there I found it. A room of magic filled with outfits handpicked especially for me, in an exquisite display of dresses, shoes, and whatever accessories that could possibly cross a person's mind.

The most spectacular piece of furniture in view was a

glass cabinet filled with extremely sexy items of lingerie, each individual one carefully arranged on its own hanger, likely to show off the fine materials they were made from. Either Ferris didn't get the message about me not sleeping with him, or he was enjoying torturing himself. One thing was for sure, he wouldn't be able to take advantage of the full package that fine pieces of lingerie like these have to offer.

I decided to try one of the teddies on, admiring in the mirror how perfectly it wrapped my body. Choosing to keep it on, I pulled an emerald green dress over it. In no time, I was in the limo, waiting for the three minutes it took me to get to Ferris to pass by.

My night was far from being over; that feeling of concern still lived within me, ruling my world and slowly placing humanity's pain upon my heart. But it wasn't the right time to stop and think of that.

My mission came first.

My family came first.

There was nothing much that I could do anyway. I had to sell my soul to save *two* people. What would the price be to save an entire city? Besides, Echo City had only been my home for a month or so, and what I had found in this place was far from worth saving.

I had to let the thought go. I couldn't take this responsibility on my hands as well. It wasn't even my responsibility. Was it?

"Wow, you look stunning," Ferris's voice brought me back to the real world. I found myself in the middle of the hallway, with warm arms coming to get a hold of me. In no time, I was safely resting upon his chest, floating in our special madness so far away from everyone else.

I was a fool, tying myself with an invisible blindfold when it came to him, refusing to see the obvious, and willingly losing myself in this spell. Maybe he was my only refuge in this stormy sea? Maybe he was just hope when I had none? But he was giving me strength while at the same time gradually breaking me.

"Come, Vanya, is waiting," he gestured, only after having captured my lips with his, making sure that I remained trapped under his charm.

His arm slid around my waist, guiding me towards the other end of the lobby, through a large corridor, and into an elegant saloon.

"Good evening, Vanya." I nodded, acknowledging my boss's presence.

"Bea, so nice to see you." She shifted from her seat to look at me while Ferris invited me to take a place on the sofa next to him.

"Wine for the ladies." As careful as ever, Ferris made sure all of our glasses were quickly filled with Dionisio's liquor. "Now that everyone is here, we can get on with our evening," he smiled, as he lit himself a cigarette. "I wanted to put all the cards on the table. I don't want any doubts or any further claims to appear later from either side."

Vanya took a sip out of her glass. "Bea can quit whenever she likes. I've never kept anyone by force. But she met you during a Pleasure, so I do have the right to a commission out of any material earnings resulting from that." She was a businesswoman, and I did not expect anything less of her.

"That's exactly why I called you here tonight. Have you brought the contract?" Ferris calmly asked.

My boss nodded. "Yes."

"Okay. I want it to be stipulated in black and white that all rights and fees will be fulfilled in full and final payment with this check." Ferris pushed a wrapped piece of paper in front of her, and as soon as Vanya opened it, her eyes glinted in surprise.

There must have been a lot of zeros scribbled down on that piece of paper since she wasn't the type to ever let herself be *surprised* by anything.

"That's a generous sum," she uttered, returning to put pen to paper, signing the contract. "All claims solved." Vanya smiled, pushing the papers back to me to also sign.

In reality, I regretted parting from her. My boss may be tough, but at least she was one of the few people who were truly honest with me.

The papers were signed by both sides, eliminating all concerns regarding the termination of our contract.

"If you ever want your old job back, you'll always be welcome." The door to The Pleasure Room was still open. But even if it was the only place I found solutions to my problems, I was certain that ever returning there would totally break me.

Ferris seemed to agree. "She won't return," he muttered, throwing her the coldest look he owned. I belonged to him now, and there was *nothing* that could change that.

"As you say. These are murky times. It's better to have friends everywhere rather than enemies." Vanya was making sure to keep the connections, especially with a man of Ferris's worth.

And even he seemed to take the diplomatic path, acknowledging Vanya's true worth in Echo City. She may not have his fortune, but information is power, and can sometimes be of greater value than a generous bank account. "Yes indeed.

It wasn't meant as an offense. It was only a statement. Bea won't need to return to The Pleasure Room."

"I'm always happy when one of my employees finds a better path." Vanya smiled, tilting her glass of wine in a small toast for the new life awaiting us. "I'll be leaving you two to celebrate." She stood up to leave.

"Thank you for everything you've done for me. I'll walk you out." I followed her out of the room only to witness her make the most uncommon gesture.

Catching me into a parental hug, Vanya kissed both of my cheeks, drawing me closer to her chest. "Be careful with him." A piece of advice that left me breathless, staring to the ground long after she left the room. She was by far the least likely person to ever do that, so the warning had every reason to be heard as loud as it was intended to be.

I've always ignored my instincts when it came to Ferris, mostly because he had his special way of convincing me that it's only a figment of my imagination, not with words, but with warm gestures. Or maybe I was just a sucker for affection after being deprived of any for so long. I didn't even know any more, although I'd always felt when it came to him that his darkness outshone his light.

But who was to say that you can't thrive in the dusk?

"Is there something wrong?" Coming from behind me, his warm lips fell to my neck, leaving a long trail of goosebumps.

I turned to cast him a smile that I didn't truly own. "Nothing." I leaned my forehead to be buried in his chest as he caught me between his arms.

"Bea…" He held on to me to kiss the nape of my neck over and over again until he managed to make the world around us blur again. "Are you sure you're okay?" he whispered while setting a little distance to be able to properly look into my eyes as I answered.

"I guess I may be more *damaged* than you initially presumed," I whispered, drowning in unknown sorrow.

"If that is the case, I have the perfect remedy for that. Wine." Ferris pressed the glass to my lips, making sure it remained glued there until I drained all of its contents. He soon emptied his own, just so he could refill our glasses seconds later. "Wine and good food." He took my hand, guiding me toward his room. "You don't mind if we dine in, do you?" He asked in a delicious tone and as soon as we reached the bedroom, he led me to find a place on the rug in front of the fireplace. An indoor picnic was elegantly laid out there, waiting for us under the light from a silver candlestick.

"This looks delicious," I uttered, raising the lid from over the plates and discovering the most appetizing dish. My stomach reminded me that I hadn't eaten for who knows how long at the same time as I found my place in front of the flickering flames.

"*Coq au vin* prepared by a Michelin star chef." He winked as if he had just pulled out the heavy artillery.

I giggled. "Oh, more wine?"

Ferris tilted his glass, emptying it again in one sip. "Wine is good for the soul in any combination. The more, the merrier." He then waited for me to follow, even though the liquor didn't seem to flow so smoothly down my throat as it did down his. Even so, by the time we finished dinner, I was on my fourth glass, feeling the hypnotic glow from the fireplace invading my whole body.

It was like I was burning from within, as the dress I was wearing seemed to be tightening on my breasts, making them ache to be set free and *ache to be touched.*

Sensing my anguish, Ferris spread his hand out for me to join him.

And how could I have said no? The next moment, my feet were stretching next to his, in the opposite direction from his own, so that I could face him. "What else?" I asked, not really expecting a surprise but that mesmerizing sensation of feeling his body incredibly close to mine.

"Whatever you desire." He gently tugged the dress over my shoulders, assuring himself of access to explore the new piece of lingerie I had on. "Whoever bought you this must have had excellent tastes," he whispered, leaning in to pamper that swollen flesh right above the cup of my bra.

"Tonight, it's my turn." I pushed him back, beginning to unbutton his shirt. A lust I never felt before was tormenting me. I wanted him. I wanted all of him in every way I thought humanly possible.

One by one, his buttons evaporated, setting free a spectacular display of inked muscles, so appealing that my tongue couldn't help itself but have a taste. And he was as delicious as I expected. His cologne was filling my senses as the muscles underneath my tongue became firmer the second I reached them. There was something happening to me. Desire was replacing all rational thought, only to take as much as he had to share with me—body and soul.

With perfect precision, his hand tangled itself between my locks as I traced each exquisite line of his chest until I could hear a long "Fuckkk," escaping his lips. The grip he had on the base of my hair only boosted that throbbing sensation that was making my pussy pulse in expectation. Maybe it was from the alcohol, or maybe the alcohol was just the fuel I needed to ignite my deepest cravings. I was lacking all inhibitions, driven by his hitched breath to enjoy that taste of him for as long as I could.

Though something stopped me, almost waking me up from my beautiful delirium as I stumbled upon two scars that crushed my soul. Two circular wounds that lead directly to his heart made me instantly dampen them with crystal tears.

Were those healed bullet wounds?

"What are these, Ferris?" I asked, my voice drowned in sadness, thinking of all the misery he must have gone through.

"Something that I won't let ruin my evening. They've ruined my life once already." He refused to let me waste any more time searching his past, preferring to focus on the *immediate* future.

I was high in the air before I realized what was happening, being carried by my *royal highness* straight to bed.

"That's a smooth way to hinder my interrogation." I giggled as I felt my dress slipping off to meet the ground, even before my body rested between his sheets.

His body came on top of me, caging me between the strength of his arms and his undeniable lips. "I know much smoother ways."

Yet the wine was guiding me to take the lead. I moved my hand to reach for his belt, his hard cock waiting impatiently under my fingers. But my prude nature managed to defeat even the alcohol running through my veins and seconds later, the realization of what exactly I was doing kicked in. My hand suddenly lost strength, but as if recognizing my plans of retreat, Ferris quickly caught my wrist. There was no backing down from this. I could tell from his hitched breath that he was waiting for me to go on with my initial plan. And guiding my hand straight back to the place of its intended target, he was making sure that this time it wouldn't retreat again.

My lips stopped moving against his own, surprised by the *strong* effect I had on him as his cock was eagerly awaiting to break through his jeans. Time froze as I glanced straight into his eyes, stroking his whole length through his pants. Everything felt so free. I felt so in control, so different than with Cole. This time I was doing it because I wanted to and not because it was a part of a deal. It was a whole new sensation, giving me the thrilling satisfaction of bringing him pleasure. Still, there was something stopping me from going all the way with him and a fragment of reality came crashing in on me. "You know that I still can't fully... You know..."

"Don't worry, we'll improvise." He grinned as the blueprints of a new plan were already set out in his mind.

I trusted him, and having a clue of what he was thinking about, I proceeded to unfasten his jeans, pushing them down and leaving him only in his boxers.

He seductively smirked, letting the top of the teddy fall over my breasts and leaning his mouth to taste the newly exposed skin. He was once again pulling me back into the arms of that intoxicating feeling that always arises around him.

Reaching for the hard part of him that hid beneath his boxers; I didn't stop until he let out a long groan, satisfying my need to know that I could please him. He was mine now, and as the single benefit I got from my experience with Cole, I had a very good idea of what I needed to do to get him to ecstasy. However, I didn't take into account his hand that tore the snaps off my teddy, reaching for the very aroused part of me and tracing a line over the whole length of my pussy.

"You were waiting for me," Ferris felt the need to state the obvious. His fingers instantly glided across my clit and then all the way down to my entrance in repetitive moves that were creating such noticeable signs of the effect he had over me. I wasn't just wet; I was melting.

I didn't reply, just kneaded him harder, feeling each vein threatening to explode under my touch. I was traveling his full erection with every stroke of my hand, over and over. And he was driving his fingers to move in the same rhythm as mine, extracting bit by bit that sweet pleasure building in me.

Unwilling to lose ground, his tongue began to circle my rosy nipples, nibbling them gradually into ecstasy until they became so sensitive that each one of his whirls seemed to shoot straight to my core. And yet, I wanted more. I couldn't even conceive he would stop as I had never felt so close to heaven before. I needed to completely surrender to him. But at the same time, I needed to hear him at least partially roaring in satisfaction. And that thought kept me going, kneading his length faster, only stopping to brush my thumb over his tip with each complete motion. It seemed to be working since his groans were becoming louder yet completely hindered by my moans. I was moments away from floating in an orgasm, and both our bodies were silently trembling, anticipating the next move. Our breaths went from nonexistent to almost chaotic, as if we had just registered for a race to total bliss.

Feeling I was close—probably from my restless hips that were arching into the mattress like they were preparing to tear it apart—Ferris returned to my lips. His tongue snuck into my mouth to properly kiss me, or maybe just to feed on my moans. I was almost lost, though I couldn't let that burdening pressure control me—not before I made sure that he was ready to join me in ecstasy.

Gripping him stronger, I slowed down my rhythm, turning my moves into much wider ones, only gradually increasing the speed until that unavoidable elation was reflected in his eyes. I instantly relaxed, allowing myself to thoroughly lose myself in his game. My hand continued to shift over his cock until my feet were moving aimlessly into the sheets. I was trying to find something, anything, to support me as an anchor, without losing focus on my hand that was tightly locked on his hard length. I didn't let him fall behind, getting his body to jolt away from my touch as that tightening sensation overcame him. His release came in heavenly unison with mine, and I could hear a loud snarl as I felt his fingers being coated by my juices.

"I'm starting to believe that you cheated," he protested, burying his face into the mattress, still trying to control the effects of his recent ecstasy.

"You did say improvise." I smiled, dragging the sheet to cover myself.

"You're right."

My vision was beginning to become blurry from the alcohol, but I couldn't help myself from casting him a smile. "Why are you showing off your fangs?" I asked, sensing the immediate *danger* as my body seemed to still be craving him.

"I'm not showing off my fangs, just saying goodnight." He disappeared under the sheets, pushing my thighs apart, to flick that tongue piercing in a long trip over my once again trembling flesh.

I felt the same damn fire, igniting all over within me, as I was starting to believe that tongue piercings were part of my blessing and my curse.

"We better stop." He resurfaced from beneath the blanket so fast that the room was still spinning around me.

My body seemed to be aching again for him, and my ovaries were about to explode, as my torment was quickly increasing. It was pure torture. "Don't stop. I want to be yours," I moaned throughout my impossible yearnings. Almost losing all rational thought, I turned to fully face him while my own hands cupped my breasts, which were in terrible agony without him touching them.

"I can't. Not tonight. You had too much to drink." He kissed my lips, then tugged me into his chest, trying to calm my heated body.

"You said whatever I desire. I *desire* you," I whined, still unable to let go of my cravings. At that moment, I had completely forgotten about the deals. There was only one thing ruling me—the needs of my body.

However, he wasn't going to let me push things further. "If only things were that simple," he said, in an almost desolate tone. "But I promise that if you don't change your mind tomorrow after the wine leaves your system, I will fulfill every single one of your fantasies."

That sounded perfect in the foreseeable future, but right then, he was just pouring salt on an open wound. Who could wait for tomorrow when my body was screaming to melt under his touch?

"Good night, Bea." That damn line again, ending my evening in complete mystery and leaving me feeling like a fish slowly meeting its demise on a bank of sand.

CHAPTER 17

T he room was spinning, the bed was spinning, and I was spinning along with them, my head pounded and felt like a lead weight was holding it to my pillow.

"Take this," I recognized Ferris's voice as a hand appeared in front of me, opening to reveal a white pill. As much as I wanted to move, my pupils seemed to be the only part of me working throughout my entire body. "I have orange juice." A glass in which an orange liquid was swirling also appeared in front of me.

How on earth was I supposed to move from my current position to one where my lips would meet that glass?

Impossible, I thought, that was until Ferris's large torso leaned on me, helping me up on the pillows. It felt like an earthquake had shattered every cell in my body. "The wine got to you." He laughed, rubbing last night's mistake in my face as if I didn't already feel the consequences badly enough. "But I lived for every second of it." The memory of me, lustfully unzipping his pants rapidly brought color to my pale cheeks, and by the wicked grin so proudly displayed on his face, he was referring exactly to that moment.

"Never drinking again," I mumbled, convinced that I

wouldn't touch another glass of alcohol ever again.

"You're drinking this, though." He put the glass against my lips right after slipping the pill inside my mouth. "Now, sleep for another hour. You'll be as good as new when you wake up."

I'm not sure if he was talking from personal experience, but he seemed to know exactly what he was saying, turning his words into my commands. My eyes closed as if I had been awake for days, allowing me to find that all-too-desired rest once again.

I wasn't entirely sure what time it was when I woke up, but it was dark outside.

What the hell had happened? And where did my day go?

"Ferris!" I called out for him as soon as my eyes were fully open, desperate to understand how I managed to sleep for an entire day.

"I'm here," he quickly returned from the balcony, putting out his cigarette and then took a seat next to me on the bed.

"What happened? What time is it? Why did I sleep for so long?' The questions just kept rolling off my tongue as a sudden state of anxiety took over me. At least the alcoholic fumes seemed to have dissipated, and my body was resuming its normal functions.

Ferris's hand began to slide through my hair, tugging a few loose strands behind my ears. "Slow down. It must be from the fatigue mixed with the wine. It's actually my fault. I shouldn't have left you to sleep for so long. It's just that you seemed to need the rest so badly."

I rushed to stand up. "My clothes... my phone." I was roaming around the room, trying to find them, completely unaware of where I had left them.

"Why are you in such a hurry to get dressed? I'm pretty sure the university courses are over by now."

"Ferris, I still need to leave," I called out to him as soon as I took hold of my dress, slipping right into it while I was staring at my phone. Six missed calls from Brax and a voice message. I was in such deep shit.

And Ferris seemed to have plans of his own regarding me. "I was actually hoping you'd join me on a short business trip. I have to go to the next town over in the morning, and I hate being out of the house. Your company would do me good. Besides, it's only for a couple of days. I'll talk to the Dean myself if that's what's worrying you."

"It's not only about the university; as I told you, I have other... commitments." My voice almost whispered, ashamed to admit whatever those commitments might imply.

Exactly as I was expecting, his dark eyes flared with a chilling gaze that pierced through to the deepest place within me. It was jealousy coated in doubt, though no matter what he felt or even what I felt for him in those seconds, I couldn't change my mind. "My family will be arriving here soon, maybe even in the next couple of days. I need to be in town when that happens."

Still, no words left his lips, so I decided to completely seal his mouth with my own. "I wish things were different," I whined, catching his torso between my arms while the thought of the voice message from Brax was swirling through my mind like a hurricane. I needed to get out of there, no matter what damage I might cause in the end. We had a deal, and so far I have been keeping my part of it the best way I could.

"Things will be different at some point, I'm sure of that." Ferris's smile suddenly reappeared, though it lacked any real sign of warmth. It was as if I said some incantation to cast him into a spell. A spell that I was starting to believe I was no longer a part of.

"I'll call you tomorrow. I promise." Smashing my lips on his again, I pulled him into a final kiss, then ran out the door without looking back. It felt like Sodom and Gomorrah; if I turned for one last look, I would turn to stone. In reality, my heart was supposed to be made of stone to live with everything I had done by now.

The second I closed the car door behind me, I pressed the phone to my ear, hitting voicemail—one message from Brax.

You probably don't care as much as you pretend to about your family.

His tone—so full of anger that it immediately instilled a trembling sensation in my flesh. It felt like the car couldn't go fast enough, even though it was only a three-minute drive. The second it stopped I jumped right out, walking straight to my new apartment. I must have called Brax five times before his ego finally let him answer, "What the fuck do you want?" He barked, as I was already an hour late to our *date*.

"I'm sorry," I whimpered, hoping that my mistake wouldn't have consequences that would affect the mission of bringing back my family.

"Yes, you will be." A threat that I knew held ground.

My voice was shaky. "I wasn't feeling well." I kind of forgot to mention the part where I was too drunk to get out of bed.

And it seemed Brax somehow caught onto my lie. "Oh, really? My driver was in front of your apartment for an hour. When I saw you weren't picking up, I asked him to go inside. But *surprise*, you weren't home."

"I... I don't live there anymore," I whispered, hoping he

wouldn't ask any more questions.

Seemed that the mighty Brax had missed a detail. "You don't?"

I had to tell him the truth. "No... I live... I live in the Hills."

"This has to be good." I could sense him from the other end, flaring his nostrils.

"There's nothing good about it. I just have other... arrangements. Nothing that could affect our *deal* though." In the end, that's the only thing he cared about—that his *payment* would still be intact when the time came for him to claim it. "I could come now if you still want me to," I lowered my tone to a more seductive one, hoping that I would get him to soften.

He snarled. "There will be consequences to this. No one keeps me waiting."

I was the only one responsible for my mistakes; my family shouldn't pay for them. "As long as *the consequences* don't affect your part in our deal."

"No... it won't be affected," he growled as I could sense all the devious thoughts forming in his mind. "Text me the fucking address." And he hung up, leaving me to stare at my phone.

In less than five his Jeep was parked outside my window. But before I got a chance to get out the door, someone was already ringing my doorbell. It was one of Brax's men, holding a large white box with an extremely elegant cherry blossom pink ribbon. Whatever was in the box must have been expensive, which left me staring at it, almost shocked.

"Boss asked me to give this to you." The man handed me the package. "That was before he almost set my phone on fire. But since he gave me no other instructions regarding it, here it is."

"Thank you," I said sheepishly, unsure of what exactly I needed to do with the gift.

A note was quietly waiting for my attention on top of some pink luxury wrapping paper.

An upgrade to your dress

Putting the note aside, I tugged at the wrapping, only to reveal an exquisite black dress. Handsewn crystals were decorating a bustier top; perfect lines were shaping an astonishing knee-length piece of clothing, while nesting beneath it lay a pair of black stilettos. I recognized the clothes brand as being one that the rich kids at the university wear. Ferris had already bought me a few pieces from the same store that were hanging in my dressing room. However, *this* dress held a different meaning.

Even though I would hate to admit it, with Ferris, the gesture of giving a gift didn't come across as an uncommon act. I even suspected that I wasn't the first to have received an over-the-top wardrobe or of being spoiled with a few expensive gifts. Let's just say that his more romantic nature inclined him toward being the type to make these kinds of gestures. But when it came to Brax, things were oceans apart. He wasn't the giving kind. Sure, he gave me a gown before, but that was only business. He needed me to wear that golden dress, while this time... this time he gifted me the dress because he wanted to. And that was exactly why the piece of clothing I held in my hands conveyed more meaning than my entire dressing room. This present didn't have a hidden purpose behind it, he didn't need to seduce me since I was already his.

To put my mind at ease, I convinced myself that he wanted to take me to a public place and that he would be ashamed of my usual clothing. A present that would still serve him somehow, as he was unwilling to allow me to spoil his image when I was beside him.

Gathering my strength, I ran to the bathroom to take a quick shower and change, slipping between the straps and crystals, fitting into the dress and the red sole stilettos. In less than ten minutes, I managed to transform the mess I was posing as earlier into a princess. A red-eyed princess since the effects of the earlier alcohol hadn't fully left my system, but still.

"I'm ready. Take me to him," I let the driver know the instant I walked out of the bathroom. Before I knew it, we were climbing into the Jeep so he could drive me towards my final destination.

As we were approaching Brax's house, I observed that the place looked extremely glamorous at night. Imposing lights underlined every line of exceptional architectural design, making it resemble one of his art pieces more than an actual home. Certainly, a building worthy of the Hills, even if the man who owned it had strayed so far from the Elite etiquette. Or maybe he was just like them, separated only by origins, but both sharing similar goals and means.

Walking up the front entrance stairs I glanced around searching for guards. I wasn't able to find any. So, without waiting for anyone to appear, I decided to knock, then stood back and waited patiently, or more likely impatiently for someone to open the door. Yet minutes passed, and nothing happened—no sign of anyone coming my way. I kept telling myself to wait a little longer, but after my third attempt at knocking failed to elicit a reply, I decided to turn the door handle and let myself in.

Already familiar with the place, I ventured to look in the living room to see if Brax was there. It would have been a little strange for him to have called me to his place without actually being here. But seconds later, I realized that maybe I shouldn't have entered. Maybe I should have just turned and left when no one answered or maybe even not come to his place at all. Perhaps I should have just tried to fix things in the morning, and he would have forgiven me. Because the Brax I knew was *gone,* leaving a steaming dragon to occupy his body.

I found him sitting on a sofa, a large glass of whiskey resting between his fingers, his gaze fixed on the screen of his TV, his mind lost in an entirely different place. There was something extremely attractive about the madness glinting in his eyes. Making me realize that I was beginning to be a sucker for the Brax package: a dominant attitude, firm muscles wrapped in a fine Italian suit, and those absinthe eyes that created a pool between my legs whenever they were pointing at me. Or maybe I was the one who was losing their mind.

"Brax..." daring to call him back to reality, I unwillingly managed to draw his wrath upon me.

His head turned my way, his eyebrows shifting into a deep frown. "Shit, I forgot about that," he groaned, noticing the way the dress *he gifted* me wrapped itself around *my* body.

"Thank you. It's amazing." I smiled, unsure of how exactly I should react after receiving such a beautiful gift from him, especially after I just messed up his plans.

"You already *thanked me* with your behavior." The disappointment in his voice answered my questions, reminding me exactly how badly I had fucked things up—maybe even to the point where I was even risking the future of my family.

One thing was clear; I wasn't even close to being out of the woods yet.

A sudden sound of shattered crystal and porcelain clattering together caught my attention, making my eyes shift to the opposite corner of the room. An older woman dressed in a black uniform was there, cleaning up some broken plates and glasses from the floor. An insane rhythm began pumping through my veins as I glimpsed a round table for two that had been thrown next to a large window. Scraps of food and the spilled contents of a bottle of champagne were covering a white mohair rug like a hurricane just swept through the place. All of these, signs of Brax's internal turmoil.

"I had plans for tonight." His words cut straight through me, assuring me that any good intentions that had been present earlier in the room had died because of my disobedience.

No public place, I guess—the dress was just for *him and me*. My failure was of epic proportions, slaughtering any hope that Brax would ever ease up on me. I was now back at square one, or maybe even worse, judging by the morbid emptiness resting in his eyes. All human feelings were pushed aside, leaving only sinful desires to take their place.

"Lucia, you can leave now," he barked, speaking to his maid without even turning to face her.

The woman immediately stopped cleaning. "But, Señor Brax, I haven't finished," she replied, almost terrified that her time was up.

Brax let out a grunt. "Did I ask you if you were finished?"

"No, Señor." Her eyes met the floor.

"Leave!" His final word before the poor woman ran out the door, grabbing her bag on the way out.

Should I have been as scared as her, or maybe even more? I had every reason to be. The image of the crumpled table wouldn't leave my mind. I hurt him, and I was damn sure that only moments separated me from learning the full price of my mistake.

"Let's get this over with." He moved his eyes to look at me, downing the glass of whiskey in one sip. "Get down on your knees."

That was it, my punishment, or maybe his plan all along.

Cole may have managed to dress me pleasuring him as a game of chance, but with Brax, things were completely different. He wanted—he received, even if tonight I may have held a small chance of changing that. But I blew it, and the only thing left to be done was getting my knees to hit the rug in front of him.

With a shallow breath, I reached for his jacket, slowly pushing it to the sides so that I could gain access to the buttons of his shirt. At least, this was the part I was secretly waiting for since the tanned skin and the defined lines of his chest had been haunting my dreams for a while.

My mouth leaned in to explore his gym-sculpted body, relishing itself with the mutters leaving his throat. He was enjoying this, I could feel it as my warm breath was making his skin crawl under the tip of my tongue. But so was I, as his manly cologne was infiltrating my senses and it seemed to gather in an arousing rhythm that was set to make my core melt.

My own satisfaction was quickly noted, and even though the pleasure I was bringing him was much too obvious, he chose to ignore it just to prevent me from finding any satisfaction from fulfilling his order. It was a punishment, after all.

"When I asked you to get down on your knees, do you think this is what I was waiting for? Unbuckle my fucking pants," he growled, treating me no differently than any other one of his cheap fucks. And this time, in his eyes, I deserved it.

For a second, I froze. The man who managed to dig a tiny tunnel into my heart was now shoveling back the rocks. "Do it, Bea, or do you want me to tell you step by step what needs to be done?" Why did all men feel the need to give precise instructions to women? If by any chance I couldn't handle this, I would have just followed Ferris's advice—improvise, even if when it came to Brax, there was not much room for that.

I didn't have any options left other than to follow his exact commands. Any signs of humanity had left him from the moment I messed up, and now I was sitting in front of the real Brax—the cold-hearted mobster.

My hands were shaking against the metal buckles, trying to control that screaming sensation igniting in my throat. I hated him, but mostly I hated myself for not being able to shake that feeling of sorrow for what those shattered plates really meant.

Pulling Brax's pants over his knees, the cross and thorns tattoo covering his entire left thigh came into sight. Such a fine irony of the situation I found myself in because there wasn't anything holy about this man.

I looked up at him, hoping that I would find clemency as I was sheepishly disposing of his boxers. Of course, he had none to give. But what surprised me was that I couldn't spot any sign of excitement or satisfaction either. His gaze—so much different than Cole's—bittered with the taste of my mistake. Although I suspected he didn't consider it to be *my* mistake any longer. He was blaming himself for *his* momentary weakness, maybe even for the overpriced present he had sent to my apartment. And that was just making things a thousand times worse.

Still, there was a part of him betraying his instinctive reactions. Human anatomy couldn't be controlled, and his hard cock began twitching under the touch of my tongue. Though his eyes remained hollow as he was focusing to remain a stone statue, unwilling to show me that I had any kind of power over him.

Without having a proper understanding of what needed to be done, I closed my lips around his thick member, moving up and down on its length, trying to take him as deep in my mouth as I could. Under no circumstances did I want to prolong this. I knew what his final goal of the evening was— to break me. And the longer it took me to make him come, the easier it would be for him to succeed with his plans.

But nothing seemed to happen as his countenance remained impenetrable, and his all-too-chill reactions were making me stumble in my movements. I suddenly became too aware of what I was doing, ashamed and humiliated by the all-too-mechanical gesture. With each bobbing of my head I was slowing down, as guilt and embarrassment were turning everything into a molten pain.

Brax probably sensed the thoughts that were taking over me, and after pouring himself another glass of whiskey, he let his hand search for a spot behind my head. His fingers loosely twisted between a few locks of my hair as my true punishment was beginning. "It's time for you to pay for your mistakes."

I felt him move from his seat, guiding my lips to meet his thrusts, amplifying their effects while his nostrils flared in evil satisfaction. It was all too clear. He wasn't searching for pleasure; he was just punishing me, harder and faster, draining the air out of my lungs until I felt that I could no longer breathe.

His muscles suddenly tensed, his jaw tightened, his fists clenched—all signs that he couldn't remain immune to me. I could sense the fire burning beneath them coming alive in his veins as his fingers moved against the base of my hair at the same pace as my mouth.

Tears were lining my eyelids as I couldn't find enough air to keep focus, my body almost limp—a puppet in his hands, the same way I was with Cole. With the last of my strength, I pressed my palms on his thighs, pushing him away. I was trying to breathe while fighting that gagging sensation that was almost making me throw up.

"Relax, so you won't choke." I could see Brax smirk because his actions were intended just for that purpose; to make me choke, to make me feel the full extent of my error.

But this time, I couldn't keep quiet, and my mouth got the better of me again. "Fuck you!" I grunted, even if, in the next second, I realized that the words that slipped from me aggravated everything.

"No, Bea, that would be my job." Without leaving me with a second more to catch my breath, his hand forced my head back to fill my mouth with his cock. He began moving against me again, only much stronger this time, as if he was set out to make me faint. "Good girl," he groaned. It made me feel cheap, like just another one of the strippers who work for him. And that was his ultimate goal—to take the last drop of self-esteem left in me.

It should have been enough to make me hate him.

I should hate him, right? Somehow, this seemed to be a question that wasn't even supposed to be asked.

Move by move, Brax's breath was losing its repressed pace, and the grip of his hand loosened to the point that it was merely resting on the back of my head. Maybe my punishment was coming close to an end, or maybe he couldn't fight that feeling any longer, but a tightening expression emerged on his face. He wasn't in control of the pleasure anymore. *The pleasure was controlling him.*

I watched how that mass of muscles moved beneath the suit. His chest was struggling so fiercely to focus on my rhythm that he seemed like a bomb ready to explode at any second. And at the same time, my own body was reacting, led by his ecstasy. Every inch of me began to cry out with the molten need for him to touch me. I needed something, anything to release some of the strange tension that was taking control of my body. However, his next gesture was so far from being one that might come to my assistance. Taking his hand off me, he downed the contents of another glass of whiskey. But instead of placing it back on the small table next to him, he hurled the glass, together with the piece of furniture across the room, shattering the crystal decanter and scattering its contents all over the floor.

"Get up!" He snapped, roughly catching my arm to set me back on my feet, then quickly pulled up his boxers, leaving his pants, shirt, and jacket to fall on the floor. Without a word, he turned to walk toward his bedroom.

It took me a long second to clear my mind, but I followed him, even though he didn't instruct me to do so. By the time I got to the bedroom, he was lying on the bed, dressed only in his underwear. "You can... resume." He pointed toward his *unsolved* erection, waiting for me to continue doing something about it.

I really had no escape. At least the light wasn't on in the room, and that was providing me with some privacy because, as I was about to discover, I was going to need a lot of it—at least so that my prude, introverted nature wouldn't make me faint.

I pulled on his boxers again, releasing his hard cock to bring my mouth over it once more. He felt even larger in this position, and I was uselessly trying to relax my jaw to take him. I was too stressed, too overwhelmed by the reactions of my own body. My breasts swollen, needing to be touched, my pussy aching with the need for a release I knew I wasn't going to receive. Brax was the last person in the world who would care about my needs or about the anguish that I didn't know how to silence.

But, surprisingly, only after a few short moves, I felt him changing positions. One of his hands was now securing my head in that same spot as it did earlier, and the other, clenched on my leg. With my mouth still tightly locked on his length, he whirled me around until my thighs wrapped themselves around his neck.

A loud pulse began vibrating in my core, his fingers playing on the delicate lines of my panties causing my legs to try and squeeze together to soothe some of the delicious pain that was taking over me. But I couldn't react in any way. Brax's hand locked behind my head, making sure that my mouth remained fully occupied, and focused on his hard limb.

Without warning, I felt my dress being lifted over my waist. My panties were being pulled aside, and the warm dampness of his tongue left a long line from all the way back to my sensitive clit. The wet trail managed to intensify the weakness taking hold of me. A place that needed to be touched, pampered, and fully explored. And I had the feeling Brax had decided to take care of that for me.

I couldn't truly process what we were doing though, not without having a full on panic attack or needing to confess my sins the second I was out the door. So, I tried not to allow myself to go there, focusing only on the way in which my body was being brought to life.

A snarl escaped Brax as I felt his tongue kneading my swollen nub, and at the same time, he was pushing himself deeper inside my mouth, seeking his own pleasure as he was building mine. My reactions seemed to be amplified with his every thrust as we were working together as one. My senses were on the verge of exploding, and my hips slowly moved against his face to find relief. His devious tongue seemed to be an expert at eliciting that crazed need for an orgasm. I could barely moan as I could feel the tip of his cock hit the back of my throat. I was ready to fall over the edge, until an unexploited spot came to life. "Brax," I whined, feeling the tip of his finger checking on his *payment* and slowly entering my channel.

"Shush." He jabbed himself deeper inside my mouth, letting his finger advance a little deeper until he caught on to my discomfort. I stiffened, feeling his digit slightly moving at my entrance, pacing the lustful rhythm of his tongue. "It's okay, Bea. I'm just playing," he continued, gently sucking my swollen nub between his lips and making me realize that something had unexpectedly changed.

He was *playing?*

What had happened to the steaming dragon? Did I tame him?

Highly unlikely. And yet, the *good girl* was gone. I was *Bea* to him.

Another finger followed, not deep enough to ruin me for him, but enough to make me feel something I had never done before. And I needed more of it, like a drug that gave me an instant addiction, I wanted to know how it felt to be fully claimed by him. I needed to know what could ease this new torment, because I had a feeling it would be nothing short of amazing.

My own lips moved only to please him. I wanted to match the silent tremble he was instilling inside me with one of his own. I wanted to create that *moment* for him, the same way he was doing it for me.

I could feel his cock growing thicker as he was aiming to thrust even deeper. My clit was sucked roughly between his lips, and I was lost, my body spasming as my orgasm took all control I thought I had. Simultaneously, I felt his cock throb sending the hot liquid of his release down my throat.

He cursed as he came, and for a few seconds, kept a hand behind my head, making sure I swallowed all of him. Marking me. The same way Cole did, claiming fake ownership over a body that was his, just as long as the deal lasted.

I felt him pulling me almost into his arms to align my body with his. I couldn't even react anymore. I was just uselessly trying to recover after the most intense experience I ever had. It was a whole new level of *everything,* bonding me to him in an inexplicable manner.

Setting a small distance between us, I leaned my head on a pillow to properly look at him. I wanted to decipher how was it that my punishment ended with my orgasm. I didn't even have the time to catch a proper glimpse before his lips hungrily smashed to mine, ferally searching for the taste of himself inside my mouth.

A kiss like never before, exposing the last unexplored corner of my heart, and altogether, unveiling Brax in front of me for the first time—even if for only a moment of total weakness. He wasn't the kind to do something so unpredictable. Everything in his world was calculated and carefully planned. While this was pure desire, uncontained passion, maybe even a feeling that he didn't know he owned.

And then, the tiny spell broke.

Suddenly, he stopped, his arms shaking as he was about to lose all control, while his lips formed into a thin line, bottling back inside everything he almost succeeded in letting go.

"You can sleep here tonight." An offer that I was certain not many received, but as always, a double-edged sword when it came to him. "I need to return to the club anyway." Leaving the bed as if it was burning him, he stormed into his dressing room.

A minute later, he walked out in a completely new suit, as if nothing had happened and our worlds hadn't just been turned upside down. The Brax I knew was back.

I wasn't entirely sure if he got cold feet or just got bored with me the second he found his release. I wasn't even sure whether I was regretting or not what had just happened. But he wasn't going to stick around to help me find an answer to any of those questions.

"I'll be claiming my payment in two days," he snarled, closing the bedroom door behind him.

Yup...the Brax I knew was a hundred percent back!

CHAPTER 18

I wasn't going to sleep in Brax's bed, especially not without him present, and certainly not after the way he had treated me.

I just needed to be alone after a night like that, sleeping between my own sheets—not that any set of sheets really belonged to me. Nothing belonged to me anymore, not even *me*.

In reality, I was anticipating things getting a lot better for the rest of the night. But it seemed that the first evening I spent away from Ferris's bed didn't feel as good as I expected. Maybe it was just out of habit, but I had the impression that I was in the *habit* of missing him.

My presence—or rather, the lack of it—seemed to have been missed at the university because the very next morning Jenna ran my way to catch me in a hug as soon as I set foot into our part of the hallway. "You scared the hell out of me. I was beginning to think that your *benefactor* did something to you. I was one step away from borrowing a phone to call you."

"What could he ever do?" I laughed. "He's not that bad. I think..."

"What happened? You never miss classes?" Jenna questioned.

I tried not to stutter. "I overslept... for an entire day."

"Who does that?" she uttered.

I couldn't hold back a giggle. "Someone who drinks too much wine."

"How much? Like a wine cellar?" Her eyes rolled all the way up.

Her question did have a point, but certain aspects of that night were a little blurry. "I can't really remember. Four, maybe five glasses."

"Oh, you're right. That is a lot... for a toddler." Jenna laughed; after all, she probably attended a lot more parties than I ever had and had her share of training.

"Then I guess I'm a toddler." I shrugged, heading to my first class. Though not without her careful supervision since we were sharing the same student desk.

By the end of the class, Jenna had gotten me to answer more questions than I could count. And the interrogation seemed set to go on and on for hours to come because I also had the misfortune of sharing over half the day's courses with her. However, I didn't let her know anything in particular about the deals I accepted—just small drops and hints that were very far away from forming the complete puzzle. What could I say anyway? That I'm seeing three men, my personal harem? That I have sex in one way or another with all of them, though surprisingly, I'm still a virgin? Highly improbable.

Altering the truth was a lot better than sharing it in this case. The only thing I did regret was the girl time I used to share with her. Now, due to my commitments, I was ignoring it completely, even though she asked me to hang out on numerous occasions.

However, she did understand my late absence since I implied between words that it had something to do with recovering what was left of my family.

Class finally came to an end, and while I was preparing for my last one, a decisive hand came from behind me and pulled me into a janitor's room. For the first few seconds, I was convinced that this was one of Cole's games. Though as the lights went on, I discovered it to be someone much more dislikeable than the king of ECU—Ace. His athletic body was blocking the entrance as a despicable grin spread all over his hyena-like face.

"What's the meaning of this?" I all but yelled at him, in the hope that it was one of Cole's tests, although deep inside, I suspected what was really going on.

The bastard smirked. "I want some one-on-one time with you. Or would you prefer me to hire you directly from The Pleasure Room?"

"You know that I don't accept those kinds of Pleasures. Now, let me go." I tried to get him to move so I could leave. But there wasn't a chance in hell that he would budge and allow me to pass.

"I want the same treatment as Cole. I can see it from the way he looks at you. He wouldn't give you a second of interest if he wasn't fucking you." Ace took a step closer to me, his eyes drowning in the most despicable lust I had ever witnessed. "You can't be too much of an expensive bitch since I know he no longer has money." I could tell from the way he said it that he didn't just want to fuck me. He was doing this because he loathed Cole—his *friend*. He wanted to take something from him, to show him he was not the ultimate king.

Taking a step further, Ace shoved me against a wooden shelf, my back exploding in sharp pain from the impact. His hands, already on my body before I could come back to my senses.

I needed to get away, but the second I opened my mouth to scream, his large palm pressed against it, almost taking all my breath away.

My own palms pressed to the center of his chest, trying to push him away, but he wasn't moving an inch. Every possible plan of escape ran through my mind, and I would have done anything to get him to back down, including knocking him unconscious. I just needed something to use as a weapon since my bare fists would have probably felt just like a caress to his massive body. My head turned to the shelf behind me, searching for something to strike him with, but at that very moment the door opened. A hand appeared through its crack and dragged Ace out, almost throwing him into the middle of the hallway.

My savior was the angriest devil of them all—Cole.

By the time I managed to get out of the janitor's closet, an avalanche of fists and knee blows to the ribs were falling over Ace. And he deserved every single one of them, but the overzealous nature of my *king* was threatening to turn everything from a well-deserved correction into a full-on slaughter.

I might have been a damsel in distress this time, but I couldn't let him go to jail protecting my honor, considering he was, after-all, the first one to make sure that I didn't have any honor left to protect.

Jason and Nick shouted at Cole to end the madness, but were too afraid to intervene. And nothing seemed to be able to make him stop. I could see it in the dark fog that was now covering the perfect blue of his eyes, he wasn't going to stop until he took his life.

It took every last drop of courage I had to jump on top of my king, climbing on his back to wrap my arms around his broad neck. I had to take any action I could to force him to stop hitting Ace before we would have to call an ambulance.

Blinded by anger, he didn't even realize who it was that was mad enough to approach him. Shaking his arms to escape from the unwanted assailant, he managed to thump me with his elbow, sending me straight to the floor.

A roar of rage echoed through the hallway as Cole left Ace almost unconscious on the ground, the poor idiot barely able to keep his eyes open. Not that I was doing any better. My own vision was hazy. I didn't even see when Cole approached me. I only realized he was next to me the moment his hand caressed the bottom of my chin, turning my head to face him.

The fall had broken my inner lip, and I could feel the blood pooling on the tip of my tongue. Cole noticed it too because his thumb snuck inside my mouth, searching for the place the sweet liquid was springing from. The bastard was getting off on my pain.

Retrieving his finger, he placed it in his own mouth as if savoring the taste of my blood, like he just claimed another piece of me. And that was forming a needy knot in the pit of my stomach.

"Walk with me, Mouse." He gave me his hand to help me stand up, then began walking toward the parking lot as if nothing had happened. But I knew better—even though beating up some unfortunate student during the break wasn't an uncommon thing for him, smashing Ace's face to the ground was. He just ruined a friendship because of me, and that was going to cost me.

Cole was walking so fast that I could hardly keep up with him as he was heading toward his car. "Where are we going?' I asked.

"Mommy wants to meet you," he replied ironically, opening the driver's door so he could get inside the car.

I needed a century heads-up for that. "Tonight?" I panicked.

"Now." He shrugged as if he couldn't give a fuck about what would happen. "Did you manage to get your family into town yet?"

My eyes stuck to the floor as I got into the right side seat of his car. "No... Not yet."

"Then you don't have any reason to say no to her. I needed to tell my father you are my girlfriend, so he won't ask too many questions about helping you. Now I'm stuck with my mother on my back. I know her. She won't back down before she meets you."

"In exactly how much trouble am I in?" I was almost afraid to ask.

Cole fully turned to look at me. "Never brought a girl home, so I'm also treading on new ground. My father does anything I ask without too many questions. But when it comes to my mom, she acts as the prosecution."

I felt like I couldn't breathe. "What if she asks questions? I literally don't know anything about you."

However, Cole seemed strangely relaxed, especially for someone who was bringing a girl home to meet the parents. Maybe because we weren't a real thing. "Do you really think that at our age, my mother would expect you to know anything except for what my dick looks like?"

Well, that part was surely covered.

"What if she asks about me? About my not-so Elite origins." I was nervously rubbing my hands against my skirt trying to imagine her look when I told her that I wasn't one of the *privileged.*

"Chill down, Mouse. You can tell her you come from the Pit. It's not like I'm going to marry you." Wow, that hurt, even if it wasn't supposed to. Seemed I was screwing material, but definitely not wifey.

"Now stand still and let me see what damage I have done." Catching my chin between his index finger and thumb, he held my head motionless until he could sneak his tongue between my lips. He was tasting me, kissing me so slowly that I was beginning to ask who this guy was and what he did to Cole. His hand was advancing to the side of my face in a gentle move, stroking the line of my jaw all the way up until his fingers rested behind my ear.

I've never been kissed like this. Not even by Ferris, and as much as I hated to admit it, I was enjoying it a little too much for my own good.

And he seemed to be doing the same. "Fuck," he breathed the words, slowly opening his eyes, stroking my cheek with the back of his finger for one last time. "It's better now." The certainty in his voice made me laugh.

"Did you heal my lip with your magic tongue?" I giggled, amused at what an exceptional opinion he had of himself.

But I only ended up setting another trap for myself. "You know my tongue is magic. You couldn't resist it for more than five minutes."

My face flushed a fiery red as he flashed me the tongue piercing again, reminding me of the precise way he used it.

Being next to Cole felt so similar and yet so different from what I had with Brax. When it came to my mobster, he had a certain way of turning himself from Antarctic cold to the scorching heat of a volcano, firing an unprecedented passion. And still, Cole was not to be ignored. The tormenting twists of his games were dissolving me with their tempestuous beat, appealing to a wild side of me—one unexplored before.

"Cat got your tongue?" He grinned again, merging our lips and sneaking his tongue inside just to bite on my own. "Oh, I guess it did, Mouse." He paused, directing all the shady thoughts sprawling his mind straight into my eyes.

"You said your mother was waiting." I felt I had to remind him of our impending visit since things were slowly slipping in a direction where I would become his slave again. And bringing him on the road to happiness in the university parking lot was not on my goals list.

"Anxious to meet the parents, I see." He laughed, getting back to the real world, likely reminding himself that dear mother was waiting. "Wish granted." He turned to face the steering wheel, driving off in a rush for his home in the Hills as if he was running away from his demons.

At least, I didn't have time to get cold feet in the time spent between tasting his lips and holding on to dear life because of his NASCAR driving. In less than ten minutes, I was to face his mother.

The next thing I knew, I was retracing my steps from two days ago. Only this time I didn't get to take the stairs. We stopped in the living room, escorted by Cole's hand that seemed to be stuck on my lower back, testing from time to time the shape of my ass. "Cole!" I warned him, ashamed that his mother might see this.

"Don't be in such a rush. You'll get to visit my room a little later." The devil smirked, knowing all too well that me calling his name wasn't about my need for some one-on-one time, but because of him testing the limits every single damn second.

"Your maid should be the one to visit that," I grumbled, remembering the ultimate chaos in his room but omitting an aspect out of the equation.

"This isn't fucking Buckingham Palace," Cole moved his hand to find a strong grip on my arm, making me realize that I might have touched a soft spot—his family probably could no longer afford a maid.

I, of all people, should have known better than to mess up like that. I had become so accustomed to all the personnel

I noticed in Brax's and Ferris's house that, in my mind, I assumed that it would be the same in Cole's case. Mistakes seemed to rule my world lately and all my actions risked angering at least one of my *kings*.

"You must be Bea," a warm voice cut all replies short, forcing me to turn my gaze to the opposite corner of the room. An elegant woman entered the room, holding a tray with tea and biscuits. I couldn't help but recognize her resemblance to Cole; same cobalt blue eyes and raven hair, only a much kinder smile than the one of my king.

"Yeah, girlfriend of the year." Cole's irony could be sensed from miles away, especially since the term *girlfriend* was more of an offense than of pride to him. He was certainly not doing this out of the goodness of his heart, just forced by the circumstances since he did promise to honor his side of the deal.

I nodded, slightly bowing my head. "Yes, I am Bea."

"I am Ms. Clayborne, but you can call me Debrah. My son is incredibly cranky," she said matter-of-factly, looking straight at Cole. "I'm starting to think he was born this way. But I guess you already noticed that." The glimmer of a smile formed as she began examining me from head to toe.

The dress I was wearing couldn't betray my origins, but it was only a matter of time before she found out who she was dealing with. After all, that was why she called me here in the first place.

"I'm starting to adapt," I replied, looking over my shoulder directly at him.

After placing the tray on a coffee table in front of us, Cole's mother took a seat on the couch and gesturing us to follow.

"Don't you two get too comfy. I'm supposed to be doing something with Nick in a couple of hours," he grunted, trying to make this visit a short one.

"*Something...*" His mother said, raising an eyebrow in annoyance. "He never tells me what he does all day. I didn't even know you existed until two days ago." I could sense the disappointment in her tone, as no one seemed to be able to control Cole. "Bea is my guest for dinner. So, if you have *something* to do with Nick, you better go now and return in an hour. Leave us alone for some girls' time."

As appealing as the idea of getting rid of Cole might have sounded, the prospect of girl time with his mother was scaring the shit out of me.

"Not exactly my plan, but I can work with that. *Chatting* isn't my thing." Cole got up from the couch, even though I was desperately squeezing his hand, implying that he shouldn't leave me alone with his mother.

Was he really dumping me here with his mother, after less than a minute of meeting her?

Not that he gave a damn about my incoming anxiety attack. "I'll be back for dinner. Hopefully, Dad will be home by then too, so I won't be in the minority," he casually announced to us while checking his phone.

"Are you sure that you have to go?" I asked the big bad shark, feeling like a fish thrown out of the water.

"If you can manage my son, I'm certain you can withstand an afternoon with me." His mother chuckled, "You're excused, Cole."

"Don't remember asking," he snarled, taking the path that brought us here.

I could hear his mother sigh. "My son is... rude. I need to be honest. I'm pretty sure you've noticed by now. He's not the type to play Prince Charming just because he found himself a pretty girlfriend."

I shook my head, then took a sip from the cup. "No, he is not."

"Not originally from the Hills, are you?" she asked.

Wow, straight to the point.

"How could you tell? Am I holding the cup the wrong way?" That was the only explanation that came to my mind since I had been inside the room for less than five minutes.

"No. Nothing that oblivious. My husband mentioned you coming from another town and about needing some help with custody." I already knew about their conversation, but admitting to eavesdropping on the *meet-the-parents* evening might not have made such a good impression.

Even though my relationship with Cole wasn't real, I felt compelled to ask. "Is that okay with you? That your son dates someone from the Pit?"

"I see no difference between humans. Unfortunately, I can't say the same about my other friends. But you don't have to worry about that. I won't be a hypocrite and tell you that I would ever want to go there. However, I do admire you for your strength of surviving in such a place." She seemed genuine. The woman was starting to make me believe that Cole was adopted, since nothing from her genes seemed to have been passed along to him.

"Thank you," I murmured.

"Now, let's leave the discrepancy between the two social systems behind. Tell me about the university. What courses do you take?"

We talked for more than an hour about teachers and courses, until the oven clock rang, letting her know that dinner was almost ready. That was about the time Cole returned, followed shortly by his father, who seemed as pleased as his wife with my presence there.

I guessed they had given up a long time ago on any expectations of Cole ever acting like a normal human being. I was the one bringing some hope. Little did they know that I was just a pawn in the most devious kind of pact. And since this wasn't the only deal I needed to honor, there was a certain someone that I still had to call.

Excusing myself, I left for the bathroom, hitting the phone's green button the second the door closed.

"Hi," I spoke in a whisper.

"Bea. Is everything okay? Why are you whispering?" Ferris asked in a worried tone, as soon as he heard my shushed voice.

I paused, unable to come up with a lie, and at the same time, not wishing to do so.

"It's okay. I understand," he continued, implying that he realized that I may be with other company. But did he really understand? Because that thought might have been pretty difficult to digest.

However, I didn't want to open that subject. "When are you coming back, Ferris?" I asked.

"Two, three days tops. The board of directors must have thought I died since I only video-call them once a year. Now they can't get enough of me. I think I have a note from every unsatisfied man in a suit that ever entered my company." He sounded exhausted.

"That bad?"

"It doesn't really matter. I know someone who could quickly help me forget all about them."

"Do I also know that person?" I was entering his game to revive his spirit.

"You might. I'm talking about a green-eyed she-devil that happens to belong to me."

"Is that what you think, that I belong to you?" The thought scared and flattered me altogether.

"Don't you?"

"I do belong to you... But—"

"But I don't want to hear the rest," he cut me off, unwilling to hear the whole truth. In the end, this is what he did best — keeping only the fragments of the reality that suited him and ignoring all the rest. Though maybe this time he should have heard it because the complete phrase should have been, *I belong to you, and to two other people.*

Still, as I mentioned, it wasn't the right time to discuss the subject, especially since I could hear distant steps closing in on me from the hallway.

"I should go...," I rushed him, not knowing who was coming in my direction. I didn't want things to look like I had to go to the bathroom to talk on the phone, even though that was exactly what I had done.

"I'll call you tomorrow. I have a surprise for you," his voice hoarse as if brewing something deliciously wicked.

"I'll be waiting," I replied, rushing to hang up the phone. The next second, the bathroom door opened, making room for Cole's massive figure to enter the room.

"What are you doing in here? Are you crazy?" I exclaimed.

"You keep asking that question as if you don't already know the answer," he casually said, advancing to melt his body next to mine. "As you may have noticed, I'm keeping my end of the deal."

"Yes, I did notice. Thank you. Now let's go." I tried to walk by him, but the confined space left me with no room for such a maneuver.

And he didn't seem to budge. "You go when I say." He extended an arm so that I couldn't move. "You know, I enjoyed it when you kissed me in the upstairs bathroom. It doesn't happen often enough lately. I don't particularly like kissing, but with you, it feels different. I just haven't figured out why yet."

I could feel he was coming up with some of his twisted ideas again.

"I want you to do it again. Like you mean it."

My mouth went dry, my heart skipped a beat, and my feet felt wobbly. I hoped he was only referring to the kissing part, not a repeat of our last indiscreet interaction in a bathroom.

Rushing to get his latest request over with, I crashed my lips on his, quickly sneaking my tongue to search for his own. Though, before I could *knock him off his feet,* he bit my lower lip until he almost made it bleed again. "Like you mean it, Mouse," he growled, apparently unsatisfied. I was just in a hurry to get out of there, and that was obviously detracting from my *performance.*

Okay... like I meant it. I pressed my body weight against him, our chests fusing while our mouths searched to embody everything that kiss meant. Passion. Lust. Pure adrenaline. And it was pure delicious, almost as if it wasn't a task anymore. "It's better now!" I stated, stopping to look at him while trying to convince myself that the rapid thump of my heart was caused solely by the fact that his parents were in the next room.

"Did you cure my moody temper with your magic tongue?" He cackled, securing me next to him with one of his arms, close enough to feel his hard cock poking me in my stomach. "Again," he ordered, and there I went again, moving on his lips until his breath became hitched with lust. "Lower."

This time I was the one biting his tongue in defiance, hearing that impossible command.

"Don't bite me like that. I might fall for you if you keep it up." He raised the corner of his lip into a smile that I was willing to bet partially hid a deranged truth.

"That would imply you had a soul, or at least a conscience," I snapped back.

"You're right, I don't. Lower," he ordered again, always eager to find new ways of torturing me.

And lower I glided, lifting the shirt that he had on, making my lips dance on the black drawings that covered his chest. Then lower, brushing over the muscles of his ribs... and then lower, straight over his navel, making him almost bow in front of me from the electric tingle that I was sure, went straight to his cock.

"Shit, Mouse. We may not make it to dinner," he chanted, catching the sides of my cheeks between his hands, slowly lifting me to face him. And strangely enough, I probably felt as lightheaded as he did, the scent of his cologne lingering on my lips while my thighs kept pressing onto one another. "We'll keep the best for later. I know you're wet by now." He bit my lip again, his hand falling to grip my ass, assuring himself that I had a heads-up to leave the bathroom.

Such a charmer, this one...

He was definitely not getting the psychopath genes from his parents.

Cole returned to the dining table a couple of minutes after I did, at least trying to maintain some minimal illusion of decency.

Despite my *personal guard*, Cole, constantly watching over me, it was a nice evening, reminding me of the family warmth that I craved for so long. Not to mention the home-cooked meal that, even if it didn't have the Michelin stars hanging above it, was as good as my mother used to make.

Except for the bathroom rendezvous, everything about the evening instilled me with hope. *Hope* that I had unconditional support when it came to his parents, even if they were unknowingly offering Cole the weapons he needed to fully control me.

Of course, as if there was a curse that hung over me,

something had to go wrong at some point. After I helped Debrah serve the desert, it was time to leave. Or not exactly. "You can stay the night if you like," his mother offered to accommodate me through the night as I felt the need for a mental facepalm.

"Oh, thank you, but I should really head home. I have to wake up early in the morning to get to school." I desperately tried excusing myself.

"I'd like it if just for once my son would say that," his father cackled, looking over at Cole who let his fork fall on the table, making a loud clicking sound.

A diabolic grin instantly spread across my devil's lips. "Then, maybe Bea will manage to wake me up on time in the morning?"

"I shouldn't spend the night," I rushed to reinforce my earlier statement.

"We're all grown-ups here. I know how things are at your age. No one believes you would abstain until marriage. No one would even believe you if you two would claim you waited longer than the second date to—"

"Debrah," Mr. Clayborne interrupted his spouse. "You'll have to excuse my wife, Bea. Sometimes she can't help herself from saying exactly what she is thinking. And the wine helps." The man pointed toward her empty glass, which strongly reminded me of my own night accompanied by Dionysus's juice.

Mrs. Clayborne stood up. "I'll make up your bed. My son certainly doesn't know how to do it."

"The bed I sleep in is just fine," Cole offered, impatient to get out of there.

"See what I was saying? I'll take this to the kitchen, then change the sheets." His mother smiled, grabbing a few plates.

I gathered a few empty bowls and headed to follow her, but before I could take another step, I felt Cole's hand stopping me. "The sheets are changed," he grumbled, then began to walk me toward his bedroom, almost dragging me along with him.

"I should help her with the dishes," I whispered, still trying to escape from his plan.

Yet, he seemed dead-set to go along with his madness, "She'll manage them this time."

"Cole..." I tried to reason with him.

"Don't make a fuss about it. She sees you like a stray puppy. That's why she asked you to stay the night, so that you don't go back to the Pit. Not because you are my *girlfriend*." He was reminding me of how his world really worked.

"At least she has a heart," I snap back. Not that I ever wanted anyone's pity. But people who truly cared were so rare these days. And I knew all too well Cole wasn't one of them. Still, there was a question that had been troubling me for a while and I couldn't postpone asking it. "And you? How do you see me?"

Amused and honest at the same time, he guided me to his room, offering me an answer I suspected long ago. "Through the eyes of the big bad wolf."

CHAPTER 19

S trange enough, Cole's room was much tidier than the last time I was here. And I couldn't hide my surprise at seeing such an upgraded version of the wolf's den. "Wow, what made you clean up the place?"

"I did it for you, *my love*." His mocking tone assured me of exactly the opposite. Still, it was a little strange that he cleaned his room.

"Always a gentleman." I replied, flaring my nostrils, proving to Cole that the tone didn't belong only to him.

"I'm happy that you noticed. Now this gentleman wants you to kiss him again. You know the rule," he rushed to remind me.

"Yeah, like I mean it," I sighed. "Why are you doing this? I'm not even sure that you enjoy it."

But I seemed to be wrong. "You have no idea how much I *do* enjoy it." He licked his lips while gazing straight at mine. "I love how your eyes flicker in repulsion. And I know it's not because you hate how my mouth fits so perfectly with yours. It's because you hate being told what to do."

He was the most devious type of demon, always coming up with a new way of torturing me.

I took a step closer to him, pressing my palms on the taut muscles of his chest. "Then, let me humor you." My lips merged with his, freeing up every emotion I had bottled up inside. I was kissing him like I meant it. Like he wanted me to. Like my body was about to catch fire.

"A week ago, I never thought that I would ever bring someone here to share my bed." He was letting out a confession in the heat of the moment, a truth that I had a feeling he had barely come to accept.

Lately, I got a lot of those kinds of confessions from the men who just came into my life. I just couldn't deal with their true meanings, and that made me try to avoid that conversation. "Maybe I should leave then." I smiled with no real intention of actually leaving. I was just playing with him.

Cole cocked an eyebrow. "Leave now? After you just cost me my best friend?"

Was he for real? "You call him your friend?" I asked with an obvious hint of disgust hiding in my voice. "I didn't ask you to defend me."

"You didn't have to. I know him; he wouldn't have stopped until he got what he wanted." From the snarl leaving his throat as he spoke, there was no way he would have accepted that.

"Kinda like someone else I know," I muttered. I felt his palm fall heavily on my ass, I couldn't hold in a small whimper, feeling the sting spreading inside of me like something toxic, yet so arousing.

He let his hand glide on the spot he hit, clasping it so tightly that the hot pulses of the pain began echoing through my body. "Your mouth always gets you in trouble," he whispered, close to my lips.

"I'll scream," I threatened.

"Do it. Looking forward to a reason to gag you," he smiled, pushing me toward the bed. I could tell how wicked fantasies were dancing in his mind while his hands rushed to my back to unzip my dress. But an important detail caught his attention, almost making him reconsider his actions even before he had properly begun. "This one is expensive. Who are you opening your legs for to receive a dress like this?"

"You don't have the right to ask that question as long as I'm only standing here because of a deal." I retorted, feeling offended by the vile way he expressed himself.

Not that he seemed to care about offending me. "Really. Is that the only reason you're here?" His palm glided down the small of my back as his eyes began burning with a madness I had never seen before.

"Y...yes," I mumbled. Trying unsuccessfully to push him away, because the words leaving my lips weren't completely honest. I wasn't sure I wanted him to stop, even if I could never make such a dangerous confession to him.

His breath thick with a passion that had my body vibrating in temptation. "Are you still afraid of me, Mouse?"

"I never was." This time, I was lying. I didn't want him to pick up on my fear because he thrived on it, exploiting it until it got him everything he wanted. I didn't only cower in front of the wicked ways in which *his* mind worked; I also dreaded my own mind when around him. And I hated myself for enjoying even a second spent together.

"Don't lie. I can tell when you're lying. I hate it when you're lying. You see, when it comes to you, I'm honest, even if that sometimes hurts. That is a quality you could learn to appreciate about me."

If I were to put my cards up on the table, he never gave me a reason to doubt that—even if in the beginning I suspected him of having some chances to not go through with his part of the deal. I knew he had the ways to help me; I just wasn't sure if he had the heart.

Slowly, Cole seemed to be entrapping me in his illusion, though not tightly enough to make me want to stray from my path. "I'm not opening my legs to anyone," I stated loudly, more likely trying to convince myself rather than just him.

Without wasting another moment, he drove his palms beneath my knees and lifted me to his waist. "You will open them for me," he whispered, keeping me still to look him in the eyes while I could feel his steel erection pressing against my panties.

"What are you doing?" I quivered, already feeling my center ache.

"Spending time with my *girlfriend*." The term was so bizarre coming from his mouth that it almost made me laugh. "Lights off," he called out, and the light sensor followed his command, leaving us in complete darkness.

He seemed to have had plans for us. My legs were forced to brace themselves over his waist, feeling my body leaning back to meet the mattress, and strangely enough, his mouth was searching for mine through the darkness, in slow, unhurried kisses. If I didn't know better, I could have thought this was Ferris, not Cole, because every single one of his gestures was emitting an emotion I never felt before around him. He was enjoying this in a very different way than he used to do during his little games. As if it wasn't just his cock that was asking him to touch me. And with every single move, I could feel control slipping away from him as he was replacing his need to dominate me with something far more seductive.

His body came to rest on top of mine, but not before he made sure my dress rolled completely off my own body. Demanding and needy, his hands yearned to explore my breasts, catching my rosy nipples through the material of my bra and twisting his fingers around them until they came to life for him.

My breath hitched, my core tightened, my mind a beautiful blur, as I searched out his lips.

I felt him beginning to move against me with primal desire, his hips rocking into mine to find even the least bit of friction, his own body tormented by the same pain I was fighting. It felt as if he was igniting his own rhythm in me, getting the pit of my stomach to instantly tremble as an insatiable hunger for him was coming to life.

"For just how long are you going to boil me?" he asked, fingers digging into my hips, almost ready to rip my panties to pieces.

"You know the deal," I whispered, unsure of what I was trying to say. And maybe that's why Cole decided to prevent me from speaking again.

His thumb gently slipped between my lips while his tongue was still moving inside my mouth. "I haven't dry-humped someone since kindergarten." I could feel him smile as his hard limb was grinding against my own needy flesh in a tantalizing rhythm. Luckily, he was still wearing his jeans and I, my panties.

"You were dry-humping people in kindergarten? What was wrong with you?" I asked, laughing, biting his finger, just as a warning. "I'm sure that you can pick anyone from the *line* that always forms behind you to solve your *problem*." I teased him, hinting at the remark he made a couple of days before about every breathing female at the university wanting to fuck him.

"My *problem* needs special treatment." I felt him sliding off his jeans as his kisses intensified their pulse to something more demanding.

That insane friction he was creating against my panties was dampening the material that covered my core, my own panting needy breath could not be withheld. "Cole, I didn't say yes," I whined as I felt him creating an undeniable delirium, which I was one step away from falling into.

His lips kept moving to search for mine, as if his soul, not just his body, craved me, almost stripping me of any power of self-conviction. "Okay," he whispered, even if his actions weren't convincing me he understood what I was asking.

Okay? Nothing could be *okay* when he says *okay*. And to be proven right, he was ignoring me completely. In one move, the lower part of my lingerie was snatched away, leaving his hand to play on that so easily aroused part of me. "Fuck, Mouse. You've got *my* pussy so wet and ready for me. Look at her dripping on the bed for me to touch her," his voice drenched with lust as I felt his fingers gathering my wetness to focus it all over my clit. He was rubbing my damn sensitive nub like he was aiming to break it until the building sensations got my own hips rocking into his hand. "That's it, Mouse, give in to me. I'll take care of you," he whispered the most alluring promise. And although he might have been able to majestically take care of me for the night, my own problems needed *special treatment*. I needed the three deals, not just this one.

I tried to push his hand and get him to stop before I got too out of control to stop myself, but not with any form of complete conviction. My hands were weak, still deciding if I wanted to end things or not. And to turn my decision into a complete torment, his carved lips opened to murmur the strangest confession. "I *need* you tonight," whispered words that revealed a juncture of letters so uncommon for him to ever use—he *needed,* as opposed to him *wanting* things.

I could feel him instinctively jab himself against my opening to the point I was beginning to think that with his next thrust, he would be inside my pussy. "Cole, slow down," I warned before he would have done something that I would have ended up regretting later on.

But all I got in return was a throated groan as his hands fell against my ass, sinking into the flesh. "God, you feel so good, Mouse."

Should I have repeated his statement? Because he felt amazing against me. Our chemistry was sky-rocketing, lifting me from over the bed and raising me so high that I was becoming certain that I had some sort of cosmic connection with him.

A sudden move made me aware that he had just become completely naked. And although my pussy flinched, craving to learn the new sensations he might have so easily offered, reality came kicking in. "Cole, what are you doing?" I cried out, pushing his weight away from me with all my strength, trying to escape to the other side of the bed.

"Obviously a mistake," he muttered, visibly annoyed that I rejected him so brutally.

I knew right away how badly I screwed things up, especially since he let the word *need* slip out in the open, exposing his most personal inner thoughts. It was probably one of the few times he showed any signs of weakness to another person, and I was certain he would do his best to fix that mistake.

"Go to sleep," he ordered, allowing me to remain in my place without any other interaction, turning his back on me.

My eyes instantly filled with tears, almost regretting a life I didn't get to live. I wished I could have been the one to decide how I spent my life. The one who got to choose who she kisses and who she shares a bed with. To be able to choose who I could say *no* to and the one whom I would tell, *"Don't stop"*. The one who makes her own mistakes. And if it came to mistakes, Cole would occupy one of the top spots on the list.

I eventually managed to fall asleep. But I felt Cole tossing and turning all night long, just as if he was sleeping in a foreign bed. Or maybe it was because he was sharing it with me. The certainty was that I managed to infuriate the last of my *kings* as if I had a special gift for doing it.

In a way, I felt guilty. I should have felt guilty if I had a drop of normality left; not because I angered them, but because the time spent alone with the guys was starting to bring me a strange excitement. Little did I know that my decisions would gradually guide me to the exact path I could have taken in the first place, accepting to go further with the Pleasures.

I only opened my eyes in the morning to stare at that perfectly carved face of my twisted king. I was breathlessly waiting to watch the blue cobalt of his eyes come to life as he would wake up. "Stop staring at me. You don't want me fucking you, instead, you pull some psycho shit on me by watching me sleep. And they say I am the one who should get his head checked."

Wow, someone definitely woke up on the wrong side of the bed.

"Get dressed; we wouldn't want Miss Goodie Two-Shoes to be late on my account," he snarled, walking to the bathroom from where he came out dressed for the university. And so was I. In the minutes he spent in the bathroom, I had time to get fully ready for school, although classes weren't exactly what I had in mind for the day. I felt off—confused, maybe even defeated. I was going to see my family, and I was going to end my part of the deal with Brax at the same time. But at what cost? Not only the price of my body but also with the price of my free will. I wasn't the one who would get to choose. And who knows, maybe by making me succumb to this deal, my king of the underworld was stopping me from choosing *him*.

It wasn't long before both Cole and I were in his car, heading toward the university. He was speeding again through the streets as if he was competing in NASCAR, while my heart seemed to be preparing to escape my chest. "Please slow down," I whimpered, trying to hold on to anything I could.

Not that my pleading was helping in any way. "You already used your request of the week last night. I get to do whatever the fuck I please now."

"For you to get to do whatever you want to would imply that we would both make it there alive," I snapped, afraid that he'd get us both killed.

"We will, don't worry. I won't let you get away that easily. I'm far from being done with you." I took his words exactly as they sounded. A threat, one that I was sure he would make good on.

"Come on," he ordered me as soon as we got out of the car.

"Where?" I asked in total confusion, seeing him grabbing the upper part of my arm and almost dragging me to the front entrance.

What on earth was going on?

I shortly received the answer to that question. Before I realized what was truly happening, I was walking beside him, right to the main end of the hallway. The place was crawling with students, and our arrival seemed to have caught all their attention. Everyone was staring at us as if they were getting ready to watch the most entertaining show. I was beginning to believe Cole was about to give them one. And I was going to be a part of it.

"Why did you bring her here?" I could hear the confusion in Nick's voice as we walked past him. He was just asking out loud a question that I was just about to address myself.

The king ignored him, guiding me a few feet away from the small group of students Nick was a part of. "Shut the fuck up, Nick," he snarled, putting his disciple in his place while I could see everybody's heads shifting to look straight at me.

I was in trouble, and I knew it.

"I have a present for you, Mouse," Cole whispered, turning me to face him.

Suddenly, I became all too aware of the wicked thoughts that were glittering in his eyes. I didn't have a chance to react. His hands locked on my waist so tightly that I felt I was losing all drops of oxygen. The pain was forcing my eyes to raise and look up at him, acknowledging his next gesture.

But it couldn't have been possible.

Why would he ever do *that*?

In slow-motion, his head tilted, unhurriedly advancing towards me, not because he was in a habit of taking things slowly, but because he wanted me to live through every last second of it. His lips were inches away from mine, melting every beating cell with his intoxicating cologne. He brought his mouth down to meet mine, publicly claiming me as his. Sure, it wasn't the first time that we kissed, but this... this was a whole new beginning, not necessarily for the two of us, but for me. He was kissing me in front of everyone, making a statement whilst placing an invisible crown on my head. "Say hi to the fans, Queen B," he whispered inside my mouth, placing me on the throne next to him.

The kiss was exactly that, my coronation, offering me with one single touch of the lips supreme power over all of Echo City University.

A power I didn't want.

A power that *he* knew I didn't want.

It was far from being a present. It was both a punishment and a god-damned curse, taking me out of the corner of anonymity I loved so much and casting me straight into the strongest spotlight.

He was consciously throwing me to the wolves, watching with amusement, to see if I was to be ripped into pieces, or if I would come out as the leader of the pack. Not that he would care. He would just drain me of whatever he was after, satisfying his own interests; then he would return to look in as an outsider at his own game.

"This isn't a present, and you know it," I muttered under my breath.

"Do I? Maybe I was just letting my feelings for you get the better of me," he cackled as if he just made the best joke.

I didn't answer. I just left, knowing exactly what his chess move had brought upon me. With that kiss, I became his *Cinderella*—from rags to riches. From then on, I had to stay away from all the witches who would envy me. But the trick was, I also ruled every single one of them, handing me with a power I wasn't ready to exploit.

I couldn't deal with spending the day at school, at least not with everything going on lately, so I left for home right before the first class began.

My clothes hit the floor the second I entered my apartment,

I headed straight to my walk-in shower. Funny, I now had a *walk-in shower* while my old apartment was entirely a walk-in-bathroom since I could bathe wherever I wanted with my *tub* being a small metal basin that I used to fill from out of a barrel.

How things have changed in such a short time. And yet, how happy I would have been to still have the life I had two years ago, alongside my family. Though I couldn't think that way, especially when everything was set to change again. By the next day, I had every chance to be standing with my brother and sister right in my new living room. And that had the power to erase everything I did to get them here.

My fingers were running through my dresses, searching for something to wear tonight. I was even thinking about wearing my old clothes since going to visit Brax dressed in something Ferris had bought me just didn't seem right. Before I got to decide on an outfit, I heard my phone ringing.

Judging from the ringtone, it was Ferris.

"I hope I'm not interrupting your classes," as thoughtful as ever, he was first checking with me that I was okay to talk.

"No, I actually came home earlier today," I confessed.

The tone of his voice suddenly sounded worried. *"Is everything okay?"*

"Yes, I'm just nervous. I think my family might come to town tomorrow." My voice trembled with the words.

"That's great news."

"Are you returning tonight? I don't think I can come to visit you if you do... I'm sorry." I rushed to excuse myself.

"It's okay. I have other plans for tonight anyway." Even though his tone wasn't implying anything, the thought that he might have made plans with somebody else unsettled me.

It was causing an abyss to form at the bottom of my stomach, threatening to swallow me whole.

But I couldn't react. I had no right to, especially since I was the one setting the rules of whatever was between us. I had other *arrangements,* so why couldn't he?

Maybe the thought just hit me more strongly because, out of all three of my kings, I considered him to be the most unlikely to find another companion. Or maybe it was because I was developing some kind of feelings for him. Then again, there could always have been the chance that I was wrong, and *his plans* involved something completely different. Though I couldn't ask, I wasn't in a position to. Asking could only increase his power over me. "I understand," was the only answer I could provide, even if, in reality, I didn't understand a thing.

"We'll make plans for the next few days. I'll share you with your family, maybe you could squeeze me in sometime after midnight?" He continued, and I could feel from his tone that his *plans* were referring to a certain something he left unfinished the other day due to my *inebriated* state.

"Maybe I'll *squeeze you in* for an entire day. That is, if you would like to meet my brother and sister," I giggled.

"That sounds amazing. Hold on; there's someone on the other line."

Holding on was the only thing I could do at that time since I felt pretty tired. "Okay."

"On second thought, I'll call you in half an hour. You aren't going anywhere, are you?" he asked, in a rush to hang up.

"No, at least not for a few hours, I said."

"Just make sure to pick up."

"I will," I chuckled, sensing a masked excitement in his voice.

And since I was already sleepy, I must have dozed off. I just cuddled up on the couch, waiting for him to call me. The phone seemed to have rung straight after I had closed my eyes, although the clock on the wall was telling me a different time.

"Sorry, I was late. I didn't want to call you from the car, so I waited to reach my hotel room," he tried to excuse himself.

"It's okay. I fell asleep on the couch anyway."

"Did I bore you to death?" I could hear him laugh.

"Not a chance."

"Then the opposite?" Ferris asked in a throaty tone that instantly changed the mood, making my back slightly arch on the couch and my ears pay extra attention.

I shall call it *the Ferris effect.*

"Yes, the opposite. You never bore me. Maybe put me to sleep." A laugh escaped my lips, "But never bore me."

"So, you miss me?" his voice hoarse, hiding a certain intonation.

"Yes," I groused, realizing exactly how much I wanted his warm arms to replace the couch. I just wished I could be sure that his *plans* for the night wouldn't lead to anyone else occupying my place in his bed. I didn't even know why I was jealous. I didn't own him; it was the other way around.

"I want to see how you miss me," Ferris suddenly demanded.

"I'll draw you a sketch." I made fun of him because, unless he had some satellite spying on me, it was impossible for him to see me.

"I have a better way." As he finished his words, there was a knock on the door. *"Answer it."*

And I did, coming face to face with a delivery man. "Sign here, please," the man handed me a delivery note and a pen. The next thing I knew, a small black box was in my hands, waiting for me to open it.

"Go on," Ferris confirmed.

I opened the package, revealing a state-of-the-art phone that looked extremely expensive.

"Did you get it?" he asked.

"Yes, but I already have a phone." Okay, the thing I was holding in my hand could barely be called a phone, but at least it still had reception.

I could hear him laugh. *"No offense, but that isn't a phone. Maybe they'll take it as an artifact in a museum."*

I huffed. "Real funny."

"I always am. And as for the very fun part, I want you to take your SIM card out of this phone and put it into the new one. You don't have to do anything else but hit call. I made sure every setup was already completed, including putting in my number, so I'll be waiting for you."

"OK." I hung up, replacing the cards—just as he told me to, then hit the call button again.

"That was quick," I could feel him smile from the other end. *"Now, I really want to see how much you missed me."*

In my world, all feelings and emotions had to be kept hidden. It was the only way to survive; therefore, confessing them to any other living being seemed like asking for the impossible. "I'm not too good with these kinds of words."

"No words. Show me. Switch to the camera," he asked.

What was up with him?

I put my tongue out at him as his image appeared on the screen. "Done."

"You look so pretty today." Such a charmer.

However, I knew he was trained to be a gentleman. "I just woke up; I'm *pretty* sure that you're just being polite right now," I said, trying to rearrange my hair.

"No, I just love the way you look in the morning."

I threw him a smile as I raised myself onto my elbows to get up from the couch. "Please, sell one of my dresses and get yourself a pair of glasses."

"Don't get up. Stay there. The way the light hits your body is amazing." What was up with all this flattery?

I found his strange behavior quite amusing. "Aww, do you want to take a picture of me? Let me fix my hair," I said, although I was starting to doubt that he was joking.

"What are you wearing?" he asked in an even hoarser voice.

I still hadn't managed to find an outfit before I dozed off, so I remained dressed in what I was in when I got out of the bathroom. "A bathrobe."

"Show it to me," he smiled, a hidden intent in his voice.

I lifted the phone so he could see me from above. "You want to see my fluffy robe? Okay... I'm pretty sure that I have a sleeping mask with a fluffy Koala bear somewhere. You must know about it since I guess you bought it. Do you want me to put that on?" I was still amusing myself when, in fact, things were as serious as they got.

"No, Bea. I want you to open the robe." His words filled with a sexual vibe made me glance straight at the screen. A tremble was taking control of my body, seeing his eyes gleaming with that same gaze I noticed before I left his bedroom the other day —only this time, it was spiced with uncontrollable lust.

"I... I'm not wearing a bra," I stuttered.

"I was counting on that."

"Ferris," I was surprised by this turn of events.

"Don't make me use my prerogatives." I couldn't tell if he was just making fun of me, or if he would ensure I followed his plan and actually used our deal as leverage. I was hoping for the first option, and that he wouldn't be the same as Brax or Cole. But then again, sometimes a stubborn heart can be blinded by the lies we want to believe.

And he was making sure I followed through. *"Do it, Bea."*

I gulped, swallowing the knot that formed in my throat, then lowered my hand to unfasten the cord that held the robe together.

"Push it aside," his instructions kept rolling, just as I thought I may have had a small chance to escape this without exposing my naked body to him. There was none, and the next gesture I made left the plush material to fall away on the sides, revealing my breasts. *"You make me want to be with you so badly... to touch you."* His thick tone brought a strange torment right where he intended—within my core.

But I could also play dirty. I brought my hand to pull my robe back together. "Then maybe I should cover myself back up, so I don't raise your appetite."

Not that he was allowing me to deviate from the course he was setting, *"No. Drag your hand lower. You know where,"*

I huffed. "Are you kidding me?"

His head shook *no*, making sure I clearly understood exactly where he was taking things.

"Don't make me do this," I whined, hoping it would get him to stop.

Instead, a grin spread across his lips. *"You'll thank me later."*

"No, I won't. I will not speak to you later," I hissed, pouting at the screen.

"I have faith in myself. I have my ways. Now, go on," he continued in the same aroused tone.

Seeing there was no way of changing his mind, my hand fell lower, reaching the hem of my panties. I needed to take a deep breath before slowly letting it slide beneath them. Maybe I could have kept the panties on and fooled him into thinking I was following his instructions.

Ferris was much sneakier than I was. *"No. Take them off."*

Shit!

"I can't let you see this," I whimpered, feeling totally unprepared for his plans.

But there was no backing off from his side. *"Oh, you will. Lower the phone and take them off."*

"You are sick," I whimpered, trying to mentally prepare to do what he wanted.

"You have no idea. I'll show you someday," he grinned. *"Now, do as I say. On second thought, put the phone on the couch pillow so I won't stress you out holding it."*

"So thoughtful of you," I growled, yet followed his instructions. There wasn't much else I could have done anyway.

"I just want to enjoy the show," he confessed, eyes flickering with anticipation.

Jesus, he was no different than Brax.

Admitting to myself that I had no way out, my fingers began moving against my sensitive folds. I was searching for even the smallest sign of dampness, but I could find none. I was too stressed to enjoy myself, especially without his physical touch. I tried, again and again, to find some stimulation, to the point where the useless movement was beginning to irritate my nerves. It was just the way my body functioned, I couldn't get off without being touched by a man. "Ferris, I can't. You know I can't..."

"Close your eyes, Bea. You are so fucking hot right now," he whispered in a tone so seductive that it was having a tingly effect on my core.

I needed him to help me out with this. "I closed them," I snarled.

He instantly felt the annoyance in my voice. *"Stop pouting and listen to me. Imagine that your fingers are my own. That I am the one touching you,"* he paused, leaving me time to get into the *mood.* I wasn't sure it was going to work, but I needed to try to end the *horrible ordeal* he was subjecting me to.

"Now, move them as you would like me to move. Like you would lead my hand.'

My fingers began skimming my sensitive skin, searching for the zones that brought me the greatest pleasure in the past and retracing the touch of my kings. I began working my fingers over them, slow at first, then faster, hoping to at least get the dampness I needed. *"I'll tell you where I would be... a little higher."* Ferris was guiding me to a different zone from where

I was grinding my fingers, right above my clit. *"A little faster. I want to see your clit swollen and blushed with that perfect shade of bright pink."* It might have been impossible, but somehow, he seemed to know my body better than I did. The spot he asked me to explore instantly made my feet buckle into the couch beneath me.

"Perfect." The excitement in his voice seemed to be reflected in my nerve endings, and every single one of his words managed to send me closer and closer to ecstasy. *"I could teach you one or two more tricks. But I'll keep them to myself for now. I want to make you melt under me the next time I see you. Would you like that?"*

I didn't answer, mostly because I was preoccupied with my current assignment but also because I was much too shy to express everything Ferris was asking of me. I didn't want the conversation to go that way, especially since I could feel him so warmed up that he was almost ready to ask for much more than what our deal offered him.

He didn't seem to be giving up. *"I asked if you would like that?"* he insisted.

Why do men always think they should receive answers when they deflect from answering women most of the time?

My answer—*the truth and nothing but the truth.* "Yes... I would." My own voice was cracking under his guidance, pushing me to the verge of falling apart as my core was preparing for that tightening sensation.

My rhythm was sublime, finding the perfect balance to shatter my inhibitions and discovering a way to be set free, while Ferris gave me just the words I needed to cross that line. *"It's my hand, Bea."* His whispers made me dream of him being next to me, helping me find beautiful rapture. And at the same time, allowing him to strengthen one of those invisible strings that were wrapping around me, binding me to him in yet another way.

"I'm starting to think that the phone was the best gift I could ever get you. Pretty tough to outshine this one. But I'll try." I could hear the playful amusement in his voice as my moment of bliss seemed to have already been noticed.

Ferris just pushed me over my comfort limit, and although that brought that insatiable tremble to my core, it almost made me die of embarrassment. "I never want to speak to you again."

"You say that now, but wait till I get my hands on you," he warned me, with every intention to make good on his word.

"Goodbye, Ferris." I hung up to the sounds of his laughter. Unwillingly, I was letting the dark side of him get to me as tiny sparkles of that special afterglow were residing in me, making me dream of the moment when he would be the one touching me. And that was leading me down a dangerous path because I was starting to feel that way about *all three* of the men who owned me.

CHAPTER 20

My limbs were trembling long after I hung up the phone, while my body seemed to have been unable to stand or even move. I was angry with Ferris, and I was even angrier with myself because I began to think I was intentionally blinding myself when it came to him. Still, I was unable to prevent it; he had a power over me that I couldn't understand or explain. There wasn't much I could do anyway when it came to the deals I accepted, just shut my eyes tightly and wait for my journey to be over and all my efforts to finally be repaid.

It must've been around seven in the evening when I woke up again, looking directly out the window only to notice it was dark outside. It was dark most of the time, but we could still tell night from day, especially up in the Hills where even nature seemed to be kinder to the privileged few.

My body was refusing to move from the spot, my feet felt like they'd been tied to the bed. Yet I needed to get myself together because time wasn't on my side. The two days were gone. It was time for Brax to collect his *payment*.

Regrouping my strength, I walked to the dressing room, attempting to finally decide on what to wear. There was still no message from Brax. He was supposed to text me with the time, or at least the place to meet him. But nothing had lit up my phone screen ever since I talked to Ferris.

Maybe he got caught up with business and just forgot, or perhaps he needed to postpone the date of the rescue operation. Although deep down, I hoped that wouldn't be the case since I so desperately wanted to see my family.

With no idea where I was going, or if I was even going to meet Brax tonight, I slipped into a red satin nightdress and put on a matching robe. All chances were that I'd wear one of the dresses I had on during my last encounters with him—either the one I purchased or the one he bought for me. I would choose when I received a message from him.

There wasn't much else I could do except sit around and wait. So, for the first time in a long time, I turned on the TV.

"I am Legacy Abbot, and I give you the Echo City evening news," the anchorman said with a worried tone. It seemed my timing to watch TV was just right to catch up with the latest events. *"Tonight, we'll start with the most important news of the evening, which we'll continue debating with a few special guests later on.*

An artisanal bomb detonated an hour ago in the Hills, destroying the front lawn and a few first-floor rooms of Mr. Delarose's house.

We are still uncertain if it was a threat or just a failed assassination attempt, but this terrorist act won't pass by without any consequences. Mr. Delarose is the main pawn in the City Board, some even considering that the mayor reports directly to him.

This act is suspected to be a declaration of war from the so-called Annelids—"

A knock on the door interrupted me from watching the complete news, but unfortunately, *for all further events*, I got the essentials.

I presumed it was one of Brax's men.

And I wasn't even dressed yet!

I'll just tell them to wait since his boss can't even find three free seconds to send a damn text. Or at least, this was the scenario playing in the back of my mind. But as I opened the door, I was unable to hide my surprise. "Brax?"

Brax himself came to *visit* me. Though, if it wasn't for the signature way he held his cigars and those to-die-for absinthe eyes, I could have barely recognized him. He was different. Not in a bad way different. He looked like a damn mesmerizing dream—just when I thought he couldn't get any more good-looking than he already was.

There was no suit this time. Just a black t-shirt, black jeans, and a jacket, leaving me to see him, for a split second, like a normal man. But I knew better, and the normality he was displaying was actually scaring me to death.

"Were you expecting someone else?" he asked, utterly annoyed that I didn't invite him in the second I opened the door.

Perhaps his new appearances have deprived me of my manners. "No... I wasn't expecting anyone. Not even you. Maybe I was expecting your car or a phone call, but certainly not you."

"So, are you going to keep me at your door just because I don't have a written invitation?" he snarled.

"No, of course not. Come in." I took a few steps backward to make enough room for him to enter the door. I just couldn't take my eyes off him. Such a huge difference from the man I usually see.

He quickly observed how surprised I was to see him like that. "You're staring," he grunted.

"Well, I have a good reason. You look different," I replied, trying to get a grip on myself.

"Yeah... I've been away on business and will be leaving again soon," he said with a certain worry coating his words.

"Soon... I thought—" I thought the night we would spend together wouldn't be something to be rushed.

"Soon as in a few hours. Don't tell me you thought I would stay the night and cuddle with you?" he said, sardonically, making sure again I understood this was only a deal.

I couldn't put a finger on what was wrong with him, but his clothes weren't the only thing that had changed. His attitude was taking a dive for the worse.

"I don't need your pity, Brax. I need your help." I tried to hold my ground so I wouldn't let him know how much his cranky mood was affecting me.

"And I need a drink. Do you have any around here?" he asked, looking around like he was studying the place, or more likely, assessing its market value.

"Wine," I pointed toward a small display shelf where a dozen properly aged bottles of wine were waiting. I just hoped he wouldn't ask me to join him because, after my latest experience, it would be a while before I would put my lips on a glass of alcohol again.

Brax didn't seem pleased with my selection of drinks. "Wine is for the ladies. Anything else?"

The apartment had a bar, but I never had the curiosity to open it.

I walked to the wooden handcrafted furniture and pulled open the door that hid the drinks. Gin, rum, vodka, champagne, and a vast selection of pretty much everything else except for whiskey—Brax's favorite drink.

"Vodka?" I asked, unsure of what to bring him.

"That will do. Search for the largest glass you have and fill it. We need to talk business first." He paused, as if he had something on his mind. "And fetch a glass for yourself."

"I don't want to drink," I quickly replied.

"Did my *request* sound like I was asking?" he snapped. The arrogant bastard always thought the world should bow at his feet. And I couldn't do anything to change that.

"No. It didn't." I poured two drinks into different-sized glasses, then handed him the largest one, as he *requested.*

"Quite a place you got *for yourself.* Did you make a *deal* to get it?" he asked, furrowing an eyebrow. I knew where he was going with this, and it was fine by me. It was the truth anyway. "Who's the lucky man?" Jealousy or envy, I couldn't quite discern.

"I can't give you his name. It wouldn't be fair." I tried protecting Ferris's identity.

"*Fair*....right." He took the last drag of his cigarette. "I don't give a fuck, as long as he's not screwing you."

"He's not," I reassured him.

"Well, in a couple of hours, you'll be free to do whatever you please," he spoke as if he didn't give a fuck about what I did once our deal was concluded.

"Yes... *free*," the word seemed so bizarre, probably because I would never be free again. My nights will belong to Ferris, while some broken pieces of me will always belong to all of them. Every one of them took a part of me, turning me into a delicate ceramic decoration wearing the signs of being dropped on the floor.

Taking a deep breath, I tried to calm myself and mask my emotions as well as I could. I didn't need Brax to know how deeply the deals were getting to me. I didn't want to give him that kind of power over me, because, in the end, I was just entertainment to him. He didn't even bother to try to find out more about whose house this was. And that came off as rather strange since I knew information meant power in his world. Information was everything, no matter how big or small you were. However, this time, it was like he was deliberately avoiding caring, taking every precaution to ensure he knew nothing more about me than he needed to.

"What happened to your hand?" I asked, looking at a white cloth that was soaked in blood and wrapped around a wound that looked like it extended across all of his knuckles.

He definitely didn't seem pleased that I noticed, let alone that I brought it up. "Rough day at work. The fucking riots are doing my head in," he muttered, clutching his fists.

"I heard about them. There was news about a bomb on TV earlier," I said, realizing that I didn't get to watch the entire news.

"Yeah, well soon that's all it's going to be on TV. You know, you're bringing your family into a burning town." Brax let out a worrying confession.

But there was nothing worse than living with my father. "I'm taking them out from a burning town."

"You're right. It's probably the whole fucking world that's about to catch fire." Brax replied, and for the first time, I saw fear and concern in the eyes of the man who showed none before.

Things were serious. It was a matter of life and death, and I could feel him losing ground. This is a war that won't leave him unaffected. And I needed him to fulfill his part of the deal before all hell broke loose. "So, when are your men going to get my family out?"

"Tonight," he took a step in my direction, placing his empty vodka glass on the arm of the sofa.

"I was expecting to see them... before..." I babbled.

But, as always, Brax was straight to the point. "Before I get to have you? You don't trust me, is that it?"

I couldn't tell him that I was apprehensive when it came to him. After all, he was a mobster. "I...I do. I just want to know they're safe."

"I'll make sure they're safe, no matter what. That's a promise I'm willing to make to you." With another step, he closed in the distance between us.

My heart was pounding so loudly, I felt as though I could hear the sound of my own blood racing through my veins. It seemed to be trying to beat its way out of my chest.

"I need this now," he pushed the robe off of one of my shoulders, letting it slowly slip down my arm and expose my collarbone. "I might not return to claim my prize."

Wait, what?

"You're going with them?" I was more startled than surprised that he was going to join the rescue mission. In a way, it made me feel a hundred times more relieved regarding the mission's success. But on the other hand, it gave me more reasons to be worried. More people to be worried about.

"If you want something done right, you'd better do

it yourself. And this has to be done right." He stated, underscoring the importance of this mission for him.

Nervously, I brought my nails to my lips to chew on them, just like a child. "So, I guess we won't be seeing each other after this."

"You will come searching for me," he smiled, showing off that arrogant attitude of his again.

But things wouldn't work out that way. "Brax, I won't, and you know it."

"Then you're smart," he said, pushing the other part of the robe off my shoulder. "Untie it." Gesturing to the cord that still held my clothing together, and since his wish was *my command*, the next second, the material was a red puddle at our feet.

A strange pause followed as the green color of his eyes analyzed every feature of my face, almost as if he was drawing a mental picture, immortalizing this moment. Maybe that's what he did with each conquest he crossed off his list —thoroughly scanning them so that he could keep them all stored up in a place where no one else but him could reach. Like a mental shelf of trophies, because that's what I was to him—a golden trophy, reaffirming that he always got what he wanted.

"Where is the bedroom?" he asked in a heavy voice, looking behind me like he was trying to guess the right door.

"Here," I turned to walk in front of him, leading him to a corridor, and then toward the bedroom. "It will be okay. Won't it? Everyone will be okay, right?" The worry that was consuming me from within forced me to ask.

"They will be here, as I promised," he answered, convinced of his success.

"I was asking about everyone, Brax," I said, stopping in

front of the bed and raising my eyes to gaze into his own, seeking the true answers I needed.

Little did I know how badly his answers would hurt. "You will probably hate me by the time I walk out this door. So, *everyone* won't be of your concern. And that's okay... You hating me. It's not love I am searching for."

"Then what are you searching for?" I asked, almost biting back a tear.

"Satisfaction. Physical pleasure."

"You can find that every day of the week with much less trouble. Maybe you should search for the truth because I'm beginning to think that you're lying to yourself." I replied, feeling hurt by his indifference, but also with a glimmer of hope that he still had something decent within him.

"Maybe *you* should search for the truth because I'm beginning to think it is *you* who is lying to yourself, Bea."

Was I? Was I fooling myself so I could cope with the weight of what I needed to do for each of my kings? Was I creating a false illusion just so I wouldn't see the men who owned me for what they really were?

"You're right. Maybe I am." The bitterness in my voice didn't go unnoticed. Still, his hand raised to find my neckline, tracing a path from under my ear to the strap of my silk night dress.

For a moment, I stopped breathing, prisoner to a consuming feeling, so different from anything I ever experienced before. His lips soon followed the path of his hand while his tongue pressed against every inch of my skin, almost impossibly slow. I wished he would waste the time he had left before he needed to leave just exploring every nerve ending of my body. But that was just the insane part of me, the masochist side that was determined to torture my soul to its greatest extent. I couldn't allow myself to fall for this man. I had no reason to even like him. Yet, I couldn't stop that maddening rhythm in my heart whenever he touched me.

A gasp that couldn't be contained escaped me as I felt his hand clutch tightly on one of my breasts. He was tugging the dress aside to search for that primordial flesh-on-flesh sensation.

In a last attempt to keep my sanity, I seemed to follow some in-built self-defense mechanisms. I tried to back away and set even the slightest distance between us, but with his palm still grasping my breast, I only managed to hurt myself by forcing him to tighten the grip.

"Bea, all sorts of shit has been happening to me today. So, I need you to behave so things won't get out of control. Okay?"

"Okay." I nodded, mostly out of fear because I could tell he was barely keeping himself together.

My confirmation brought the pressure he held on my breast to lessen, as his thumb began slowly moving, skimming my hardened nub. "Good." His lips descended to attend to the round shape he just mistreated, lustfully moving his mouth on its entire surface, until he stopped to take my nipple between his teeth. A move, almost brutal, but altogether so arousing that I felt my core tighten.

My legs pressed together in the most useless attempt to subdue the craving that had begun controlling me. My dress slipped, abandoning my body and puddling at my feet as his hands and lips were so focused on my breasts that I felt I was going to melt alongside the fabric. His mouth slid lower, reaching the side of my ribcage, his tongue gliding across my sensitive skin, causing goosebumps to decorate the path he was creating, pleasure shooting through my body to my core.

I know he asked me not to move, but how could I remain still when my body wasn't obeying me any longer?

He immediately noticed my thighs rubbing together in anticipation. "What did I just say?" his tone demanding. His grip was so hard on my waist that it would certainly leave bruises come morning.

Crushing me to him, his teeth dug in to graze my flat stomach, a few of his fingers strode over the material of my panties, moving through the wetness coated there to bring me unimaginable pleasure.

I replaced any answer with a tremble. A shiver ran across my body, making me almost cry out in both anger and helplessness. I wasn't helpless when it came to Brax; I was helpless when it came to **me**, *unable* to control my inner reactions. Yet somehow, totally *able* to allow his lips to ignite every cell in my body.

Then he decided to break me, with magical incantations made by the twists of his tongue as if he was writing them along my skin. His mouth descended toward my navel, while at the same time, his hand was gliding somewhere around the hem of my panties.

Deep down I feared what would come next. I knew from Ferris that his tongue was going to press against my belly button, creating that lightning bolt again to split me in half as it traveled straight to my core. And the sensation was there again as his fingers pushed my panties aside, sneaking between my folds and grinding over that tiny nub that would make me instantly bow in front of him.

I let my palms search his shoulders for support, taken by surprise by the quake he had raised within me. I expected him to be angry, infuriated by my lack of control since I wasn't able to listen to his command and remain still. But in response, he raised his eyes to glance at the tremor my own two orbs reflected. "It's okay, Bea. It's okay." He let out a devious grin, turning his fleshy lips to a thin line. His fingers drove to play between my damp flesh as his tongue went up to taste the curves of my breasts again.

Somewhere between the nibbling of my nipples and that intensifying sensation in my throbbing core, I found myself being lifted to his waist.

He slowly laid me down on the bed, then *my beast* moved on top of me, muscles fully tensed, arranging himself between the tight grip of my thighs. Hauling his black t-shirt over his head, he threw it to the floor, returning to tend to my needs before he got a chance to take his next breath.

"I forgot about these," he said as he toyed with the edge of my panties. The problem was quickly solved as he raised my legs over his hips to tug the unwanted material over my ankles, while he unbuckled his belt.

The sound of the metal buckle coming undone brought me to my senses, as I was becoming all too aware of what was to happen next. "Did you bring... you know..." I was such an idiot that I was too embarrassed to even ask the question all the way.

"A rubber?" Brax and his big mouth, always straight to the point, while the conversation seemed extremely awkward to me. "I don't want to use one with you."

He looked at me as if I was the forbidden fruit, and he was about to enter The Garden of Eden. "But I do use one with everyone else, so you don't need to worry. When was the last time you had your—"

I cut him off again. "I've been on birth control for awhile. My doctor prescribed it to fix some.... how should I say this? Monthly issues."

"Good, 'cause I want things to be perfect," he said with a hindered breath, leaning on top of me as I felt his pants slip over his feet.

Perfect? He had a lot to learn about what the term *perfect* meant.

Before I had any possibility to act again as the awkward introvert I usually am, his lips regained their position, as did his hand, moving even stronger than before as if he was aiming to make me squeal out in ecstasy within seconds.

Without warning, I felt one of his fingers gliding within me. Instantly, I arched against the mattress, buckling up to try and endure the pain I knew was coming. But the second Brax felt me tense, he raised his head from over my breasts to glance straight at me.

The discomfort was preventing me from finding pleasure, even though, when it came to provoking pleasure, I did not doubt that he had a master's degree on the subject. He began to move slowly while another of his fingers slipped inside me, and then another, stretching me to the max. The intrusion made my gaze become a blur. I couldn't even see him clearly anymore. In fact, I couldn't see anything. I just needed to close my eyes and survive the night.

"Look at me. I want you to see me as I make you mine in every way," he growled, bringing me back to my senses. If only so that I could stare into the depths of the absinthe color of his eyes. He was searching for something within the lines of my face. Maybe it was the way my lips were parting as I was trying to deal with the pain caused by his fingers grinding within my walls. Or, maybe it was the way I was clenching my teeth as I felt him so intimately close. I couldn't tell, but I noticed flickers of anxiety glittering in his eyes each time a new emotion passed over my face.

Slowly, the pain began to subside, being replaced by consuming need. And as I came to think about it, Brax was probably waiting for just that moment. He wasn't there for my anguish; he was there for my ecstasy.

His thumb moved over my throbbing clit, sending a whole new sensation racing through my body. Converting the pain to pleasure, and with each move, I seemed to be relaxing. My breath became shallow, my pussy needed to swallow his fingers whole.

Just as I was falling prey to that rhythm, I felt him move to dispose of his boxers. With one long move, he replaced his fingers with the hard part of him that wanted me so badly. That impossible-to-bear sensation was back again, chasing away the elation and bringing back that quiet anguish.

The strange discomfort made me wrap my arms around his broad neck, hoping I would get him to slow down or maybe even stop. He didn't. Brax was set on claiming his payment while making good on his word; this was only physical pleasure to him. With my head buried against his shoulder, he quickly breached the last bit of distance between us, impaling me on his hard cock.

I didn't even know which one was more intense, the necessity to have him inside me or the sensation that his cock was in danger of splitting me in half. But even if I didn't want it, I *needed* more of him.

One of his hands closed around the back of my neck to keep my head against his shoulder while I could hear his jaw clench, teeth almost breaking under their strength. My own teeth were sinking into his inked flesh, trying to withstand the sensation of being so full yet still wanting all of him. But there was something bothering me even more than that, I was giving him my virginity as the result of a deal, and not as my willing choice.

Brax seemed to be avoiding my lips. From the second he entered that door he never kissed me once. Perhaps it was my paranoid nature, but I had a suspicion it had something to do with him not wanting to get attached to me... you know, catch the plague called *feelings*. And whatever danger I may have posed to him, he was disposing of it second by second, removing every form of emotion from the room with every single one of his rough thrusts.

Still, no matter what my mind wanted to believe, the fluttering tingles beneath my waist were letting me know that my body didn't agree with the rational part of me. It had just switched over to the enemy lines without showing off a single form of regret.

With every one of his moves, my teeth needed his shoulder for his support less, although they were leaving behind a red trace to tattoo themselves next to some of the black drawings inked on his skin. As always, Brax took advantage of the moment and shifted his head lower to reach for my hardened nipples once again, as if he were trying to complete a circle that would cause some kind of addiction to him.

Reality became a blur. My king was so mesmerizingly close to me, like a part of the puzzle that was missing all along. Sure, I knew that it was just me feeling this way, but for a moment, I needed to believe it to be true. I needed to find a reasonable explanation for what I was doing, anything except for succumbing to the cruel reality—I was only exchange currency in a deal.

I felt him move like a tidal wave that crashed on the rocks, over and over again, with lost breaths and eyes tightened until I couldn't breathe myself. My core felt ready to explode, my feet were moving aimlessly between the sheets, my limbs only tangling further into the sea of silk in a useless hope of anchoring myself. I was becoming clay in his hands, and he, my most skilled potter.

Sensing I was losing all contact with reality, his arms wrapped around me and whirled me around. He was raising my body on top of him until he was sitting on the pillows, and I was facing him, with my knees gripping both sides of his waist. From that position, he seemed even larger, in fact, so big that I couldn't even move—though that wasn't a problem since he decided to do it for me. "This little cunt will need to suffer a little for pleasure," Brax groaned, gripping my waist. Contrary to his rough tone, he was handling me like a snowflake. His muscular arms were guiding my body to move against him slower, then faster, until feeling him inside me was becoming a pleasure I could barely handle. Yet, I still craved every single motion, each thrust aimed to make me discover what I was *missing out on.*

But, as usual, his *unique* nature had to ruin things. "Good girl," he groaned with the satisfaction of the man who knew exactly what he was saying.

"Fuck you, Brax," I muttered since he knew damn well I didn't like when he called me that.

He suddenly stopped, taking his hands away from my waist and placing them on the sheets, on both sides of his body. "Go ahead, do it. Fuck me!" he snapped, waiting for me to go through with my words. "Move," he ordered again, using his specific accent of superiority.

He was pushing me over my limits, and this time I couldn't help myself. I let my palm fall over his face, filling the room with a powerful clasp.

Maybe I was utterly insane, but I wanted to do it again, to bring some sense into him.

I never got a chance to do it the second time. Brax caught

my hand, drawing it behind my back as his lips finally came crashing down on mine. He was devouring everything in me. I could feel us vibrating like two magnets uniting, stronger and stronger every time he pushed himself inside of me. That impressive mass of muscles was flexing to keep me moving against him through faded moans and victorious groans. Tiny drops of our sweat were moistening the sheets beneath us. It felt more than just amazing. It felt like we were supposed to be doing this all along. Like our bodies together were designed to do this all along.

There was passion, and there was lust, no one could deny that, not even Brax. And for the first time, I saw another side of him. He was kissing me like there was no tomorrow, entrapping a part of us forever in this room. For that moment in time, he wasn't *fucking* me, as he liked to believe, he was making love to me. Sure, the movements were meant to drive our bodies over the edge, but passion was fueling our hearts.

The fire I knew always burned within him was torching me with its flames. Consuming me. Breaking me. Building me.

It was so far from being just a deal at that moment, the same way we were far from ever being two strangers. The ropes of fate were tightening around us with every moan of incoming ecstasy, with every kiss that wasn't in any way mechanical. It was heartfelt.

But unexpectedly, just as everything was reaching a new peak, his lips broke away from mine, and he began shaking his head as if some kind of monster got inside of it.

It took only a short second from when he had *disappeared* until he returned to me, yet he seemed to have lost a part of himself along the way. Brax had allowed me to get too close to him, and I was about to pay the price for his mistake. His mouth was suddenly too far away for me to reach it as he whirled us both until my back was the one resting on the sheet.

He was on top of me again, staring straight into my eyes, trying to establish total dominance.

"Look at me," he groaned out in between thrusts. My eyes were refusing his command, being driven by a much stronger force to wander across the room in search of something, anything to keep the tormenting rapture that was building inside of me under control.

"Fucking look at me," he barked again, driving his hand under my chin to get me to face him.

I recognized exactly what he was doing. He was waiting to see that pleasure ignite inside of me again, gathering the results of our carnal encounter, yet at the same time, casting away all feelings. He needed to prove that he owned me, but he also needed to prove that he didn't care.

Once again, he was ice cold, taking only what he came here for—another thing to add to his collection. It was then that I realized that no matter what happened today or tomorrow, or maybe even for the rest of his life, he wouldn't ever let anyone in.

I felt a tear falling from the corner of my eye, rolling down the side of my face, and dropping on the silk sheet. I was feeling sorrow, though it wasn't for me. I felt sorry for him. He was willingly choosing to be forever empty.

In a way, I wanted to stop him from obtaining what he wanted. He could have my body because that was a part of our deal, but I didn't want to give him the satisfaction of seeing me enjoying having him inside me. Yet I couldn't help myself. His hips were moving harder and faster, working on that damned spot that made me disintegrate, until his gaze darkened with animalistic thoughts, forcing my own body to betray me.

A level of pleasure I never felt before was making me feel lightheaded, as if the world around me disappeared and all I could feel was his hard cock grinding against my walls. Suddenly it was all too much, all too devastatingly perfect. Against my will, I felt myself tightening around him as waves of sinful euphoria ran through me, making every cell inside my pussy shudder.

Brax's deep groans quickly filled the room, making him break eye contact and push his head against my shoulder as the same consuming waves of pleasure were also devouring him.

My end of the deal was finally completed, and the price I ended up paying was greater than just my body. Brax was taking away a part of my soul, and that was leading me to ask the impossible of him. "Would you stay for just a little longer?" I knew all too well that I became just a name on the list as soon as he was done with me, but I was foolish enough to think that maybe I could have been enough to make him reconsider. He had a few more hours left before he needed to leave and get my siblings.

But my request managed to elicit the opposite response from him. The next second, he was pulling up his pants as if my words just burned through him. "Bea, there's something you should know about me. I'm a monster. And you're not supposed to love a monster. You're supposed to fear it." His black t-shirt was back on before I knew it, and he was already heading to the door. *"I'll return with your family."*

CHAPTER 21

I must have remained in bed for hours. The hours I wanted Brax to lay there with me. I might even have cried a little, but then something beyond crying came; a silence that was akin to Ferris's madness. Maybe I needed that, considering the alternative, me having feelings for Brax. Because I could feel there was so much more to him beneath his perfectly practiced coldness. I could feel the passion he tried so desperately to hide and the fire he wanted to extinguish. Anyway, what was done was done, and nothing could turn back the clock. I just needed to go further, even if I knew it wasn't going to be that easy. Despite spending an extra hour in the tub, I still felt like a used object. I was broken. But I was soon to be whole, with only ticks on the clock separating me from seeing Natalia and Sebastian again.

I suspected it was going to be sometime in the morning. The only thing I knew was that I couldn't sleep. So, I decided to do something with my time. Deep down, I already knew what I was doing with *my time*—I was letting my heart break because of Brax. The sensation of *him* still lingered between my thighs, serving as a permanent reminder of the price I had paid and of the man I would probably never see again.

Knowing I had some lounge joggers somewhere in the dressing room, I went and put them on along with a tight shirt and a zip-up black hoodie. No more seduction for the day. I considered I might have overused my quota for the evening.

I walked into the kitchen to make something to eat. I wasn't hungry. I was just going to prepare something to be ready for when my family arrived since I suspected that they wouldn't have eaten a decent meal in days.

The selection of groceries was so wide that I couldn't even decide what to make for Nat and Seb. Alfred had someone hired to restock the kitchen with pretty much everything you could think of. I didn't even see the person who restocked ever coming in. If I didn't know better, I would believe that food might magically grow there. After all, everything felt like a spell when it came to Ferris. *A spell that had just been broken.*

Pot roast with beef and vegetables. That's what I decided to cook, although I was 100% sure that they would prefer some French fries. I just didn't want to spend time in the kitchen when they arrived, and since that was a dish that almost cooked itself, I wouldn't have to.

There was the option to order in, but I needed to do this. I needed to make things seem normal, like they were just out on a short vacation and were coming back home. Yes. That was it, just out for a while and returning to an improved version of their home. Everything would go back to normal. Cole's deal would end soon, and then there would be only Ferris. I could handle him. Or maybe I couldn't, and we'd let fate decide. One thing was certain, I was walking into a whole different era, for one last time.

I had just finished in the kitchen and was returning to the living room to turn the TV on—when a large thump echoed somewhere in the distance. A tremor that shook all the windows of the house followed. It was so strong it made me fall to the floor. Scared to death, I covered my head with my hands, trying to make sense of things. A loud roar became the new background noise, and although I still couldn't tell what was happening I realized it was coming from outside. Crawling to the window, I noticed that people were leaving their apartments to see what was going on while a large cloud of smoke was rising into the air a few streets down the hill from mine.

I didn't get to leave my apartment and join the crowd as I spotted a police car traveling the street with a megaphone.

Everyone, please remain in your houses for your own safety.

We have the situation under control.

Please return to your homes!

The message went on and on as people were listening to the orders and returning to their homes, leaving just the mysterious cloud of smoke filling the air.

The TV was my only option to figure out what was happening, as I turned it on a special edition of the news was just beginning.

"Good evening, I'm Legacy Abbot, and I bring you a special edition of the recent events from just a few minutes ago. It seems there has been another explosion in the Hills. Our news crew is already heading to the location of the fire, where it is believed that the police chief's car was just blown up by a terrorist group.

We have received assurances that everything is under control now... but then again, we received the same assurances before, when a similar bomb was planted in the Hills.

*In a few moments, we'll go live to the mayor, who'll give us a few words about the **official** version of what is going on out there."*

I didn't get to listen to the mayor or his made-up lines. As my phone began vibrating with an incoming call.

I ran toward it since I'd left it in the kitchen, hoping that it was Brax with good news. Instead, I found that it was Ferris. *"Are you okay? I just heard about the explosion."* His voice was full of worry.

"News travels fast," I replied, knowing he wasn't even in town yet.

"Alfred called me. He said that he could see the smoke from the house."

"They just said on TV that things should be under control now. It has something to do with the rebels." I tried to tell him what I knew.

"I'll send two men to check the area. I have more men than I need at the house. They will be there in a couple of minutes. Or if you want, they can escort you to the mansion." Ferris offered.

But as much as I would like to find refuge in his fortress, I couldn't leave the apartment. "I can't. My family is on their way."

"That's great news. But all the more reason for security."

That I agreed on. "Okay, send them, please."

"I'll make the call now." I felt him in a rush to hang up so we wouldn't waste precious time.

"Thank you, Ferris," I whispered.

"We'll talk tomorrow... and Bea, if there's anything you want, just ask."

"I will." I hung up the phone, getting back to the news. The word rebellion was instilling a new kind of fear inside me. The revolution was about to break, and I was bringing my siblings into a battlefield.

I kept watching the news until morning. Witnesses were giving testimonies about the rebels, the politicians were lying, and so many people were expressing so many different opinions that I didn't know what to think anymore.

One thing my mother had taught me—*the truth is often to be found only behind closed doors.*

If that were accurate, then almost everyone I knew was in deep shit, including myself. And it was making room for a strange idea to form in the back of my mind. It was something similar to one of the strategies rich people play on board games, but I cast it quickly aside. I need to focus on the return of my family.

The food was ready, and as if on cue, the doorbell rang. I froze, barely able to swallow the lump I had in my throat ever since Brax left, then gathering all the strength I had left I walked to the door.

Praying to all the saints that my family was finally safe, I turned the lock and grasped the doorknob. I wanted the door to open immediately, but the fear of what would happen when it did was making me almost collapse on the floor. Closing my eyes, I pulled open the door, and as soon as I opened them back, I realized *Brax was right. He did it!*

"HE DID IT!" I screamed as two pairs of arms instantly wrapped around me.

Natalia and Sebastian!

My family!

We all collapsed to our knees on the entrance hall's floor for a few minutes, holding each other in a hug that had been delayed for too long. I only parted from the embrace so I could look at their faces from time to time. I just somehow needed to confirm in my head that this was real, and it was truly them.

"I'll be leaving, Miss. If you consider everything to be okay." A voice pulled me back to reality. A voice that struck me as strange, especially since the word *Miss* wasn't in Brax's vocabulary. It wasn't until I raised my eyes to look towards who had just spoken to me that I understood the reason—it was Erick, not Brax, addressing me.

"Where is Brax?" I asked while a strange feeling washed through me.

"Boss had an emergency and had to stop at another location." The man said, confirming my suspicions. Brax didn't want to come and bring my family himself because he didn't want to see me again.

"Thank you." I nodded as I had received all the information I wanted. I wasn't going to let Brax's absence cloud my day. Not today of all days.

"Let's get you two inside. It's not that safe here lately." I pushed the apartment door open to let them into their new home.

"I know," Natalia let out a sigh.

"What do you mean *you know*?" I asked with concern.

"I saw a number of vehicles as we entered the city. Cars filled with men moving in and out of town. Sad men. Dangerous men, Bea," my sister's voice saddened as she couldn't keep from showing her concern.

"It will all be okay. We will be okay. I'll see to that. Now, smile. We're together again, and nothing. I mean NOTHING can keep us apart any longer."

I must have used up a century's worth of hugs during those hours. I just couldn't satisfy my need to feel them close, as if nothing I would've done could silence that fear inside my heart. This wasn't over, and deep down, I knew it. However, there was something that was worrying me, "Did they hurt you when they took you out of there?" I asked my sister, noticing a few bruises on her face and the bare part of her arms. But upon closer inspection, I realized that the bruises were not fresh, they seemed to be older injuries.

"No. A couple of nights after our phone call, I tried to run. I didn't want you to get in trouble because of us, so I tried to escape while one of the guards was sleeping. I didn't even make it to the door. And this—" a crystal tear ran down her face, "this was my punishment." She lifted her sleeve high enough to reveal an almost open wound that was running from her elbow to her shoulder.

"What the hell is that, Nat?" I could hardly breathe. My blood was boiling so strongly that I was beginning to think it would burst through my nose. "Who did this?" I screamed, so furious that I was only seeing red.

"Our father. Bea, he is so out of control. When he found out I tried to escape, he threw me in a makeshift cage, but there was a metal sheet protruding from one of the corners. I cut myself on that. After he saw me bleeding, he beat me for injuring myself and making my *market value* drop," my sister said, telling me the gruesome story of what our father had become.

"Jesus," I uttered.

"Bea, it's okay. It doesn't hurt that much anymore," she tried to reassure me.

Yet, looking at her wounds, I found no reassurance, I only felt pure anger. "It doesn't hurt *that much* anymore? I'm going to kill him! End that miserable life of his for good!"

"Bea," Nat whispered, rolling her eyes in Sebastian's

direction, who was gazing straight at me, one second away from crying.

"Sorry," I let my palm cover my eyes. Maybe I've been around Brax for too long. "Or maybe our father is already dead? I didn't get a chance to ask what happened back there," I whispered to Nat so that, this time, Sebastian wouldn't be part of our discussion again.

"I'm not a child, you know," my brother muttered.

Great, he was grown up all of a sudden. "Oh yeah? What are you then?"

"Old enough to be involved in whatever is going on here." Sebastian always had an attitude, and apparently, it hadn't remained back in our old town.

"Seb, *I* am not old enough to be involved in whatever is going on here." I was just winging it, one day at a time, living life as it came. Living the life I had created for myself as it came. "But since you're *old enough*, I guess you won't be needing the brand-new remote-control car that I just bought for you. It was waiting for you to play with it on my bed, but I think I'll have to return it in the morning. Since you're *old* enough to stay here and be a part of this conversation."

Reverse psychology always did the trick. "Come to think about it, you two are boring." He giggled, running around the house trying to figure out where my bedroom was.

Although, I needed to tone him down a little, "Stop running!" I called out because his medical condition didn't allow him to jog. I turned back to my sister, "Go ahead, Nat. Tell me. Tell me what happened," I insisted.

"I don't know much. All I know is that I heard loud noises, then gunshots."

My heart skipped a beat. "Gunshots?"

After a deep breath, my sister continued. "Yes, a few. And then two men came and put some blankets over our heads. The next thing I knew, Seb and I were in an ambulance. One of the men took the blankets off and assured us that everything was going to be okay. We were to meet you in a few hours. Then he got out, probably to go in a different car."

I couldn't help myself from asking, "What did the man look like?"

A large smile appeared on Nat's lips. "He looked like God had placed two emerald jewels in his eyes."

"It wasn't God who placed them; trust me on that." It was more like the devil since I was sure she was talking about Brax. "What else did he say?"

My sister furrowed her brows as if she was trying to remember everything. "Nothing else. It seemed like he wasn't feeling too good."

"Okay, Nat. Thanks," I said, wanting to change the subject.

But Nat seemed set to ask more questions about her savior. "You know him, right? Who was he?"

"One of the men who saved you, nothing more," I tried to cut her short again.

"A good man," she stated, seeing him as her hero.

He might have been her hero, but when it came to me, he was the villain. "No Nat, not a good man."

"Well, I think he must be a good man since he had pizza waiting in the ambulance for us," she said, placing both hands on her hips and looking at me like I had no way of winning this one.

"Did he now?" I hissed, hoping she would sense the irony in

my voice and drop the subject.

Which, of course, she didn't; on the contrary, she was starting to pry. "Is he the one who got you this apartment?"

"No," I uttered, making her understand that the Brax chapter was over.

"Who did then? Your boyfriend?" And another interrogation began.

I needed to distract her. "Not exactly. You know what, Nat? I think there's something on the bed for you too."

"Do you think I'm Sebastian? I can see what you're trying to do," she said, while giving me that *I know better than to fall for that* look.

"A new dress," I continued.

Nat still seemed set on finding out everything that was going on in my life. "Not giving in until you answer my questions," she said, holding her ground.

But I came with hidden weapons, "New shoes."

"Not interested. I'm not moving until you answer." She crossed her arms.

"And a large bag of glittery notebooks, pens, and who knows what else in there," I continued, extending my offer.

Game, set, and match!

"Okay... Bye!!!" She was running faster than Sebastian, searching for the presents I got for them out of the money I had left from the Pleasure Room.

I let them enjoy the gifts for a while, then called them to dinner, which had already turned into breakfast since the sun was high in the sky by the time we got to eat. My siblings were exhausted, and so was I. But it didn't matter anymore.

Nothing ever mattered, as I would have done everything again ten times again over, just to live this moment and have them by my side.

"Let's get some sleep," I rushed them as soon as the dishes were done before I could fall from my feet. "You both have your own room." I couldn't get another word from that point on, at least for a few minutes as their cheers lasted. "But can we please stay in one bed today? Like we used to back home?" I needed to feel I wasn't alone anymore.

"Sure," they both nodded with large smiles plastered all over their faces.

But I couldn't be in my bed, at least not for today. "Nat, we'll sleep in your room. Your bed is larger than Sebastian's."

"Why does she get the bigger bed?" Seb retaliated.

Here we go again. I might have been a masochist, but I missed this part.

"Because I'm bigger!" Nat stated proudly.

"It's not because she's bigger. It's because you need more room to play ball. So, a smaller bed leaves you with a bigger space."

"I win either way," Nat was just adding fuel to the fire.

"No one wins. Let's go to bed or you'll both be sleeping in the living room." One final threat did the trick. It didn't take long before we were all heading to dreamland, embracing one another as we used to, just as if nothing had changed. When, in fact, everything had.

Now, they are here. They were finally mine. But this also brought along with it a huge responsibility, leaving room for something that I had kept bottling up inside of me to surface. I needed to protect them. It was making me face an unwanted truth. Over the last couple of weeks, I've come to know things. I was ashamed to admit how I learned them, but hearing Cole's parents talking, then Brax with his associate, plus the recent events, all pieced together were leading to a greater scenario. A scenario I couldn't ignore any longer.

I was beginning to think it was fate that wanted me to learn the things I did. There was an end coming our way. And I was one of the few people who had the knowledge and the means to try and prevent it. Even if I failed, even if there would be nothing left of me after everything was over; it was my burden. No matter what, I needed to know I did everything possible to keep my family safe, and this city along with it.

But for the night—or should I say, *the* day since it was morning—I just closed my eyes and found a few hours of peace in a time of war.

Ferris called at one point, just after we had woken up. It was late in the afternoon. Nat, Seb, and I were spending our time together telling stories and playing silly games. I wanted to invite him over. It was his place, after all, but something made me ask him for one more day alone with my family. I needed to spend the night with my thoughts. I needed to reflect on things and on my greatest flaw; that I took everyone's pain. It seemed like *empathy* was turning into a critical condition in my case.

They say everyone has his or her moment of greatness. Well, this was mine. Or maybe it was madness in my case; who knew? But I'd reached a decision. I *would* be the one who made that difference. The one who would end this madness. And to do it, I needed *all* of my kings.

The next day, I asked Nat to look after Sebastian and remain in his room for a while. I was expecting some visitors, and let's just say they weren't so appropriate for family time.

I had to insist with a few phone calls to get my green-eyed mobster at my doorway again. Even so, I wasn't a hundred percent sure he would show up. But he surprised me. "What's this about?" He asked even before coming inside the apartment while lighting himself a cigarette.

"I'll explain in a minute, please come in." I led him into the living room, noticing that he had a little limp in his left leg as he was walking. "What happened?" I asked.

As usual, his answer didn't give away too many details. "Work accident."

I suddenly remembered my sister mentioning that he wasn't feeling well the other night. "Is this from when you went to recover my family?" I couldn't control my curiosity.

"Is that why you asked me here today?" he muttered, taking a drag off of his cigarette, then looking at his watch as if he was already in a hurry. I recognized his tactics—he was forcing me to stop pushing him with my questions.

I smiled, trying to play along until I achieved my goal. "I want you to meet someone."

Brax never enjoyed being caught off guard, "Who is it, one of your fuckboys?"

"You should know better than that, especially after the other night. I haven't *fucked* anyone other than you, Brax," I replied, feeling somewhat offended by his tone.

"Yeah," he grunted like that was in the past already.

"I need to tell you something first. To clarify the reason we are all here. This isn't a cockfight. This is about what's going on out there, in the streets." I needed to clarify things before the war would start inside my house.

Brax took another drag of his cigar. "What do you know about what's going out there?"

I couldn't reveal the whole truth yet, but I needed to get his attention, "Much more than you think."

That got his attention as his eyebrows raised, eyes pointed straight at me. "I'm listening."

"I have a plan. A plan to stop this," I said, preparing for whatever was coming next.

"Who said I want it to stop?" He was playing dumb.

But I wasn't going to play along. "I do. It will affect you and everyone around you."

"I'll adapt. I always do," he said, confidently, while huffing like he was about to lose his patience.

I just couldn't with this man. "Not this time, Brax. Please listen."

"I would be out the door by now if I wasn't willing to do that." Irritation bleeding through his words.

The challenging part was coming up next. "I will need *all three of you* to do this."

"All *three* of us?" Yes, I knew he had no idea what *all three of them* meant, but he was about to find out.

"Yes... All three of you. While working at The Pleasure Room, I accepted two other deals aside from yours. But I assume you're already aware of that."

Although he seemed intrigued by the reasons I called him here, my personal life played no importance to him. "There's a complete report of every second of your life since the day you met me until now. It's sitting on my desk. I didn't open it. Do you know why? Because **I don't care**." Brax *did care* to emphasize that last part.

"Fair enough. Then you will probably get the short version of what I've been up to really soon." I was laying my cards out on the table because from that moment on; it was how I needed them to play too. "You see, individually, you are weak—"

His ego instantly surfaced. "Weak? Are you fucking kidding me?"

"Please, hear me out first," I was asking for his patience again. "Weak in front of everything around you. You *all* are weak alone. But the powers of all three of you combined—"

"I'm one minute away from leaving," he threatened.

"Then I'll find someone else. Probably make another deal. I don't know. My family is still not safe. And you know I would do *anything* to keep them safe!"

"None of us are safe anymore. You have five minutes before I start asking for compensation for my time." As always, Brax needed *extra* currency.

"Deal. Five minutes." I nodded. "You all have strong attributes. Together, we can fight this. Everyone plays a part—finances, political connections, underground connections. You will need each other. And I will need all three of you to make this work."

"Who are the *three* of us? That's what I want to know," Brax insisted.

"I'll show you, though one of you is a little late; I'll save the introductions until he arrives. This way." I opened the door that led to a dining room for guests. A room in which Ferris was already waiting. I talked to him earlier and asked him to come, though without telling him much about what was happening. Same with Cole, who was proving to be a little late, likely trying to make himself seem more interesting. That didn't even matter anymore. I just needed him present before Brax got pissed off and left.

But it seemed I had something that was going to make Brax stick around for a while. *"Ferris?"* The shock in Brax's voice made me pay full attention to them. He seemed to know my royal highness's name without me even getting the chance to introduce them. "Ferris! I can't believe it's you!" Brax walked over to him, keeping that limp in his left leg, as Ferris's gaze appeared to have turned to stone. He was in as much shock as Brax initially portrayed as my mobster's arms came around him, engulfing Ferris in a genuine hug. This was the first time I had witnessed Brax manifest any kind of human emotion, totally unaffected that there was another person in the room —me. A strange mixture of pain and happiness appeared on both of their faces, reminiscent of the one I think I had when I reunited with my family.

The roles had suddenly changed, and I was the one who needed to ask questions. However, before I got to open my mouth and say anything, Cole walked through the door. "Mouse, don't tell me you're planning a surprise—" He too suddenly stopped in the doorway, eyes bouncing between my two other men. *"Brax? Ferris?"*

What the fuck was going on?

End of Book 1

The Pleasure Room reading order:

1.Kings of Desire

2.Kings of Lust

3.Kings of Seduction

4. The Book of Kings -optional (Kings' POV)

5. Kings of Destiny

About The Author

M.O. Absinthe

Ascending author with a sweet tooth for alpha males, and a guilty pleasure of making your darkest fantasies come to life.

Follow me on:

-Instagram: @m.o.absinthe -for sneak peeks and events

-TikTok: @m.o.absinthe

-Facebook Page : M.O. Absinthe
-Facebook Group: M.O. Absinthe's Dark Sinners

-Email : absinthe.is.writing@gmail.com

Sign up on my website www.moabsinthe.com to my newsletter to get a FREE extra-steamy bonus scene featuring Bea and her kings

BOOKS BY M.O. ABSINTHE

The Sin of You

A vampire dark romance that will make you shiver in unknown temptation

The book is suitable for a mature audience.

I invite you to take a dangerous path where nothing is forbidden. Desire, lust, deceit, and betrayal revolve around an ancient prophecy that can build or break destinies. You're soon to find out if passion and love are enough to stand in the way of antique forces, or it will all be dust with the first ray of light.

"The room darkened with his presence as every step he made towards me took me closer to my downfall. He was death, and life merged in a predator's body. Strength and dominance oozed from his every pore. But it was something else too... Something more that made a cold chill flash through my body. His beautiful absinthe eyes captured the depths of time, making him irresistible, undeniable, but also fatal. All of my instincts were telling me to leave as fast as I could, but there was something stronger that kept me frozen to the spot. An unspoken link from the dawn of time brought me here, in this place, meant to fulfill my destiny. He is the living dead that people whispered about while looking, with fear, out the window... He is a vampire."

Il Capo's Seduction

An enemies-to-lovers passionate mafia romance.

The book is suitable for a mature audience.

One dreadful night changes Angelo's and Elise's lives forever, sharing a dark secret that can never be revealed.

After her mother's tragic death, Elise finds herself trapped in the dangerous Italians' penthouse caught up in a wicked game of smothering lust and wild passion - mind versus feeling.

To escape, she has to win his trust -yet she ends up losing her heart in the process.

"The water drops path while rolling over his inked body was becoming mystical. A sparkling road her famished hands craved to thoroughly follow, to feel his ripped muscle tense beneath them while sliding her fingers towards the wet towel. It felt like a sin, just to be looking at him. "

Printed in Great Britain
by Amazon